FLANAGAN

By

James H Longmore

A HellBound Books Publishing LLC Book
Houston TX

A HellBound Books LLC
Publication

Copyright © 2018 by HellBound Books Publishing LLC
All Rights Reserved
2nd Edition

Cover and art design by Phillip Bleacher for
HellBound Books Publishing LLC

www.hellboundbookspublishing.com

Printed in the United States of America

Other James H Longmore Books

'Pede
Tenebrion
Blood and Kisses
And Then You Die
Buds
The Erotic Odyssey of Colton Forshay
Feeder/I Am Joe's Unwanted Penis

Visit

www.jameslongmore.com

Dedication

To my wonderfully stubborn wife, Jennifer – without your unerring belief and browbeating, this story would not have seen the light of day.

FLANAGAN

PROLOGUE

The First Couple

"They're going to kill us," it was the woman who broke the silence first, her voice weak and dry.

"I won't let them do that, baby. I promise," her husband tried his utmost to reassure.

The woman shook her head and tears welled up from around her sun-baked eyes and mixed with the congealed blood that had oozed from where her eyelids had once been. The tears offered a modicum of relief against the constant, prickling pain that burned her drying eyes, and for that much at least, Trisha Carey was grateful. She stared at her husband. "You can't promise me that," she said, able to speak now that sweat had loosened the fat strip of silver duct tape that had been used to stick her mouth closed; the tape remained adhered to just one cheek and flapped like a second mouth as Trisha spoke.

She was right, of course; it was painfully easy to see that that Daniel was in no fit state to make such a rash undertaking.

Her husband had been chained to a thick, wooden stake hammered deep into the parched desert floor and he was suffering unspeakable pain. He was naked, beaten and had bled profusely from everywhere that his skin had cracked and split. Worse, his penis had been sliced vertically in two from tip to base and his prolapsed rectum lay drying on the hot sand; reeking, sticky with dark blood and crawling with insects. He'd long since given up on trying to move the insects along, and had succumbed instead to the maddening torture of their tiny, prickling feet and probing mouths as they rooted and jostled around in his exposed flesh.

Daniel sat there, staring helplessly at his wife of just two years, the pain in his heart equal to that of his violated body. He struggled to see her clearly through the blackened, bruised eyes that had been pummelled by merciless fists until the swelling had all but closed them, but he could see enough to comprehend his wife in her pitiful state; and it was beyond torture for him to be in such a predicament as to be unable to save her.

Daniel turned his head away.

Trisha was staked out opposite him, less than three strides away. She was spread-eagled with her back pressed against the desert floor, her body slick with sticky sweat, her ebony skin a shining contrast to the crowding summer Bluebonnets that surrounded them in that vast field in the dead centre of nowhere, Texas. She was as vulnerable and naked as her husband, arms and legs strapped to four iron stakes that had been pounded into the hard-baked ground and deliberately spaced for maximum discomfort. The insects and crawling things had been equally as quick to home in on Trisha's exposed and torn flesh as they had her husband's; flies darted over the entirety of Trisha's ruined body, settling on her raw, bloody flesh and driven to a frenzy by the metallic scent of her blood. There, they braved the early evening heat to crawl, feast, fuck and lay their eggs.

As the sun continued to sink towards the horizon it afforded an eerie backdrop to a trio of ugly, black buzzards who wheeled patiently overhead. They soared high above the grim tableau in patient anticipation of their next meal and their immense shadows passed from time to time across the couple's bloodied faces.

"They said they'd kill us at a quarter after seven," Trisha's voice trembled. "And I think they meant it." With soulful eyes, she glanced at the old-style alarm clock that sat quietly ticking by her head. It was increasingly difficult for Trisha to see now as her eyes were all but dried out, but she could make out the vague shape of the round faced, old-style wind-up clock that sat less than an arm's length away from her face. The clock was the kind with twin steel bells that rattled tiny hammers to sound the alarm, creating an annoying tinny noise that was guaranteed to awaken even the most ardent sleeper. The clock had a time-yellowed façade, plain black hands and Roman numerals for numbers. It went about its almost subliminal ticking as if it were mocking Trisha and Daniel from its perch on the green, plastic gas can. Above the foul, metallic stink of her own blood and waste, Trisha could smell the unmistakable acrid stench of the gasoline fumes that seeped from the can; and along with that came all of the terrible implications that the smell conjured.

"They only said it to mess with our heads, part of their sick game," Daniel croaked. "We'll get out of this, I promise," but he sounded like he couldn't even convince himself.

"They're not just going to let us go," Trisha told him, and there was a sad resignation in her tone. "Not after everything that's happened."

Trisha Carey – the one true love of Daniel's life – was battered and bruised almost beyond recognition, no longer was she even a passing resemblance to the dark-skinned, doe-eyed beauty he'd fallen so heavily in love with a lifetime ago. There was a sickly odor wafting over from her; strong and pungent - the blend of fear-sweat, wastes her body had abandoned control of somewhere between being dragged from the trunk of the car and having her eyelids sliced off - and the acrid, copper tang of blood.

And then there were her eyes. They'd been the first thing about her to have caught Daniel's attention when he'd met Trisha in the darkened nightclub a lifetime ago and she'd introduced herself as Patricia and told him that if he called her that she would *never* sleep with him; wide, brimming with an eager lust for life and so darkly brown as to appear almost black. But now they were just wide orbs, staring and daubed with clotting blood. Daniel thought they made his wife look like a crazy person.

As hard as it must have been for Daniel to look at his wife, he simply couldn't tear his eyes away. It was as if he felt that he at least owed her that much for having been powerless to prevent the atrocities that had been inflicted upon her. To see his beloved pinned out in the desert like some vivisected laboratory specimen, caked with congealing blood and snot and semen and dirt was an ordeal for Daniel that surpassed even his own violations. It was a torture all in itself for Daniel to see her full lips split and bloodied, front teeth smashed into crooked nubs, and her once flawless, ebony skin spoiled by the innumerable, seeping cuts that criss-crossed and flowed into one another. They looked to him like ghoulish lay-lines, contrasting dark skin with the raw, red flesh that pulsed beneath.

It hadn't passed Daniel by that the visual torture was as much the point of their ordeal as the physical.

Both of Trisha's dark, neat nipples were gone. The left one had been sliced away and had left a blood-filled hollow at the tip of her pert, pointed breast. The blood that had poured so profusely from the wound had streaked her side and belly with crimson until it had finally clotted and now the wound simply oozed a clear fluid that set like amber in the dry desert heat. Her right breast was gone completely; nothing more remained than a bloody hollow on her chest through which glinted a hint of white rib bones.

Daniel sobbed and tugged hard and in vain at the chains that held him fast. He ground his teeth against the sharp pain that burned up from his legs as he struggled and he tried to ignore it, undoubtedly focused by the need to break free, be the hero and save his woman.

But Daniel was going nowhere. Even if he managed to break free of his shackles, his legs had been rendered useless. The skin on both of his calf muscles had been neatly sliced away and rolled down from knee to ankle. There the loosened skin rested against his bare feet like gruesome socks. The naked muscles ached and throbbed as they dried out and died, and every grain of wind-blown sand was a vicious shard on the exposed nerve endings.

Nausea washed over Daniel in thick, suffocating waves and countered the consciousness that would have had him asleep and out of this horror. His hands, sticky with blood, wriggled with sad futility behind his back, desperate to be free of the cuffs that dug cruelly into the soft flesh of his wrists. "I'm sorry, baby," he sobbed, "I really am truly sorry."

"It's okay, Danny. It's not your fault." Trisha rolled her head to one side and faced her husband.

Daniel shifted his weight in a vain attempt to alleviate the intense pain that twisted up his bowels. The blood-soaked sand beneath his ass squished and a fresh, trickle of blood and liquid shit oozed from his split anus. A mosquito settled on his neck to feed and the angry, red bump created by its pin-prick proboscis simply blended in with the rest of the angry wheals on Daniel's lacerated skin.

"If I hadn't made you come out here -" he said.

"You can't punish yourself with *ifs, buts* and *maybes*," Trisha said. "Life's far too short for that." She gave him a wry, pained smile along with a glance at the alarm clock.

The time was now ten after seven.

Five more minutes.

"You can't just give up. Not like this."

"Why not?" Trisha replied, and there was anger in her voice, "what else is there to do, Danny?" Fresh, soothing tears sprouted in her spoiled eyes. "If there had been any way out of this mess, we should have found it before now. Before – this," she sounded way too rational. "Either in the motel last night, or when they brought us out here." Her voice hardened - more with resignation than resolve. "Just look at us, baby, we're in no fit state to escape even if we could. We'll be better off –"

She stopped herself, her meaning loud and clear.

Dead.

We'll be better off dead.

Their ordeal had been brutal, beginning as it did with the violent intrusion into their peaceful sleep. From there had followed the relentless night of demeaning indignities, and sickening sadism which culminated with the cramped ride in the trunk of the car and the heinous late afternoon under the mercy of the desert sun.

"You mustn't talk like that." Daniel's chastisement was almost a whisper, cracked through with raw emotion. "Perhaps someone from town will find us before those crazy bastards come back."

The ever-patient Trisha shook her head at her husband in that same endearing way that she had always shaken her head at his crackpot ideas; *'let's adopt another dog', 'I've decided to fix the car all by myself', 'let's try swinging'*. "No one's going to come for us," she said, "they drove us God only knows how many miles out of Flanagan, in case you didn't notice. And that place is a one-horse town at best."

"Only without the horse." Daniel cracked a smile that sent shards of pain through his face. "I remember."

Flanagan, where they'd stopped the evening before was a deadbeat town in the middle of Christ-only-knew-where and the only indication of civilization at its outskirts had been the old tin-plate sign nailed to a diseased, skeletal tree and shot through with bullet holes: *'Don't Mess with Texas'*.

Daniel and Trisha shared a shallow, sad laugh. It was a desperate gesture amidst the pain and the hopelessness; one of the human animal's more peculiar reactions to adversity.

Trisha's throat was beyond dry which made speaking increasingly difficult as each gulp of stale evening air further parched her larynx. "We'll not be missed for days - and we're too far away from the road to be seen."

Until their corpses were burned using all that nice, fresh gas in the gas can, that is. She and Daniel had been in the trunk of the car when the crazy people had stopped at the gas station to fill it – it was as if they had wanted their victims to know what fate awaited them as further enhancement to the torture. Once the fire was lit, it was an almost guarantee that folk would see the smoke for miles and come running – albeit too late to help.

Trisha groaned and twisted her body against the restraints that held her tight. The unrelenting sun had made her skin sore and tight to the point that she feared it would split in places anew whenever she moved; new sores to join the heinous wounds that had already been inflicted upon her throughout the night. That agony must have been ten-fold for her poor, Caucasian husband; after so many hours in the Texas sun, what remained of the skin on his shoulders, belly and thighs was an angry, scarlet red that bubbled with blisters that wept a clear, viscous fluid.

Mercifully, the sun beginning to set; a garish, bloated orange globe that painted the sky a vivid salmon pink. Its heat dissipated a little too, which provided slight relief for Trisha and Daniel's tormented skin.

"Just remember that I love you, more than anything, ever," Trisha told her husband. She attempted a smile that made her mouth throb.

"And I love you too," Daniel replied, "I always have." He tried to look into Trisha's face but couldn't. Instead, his eyes diverted away as if with a mind of their own to gaze over Trisha's body as if trying to see it as it had been before all of – *this;* less than twenty-four hours ago.

All of his wife's toes were missing.

"Time to find out if you're a foot guy or not," they'd said to him as they waved the secateurs in his face. Daniel had attempted to struggle free at that point, but they had him tied too tightly to the shitty motel bed that reeked of sweat and blood. "Fingers or toes, Mister, you choose."

At first, Daniel had refused to play their nasty little game, no matter how hard he'd been beaten or how much his body was violated. But when their attention had turned to Trisha and they'd threatened to do such horrific things to her, he'd had no choice but to comply. Fingers or toes?

Although it was a choice that he'd never thought he'd be faced with, Daniel had always preferred his wife's fingers to her toes. He'd never been able to understand the whole foot fetish thing, but then again, Trisha did have spectacularly unsexy feet. The way her second toes were almost a knuckle longer than her big toes had always creeped him out.

Not anymore, they didn't.

Given the decision to make, Daniel would keep Trisha's slender, French-manicured fingers every time as often he preferred them around his dick to being inside her, such was the magic she could weave with those digits. And so, like some poor schmuck contestant on a masochistic game show, Daniel had - finally - chosen toes.

Trisha had filled the stale motel room air with shrill, guttural screams as each and every one of the toes her husband had chosen for amputation were deftly snipped off and lay oozing blood on the cracked tiles of that cheap motel bathroom floor. Until there was nothing left but ten raw, bloody stumps.

And they'd made Daniel do it; he'd snipped them off one by one and cried as the blades sliced open the delicate skin and the bone crunched and splintered; and he'd felt each and every one through the rubber- coated handles.

One minute to go.

"It's important to me that you know I don't blame you," Trisha whispered, "I don't want to die knowing that you blame yourself."

"Don't talk like that, baby. Please," Daniel implored, his eyes filled with hot, stinging tears.

"I'm just being realistic, lover," she told him, "think of it as a mercy when they - you know - when they come back. I wouldn't want to live like this." With a weak incline of her head she indicated the ruined mess of her body.

"There's still hope," Daniel – ever the optimist of the two – ventured. "They may not come back at all, and they might not kill us if they do."

Since childhood, Daniel had always been a firm believer in while ever there was a breath left in a body, there would *always* be hope. It was how he rationalized how come people could walk so calmly to face their execution. There was always the thinnest grain of *hope* – perhaps the rope would snap, the electricity fail, or there would be that much prayed-for last minute telephoned reprieve?

"We can get you fixed up." Daniel said. "It's amazing what doctors can do these days."

Grasping at the most ephemeral of straws.

"Thank you, darling." Trisha raised her head slightly to smile at him, an unnaturally calm tone to her voice. "They could fix up the boobs; probably even get me some fake toes." Sadness choked her throat. "But not this, they couldn't possibly fix this." She didn't have to indicate the lacerated, bloodied mess between her legs, the raw flesh where her vagina had once been, for Daniel to know exactly what she meant.

"I'm so sorry, baby," he sobbed, "I didn't mean –"

The alarm clock rang out in the tranquil desert, its tinny chimes resounding loud and harsh in the cloying heat.

Trisha Carey laid her head back on the hot sand beneath the light of the dying sun and she looked resigned to her fate.

Trrrrrrrr.

This was it; not exactly how Trisha Carey would have pictured her demise, but there's life's' rich tapestry for you.

If Trisha could have closed her eyes, she no doubt would have. She relaxed against the burning ground as an embracing calm enveloped her, as if she had summoned an inner peace rather than the adrenaline-burst of panic.

A shadow grew long and nebulous from the desert and blocked the sun from Trisha's grateful eyes. There had been no audible footsteps; perhaps her tormentors had been skulking just out of sight all along to better enjoy the spectacle of the torments they had facilitated.

"I love you, Daniel," Trisha's voice was as strong as her parched throat and courage could muster, her urge to protect her husband from all the bad things that the world had to offer remained steadfast; she didn't want Daniel to suffer.

And then.

"Oh my God! Please!" Trisha whimpered, as her nerve crumbled, "I don't want to die! Pl–"

The first punch broke her nose. The second, her orbital bone and smashed her eyeball into a bloody, oozing pulp. The next blow shattered the remainder of Trisha's front teeth and she gagged on the splintered enamel that cut into her throat like fine slivers of glass. Blood poured from the back of her nose and into her throat; hot and metallic, it made its way into her lungs and she began to choke.

As the relentless, rhythmic, punches from the gloved hand crushed her skull, Trisha quickly gave up her consciousness and for her at least the torment was finally at an end. But still the blows rained down on her, one sickening punch after another; the dull thwack of splintering bone, the fat gobbets of blood that flew skyward as Trisha's face caved inwards and the concave filled with her blood and brains.

Daniel screamed out and cried as he watched his wife die. He begged, he pleaded, but her assailant just wouldn't stop. It was a mechanical, emotionless, and efficient attack; there really was to be no reasoning with these people;

We're just doing what we said we were going to do.

Daniel's face registered a delayed reaction akin to surprise as the cool steel of a keen blade stuck into the side of his neck and sliced forward through his gullet; he hadn't even realized there was somebody behind him until he felt the warm desert air invading his exposed throat.

And so, Daniel Carey sat helplessly near the twitching corpse of his beloved wife in the sun-baked Texas dirt as he slowly drowned in his own blood.

Impending death was merciful for Daniel. He'd watched the one love in his life murdered for another's delectation against the picturesque backdrop of the pink-stained evening sky; his final indignation in this hellish nightmare had been to watch his wife die, and hers had been in knowing that he was watching.

As Daniel Carey's life left him, the cooling dessert air rang out with the relentless ringing of the clock's little brass bells; it was the sound of the happy times of high school and the bell that would signal freedom at the end of each class.

Trrrrrrr...

ONE

At the School

The following March.

The school bell's shrill, whining drone was piped through the school's Tannoy system which helped to make it sound like something akin to an old-time fire engine – the ones they overdubbed in the old *Keystone Cops* flicks. The noise had that unpleasant, aggravating tone, which bit deep into the heads of both students and staff alike with all the penetrating *screee* of a dentist's drill.

Helen Sewell winced at the irritating din, partly because the sound went straight through her like fingernails on a chalkboard and partly because the alarm signalled the end of the final class before her class's much anticipated inevitability of Spring Break.

Since her first day teaching there, the Cy-Spring High bell had always reminded Helen of those old-style alarm clocks from the black and white cartoon shows; the ones with the tiny twin hammers that clanged on shiny metal half-bells on either side of the clock's round, grinning face as the clock jumped comically around whilst some animated character attempted to silence it - usually with a mallet.

"Okay class!" Helen raised her voice above the cacophony of scraping chair legs, "the bell doesn't mean you can just get up and go -"

"- it's just a guideline!" the class repeated Helen's catch phrase back at her with broad smiles on excited faces and the quick few that had almost made it to the classroom door slunk, shamefaced back to their seats.

Helen ran a hand through her spiked short, brunette hair and smiled. It was gratifying that her pupils respected her enough to sit their asses back down when asked, even though they still stared anxiously at the clock above her head and clutched their books tight to their chests as if they were awaiting the apocalypse and two inches of hastily- scribbled Biology notes were their only protection.

It was Friday afternoon - two-thirty; high time for the studying to stop and for partying to begin.

Helen addressed her distracted students as sternly as she could pass-muster. "I know it's quitting time, and I'm well aware that I have the dubious honor of being your final class before the hedonistic chaos that is Spring Break; but you guys know full-well that the period isn't over until I say it's over."

"Neither is Katie Hutchins's, Miss!" Michelle Simmons shouted out, much to the amusement of the rest of the class, "*her* period's not over yet and she sure as heck can't wear Kotex with a string bikini!"

The class descended into laughter as Katie Hutchins's face turned a most unnatural shade of puce and she mouthed *'bitch'* at her best friend. With friends like these, and all that.

"Okay, okay, calm it down!" Helen raised her voice above the ensuing hubbub of laughter and catcalls. She folded her arms across her chest and pursed her lips. "It's your own time you're wasting," she said with the comic timing of a seasoned stand-up.

The students cheered at the well-worn phrase, which was a sure-fire winner from their favorite teacher. And, with that, they were deftly back in the palm of Mrs. Sewells' expert hand.

"Listen up guys, serious time," Helen announced to her hushed, mostly attentive students. "Please don't forget the assignment on DNA. It's due in the first Monday back after the break."

Collectively, the class groaned.

"This one is important, people! It's heavily loaded towards your final grade, so please put some effort in and who knows - you might just learn something."

She smiled at the array of forlorn faces before her; there was only one Biology on their minds right now and that certainly wasn't anything to do with Watson and Crick. "And no cutting and pasting from Wikipedia this time!" Helen chastised, "I'm not naming names, but do keep in mind that I'm still young enough to check your work online for any more blatant plagiarism."

At this, Johnny Perkins, the class jock punched Ed Smithson hard on the arm and mouthed something about getting his money back. The nerdy kid bleated and rubbed at his non-existent bicep.

Helen studied her class with an almost maternal fondness. Twenty-three of Houston's very finest in their final year of high school sat before her, bright-eyed and attentive; each and every one of them on the verge of being swallowed up, chewed and spat out by the Big Bad World. The poor, naive saps really had no idea what they had coming to them.

And how Helen envied them that.

Helen Sewell was your archetypal, dyed-in-the-wool *Popular Teacher*. She was invariably well- loved and respected by her students but knew the game well enough to understand that she would never really relate to them on their own level. As well as the divide of years, there was always that teacher/pupil divide that separated adults and children, just as it was supposed to be.

She'd never had much professional respect for those amongst her colleagues who chose to breach that line and had become over familiar with the students in some desperate need to be *'one of the kids'*. And on far too many occasions, Helen had seen that precarious path turn all too quickly into accusations, suspension and on more than one occasion, jail time.

Still, it didn't mean that Helen's days of longing for the unabated hedonism of this particular holiday week were over – she wasn't quite *that* old just yet. Although, it did seem to be an awfully long, long way away in life's rear view mirror these days, whilst at the same time it only felt like yesterday that she was dating spotty, over-confident assholes like Johnny Perkins and squeezing her trim, teenaged body into bikinis a couple of sizes too small.

"And I'll be keeping a close eye out for your shenanigans on *YouTube*!" she said, determined to end on a light note and keep 'em coming back for more. "And on *'Girls Gone Wild'* for you, Michelle!"

Again, the cheers, catcalls and whistles. Revelling in the attention, Michelle stood up and wiggled her ample breasts at her classmates.

"Now get the heck out of my classroom!" Helen dismissed the students and they all fled like their asses were on fire. "And don't do anything I wouldn't do!"

She couldn't resist yelling after them and there was a most un-teacherly smile on her lips.

Helen gave a sagely shake of the head as she watched the last of the Biology 1A students scamper from the drab classroom and out into the glare of the sticky, sweltering Houston mid-afternoon.

If past experience was to be a reliable indicator; of the twenty-three kids in Helen's class, roughly half would have the DNA assignment done and handed in on time. Of the others, they would appear on her desk in dribs and drabs throughout that first week back; and Johnny Perkins would hand his in the week after everyone else, just as soon as he'd 'coerced' one of the physically weaker kids to write the paper for him. Helen felt for the Perkins kid, he really wasn't the brightest button on the shirt and it was a damned good job that he was a genius on the football field.

Helen had been teaching at Cy-Spring High for ten years, five of those alongside Chris, her English teacher husband – and it was astounding to think just how quickly those years had gone by. It seemed to her to be just yesterday that she'd first pulled up outside that imposing, windowless, red-brick building. Then, she'd been full to the brim of hopes and dreams of shaping young minds and imparting that wonderful thirst for knowledge that the years had never managed to dull within her.

She'd quickly established herself as the teacher that all the kids loved. She had that easy demeanor and a firm-but-fair approach to controlling a classroom; if Helen were to be played in the movie of her life, it would be by Gwyneth Paltrow or a young Julia Roberts (Julia Roberts?! Most of the kids she taught had never even heard of Julia Roberts! Talk about showing your damned age!).

It was common knowledge throughout the student body at Cy-Spring that Mrs. Sewell was the school's *TILF* - that's *'Teacher I'd Like to Fuck'* for the uninitiated. She'd read the evidence for herself, written on various lavatory walls around the establishment and she'd actually had to ask the Principal what the acronym meant – much to her embarrassment, and his amusement. It was difficult to decide exactly how she should feel about that particular epithet as Helen didn't feel quite ready to be anybody's fantasy Older Woman just yet. Even so, there was that vain, girlish part of her that was flattered that boys almost half her age still found her fuckable; although she remained realistic enough to know that a pail with a hole in the side would probably have incurred the same level of adolescent lust in the majority of them.

On the other side of that particular coin, it saddened the *Teacher* part of Helen to have to face the harsh fact that as hard as she tried to engage her student's brains, the male half of her class – and some of the female, according to some of the more imaginative scribblings on the twelfth-grade girl's restroom walls – spent class-time trying to peer down her shirt and wondering if Mrs. Sewell shaved her pussy or not.

Of course, the hormone-laden throng of pubescent boys (and not forgetting a handful of the girls, too) should find her hot. Still on the right side of forty, Helen was tall, but not too tall, slim with shapely legs and large, natural boobs that her husband always referred to as *bountiful*. Whilst she took great care not to put any of the goods on display in a manner unbefitting her status as schoolmarm, Helen always dressed well for work and made sure she looked her best in school at all times. Even so, she would often find herself deflated at the fact that she was already thirty-six, and that the big four-O was looming large and menacing like a hangman's gallows on her horizon.

Helen shoved her textbooks and stray pens into the tan leather satchel that Chris had bought her on the occasion of reaching her tenth year of teaching – or *surviving*, as her husband had so eloquently put it at the time. She glanced at her reflection in the broad, dusty window that looked out onto the football field and wondered where all the years had gone.

A knock on the small window of the classroom door startled Helen and broke her wool-gathering. The door creaked open.

"Hey there, Helen!" David Trevino poked his beaky nose into the room. "Haven't you got a home to go to?" He laughed at his own would-be witticism; that same old nasal laugh that never failed to set people's teeth on edge – the same effect as chewing on cotton balls. He slunk into the classroom.

"Oh, hi, David." Helen forced a smile.

David Trevino had taught Geography at the school for thirteen years, ten as a colleague – and not so secret admirer – of Helen's. He was the type of guy who carried the unfortunate capacity to creep people the fuck out just by occupying the same room; he had oddly thin, polecat features, an oversized schnozzle, squinty eyes and gaunt, pinched features that made him look somewhat alien. And yes, Trevino was living proof that one could still buy those horrendous, brown hound's-tooth jackets with leather elbow patches – most likely from some grubby back street store named *Clichéd, Prematurely-Aged Geography Teachers 'R' Us.*

"Are we still good for tonight?" Trevino enquired, "Ann and I always look forward to your and Chris's anniversary dinner parties – how many years has it been now?"

"Far too many, David," Helen gave the rote comedy answer that always seemed to crack Trevino up.

Trevino laughed his terrible, whinnying laugh and fought to catch his breath.

"Yep, all's good for tonight," Helen persevered above the man's hoots of forced laughter. "We're looking forward to seeing you both," Helen replied courteously, although the very thought of the dinner party filled her with dread – especially so now that Trevino and his God-bothering, mousey wife were confirmed; and to think she was having to give up her weekly Taebo class – her one bit of *Helen time* – for the privilege of spending the evening with the same old crowd.

Helen had been forced into tolerating the Trevinos because David and Chris were old friends from way back in the heady days of teaching college. Chris had tried to assure Helen time and again that David Trevino was one of the good guys – deep down; but she could never seem to get past his smarmy demeanor, dull conversation and habit of perpetually trying to peep down her cleavage.

The poor sap had had a hopeless crush on Helen for as long as she'd known him, and whilst she was used to being stared at – found it flattering on so many levels – it saddened her to think that no one seemed to be capable of subtlety anymore, not even her husband's best friend. Chris didn't seem to mind, of course, he too found it flattering, plus it massaged his ego to be married to an attractive woman who was desired by all; just as the Bellamy Brothers sang, *when you're in love with a beautiful woman…*

"We'll be bringing along a little surprise to help the evening go with a *swing*." Trevino grinned, as he slipped in his ubiquitous and not-so-subtle hint at sexual shenanigans that were never going to happen in Helen's lifetime. He'd read a book on Neuro Linguistic Programming back in his student days and firmly believed that by inserting the desired word into otherwise mundane conversation, he'd be able to bend people to his will. So far, his ploy had remained spectacularly unsuccessful so far as Helen and Chris went. "If that's okay with you guys," he added with his eyes fixed firmly on Helen's chest.

"There's really no need to go to any trouble, David. We're just happy that you're bringing yourselves." Helen smiled at this; the Trevinos' idea of a *little surprise* usually comprised a cheap bottle of Pinot Noir from *Specs* or some piece of religious embroidery that Ann had slaved over for weeks. "But you do know how we love your little surprises," Helen teased with a sly grin, as she recalled that time David and Ann had brought along a wildly inappropriate sex game and claimed that they'd been given the wrong box at the store and that it was supposed to be 3-D *Mah-jong*.

"You need help with those?" Trevino nodded towards either her books or her breasts; it was sometimes difficult to tell with the man.

"Thank you, no," Helen replied.

"Well, let me at least escort you to the teacher's lounge. I hear a rumor that Coach Dabney's brought in a crate of Lone Star to help get us all in the Spring Break mood." David gave a little bow and swept his arm with dramatic flourish towards the door that he held open with one brown-socked foot set in a grubby, tan *Croc*. "And besides, we don't want you getting swept away in the crowd now, do we?" He smiled at Helen again and indicated the heaving mass of raucous students that flowed rapidly towards the school's main doors which spewed them out into freedom.

Helen cringed. "Thank you, David. That's most kind of you," she said as she clutched her bag and bustled out into the hallway after the geography teacher.

TWO

In the Teachers' Lounge

Ever the chivalrous one, Trevino held open the door to the teacher's lounge for Helen. Okay, it was part chivalry and part ruse to check out the woman's shapely ass - but it was at least a chivalrous gesture.

"Hey hun," a gruff voice greeted her. Chris sidled up and slipped an arm around his wife's waist.

"Hey babe," she replied and kissed him full on the lips with a look of relief on her face at finding that he'd made it there before her; her husband's presence was normally guaranteed to send Trevino into retreat and thus rescue her from further banal chit-chat and eye-humping.

"I can't believe it's finally here!" Chris enthused. "An entire week away from those goddamned kids!" he exclaimed with a broad grin; Chris Sewell was most definitely amongst the vocal majority of teachers who figured that their job would be so much better without having students around to spoil it. "What say you Davy-boy?" He smirked at Trevino.

Trevino gave his little polecat grin which showed off his yellowed teeth to perfection. "Couldn't agree more my friend, couldn't agree more," his voice was somewhat subdued; he was clearly intimidated by his friend's show of affection towards Helen. Trevino's eyes darted around the room to seek fresh quarry.

"I've got a few short stories to read through over the vacation – a few of the kids wrote them 'specially and asked if I wouldn't mind giving 'em the once-over," Chris told Helen.

"Careful," Helen warned, "you're beginning to sound dangerously like you actually care about your students." She tipped her husband a wink. Perhaps some of her Julia Roberts-esque idealism was rubbing off on the old cynic after all?

"Shouldn't take me too long to zip through the stories, most of 'em are complete crap," he replied and Chris Sewell, Cynical English Teacher, was back in the room.

David Trevino snorted and screwed up his eyes. "I thought you were going to spend some time on your novel this vacation, Christopher old friend."

Chris smiled at his friend. "If I get an hour or so to spare, I may knock out a few chapters," he said. Chris's supposed contribution to the ever-expanding list of Great American Novels – *Resurrect* – was already eight years and counting in the writing and still only half-finished. The plot line had become far too complicated with the passage of time and the long breaks between sessions at the typewriter and the truth was that Chris had all but given up making any sense of the thing.

"I wouldn't hold your breath, David," Helen chipped in. "We'll all be cold and in our graves before that thing sees the light of day." The three of them laughed, but Helen saw that her husband had just a tiny hint of hurt in his eyes.

Chris patted the geography teacher on the back. "We're looking forward to seeing you and your good lady wife tonight," he gushed. "Eight o'clock sharp?"

"We'll be there," Trevino told him. "You know Ann and I wouldn't miss one of your dinners for the world." He smiled. "Now, if you'll excuse me, I wanted to have a few words with Dolly Chaberek before she leaves." Trevino made an exaggerated movement to push between Helen and Chris, arms tight by his sides, shuffling on tippy-toes. They parted to let him through and he made his way across the crowded lounge.

"Dolly's not coming back after the break," Chris informed his wife. "Her cancer came back."

Helen cast a glance over at the elderly lady who sat alone on the battered couch at the other side of the room. Dolly's broad ass filled a good two-thirds of the couch and wobbled like Jell-O as she guffawed loudly at something Trevino whispered in her ear. But, despite the outward show of bravado, there was a fearful look in the old girl's eyes; perhaps it was the sadness of knowing that she would not be sitting on that couch again.

Dolly Chaberek had been School Administrator pretty much since the place was built; in fact, popular legend had it that they'd actually built the school *around* the old broad.

"That's terrible," Helen said, putting on her sad face. "She's been here forever."

"You never really liked her though, did you?" Chris teased.

"She never liked *me*, you mean?" Helen said with a defensive tone. "Not since my first day here."

Chris smiled and his mahogany-brown eyes twinkled. He tousled his unruly mop of black hair with both hands and laughed. "I remember that," he said. "She thought you were all *'overconfidence, legs and tits'*. Quote, unquote."

"I really don't know why she ever thought that, I've never been one to play the big *I am* or flash my goodies," Helen protested.

"You don't have to, my love." Chris cuddled his wife and kissed her cheek with affection. "You exude confidence from every pore, and no matter how much you try to hide the gals, it's blindingly obvious you've got 'em. You only have to look at the effect you have on Dave!" Chris laughed a hearty laugh and several heads turned in their direction.

Helen flushed, self-conscious. "Shh, everyone's looking," she chastised her husband and slapped his broad chest with the flat of her hand.

"Ah, let 'em!" Chris guffawed.

"So, I guess everyone's confirmed for tonight?" Helen changed the subject before Chris got a little too raucous – sometimes he could get as giddy as the students come break time. "Dave just let my boobs know that he and his dull little wife are straining at the leash to get to our house."

"I guess everyone's coming then." Chris smiled and shrugged. Between himself and Helen, Chris was never the one who got overly stressed as to whether invited guests showed up or not. "We'll see who comes when they come."

This was typical Chris, nonchalant to the extreme when it came to social gatherings – although he was apt to be a total control freak in other respects. Helen had been planning the anniversary dinner for weeks – at her husband's insistence, no less – she had organized the menu with the caterers, bought in the best selection of wine she could lay her hands on at short notice, and re-confirmed with all invitees at least twice. Chris, on the other hand, had contributed the square root of squat to the proceedings; except, of course for the promise of freely-flowing booze, crude jokes and many a ribald story on the night. He smiled his whitest smile at Helen, his teeth almost luminous against his dark, tanned skin. "Quit worrying, Helen. If people come, they come – if they don't they don't," he said, and Helen wondered that with such profound insight, perhaps her husband had missed his calling and should have been a philosophy teacher? "At least we know that Dave and Ann are gonna be there, even if nobody else shows."

"That's what worries me," Helen said. "I really don't think I could bear an entire evening of just those two."

"You mean just those two, *and* their good friend, Baby Jesus?" Chris laughed. "You know it wouldn't be a dinner party without Ann trying to save at least one of our guests' eternal souls from hell-fire and brimstone. And you know she's always a good source of after-dinner jokes!" Chris grinned that foppish grin of his. "If only as the brunt of said jokes," he added with a chuckle.

Helen shook her head and glanced over at Dolly Chaberek. All things being equal, at least the worse thing she faced right now was the prospect of a terminally dull dinner party with the Trevinos, and not the death sentence that had been handed out to poor old Dolly. It was a circumstance that appeared to brighten Helen's countenance.

"Okay," Helen raised her voice above the hubbub of the lounge. She shot Chris one of her special winks.

"Who do I have to sleep with to get a damned beer in this place?"

Every male teacher in the lounge thrust a beer bottle in Helen Sewells' direction.

THREE

A Dinner Party

The Sewell residence stood back from the quiet street and was nestled comfortably amongst immaculate, manicured gardens. It was a two-storey redbrick house topped with real slate roofing and it boasted a facade wider than some country house hotels. A pair of neatly trimmed bay trees stood sentry either side of the impressively wide doorway, as if to protect the inhabitants.

The driveway leading up to the Sewells' triple garage was cluttered with cars, three of which belonged to Helen and Chris, the remaining two to their dinner guests.

There should have been three guest cars by now.

Helen checked her watch for the umpteenth time, her impatience quite noticeable; it was already eight-thirty and there were two empty places at her table. The Felchaks were already seated and were politely eying the aromatic banquet of Indian food laid out before them; practically salivating on the crisp, linen tablecloth.

David and Ann Trevino had showed up – as predicted – with their special not-so-surprise of a warm screw-top bottle of Pinot Noir and something in a Circle K carrier bag that looked suspiciously like the Houston edition of Monopoly. It was indeed going to be a long, long night.

The dinner guests' chatter offered little in the way of distraction for Helen's anxiety, it was pretty much the same old, banal background noise as always; *'it's been far too long since we got together'*, *'isn't Chris and Helen's house nice?'*, *'it's great that they didn't let the money change them'*, etcetera, etcetera. Same old friends, same old prattle.

Roger Felchak had begun holding court almost as soon as he'd arrived, as was his wont. "So, my assistant – Janice – interviewed this guy for the mailroom position. I was far too busy to bother, as per usual. So, I delegated." Roger was middle management at an oil drilling company that was housed across several floors of an ostentatious mirrored glass-fronted, downtown office block. He was the typical white collar, low pay grade who liked to talk like he was J.R Ewing.

"And then Janice, my assistant, told me he wasn't suitable for the position."

"And why was that?" Ann Trevino asked, forever the perfect foil.

"Wifebeater," Roger told her. "So I said to Janice - I don't really think we should discriminate against the guy just because of the shirt he's wearing!" Roger erupted in a hearty chortle at his own joke, even went so far as to slap his hand on the table to emphasize just how funny the gag really was. In the midst of his mirth, he made eye contact with the others around the table to initiate their less than spontaneous, polite laughter.

He'd been working on that one for quite some time; it was part of a new segment in his comedy routine.

Roger Felchak fancied himself something of a natural comedian; he'd even gone so far as to appear at a couple of open-mic spots at the local fleapit comedy club - the somewhat aptly named *Laughing Stock*. He'd guilted Helen and Chris into going along to support him on several occasions, until Helen had found a human tooth on their table one night and refused point blank to ever set foot in the place again. In a boost to his over-inflated ego, Roger had gotten a few cheap laughs with a line to a middle-aged couple that were oblivious to his outstanding comedic talents and had dared to talk to each other through his allocated five minutes.

"Say buddy, mind if I disturb you?"

The guy in the audience had looked up, shocked to find himself all of a sudden the focus of the room's attention. He'd shaken his head. No, he didn't mind being disturbed at all.

"I'm wearing your wife's panties. Now, how disturbing is that?!" Roger had blasted the clueless guy with the well-rehearsed ad-lib. Inexplicably, the room had erupted into uncontrollable mirth and now Roger Felchak thought he was Lisa Lampanelli with a dick.

"And I caught Phil, the office junior looking at transsexual porn the other day." Encouraged by the ripple of laughter his previous gag had solicited, Roger now slipped into full stand-up mode. "So I told him, that's not chicks with dicks you're looking at there, buddy." Pause for effect. "It's guys with boobs!"

Everyone laughed, of course. It was the polite thing to do under the circumstances, even when Roger ended with, *"You should have seen his face!"* eyed the Indian food on the table and –

"What, no chopsticks?!" And Roger Felchack laughed long and loud at that one.

Chris bustled into the dining room, talking quietly into the iPhone he had stuck to his ear. He walked up behind Helen and stroked her bare arm as he walked by, mouthing *I'm sorry.*

Chris spoke firmly into the phone, his face a picture of concern, "don't stress about it, Mike. Sounds to me like you've got enough to deal with right now." He paused to listen. "Yes, yes, I'll tell Helen." Paused again. He then made a point of circling the table to walk by David Trevino who had popped a cigarette into his mouth and was poised to light it.

"Take it outside, Buddy," Chris whispered to his friend. Trevino plucked the offending cancer stick from his mouth and gave his host a sheepish grin by means of an apology.

"Quit worrying, Mike," Chris said, "she'll understand. Now go sort your shit out – everything's gonna be okay, man. I promise." Chris hung up the call.

"They're screwed," he grimaced.

"I guess they're not coming, then?" Helen asked and there was just a soupcon of petulance in her voice.

Mike and Chrissy Robertson were more Helen's friends than Chris's. She'd worked with them both at the middle school where she'd done her teacher training, long before the heady days of Cy-Spring High. They were to have been her welcome party relief from Polecat Trevino and his Jesus-loving wife and the freakishly fertile Felchaks with their whole, inane *the-world-revolves-around-the-kids* conversations that were invariably on their way once the wine began to take effect.

"Nah. They're at the police station with Trevor," Chris informed everyone. "Again."

"That's the forth time this month," Helen voiced her concern, "what's he done this time?"

"Same old," Chris told her, "Mike's busting a goddamned blood vessel trying to get him out of this one."

Trevor, the somewhat problematic seventeen-year-old son of Helen's good friends had been careening helplessly out of control ever since he'd hit puberty late at fourteen. Drugs, drink, truancy and a violent temper had gotten him more acquainted with the Houston Police Department than his parents would have preferred, which had become a major source of embarrassment for his attorney father. Hell, Trevor had been taken home in police cars so often, his folks had on more than one occasion voiced their surprise that the City didn't charge him Uber rates!

"How much this time?" Helen asked.

"Three ounces," Chris replied.

"That's bad, isn't it?"

"I'm afraid so. One reefer and the cops'll just take it off you and smoke it themselves in their break room," Chris explained with a wry, knowing smile. "Three ounces is *intent to supply*. They're gonna throw the book at the poor bastard this time."

"Chrissie must be frantic, I call should her," Helen said.

"I wouldn't," Chris replied with firmness in his tone. "I'd give them 'till tomorrow. It looks for sure like young Trevor's facing Juvenile Detention." The Robertson's boy had had innumerable *final* warnings from the police as they'd attempted to scare him straight – each one of which Mike had managed to prevent from turning into a misdemeanour rap. But not this time, by the sounds of it; Daddy's legal prowess wasn't going to be able to talk Trevor's way out of this one.

"Perhaps it's for the best," David Trevino ventured. "It might give that boy the shock to his system he really needs." This was typical Trevino; always quick with the judgment call, despite the fact that he actually only knew the Robertsons from the Sewells' gatherings.

Helen glowered at Trevino with a look that left everyone in no doubt that right then she could have quite merrily ripped his rodent face off his skull. But instead she said in her most pleasant manner, "Perhaps you're right David, but I'm sure it's not a pleasant thing for Mike and Chrissie to be going through right now."

"I think it's high-time that they legalized the stuff anyways," Roger Felchak piped up.

"Roger!" his wife castigated whilst digging him sharply in the ribs with her bony elbow.

"Sorry, my dear," Roger apologized, rubbing at his flank and with a look on his face that made it quite clear that he didn't mean it. "Look, all I'm saying is that there'd be far less problems with today's teenagers if marijuana was legal. *And* it would give the police more time to tackle serious crime."

"I can't believe you just said that!" Sue Felchak snapped. "You know perfectly well that it's a gateway drug!" Her lips pursed, as if daring her husband to defend himself. "One minute they're smoking bud, and then they're chasing the griffin and burglarizing old people's houses!"

Roger grinned at his wife's ignorance. "That's not always the case, my dear," he told her, his voice lowered. When Roger was in the right – which was not all that often where his good lady was concerned, he'd be the first to admit – he knew that he had to tread carefully. "Most weed users only ever smoke weed, and never go on to harder drugs. *And* it is far less addictive and physically harmful than tobacco or alcohol." Roger offered his wife a subservient smile. "And it's chasing the *dragon*, not griffin. Unless of course we're talking *Harry fuckin' Potter and the Drug Cartel.*"

Sue gave Roger a *how-dare-you-correct-me-in-front-of-our-friends* look that could have melted tar. Without intervention from a benevolent outside influence, Roger Felchak was currently a dead man talking.

"Roger makes a good point," Chris interjected. "I've smoked weed pretty much since tenth grade and I'm not a Category-A addict," so saying, Chris plonked himself down at the table next to Helen and opposite Sue. He smiled as he dolloped a heaped spoonful of lamb jalfrezi onto his appropriately patterned plate. Two spoons of rice quickly followed, which almost completely covered up the delicate, hand-painted scenes of rural India. Damned good caterers, Chris mused, they've thought of everything.

The guests and Helen followed his lead, over-hungry and eager to fill their rumbling bellies with the wonderfully aromatic banquet.

Chris slipped a free hand beneath the table and squeezed his wife's thigh.

"It's not been all fun and games though, has it my dear?" Helen smiled her sardonic grin at Chris and stroked his muscular arm. "We all know what happened to you in 'dam, don't we?" she said, and everyone smiled in anticipation of the retelling of the favorite tale that never failed to embarrass Chris.

****

It had been the summer vacation immediately before college, and Chris had flown over to Amsterdam to visit with Si Westbridge, a friend of his older brother's. Chris had just split with Charlene Caine, his High School girlfriend and was enjoying the freedom that his newfound singledom afforded; perhaps a little too much on occasion.

Then there's the age-old adage; when in Rome... this Chris took to apply to the wonderfully liberal city of Amsterdam; it was all Europe, after all. Thus, ensued a week of smoking some of the best – and ever so legal – Mary-Jane on the planet, taking full advantage of the lower drinking age, frequenting the sad, sordid sex shows and of course, enjoying the full benefits of legalized prostitution.

On his third day into the trip, Chris had spent most of his time in the coffee shops with Si – and therefore had spent the majority of the day as high as the proverbial – he'd espied the woman of his dreams standing in one of the gaudy, red-lit windows.

She was tall, made even taller by her steel-spiked heels. She had her dark hair tied up in a severe bun and she was wearing an expensive, light gray pin-striped suit that made her appear like a wet dream come true for Chris. Behind the woman, mounted upon the ox-blood colored wall, there had perched a mind-boggling array of whips and paddles, along with myriad leather things that were adorned with chains and spikes; for someone of Chris Sewells' burgeoning proclivities, there could surely not have been a vision more erotic.

It was no surprise that the teenaged Chris, fuelled by testosterone, warm beer and soft drugs, had all too quickly found himself in the suited woman's tiny room; a space little more than forty square feet and lit by a solitary, red light bulb. There had been an all pervading, ingrained stink of stale cigarette smoke and used condoms that clung to every surface and invaded every pore of exposed skin.

The dominatrix had smiled sweetly and taken Chris's cash. Upon counting it and secreting it in a small safe beneath the iron-framed bed, she had closed the dusty velour curtains to shut out the busy street beyond.

She'd instructed him to strip naked. Chris had eagerly obliged and the dominatrix had pushed him to the floor. Then, she'd trailed along the front of his body with her foot, the pointed heels of her shoes rough against his skin. When finally, the heel had arrived at his genitals, she had ground his scrotum into the cheap carpet until Chris had begged for mercy; it would be the next morning before he discovered that she had made him bleed, waking up to find a splash of dried blood in his boxers.

She'd straddled him after that, her suit flapping tantalisingly open to reveal a hint of what could have been a leather bustier, although not once did she allow Chris to see or touch her body. She'd gripped both of his nipples between long claw-like scarlet finger nails and twisted and pulled on them until Chris had cried.

The dom' commanded Chris down to his hands and knees and once he was suitably prostrate, she'd carefully selected a black, leather riding crop from the wall.

His all-fours position had put Chris at eye level with the prostitute's patent black shoes, perfectly manicured toes and muscular legs that appeared to go onwards and upwards forever which along with the delectable pain she had inflicted meant that it was safe to say that his dick had never been harder than at that particular moment in time.

The first swish of the crop on Chris's bare backside had made him jump. He yelped a little at the sharp twinge the harsh leather had left behind on his delicate flesh. He'd braced himself, the second strike was harder, the third harder still.

It was at the point of the fourth lash that Chris had begun to crawl away.

The woman in the suit had barked something at him in Dutch, and indicated that he come back to her and the look on her stern features left no doubt at all that she fucking well meant it.

And, as Chris crawled back to his fantasy woman who was in the process of selecting a particularly evil looking cat 'o nine tails that sported silver studs; he'd experienced his very first marijuana-induced panic attack.

It had hit him from nowhere, and filled him with an overpowering sense of dread and a desperate urgency to flee. Chris had jumped like a kicked dog and scrabbled to get to his feet.

The dominatrix had kicked him back down to the rough carpet. Perhaps this was part of her client's game? Perhaps not. Either way, it was her job to remain in full control of the scene. She'd brought the cat down – *hard* – across Chris's buttocks to create ugly red welts as it broke the soft white skin and there were speckles of blood in several places.

Chris had squealed like a soul in torment and struggled to his feet. He'd grabbed his clothes from the floor as the woman he'd paid to thrash him – thrashed him.

****

And that's where the recollection of that particular evening's aborted entertainment became conveniently foggy and Chris's for-public-consumption-only story came to an abrupt end. As far as his friends were concerned, he'd simply grabbed his clothes and ran from the red-lit brothel, *sans* socks.

"I can't believe you left your socks behind!" David Trevino laughed until he all but choked on his crispy poppadom. "How does one leave one's socks behind?"

Chris laughed along with him, as he always did when Helen recounted the Amsterdam story, no matter how many times she'd done so now.

"And he just kept on running!" Helen continued, clearly revelling in the re-telling of one of the group's favorite stories. "What on earth possessed you, Chris?"

"I guess it was my bad." Chris put on his little-boy-lost expression. "How was I to know that the items displayed on the wall behind the hookers are an indication of what services they offer?" Chris sighed with a dramatic exhalation and waited for the laughs at his expense.

"And the severely-dressed dominatrix in the fuck-me heels didn't give it away?" Sue Felchak joined in; the wine beginning to loosen her up somewhat.

"Nope, I guess not," Chris said. *Here it comes, folks; roll up, roll up – it's the punch line you've all been waiting for!* "I liked her suit. I thought a woman in an expensive suit like that would be nice."

And cue laughter.

Everyone giggled at the well-worn tale, even Chris laughed along at his own expense; there can be nothing quite like a favorite, mutually-shared joke to dispel the inevitable social tension at a gathering such as this. Helen winked at Chris.

Thank you.

Helen visibly relaxed and Chris smiled to see her lighten up. The ice had been broken by the familiar and Helen's tension over the no-show Robertsons had been duly dissipated. Now it was time to sink a fistful of beers, fill up on damned fine Indian food and enjoy the rest of the evening.

Chris's Amsterdam story had begun life as a cautionary tale on the Evils of Marijuana, but had transformed across the years to become the group's favorite in-joke. Sure, Chris laughed along, even though the memory still made him uncomfortable; although the truth behind what had actually happened was something he and Helen kept secret between them.

And that truth was – Chris had *fought* his way out.

The paranoid attack under the influence of the weed had turned Chris into something akin to a trapped animal; desperate to escape no matter what the cost. It had been an unfortunate meeting of circumstances - he had been gripped by the urge to flee and the dominatrix was simply doing her job in preventing that.

And so, he'd hit her.

Hard.

Chris had thumped the poor woman full in the face, so hard that the skin on his knuckles had split and he'd felt her teeth crack beneath his fingers. She'd had a *surprised* look on her face as Chris's fist had connected full force with her nose on the second punch and she'd still made no sound at all. She just staggered back a step or two, her mouth a perfect 'O'.

As Chris had scrabbled around to collect his clothes (minus those eternally famous socks, of course) the dominatrix had stared down with utter disbelief at the blood that poured from her broken nose to stain her exquisite suit a sickly, dark crimson. And once he had most of his clothing, Chris had shoved the dom' roughly aside and ran like the Devil himself was chasing his ass.

And he'd not stopped running until he'd found a cab and made his way back to the apartment. Thankfully, Si had not yet returned home from work, so Chris had had the time for the drug to relinquish control over his brain and for the paranoia to settle down.

Apart from his utter shame at having hit a woman, there was a good reason why Chris and Helen cut the story off at the abandoned socks. For following the physical altercation with the dominatrix, Chris had found himself back at Si's apartment with an erection so fierce that it had been painful.

He'd never been so aroused in his entire life.

Chris had thoroughly enjoyed his experience at the hands of the sadistic dominatrix, right up until the panic attack – and he'd gained immense pleasure from striking the poor woman; it was the marijuana that had spoiled it for him. And from that day to this, Chris had never touched the stuff again.

"So, what are you two going to do with your well-earned vacation time?" Ann Trevino changed the subject. She was never overly comfortable when the group's conversation veered towards drugs or sex and she'd not yet had her fill of wine.

"Pardon me?" Chris stammered. He'd not really been paying that much attention and had a mouth full of the most delicious naan bread stuffed with almonds and raisins.

"David and I are spending ours at Bible Camp again this year," Ann announced. "You two really should come along with us sometime – it's always fun isn't it, darling?" She broke into her husband's conversation with Roger – something dull about the current Government's fiscal negligence and the potential of a financial meltdown in China.

"Huh? Oh, yes. Yes, dear, they really should." David made eye contact with Chris and gave him a glare that screamed *no, you shouldn't! It will destroy your soul!*

For ardent atheists such as Chris and Helen, the words *Bible* and *fun* really didn't belong together in the same sentence; much like *family* and *vacation*. To them, vacations were something to be taken to get away from your goddamned family – isn't that what makes them vacations?

Ann prattled on, extolling with enthusiasm the virtues of Bible Camp and the brilliant young pastor that ran it each year. She even pulled up a picture of the guy on her cell phone and everyone agreed that he looked like a child molester, much to Ann's chagrin. In the background, The *Bee Gees* played on Helen's iPod and filled the house with their stirring, falsetto harmonies. Yet somehow, following the demise of two thirds of the group, *'Stayin' Alive'* seemed to be a weirdly inappropriate score to Ann's attempts to save everyone's eternal soul from the fiery, brimstone pits of Hades.

"We're driving up to San Manuel," Helen replied to Ann's earlier question in order to cut the woman off mid- flow before she bored everyone off of their food. "It's just across the border, in Arizona."

"You guys visiting the desert? Not much to see there but shit-loads of sand and scorpions," David Trevino chimed in, clearly bored of his conversation with Roger. Ann shot him a look that told him to mind his cussing.

Helen looked a little coy. "No David, we're going to a couples' resort," she told him. "We're going to take some time out to unwind and reconnect – it's my anniversary gift to Chris."

"Ah, a *couples'* resort?" Roger's voice adopted that all too familiar, lascivious tone that no one loved. "We've all heard about those kinds of places, haven't we guys?"

Helen's face flushed. It was always a mistake to let Creepy Roger in on anything remotely suggestive – although he could still take something entirely innocent and make it appear vulgar; on occasion, it did strike her as odd that a large contingent of their friends were smutty-minded creeps. Helen knew that for the remainder of the evening they were going to have to contend with all of the suggestive comments and *nudge-nudge, wink-winks* from Roger and David, along with accompanying disapproving glances from Ann and Sue.

"I hear that those places are all tantric sex lessons, nude pools and toga parties," David Trevino said. He grinned broadly and stared directly at Helen's breasts.

Odd how Ann never seemed to pick up on him doing that, Helen thought.

"I'm certainly hoping so," Chris played along.

"You two are going to a naturist resort?" Sue Felchak asked Helen and there was an element of shock in her voice.

"A nudist colony? *Shut the front door!*" Ann Trevino exclaimed and Helen stifled a smirk. 'Shut the front door' was as close as her pious friend ever came to swearing; at least until she was so drunk that Roger had to carry her home. Helen figured that the woman must have been feeling pretty shocked at the thought of Helen and Chris *au naturel* in a resort full of strangers to wheel out that particular expletive.

If only she knew the half of it.

"Yes, it is clothing optional, which does not necessarily mean that we'll be getting naked. At least not all the time," Helen replied, and smiled at seeing the pained expression on David's narrow, sweaty face. "The resort is much more than that –"

"– I'll bet it is, I'll bet it is!" Roger chimed in with what had to be the world's worst Monty Python impersonation. "I'd love to be there to hold your coats!"

"You're just a sad old pervert, Roger!" Ann scolded.

"Hey!" Felchak feigned umbrage. "Less of the old!"

Everyone laughed at this, Roger the loudest of them all.

"You two are *so* adventurous!" Sue enthused, and looked for all the world to be genuinely in awe of her friend. "But, then again, I thought you were decadent when Helen got her nipples pierced."

Ann Trevino sat forward, a little more composed now from the initial shock of Helen's impending spring vacation in Sodom. "I don't see what all the fuss is about," she preached. "The Good Lord put us on this Earth naked, and Adam and Eve would have stayed that way were it not for Satan and his vile temptation. Perhaps Chris and Helen are closer to God than they would care to admit." She smiled her pious smile. "As long as you do both remember that adultery is a sin," she added with a sage nod.

"It's not a swinger's resort, Ann," Helen defended. "And even if it were, Chris and I are going there to reconnect with each other, not other people."

"Well, I still think you are incredibly brave, Helen; letting it all hang out for everyone to see," Sue gushed. "I would never even dream of going to a place like that, not with four kids-worth of stretch marks to show!" She laughed.

"She's not wrong there, folks," Roger interjected, "and there'll be even more soon, now that the old bod's gonna get stretched all out of shape yet again!"

Silence.

Sue shot her husband a glance. If looks could kill, they'd be measuring Roger Felchak up for a pine box within the hour.

"I am so sorry, Helen." Sue looked mortified. "I specifically told Roger – I didn't mean to –"

"It's okay, Sue. Congratulations guys," Helen said as she put on her bravest smile.

"Jeez you guys!" David Trevino teased, "All you two have to do is share the same bath water and *pow*!"

He laughed at his own joke. He was, sadly either too drunk or too stupid to realize what he'd blurted out until it was out there, hanging between the six friends like a particularly noxious smell.

"Oh shit, I'm sorry, Helen. Chris," Roger sputtered. "It just came out; I really didn't mean to let the cat out of the bag." He looked at his wife for support and Sue's eyes made it painfully clear that he entirely was on his own with this one. Right now, she was more concerned for her friend's feelings than her loose-mouthed husband. Roger didn't seem able to stop taking, "it's not even like we've even decided if we're going to keep it yet or –"

"Roger!" Sue admonished with a sharp bark. "You are *not* helping!"

Helen stood up from the table, her eyes brimming.

"Please excuse me," she said, emotion dampening her voice. She stood up and hurried from the room.

Sue shot Roger another glance that promised a whole world full of hurt was heading his way, when she got him home. She got to her feet and followed her friend out of the dining room.

****

Helen leaned on the restroom sink and rested her head against the cool glass of the gilt-edged mirror that hung above it. She bonked her head gently on the mirror in a show of sheer frustration, as if to knock out the thoughts that wheeled around like crazy things inside her mind. Then she squeezed her eyes tight shut and concentrated on the sound of the water gushing from the tap she'd turned on to full.

It was impossible for her to comprehend that Roger had run his mouth off like that, never mind that he had impregnated Sue.

Again.

Helen had been so incredibly happy for her best friend way back when she'd announced the first Baby Felchak, even more so for the second. But, as time had marched on and Helen's biological clock had continued to tick along unfulfilled, her delight for Sue's wayward fecundity had dwindled somewhat. Two kids for those people, Helen was able to handle, three was pushing her tolerance a little too far for being so brutal a reminder that she and Chris remained childless.

But five! For Helen, a woman having five kids was just Mother Nature rubbing her face in it, plain and sinple!

And for it to come out like that, at a dinner party she'd not wanted to have in the first damned place.

Helen sighed loudly. She was never at ease hosting social gatherings and was angry with herself for giving in to her husband's nagging to arrange this one on the day before they were due to leave for their vacation, anniversary or not. Helen couldn't cook so it was always caterers, she hated the cleaning up afterwards, and she hated the invasion of her home, her private space. And most of all, she'd grown so weary of those same old jokes, stories and conversations. She was worldly-wise enough to know that in the natural course of things, people outgrew their friends and found new ones, with new stories and a fresher perspective on life.

Only, sadly, no one seemed to have let Chris in on that particular life-hack.

Roger, Sue, David and Ann very rarely had anything new to say anymore; their lives taken up with kids and jobs and dull little hobbies that neither Helen nor Chris could identify with. The Sewells didn't - *couldn't* - have children and they refused to allow their jobs to rule their lives, but although their own interests were far from dull, they were not exactly appropriate dinner party fodder.

But, right now the bland, repetitive, over-familiar banter would have come as welcome relief for Helen; Roger's story of how his dry cleaner had tried to make him pay for a suit that had been stolen from their store on the premise that it had been cleaned *before* the break-in; David's asinine pontificating on the best route to drive *anywhere* in America; and Ann's often hilarious scripture misquotes and pious judging as drinks were downed and everyone became less inhibited and forgot just how much the woman hated the *cusswords*.

Maybe this was the real reason people put themselves through this kind of social hell? To hang out with the same people, tell the same stories, and seek comfort from familiarity against the shifting background of an ever-dynamic, unpredictable world?

Unpredictable? There was an understatement if ever there was one! No way in a thousand years would anyone have ever predicted Roger's cack-handed pregnancy announcement!

Kids this, kids that, what happened at work since last they had gathered (more often than not, it was nothing at all) and if they were really, really lucky, one of the group had seen a movie that they could all chat about; that was usually a good one to kill an hour or so until the alcohol kicked in to dull the senses.

And then there was always – *always* – that part of the evening where everyone came down with an attack of the *sinceres* and had the irresistible urge to say just how pleased they were that Helen and Chris had kept their feet on the ground after the Lottery win; that they were still the same people now that they were before they got so lucky.

Lucky?

The Sewells had enjoyed a modest win on the State Lottery five years ago. It had been enough money to buy them the nice house in the gated community, fully paid-for cars and the ubiquitous round of world cruises.

Forever the sensible one, Helen had insisted that they squirrel a chunk of their winnings away for their old age, kid's college funds (ha!), and rainy days. And they'd both made the decision to stay working, even though they were comfortable enough to not to have to. Helen was level- headed enough to understand that twenty-four-seven staring at the same walls – no matter how nicely decorated – and each other would have driven them both slowly, but very surely insane. And there are only so many damned cruises you could go on.

Who was it that said *wherever you go, there you are?* Buddha? Poe? Oprah? Whoever it was, they must have done the cruise thing a million times. The whole world at your disposal, every country, every culture. And still it was you, your husband and a fucking big ship.

Roger actually had a cheesy old joke about cruises – one he had worked into his act; *'we went on a cruise around the world last year, and now the wife wants to go somewhere different'*. As corny as it was, there was a whole world of significance in Roger's old gag.

So, after their initial wildness with their newfound (yet modest) wealth, Helen and Chris had settled back into the everyday, pledging to live well, enjoy life and be sure to afford themselves the occasional, extravagant indulgence.

Yet, as with any woman in her predicament, Helen would have traded every penny in a New York minute for that desperately-wanted twin blue stripe on the pregnancy tester.

A knock on the bathroom door - timid.

"I'll be out in a minute!" Helen called out. She dabbed at her eyes with a tissue, taking great care not to smear her mascara.

Sue's voice, "Helen? It's me – Sue" As if Helen wouldn't recognize her best friend's voice after twenty years.

Helen unlocked the door and let her in.

"Helen –" Sue started to say, her voice tearful.

"It's OK." Helen forced a smile. "*I'm* okay. Just being silly and over-sensitive." She pulled Sue to her and hugged her tightly.

"I didn't mean for you to find out like this," Sue sniffled against Helen's bare shoulder. "Especially since Roger and I have not decided anything for definite yet."

"It's okay, Sue," Helen told her. "I'm really happy for you guys, honest."

Sue Felchak pushed Helen away, and held her at arm's length. "Now don't you dare bullshit me, Helen Sewell," she scolded. "I know my big-mouthed, asshole of a husband upset the shit out of you and I couldn't feel any worse about it."

"Nah," Helen laughed with false bravado, "how could I possibly be upset? After all, you're the victim in all of this." She smiled at her friend. "I've still got my freedom to do whatever I want, when I want, how I want – with no rugrats to tie me down," she regurgitated her defensive retort. "You're the one who's going to get your body pulled all out of shape yet again and who's gonna be stinking of puke and baby crap for the fifth time, not me." Again, Helen laughed and again, it was not a convincing laugh for either of them.

"When you put it like that, yeah, I *am* the fucking victim. You should consider yourself lucky, Helen," Sue agreed although it was glaringly obvious that Helen considered herself anything but. Sue smiled at her friend, *for* her friend; as if something as simple as a warm smile could melt away ten years of disappointment.

"Yeah, you poor bitch," Helen said, as she wiped away the last of her tears and inhaled deeply.

"We're good?"

"Yeah. We're good."

****

"So, where is this nudist colony?" Back at the table, Trevino was attempting to lighten the mood. Never one to let anything even vaguely lascivious slip by, he was interrogating Chris between forkfuls of Bombay aloo and garlic naan.

"It's not a nudist colony, David, it's clothing optional," Chris attempted to explain for the umpteenth time. "And that means –".

David Trevino shook his head; he was not the kind of guy to be easily dissuaded from his conclusions, once he'd jumped feet first into them. Quite possibly, this was because he preferred to imagine Helen outdoors and naked than absolutely anything else on the face of God's green earth. "You can say what you want about it, Chris, but I think we all *know*." He grinned.

"It's just outside San Manuel, over the border in Arizona," Chris repeated himself to deflect Trevino and a look of dread spread across his face the second the words left his lips; he knew full well what was coming next.

"So, I suppose you're taking the I-10 route out of state?" Trevino enquired, his chest all of a sudden puffed out with self-importance.

Chris nodded meekly.

"Well, I suppose you could go *that* way," Trevino addressed Chris as if he were one of his own less-able students. "You do realize that you're looking at a V what – fifteen-hour drive?"

"Sixteen, without stops," Chris corrected.

"Well, I hope you're not planning to attempt that all in one go?" Trevino actually sounded pompous now.

Chris, normally tolerant to a fault with his friends, looked like he wanted to hit the man.

"Especially, if you've decided to go *that* way," Trevino failed to pick up on the signals and continued on.

"Nope, we're stopping overnight, halfway." Chris hid his exasperation well, his tone remaining pleasant beneath the buzz the wine had given him. "A little place north of Fort Stockton."

Trevino's chest inflated still further and he looked like the rooster who just got the keys to the hen house – there was nothing quite like a geographical conversation to feed the little man's self-importance. "Oh really? I'm quite familiar with that particular locale, as it happens."

Chris sighed. David Trevino (and his sad, desperate ego) was the only person he knew who would ever use the word *locale* outside of the geography department. Perhaps the man genuinely didn't realize just how irritating he could be with this portentous attitude? Then again, Trevino was only too happy to openly ogle a married woman's tits when he knew damned well her husband was looking, so perhaps his moral compass may have been somewhat skewed.

"We picked the place because it holds a fantastic flea market on the weekends," Chris told him. "It's some little backwater town called Flanagan."

"Hmmm," David Trevino – geography teacher extraordinaire – stroked his chin and cogitated a second or two, "never heard of it."

FOUR

Sex With the Sewells

There can be quite possibly nothing more demotivating in life than the ever-desperate rubbing of one's wife's unresponsive, bone-dry pussy.

Sadly, the night's performance was what had become typical of their sex life to date. As was usual, Chris lay on his right side by Helen. He was manipulating her dry, unresponsive sex with his left hand whilst his squashed right arm went to sleep beneath the weight of his own body. He had gotten to the point at which he was pretty much just going through the motions in the losing battle to get his wife heated up and garner some – *any* – form of enthusiasm from her. Helen's apparent disinterest aside, at least he got to grind his erection against her smooth thigh and enjoy the warmth of her skin.

Chris, as usual following a dinner party, was as horny as hell and single-minded in gaining his release.

As a couple, over the years they had become programed

to expect sex after any kind of party or social gathering; in much the same way that a body demands popcorn at the movies, or beer at a ball game. It was a habit they'd simply fallen into; no matter how late, or how drunk – or how disinterested.

This was a routine that had begun back in their early days together, when there had been many, many parties and Helen would dress so seductively for him that they couldn't wait to get home and tear each other's clothes off. Twelve years on and Chris was still like Pavlov's dog, conditioned to salivate at the tinkle of a dinner bell; dinner party equals sex, it really was as primitive as that. But, as for his wife right now, Chris couldn't be entirely sure if Helen was still awake or not.

"You okay, baby?" he whispered as he nuzzled her ear, nibbling on the soft lobe.

"Yeah," Helen replied.

Was that boredom in her voice? If so, at least she was being honest enough with her husband not to attempt to fake any sort of interest in the proceedings. Although, that would have been particularly difficult given the current circumstances; all the moaning, cries of passion and clawing at Chris's back in the world wouldn't distract from her tell-tale dryness.

Helen was simply not in the mood for sex following the Felchak's gaffe at dinner. It had brought her down with a crashing thud and she'd not been in the best of moods in the first place, what with Chris practically *bullying* her into organizing the party for the day before they left on their trip.

Chris redoubled his efforts on his wife's clitoris and attempted to dip one finger into her impassive vagina; there had been a time that by this juncture in their foreplay, Helen would have been as juicy as hell and begging for him to be inside her.

Instead, she felt dry inside; warm and rippled, like pussy jerky. That thought brought a wry smile to Chris's lips and he made a mental note to jot it down in the morning for Roger.

Helen's flesh simply refused to yield to Chris's probing digit, keeping him locked well and truly out. *Closed up tighter than a duck's ass,* as his good friend David Trevino would have put it, *and that's fucking watertight.*

Helen lay still as Chris worked away at her increasingly sore clit. She felt nothing even remotely analogous to sexy and so just stared blankly up into the darkness of their bedroom while her husband did his level-best to get her in the mood for something – *anything.* As a biologist, Helen knew the clitoris to be a unique biological marvel, the only organ in the entire animal kingdom that had evolved for the sole purpose of providing pleasure.

So why wasn't hers obliging tonight?

No one really knew the reason *why* evolution had deemed this particular accessory necessary. Was it that women were such selfish creatures that they would refuse to procreate if there were no fun in it for them? Or could it possibly be the appropriate compensation for the unspeakable horrors of childbirth?

Which was ironic since it had been the Sewells' tireless quest for getting Helen impregnated that had made them lapse into this unsatisfactory, perfunctory sexual routine in the first place.

What Helen wanted – what she *really* wanted – was for that head-swimming delight of intense arousal; that giddying point at which one's whole being is consumed with that overwhelming *need* to fuck - and to be fucked. Either that, or for Chris to quit what he was trying to do that was making her sore and let her get some shut-eye.

Years upon years of sex-by-the-biological-clock, temperature taking and mucus-watching had taken a great deal of the fun out of sex for Helen and Chris, and had most definitely wreaked havoc with their whole concept of spontaneity.

Add to that the innumerable times Helen had listened with faux-sympathy as her friends complained about how having kids had destroyed the spontaneity of their sex-life – they ought to try the rigmarole of trying to conceive when deep down you know it's never gonna happen, and see what that does to their precious libido!

And then there were those well-meaning friends who would take great delight in saying that with all that great sex she and Chris were so obviously having, it must be loads of fun trying. If they were there in the Sewells' bed right now, they'd be able to see for themselves that it most certainly was not.

"I want to fuck you," Chris mumbled in her ear. "I want to come inside you."

With his hot, hard dick digging into Helen's thigh, that much at least was fairly obvious.

"Want me to get the *Ultra Glide*?" Chris offered, wincing against the twinges of cramp that had built up in his fingers.

"No thank you," Helen replied with curtness, "you know how I feel about that."

"Come on, babe, it's not like it's *really* cheating," now Chris was beginning to sound like a huffy child denied his favorite dessert.

"If you can't get me wet then you don't deserve to take the easy way out," there was a firmness to Helen's voice that wasn't hidden all that well by her jokey tone. There was an old joke Helen had taken to heart some years ago – she'd heard it from some hack comedian she and Chris had seen in Vegas; *how was it that when a man can't get hard, it's his fault, yet when a woman can't get wet, it is also his fault?*

Poor old Chris, he really had no chance at all.

"Lube is for special occasions only, my lover; and before you ask, no, I don't want to turn over," she sighed.

At this, Chris's erection diminished once again. He switched his index finger for his middle finger on Helen's clit, frustrated at the lack of excitement down there. Apart from parting her legs at the start of what was turning out to be somewhat of an ordeal, she'd not so much as made that adorable, whimpering purr that she would make when he hit the right spot – and experience had taught Chris precisely where that spot lay. He parted her labia with expert fingers to fully expose his target and mounted a multi-finger, full-on, over-the-top, gung-ho assault at the most sensitive part of his wife's anatomy.

"Jesus Christ, Chris!" Helen jumped out of her skin. She grabbed roughly at his hand to put a stop to the torment. "What the fuck are you trying to do down there?"

"I'm sorry babe, just trying to give you some pleasure." He replied and even in the gloom of their bedroom, Helen could see the pout on her husband's face.

"I want to be deep inside you, I want to make my baby come," Chris, forever the die-hard optimist, continued with the sexy talk.

Helen placed her husband's hand on her taut stomach and well away from the unpleasant throbbing he'd created between her legs. She reached for his penis and grasped it firmly in her hand and it twitched to full attention in her fingers.

"Oh baby, I love your hand around my cock," Chris moaned, never one to give up.

Although Helen wished Chris would just shut the fuck up and let her sleep, she knew full well that he'd not quit pestering her until he got his way, and she was feeling just a tad guilty that this time it was her own failing that was frustrating him.

She was also pragmatic enough to know that if Chris didn't get his release he'd be way beyond grumpy for their early start and long drive in the morning. Not a great start to their vacation.

Giving in to her sense of duty, Helen tugged on Chris's dick to indicate that he should move upwards towards her ample breasts. As any attentive wife, should, Helen knew what her husband liked; and at least this way, she knew that his delicate ego would be safeguarded, he would get the relief he so obviously needed and she could get the sleep *she* needed.

Taking Helen's direction, Chris straddled his wife's chest until his dick rested between her breasts. He let out an involuntary sigh and looked down in the tiny green glow of the bedside clock to see his erection nuzzling between the delicious twin mounds.

Tits, titties, boobies, breasts – Helen had heard all of the euphemisms since she'd hit puberty hard and fast at twelve. They were *tits* when she and Chris were playing dirty, *boobies* in playful fun and *breasts* when they wanted their sex talk to be erotic and sensual. And tonight, Helen knew just where to take it.

"Wanna fuck my tits, lover?" she whispered in that deep, husky voice that drove Chris wild. She thought that it made her sound like a cheap streetwalker, but it certainly did the trick as far as her husband was concerned.

"Oh, God yes," Chris's reply was breathless, he was undoubtedly aroused and ready to go despite resigned to acquiesce to second base.

Helen pulled Chris's dick towards her left nipple. She rubbed it's thick, rubbery head against the stiffening peak and silver nipple-bar. Her husband moaned and she smiled as she teased her nipple with him, relishing the feel of his smooth penis on the sensitive tip of her breast. Helen alternated between her nipples and began to enjoy the effect it was having on Chris, more so than her own minimal tingle of pleasure. As much as she needed sleep, her obligation to perform was a strongly ingrained one; Helen still wanted to please her husband.

"You ready to fuck my tits now?" again with the hoarse slut-voice.

"Yeah, I wanna fuck your big, firm tits," Chris's breathy reply came out of the dark and Helen thought he sounded like some especially bad 80's porn movie. For an English teacher – at times like this – Chris's command of the language could fail him spectacularly.

Helen raised her head from her pillow. She pushed Chris away a little, moving him from her chest. She then spat as delicately as was possible when spitting on one's own breasts and her warm saliva trickled down into her cleavage and made her shiver. She spat again, then a third time, and each time she felt Chris twitch in her hand.

She then pulled him back towards her chest and slid his dick into the deep valley of her spit-slicked cleavage. Her fingers released him there and she placed a hand on each of her breasts and pushed them together to envelop his penis in their delightful flesh.

Chris groaned as the warm, moist flesh swallowed him. He shuddered at the feel of the liquid movement of the succulent breast tissue that surrounded him and all thoughts of his abortive attempt to arouse his wife were forgotten.

Involuntarily, Chris began to thrust, his hips rocking back and forth in the timeless rhythm of sex.

Perfunctory.

It was just the perfect word for the act they were performing; an act far more about sexual release than love or bonding. The word loomed huge and heavy over Chris and Helen like 'cunt' in a convent; it was a word that neither of them had the strength to admit to, let alone voice. It was difficult to imagine just how they had come to this point in their lives, at which being with Helen had become such hard work, when there had been a time – not so long ago – when just the right look or the right word from Chris would have had her sopping wet and ready for him.

Perhaps the first sign of things going slightly astray – sexually speaking – for the Sewells had been during their first trip to Vegas together.

****

What happens in Vegas stays in Vegas. Isn't that how the saying goes?

It had been four, almost five years ago, long before all the infertility crap had consumed their lives.

Chris and Helen had spent most of their short vacation in the sinful city wonderfully naked on the widest hotel bed they'd ever seen, cocooned by bleached, white sheets that Helen and Chris had left rumpled, askew and stained. Helen had just adored lounging around on that bed *au naturel*, her bare breasts pointing their defiance of gravity and nature at the mirrored ceiling and her freshly shaved pussy pouting and glistening in a way that made Chris ache.

On their second night, they'd paid for a hooker to visit them in their luxurious room.

The hooker had been around their age with milky skin, spiked blonde hair, deep blue eyes, and a gorgeously proportioned, petite body. In short, she was as exquisite a creature as their newfound wealth could buy.

It was unfortunate, then, that their evening had been brought to a premature, abrupt end.

Chris had escorted the hooker out of their room less than two hours into their allotted time (they'd paid for all night) and paid her handsomely in cash for her services.

The hooker had dressed quickly, gathered her purse and walked across the room to join Chris at the door. She limped and winced with each step, favoring her right leg as she walked. Her face was swollen and already beginning to bruise down one side, her top lip cut and oozing blood. There were scratch marks down her arms and across her back, almost – but not quite – hidden by the skimpy pink halter-top she'd pulled back on in haste. The girl's neck and shoulders were also decorated by gaudy red and blue bite-marks, the insides of her thighs similarly bruised.

"I am so sorry," Chris had whispered to the prostitute. "I've added a little extra for your trouble. I'm sorry –"

"Just give me my money," the hooker had croaked, her voice strained. She'd absently rubbed at her throat, which had drawn Chris's attention to the large, red hand imprints he'd made around her slender neck.

Chris had paid the girl and she'd left with not so much as a backwards glance at Helen who had returned to the bed and lay face down with her head buried in the plump pillows. There was always the possibility that the hooker's pimp may come knocking on their door, angry at the mess Chris had made of his best girl and demanding further compensation, but Chris had been confident at the time that they'd more than paid her with generosity – in full for the whole night, plus that little extra for the discomfort she'd no doubt be feeling for the following day or two.

There'd be no repercussions.

Their evening's entertainment had begun with much promise. The hooker had been fully briefed beforehand as to what would be expected of her, and she'd risen to the occasion with aplomb. She and Chris – under the watchful and aroused eye of Helen – had gone at each other like rabid animals; biting and clawing, slapping and scratching at each other like things possessed.

Helen had watched with increasing discomfort, as Chris had bitten the hooker's tits until they were a patchwork of teeth imprints and bruises, and one of her nipples was bleeding. The hooker had in turn spanked Chris's behind so much and so hard that his buttocks – and her hand – had glowed bright red. She'd also raked her long, fake nails down along the tender flesh of his butt and broken the skin in places. In her throes, the hooker clamped onto Chris's nipple, biting into it so hard that he screamed out and tried to pull away but she'd held firm. And for as much as it made Chris squirm and his eyes water, the pain appeared to only further inflame his passions.

There had come a point during that brutal, sweating exchange when Chris had invited – begged – Helen to join in with the hooker and spank him, bite him, anything to inflict pain. But Helen had shaken her head and simply looked on from her place on the bed, fingers busy between her own legs whilst Chris had demanded his pleasures from the hooker, leaving her wrung out, exhausted and spent.

And then Chris had pinned the hooker to the bed with her face pressed into the mattress; grinding his dick hard into her with his hands clamped around her throat.

Tight.

So much so that the hooker had made muffled, choking noises and had started to panic. Yet the more she'd panicked, it had seemed, the more inflamed Chris's lust had become and the more frantic Helen's masturbation. The hooker had flailed her arms and legs and bucked like a trapped animal to free herself.

"Hit her," Chris had growled at his wife.

"Me?" Helen had been somewhat taken aback by the unexpected command.

"I said, hit her." He nodded towards the struggling hooker, his hands still surrounding her throat.

Helen had looked at her husband, at the struggling hooker, her fingers still buried deep inside her own vagina. Slowly, she pulled her hand away from her own sex, crawled across the bed and slapped the hooker's ass with her wet hand.

"Harder."

Helen raised her hand high and brought it down on the hooker's left buttock, hard enough to leave a red hand print on the soft pale skin. The hooker had squealed and wriggled some more beneath Chris's weight.

Chris had then turned the hooker back over, keeping one hand at her throat to press her to the bed.

"Again, baby," he'd grunted at Helen and pointed at the hooker's mascara-streaked face with his prick. "Hit her again."

Swept up in the moment, Helen had obeyed and given the hooker a light slap across her cheek. The hooker had looked up at her with surprise in her baby blue eyes that bulged ever so slightly in their sockets.

"You can do better than that," Chris chastised.

Helen swiped the hooker across the face again, this time with a little more force.

"Ow!" the hooker protested.

"Oh, for God's sake, Helen!" Chris had voiced his annoyance. "Like this!" He'd then punched the hooker full force in the face, closing her eye and bursting her lip.

Helen had recoiled, unused to seeing the man she loved behaving like this. "I can't!" she'd cried out, as she clambered from the bed and ran naked to the bathroom.

Chris had heard the bathroom door lock engage and knew that the games were over. Helen wouldn't be making an appearance now until the hooker had been dismissed. He'd looked down at the hooker who was still pinned beneath him, her pert tits embracing his cock and he'd seen genuine fear in her eyes.

He'd had the hooker finish him – quickly – between her breasts before he asked her to leave; there could be nothing worse than leaving a job half done.

****

At that thought, Chris came.

He pumped out his semen in a half dozen lack-luster spasms onto Helen's breasts. Some of it squirted beyond the fleshy valley between and onto her throat where it pooled in the cute little hollow just below her larynx. Chris groaned loudly as the relief washed over him, his objective finally achieved.

And then Helen was up.

She pushed Chris off her without ceremony, and climbed from the bed. She padded across the darkened room to the en-suite to wash off; holding her breasts with one hand to prevent her husband's come from dripping onto the plush and incredibly expensive carpet. At least now that was over and done with she could get some sleep.

Chris flopped down onto the bed. The pleasant, post-coital (or whatever the appropriate term was under the circumstances) fatigue closed his eyes. The rigmarole that had been his failure in 'The Arousing of Helen' went with him into sleep; he'd had his pleasure now and there'd be time for the inevitable pang of guilt in the morning.

Chris was asleep before Helen returned to their bed.

FIVE

Road Trip

It was a quarter after eleven on the morning after, and the unrelenting Texas sun shimmered off the long desert road to make a picture postcard sight of the sand-blown road and the sparse, gray vegetation. The immaculate, bright yellow Camaro – canvas roof down – raced by a large, black vulture that had been mashed into the tarmac. As the car passed, a wing flapped lazily in the draught as if the poor bird's flat, desiccated corpse was trying to take flight.

Chris held the car to a steady eighty on the speedometer. There were no cops around, and even if there had been, they were well-known to not give much of a flying shit about speed limits on this particular stretch of road. It was a long, straight and monotonous chunk of sun-baked tarmac and practically the only thing one could do for fun on it was to break the speed limit.

Helen lifted her head to catch the hot rays on her face – eyes squeezed tight shut behind her Ray-Bans –

and revelled in the warm, dry air as it whipped through her hair. They'd been on the road since six that morning to avoid the worst of the Spring Break traffic, although it did feel to her like it had been an awful lot longer. Helen checked the dashboard clock for the thousandth time; there were approximately three more hours to go before they got to their first stop.

Helen had always enjoyed the road trips that she and Chris took together; the solitude, the togetherness, the time doing nothing that they could take advantage of to get to know each other all over again. This was just what the two of them needed following the hellish couple of years they'd just been through. Never more so was that as achingly evident as it had been in bed the night before; Helen and Chris needed this time away more than ever. Helen felt incredibly relaxed, had been from the minute she'd sat in the car and they'd left the neighborhood behind them. No work, no inattentive, rowdy kids, no timetable to adhere to, nor clocks for them to watch. It was just the two of them.

Perfect.

Chris took his eyes from the straight, glaring road to glance across at his wife. She looked breathtakingly beautiful, an absolute slice of heaven, and Chris had always secretly enjoyed the way that safety belts lifted and separated his wife's ample breasts. It had the effect of making them appear even more alluring to him – if that were possible – than they already were. He smiled at Helen and reached over to place his hand on her bare knee. Her hand joined his, squeezed his fingers.

It was only on the rarest of occasions that Chris took the Camaro out of mothballs for a trip. It had kind of become their special car for their extra special times together. It had been his first – and only – big Lottery Win Indulgence; the instant the cheque had cleared the bank (*Chris had actually waited – he'd always been always the consummate pessimist!*) Chris had high-tailed it down to the local dealership and treated himself to the vehicle – brand-new.

And for cash.

The Camaro was manual drive – Chris had paid extra – because he truly believed that a car such as this deserved to be *properly* driven; coaxed and teased and played like a thoroughbred racehorse.

And Chris had insisted on yellow because he'd been a massive *Transformers* fan as a kid, and what ten-year-old boy didn't want to own *Bumblebee*?

"Armadillo!" Helen shouted, "two to me, one to you!"

"Dammit woman!" Chris thumped the steering wheel in mock annoyance. "You're distracting me with *those*!" he shouted at Helen above the roar of the baking wind that roared through the car and he cast his eyes down to her bountiful chest.

Helen smiled a playful smile at her husband and nodded down to her breasts that strained against the white halter top that bared the flawless skin of her back and the deep valley of her cleavage. She blew him a pouty kiss.

Chris grinned broadly. He was living in the moment, enjoying his beloved wife, the open road and their childish silliness at playing *Roadkill Bingo;* a game that had been conceived a million years ago on some arduous cross-country trip they'd taken between Miami and Houston. Back then, they'd owned a battered old Tahoe that had an ancient radio that only seemed to pick up the Hellfire and Damnation stations, no matter where or which state they happened to be in. And the rules of the game? They were easy; the first one to identify five different, dead animals on the road won - it really was as simple as that. However, spotting the unfortunate creatures was the easy part – there were plenty on the desert road – shouting out first, and loudest, was where the skill came in.

It had been Chris who'd spotted the first one – a squished raccoon spread over an easy twenty yards of the highway, its guts ground into the gray road in a splash of dry, dark red. Had it not been for the creature's distinctive striped tail, it would have barely been recognizable as a 'coon, let alone as having once been a living organism. Helen had picked out the next unfortunate; the fresh remains of a possum that was surrounded by a flock of ugly, black buzzards that picked at its still bleeding flesh. And now Helen had called the armadillo. Chris had completely missed the thing; he'd been so entranced by Helen's hypnotic cleavage and the denim shorts she had on that were so inadequate in size they would have made Daisy Duke blush.

"When you've got it, you've got it!" Helen replied with a hearty laugh. She pulled down her sunglasses and peered over the top at Chris, letting him know she was undressing him with her eyes. She let her eyes roam over Chris's deliciously tanned skin that was visible through his loose, white cotton shirt while taking in the way his muscular legs flexed ever so slightly in his tight Levi's as he drove. Yes, indeed, there was most definitely something about an open road, fresh air and the hot sun on bare skin that made a person feel inexplicably horny.

"Music?" Chris asked, fully aware that Helen was staring at him with that primal, wanton look in her eyes.

"Sure."

"Jeff and the boys?"

"Is there any other?" Helen smiled at her husband, her face radiating the sun's warmth.

Chris clicked on the Bose he'd paid a king's ransom for and loud, bass-heavy music spilled from the ten-speaker system that was buried around the car to make his chest thump. Then came the unmistakable strains of the *Electric Light Orchestra's* shrill violin rift that opened *The Way Life's Meant to Be* as it soared out across the desert, and Chris sang along at the top of his voice.

Helen joined in, singing at the top of *her* voice. This was their shared guilty pleasure; music that had not been truly popular for almost thirty years.

There wasn't an *ELO* album the Sewells didn't own between them, most of the early records they had were in the original vinyl format. Many of their collection had been doubled up when they'd finally moved in together, as they had both been big fans long before they'd met.

For Chris, it was difficult to imagine that there had actually been a time before *Helen 'n' Chris*. And like most men within a relationship, he kept his mind firmly closed to the notion that there had been other people in Helen's life before him, whilst remaining comfortable with his own history; an arm's-length list of conquests that ranged everywhere between one-night-stands to relationships that had lasted for just over a year.

And each and every one had ended the same way.

Boundaries.

Chris had always been the one to push the sexual, physical and psychological boundaries with every woman he'd known; both theirs, and his own. Some of Chris's lovers had had strict and restrictive limits from the beginning and he'd quickly grown tired of them, all too quickly bored with settling into what he considered to be staid routines so fresh in a new person.

The closest to a no-boundary relationship Chris ever gotten was with Debbie Holmes. She was a free-spirited, try-anything-once kind of girl who had few morals and even fewer limitations in her sexual tastes. Everything and anything he'd suggested; she'd been game on to try. Anal sex, along with sex in public places had been the first taboo they'd broken – simultaneously, as it transpired. That had been followed in quick succession by BDSM, mutual torture and humiliation, watersports and orgies. They'd cruised for prostitutes together, picking the streetwalkers up from street corners to take home and fuck – they'd even been cautioned for curb-crawling on one occasion; the cop had barely been able to hide his amusement. And towards the end of their time together, Chris and Debbie had also experimented with each other's bisexuality, performing with people of both sexes for each other's pleasure.

And then, one day Chris had politely asked Debbie if she wouldn't mind taking a dump on his chest.

He'd seen a scat-play movie in one of the tiny, reeking theaters in Amsterdam and the idea had always intrigued him. It was more about the why, than the how, but the subject had intrigued him enough to have remained in his psyche for a long, long time.

So, in their true spirit of giving anything and everything a try, he'd asked Debbie to indulge him.

She'd wrinkled her cute button nose at him and said no. Chris had told her *it's okay, no problem, just thought I'd ask*.

And that had been that.

He and Debbie had carried on for about another three months or so, but the spark of limitless excitement had been extinguished the moment the word *no* had left her lips. After that, their *thing* – it was doubtful if it could still be described as a relationship beyond that point – had rapidly degenerated into little more than mutually consenting sexual abuse. Chris had used her, she him. They had taken their regular patterns of play to the extremes, but that elusive promise of a never-ending sexual frontier was gone forever; the endgame had already been reached.

Oddly enough, it was not because Debbie had refused to defecate on him. Chris really didn't care about the act itself, had no burning desire or fetish for shit-play. In fact, he'd never given that a second thought afterwards. He had closed down on the delectably hedonistic Debbie simply because they had reached her boundary; gotten to the place that marked her limits. And as far as Chris was concerned, with nowhere else to go from there, there was little point in carrying on. Credit to the girl, though, she'd gone farther – much farther – than any of the other women he'd been with before.

Until Helen that is.

For her part, Helen too had had her fair share of experimentation and exploring of boundaries, much of which she had regaled Chris with during their tell-me-about-past-lovers phase; that point in every marriage where past conquests no longer matter and the insecurity of past partners has long since dissipated. In truth, Chris often found Helen's erotic tales quite the turn-on when he was in that kind of mood.

Jason had been Helen's boundary-pusher and *Older Guy*, being fifteen years her senior. She'd been in her early twenties and he had been previously married. Jason had certainly put Helen through her paces; within a month of hooking up, he'd had her along to Japanese Rope Bondage classes, exclusive swinger's parties and private dates with like-minded couples. He'd introduced her to the sapphic delights of her bisexual side, encouraged her to dominate him and to expose herself in public places for his delectation.

Things had moved quickly and Jason moved Helen into his two-storey house in the 'burbs and was certainly well on the way to making her his second wife before things came to an abrupt end. He'd instilled certain tastes in Helen that her subsequent lovers – Chris included – would find indelibly intoxicating once they got an insight into her complicit brain.

There came a time towards the end of the relationship, when Jason would fantasize about the time he'd picked up a girl and killed her just to see how it would feel, regaling Helen with how the adrenaline and endorphin rushes had been phenomenal. Of course, Helen had played it down at the time nothing more than kinky boudoir talk and figured that Jason was merely voicing a warped fantasy. But there would always be that uneasy niggle that skulked at the back of Helen's mind; *what if Jason was disguising truth as fantasy?*

It had all come to a sudden end on the day that Jason ran a quick errand to The Home Depot to buy a pack of wood screws; it had become necessary to fix a dog gate to the bottom of the stairs to stop his ageing Beagle-cross from letting itself upstairs to pee in the bedrooms. Being the pragmatic type, Jason had taken a sample screw along with him to ensure he got the right size. Slipping the screw in his pocket, he'd kissed Helen farewell and headed out.

On the way home, there'd been some old Asian lady in a beat-up Corolla who'd pulled out of a side street and right in front of Jason's car. No big deal, a quick stamp of the brakes, a polite shake of the head to the embarrassed woman, and Jason was on his way back home.

No one would know for sure at what point Jason might have realized that the loose screw in his pocket had stuck itself into his leg. Perhaps it was when he pressed on the accelerator pedal and felt a sharp twinge of pain in his groin? Or perhaps it was when he felt the spreading warm, sticky wetness soaking through jeans? Either way, the sharp metal point had pierced his femoral artery and perhaps if he *had* realized he would more likely have called 911 and not simply driven home.

Jason – Helen's tutor in pleasures of the flesh to that point in her formative years - had made his way to the home that he shared with the young woman who would later blossom into Mrs. Christopher Sewell and finished bleeding out whilst sitting in his Chevy Suburban in the driveway.

Chris contemplated his beautiful wife. "Penny for 'em?" he said as he smiled at her.

"Just that I'm looking forward to our break." Helen told him. "It's been far too long. We both need this." She squeezed her husband's thigh.

Chris nodded his agreement.

There was certainly no doubting that Chris and Helen were very in much need of some rest, relaxation and quality reconnect time, not to mention a fat dollop of fun too. And the *Quercus Heights Couples' Retreat* certainly promised all of that – and more. Helen had been particularly zealous in doing her research this time around, since the last *clothing optional* resort they had visited – Chris's selection – had harbored far too much old, wrinkled skin and too many exposed, saggy septuagenarian body parts for their liking. They'd made their excuses and left after the first day there.

A contented silence passed between Chris and Helen, for now they were a couple just happy in each other's company. On the sound system, Jeff Lynne sang his ode to the *Evil Woman* and the bland desert landscape zipped by. Chris hummed along to the song – it was one of his favorites, he always told Helen it could easily have been written about her – and tapped along to the beat on the steering wheel with his fingers. Helen gazed out over the desert, mesmerized by the barren, heat-hazed sand, her mind happily in neutral.

They saw their first sign for Fort Stockton in what appeared to be the absolute middle of nowhere. They'd seen but a handful of other vehicles in the past hour or so, and so it came as a welcome relief to see some indication of civilization.

"Fifty miles to go!" Chris chirped merrily above the music and wind noise, "almost at the halfway mark, babe!"

Helen smiled at him. "Thank God for that, my bladder's starting to complain!" she told him.

"We could stop anytime, just say the word."

"And pee in the desert with the snakes and scorpions?" Helen laughed. "Thanks, but no thanks."

"Once we hit Fort Stockton, it's only a few miles off I-10 to Flanagan; we'll be there in just under an hour." Chris smiled at his wife.

Helen reached for the stereo's volume button and twisted it all the way to the right. The *Electric Light Orchestra* blasted out their tune even louder into the desert. The song, *Bluebird* was Helen's all-time favorite and beaming like a giddy school kid, Helen sang along at the top of her voice.

****

It was a little after two in the afternoon by the time the Sewells finally hit Fort Stockton.

"I guess this is where we get off." Chris nodded towards a battered sign with buckshot holes in it:

FLANAGAN

He pulled the Camaro off of the Interstate and headed up along the smaller road, a golden plume of parched dust kicking up from the tires.

Helen turned down the music, suddenly conscious of the overbearing volume now they were away from the Interstate and driving along a quieter road. Of course, there was nothing much here to disturb, and even the buzzards refused to be perturbed by the presence of the noisy, bright yellow vehicle. The unsightly birds merely wheeled high above in lazy circles and peered down at the Camaro with black, curious eyes.

Two shakes of a lamb's tail and the Sewells reached the town's boundary.

Chris brought the car to a smooth stop at a deserted three-way intersection on Flanagan's outskirts. "Okay, lover, your choice," he challenged.

"Between what and what?" Helen asked.

"Straight to the motel, check in and *then* to the flea market, or we go directly to the flea market – do not pass go, do not collect two hundred bucks?" Chris laughed lightly, delighted that this was their biggest dilemma of the day thus far.

"Well, it is after two, and the flea market ends at four," Helen mulled over her choices. She glanced at the hand-made sign cable-tied to a scrawny looking tree by the side of the road:

FLANAGAN FLEE MARKET THIS WAY:
8am-4pm Sat/Sun

And scribbled beneath that in green crayon:

Art car exibition Sat only

"I'd hate to miss out on any bargains," she said with a smile.

"And the old bladder, my love?"

"I think it can hold on awhile yet, thank you. And less of the old," Helen admonished and patted Chris's knee. "And I'm sure they'll have restrooms at the flea market."

Chris put on his serious face. "Yeah, but what if they only have those chemical port-a-potties?" he ventured

"You know how much you hate those things."

"Just because I said I'd rather pee behind a bush and risk poison ivy where nobody *needs* to get poison ivy, doesn't mean I *hate* port-a-potties." She grinned.

"If you're sure, babe." Chris winked at her. "It does mean squatting over a slop pool of other people's waste." Now, he was just trying to gross her out.

"Sure, I'm sure," Helen assured. "And besides, maybe I enjoy looking down before I go, just to get a look-see at what other people have done."

It was Chris's turn to wrinkle his nose. "And if they don't have port-a-potties?"

"Then it's either in a field or in my shorts." Helen let out a lascivious laugh.

"Now you're talking my language, baby." Chris slipped the car into gear and drove off in the direction of the *'FLEE MARKET'* arrow.

They hit the outskirts of Flanagan within a minute or two. A battered, tin name plate proclaimed the town's name and the numbers next to *'population'* had been shot out.

The outer edge of Flanagan was much like the rest of the small town: white-board houses and double-wides adorned the roadside like some giant kid's haphazard play set. The shabby dwellings were nestled in oversized plots of hard dirt, dust and stubborn ragweed that appeared to pass for gardens, the houses themselves – for want of a better word – ramshackle. Their once-white paint peeled away like long strips of curled skin from the heat-shrunk flashing and each and every window frame was rotted and crumbling. Several of the homes even had large chunks of roof missing, although they still appeared to be inhabited – the holes patched up with faded blue tarp and plywood; a legacy from whatever tropical storm had last paid a leisurely visit to the kind folk of Flanagan.

The afternoon heat was obviously oppressive enough to keep the residents indoors, as there was not a soul to be seen. The blue, cloudless sky allowed the harsh rays of the high sun an unhindered access to sear everything in sight, and as a result the entire town was eerily quiet. It was like a scene from an old, clichéd horror movie where some cataclysmic apocalypse has occurred and all the people have either mysteriously disappeared or turned into zombies and wandered off in search of warm flesh.

"Hey look!" Helen pointed to a shiny new road sign resplendent on its own – and equally new – metal pole. "Please drive slowly," Helen read out, "we love our children." She giggled at this. The word 'love' was depicted on the sign by a large, red heart. "If they love their kids so much, how come they let them play on a main road?" She laughed heartily at her own joke.

"You're a bad girl, Mrs. Sewell," Chris joined in with his wife's merriment, laughing along and slapping her bare thigh with the flat of his hand.

And then the houses were gone and it was back to the bare, baked-dry land with its sparse, desiccated shrubs and scabby-looking *Opuntia*.

Ahead, the flea market loomed.

"I'm guessing this'll be it then," Chris announced, always the first to state the obvious.

"What gave it away?" Helen asked with playful facetiousness in her tone. "All of these cars parked in a field, the undercover stalls or the big, fuck-off sign saying *flea market*?"

"There's no need to be like that," Chris replied, faux-wounded.

"Oh, I think you'll find that there is *every* need to be like that, Chris."

They laughed together; it had been a long time since they had laughed so much.

SIX

At the Flea Market

I t was at the Flanagan flea market that the first of the odd occurrences happened.

Chris parked up next to a camper van that had been liveried up to look like Scooby-Doo's Mystery Machine. He and Helen clambered from the Camaro; Helen stretched her long, muscular legs and discretely pulled her shorts out from where they'd ridden up into her crotch.

"Most elegant, m'lady," Chris declared through a smirk. "And you claim not to be of royal descent?"

"You weren't supposed to see that!" Helen retorted and slapped her husband's arm.

"Ah, but I did, didn't I?" Chris cast an admiring glance at his wife's body; her endless legs, toned, flat belly, perfectly proportioned breasts and beautiful face. There could be no mistaking the look of pride on Chris's face, he'd looked at Helen that way since the first day he'd set eyes on her.

"Well, you shouldn't have been looking." Helen castigated her husband, although the chuckle that followed gave away her delight at being the object of her husband's desires.

After so many years of marriage, and everything they had been through together, it was a marvel that Chris and Helen could still consider each other with lust; lesser couples would have drifted apart following the fruitless years of intrusive fertility treatments. Helen loved to play to Chris's attention whenever – wherever – the opportunity presented itself, she had long since learned to embrace her inner exhibitionist and delighted in showing herself off for her husband's delectation.

With that in mind, Helen had deliberately dressed provocatively for their trip in a cleavage revealing, white halter top, pristine, white K-Swiss and the tightest pair of shorts that allowed a hint of ass cheek to peek out when she walked. Helen's toned, tan midriff also flashed when she moved, glinting with a light sheen of sweat that had appeared in response to the oppressive Texas heat and which added to her sensual allure.

Of course, Chris was delighted when Helen chose to play to his vicarphilia – the thrill he got when his wife dressed provocatively – rather than be offended by it, and was most pleased with the admiring glances that she was already attracting.

Chris had dressed well to complement his wife's attire; expensive, tan Vans, khaki knee-shorts and white polo shirt emblazoned with a crocodile logo that grinned its toothsome grin from just above his left nipple.

They walked through the dwindling, late afternoon market crowd. These were presumably the ordinary, everyday folk of Flanagan and its neighboring and similarly drab towns. The overflowing trash cans by the market gates indicated a far busier morning; the majority of visitors having preferred the cooler part of the day in which to buy their used goods, bric-a-brac and funnel cake.

"Okay, sweetie, let's go take a look over here." Chris offered Helen his hand.

Helen took it, snuggled up to his side like a love-struck teenager and walked in step with him towards the rickety wooden outbuilding that covered most of the market stalls.

It was a relief for Helen in every sense of the word to find that the market – as characteristically primitive as it was for such a backwater place – had proper restrooms; flushing toilets, running warm water, hand soap – the whole nine yards.

After emptying her aching bladder, Helen forced Chris to buy her a bright-blue slushy that tasted of artificial raspberry and sugar, and some funnel cake which she wolfed down as if it were her first meal in a week.

"Where do you want to go now?" Chris asked.

"Let's go see the art cars," Helen decided, "before they pack up and head home, it's getting close to three now."

"Your wish is my command ma'am," Chris said with a flourish and paused to brush the powdered sugar from the sexy little creases at the corners of Helen's mouth. "Let's go see us some *fanceee* cars," he said in his very best redneck accent – the one that never failed to make his wife smile.

The art cars were as art cars are the world over. They were arranged beneath the shaded protection offered by the corrugated tin roof, all clustered together to stay out of the blazing sunlight. There was an ancient Cadillac which had tiny pieces of broken mirrors glued to absolutely every square inch of its body, an ancient

Land Rover fitted out to look like a giant cockroach – complete with moving antennae; and of course, the ubiquitous Volkswagen Beetle covered hood-to-trunk with plastic, singing fish that were hooked up to a motion sensor that made them strike up their cacophonous chorus every time someone walked by.

"Adolf Hitler must be spinning in his grave," Helen observed, as they made their way past the Beetle. "It's a shame he never lived to see his creation turned into this. I'm sure the frustrated artist in him would have approved." And she smiled that enigmatic smile that only surfaced once in a while.

"Loud and proud!" Chris said randomly, inciting a fit of giggles in his wife.

"Oooh, look at this one!" Helen exclaimed as she bounded over to an antiquated hearse that was adorned with what was quite possibly *thousands* of haphazard trinkets.

Chris eyed Helen as she moved; she could sometimes be almost childlike, yet still infinitely graceful. And he noted with a thrill that there were other eyes on her too; guys pretending to be interested in the cars, yet peering at his wife's perfectly rounded, shorts-clad bottom with that tiniest hint of alabaster ass-cheek that peeked out from beneath the frayed hem.

It was simply amazing to Chris that Helen Sewell could dress like total trash and still look incredibly classy.

There were innumerable, old plastic McDonald's toys stuck to the hearse, along with dismembered pieces of Barbie dolls, commemorative key fobs, shells and ceramic figurines that were looking the worse for wear for having been glued to an automobile for Christ only knows how long.

"Wow! Spongebob!" Helen squealed with delight, pointing at the complete collection of Bikini Bottom characters that stuck out from the vehicle's dashboard.

"Stuck 'em all there ma'self, missy." The hearse's owner appeared as if from out of thin air. "Ya can git in and take a gander, if ya like." He grinned inanely at Helen, showing off the gaping hole where his front teeth were supposed to be.

"Can I? Really?" Helen gushed. It was difficult for Chris to tell if his wife was being sarcastic or not with the guy. If she was, the old boy appeared not to have noticed. Instead, he wiped a greasy hand on his sleeveless used-to-be-white shirt and offered it to Helen.

"The name's Donny," he told her, "Donny Cano – this here's ma ride."

The man was a stereotype – no, he was *the* stereotype. In every picture dictionary in the world, next to the word *'Redneck'* there would be a picture of Donny Cano the Hearse Guy.

"Pleased to make your acquaintance, Donny." Helen shook his hand politely, her breasts jiggling pleasantly as she did so. "I do love your car!"

"Took me the best part of six years to fill all the gaps up," Cano said proudly. "There's near-on three thousand trinkets on her, each of 'em different."

"I can see that," Helen sounded suitably impressed. Again, it was impossible to tell if she meant it or not; she was too damned good at the whole disingenuous kick.

"You sure I can sit in her?"

"Please." Cano opened the door. "Do that."

Helen clambered into the hearse and her butt sank into the soft, red velour seat. She clasped her hands on the steering wheel and stretched out her legs.

"Wow, so much leg room," she enthused, wiggling her feet. "I *love* this!" She smiled up at Cano who had leaned himself into the doorway. He'd pushed his baseball cap upwards and was supporting himself with his right arm on the vehicle's door.

"Yep," He agreed with a broad smile, "needs to be comfortable fo' when you're transportin' the *deee-ceased*." Cano enunciated as he leaned a little farther in. "An' jus' perfect for those long, long legs of yours." He grinned.

Helen looked up at Cano and returned his smile. "So, you collected all of these yourself?" She pointed at the Squarepants diorama he'd so diligently Superglued to the dashboard.

"Yep, I stuck 'em all there one by one, as I got hold of 'em," Cano sounded so very proud of himself. "Plankton was the hardest one to find; had to get one from a diff'rent collection." Cano reached over Helen to prod at the little green plastic figurine.

Helen could see that the Plankton character was, indeed, a little off scale from the other characters Cano had assembled into a scene of the cartoon show. She also noted that he had leaned so far into the car that his crotch was almost resting on her arm. She could feel – and smell – his warm, acrid breath on her skin, and the light touch of his spittle on her exposed back as he spoke.

Chris hovered in the background. He pretended to be examining the minutia of Cano's ridiculous hearse, but all the while he kept a watchful eye on his wife. Naturally, he could clearly see what was going on with her and Cano; the redneck was getting more than a healthy eyeful of Helen's breasts and long, smooth legs, whilst at the same time revelling in the jealous looks he was receiving from the other art car owners.

It was a game that Chris had always enjoyed. It turned him on to see Helen dressed provocatively and attracting attention in this way; he found it to be the perfect trigger and soon he would experience the familiar stirring in the corner of his brain where his darkest fantasies lurked.

"And this here's ma beer cap collection." Cano indicated with his grubby thumb the myriad beer bottle tops glued to the drop-down glove compartment door. "Took me three years to collect, each one's different, see?" He leaned in a little further, now he *was* resting his crotch on Helen's arm.

Helen glanced over at Chris and her eyes momentarily met with his. *Help me,* she mouthed.

It was the feel of the hard lump in Cano's loose-fit jeans against her arm that told Helen that this particular game had to be over now. She knew how much Chris enjoyed playing this game – her all flirty and looking hot, guys drooling over her (literally in Cano's case), and it was fun while it lasted – but enough already, the guy wasn't even vaguely attractive.

"Come along, darling." Suddenly Chris was there and leaning over Cano's shoulder.

The redneck shot Chris a nasty glance and in that instant, it appeared that he was actually getting possessive over Helen.

"Hey there, son," Cano growled, "I wus jus' showin' your good lady *waa-af* ma beer caps."

"How fascinating." Chris smiled at the man and stepped into his personal space; Chris a full six inches or more above the redneck's hunched, wiry frame. Chris shot a quick glance at Helen who now looked decidedly uncomfortable sitting so low down in the gaily decorated hearse. "Perhaps you'd like to see more of

Donny's knick-knacks, my love?" he said with a wicked, teasing smile.

"Er, no thanks, I've seen plenty." Helen forced her most pleasant expression. "I think I'd like to go see the puppies now."

"Well, thank y'all for stoppin' by." Cano's attitude shifted back to cordial once more. He stepped back slightly and held out a hand for Helen to climb from the car.

As she got out of the hearse Helen gave Cano a final, inadvertent flash of her magnificent cleavage. Cano leaned in once more, so close that droplets of his sweat dripped onto her chest and trickled down the deep valley between her breasts.

"An' if ya fancy one o'the pit-bull pups, tell Jacob that Donny sent ya an' he'll give y'all a deal." Cano's face split ear to ear in what could only be described as a shit-eating grin.

"Thank you for showing me your car," Helen said once she was away from Donny Cano's creepy, lecherous gaze.

"No, missy, *thank you.*" Cano still had hold of Helen's hand; he raised it to his toothless mouth and kissed the back of it, leaving a damp spot.

Helen reclaimed her hand and composed herself.

"Puppies?" Chris asked as he slipped an arm around his wife's bare, sun-reddened shoulders.

"Please," she replied, and looking directly into Chris's eyes her relief was apparent.

"I hope you enjoyed that as much as I did?" Chris whispered to her.

Helen chastised her husband with a stern expression beneath which lurked a sly, knowing smile.

And with that, Chris and Helen bade farewell to the inimitable Donny Cano and his decidedly disrespectful hearse and walked away, Helen clinging on to Chris' arm, their steps in perfect synch.

"Oops, sorry buddy." A guy walking in the opposite direction collided shoulders with Chris.

"No worries," Chris replied politely, yet bristling a little at the guy's clumsy intrusion of personal space.

"Say, you wouldn't happen to have a light, would ya?" the clumsy guy asked from behind.

Chris turned around, spinning Helen around with him by her shoulders. "Pardon me?" Chris eyed the middle-aged guy up and down. The man was of slight build, and wore rumpled brown pants that looked to be part of a suit, a white shirt damp with fresh sweat and a tie he'd loosened to unfasten the top two buttons of said shirt. His face was an honest looking face, rendered a bright, ruddy crimson from the sun and he had a mop of fine, white hair that wouldn't have looked out of place in a nursing home.

"A light? Do you have a light, please?" Ronnie Gagliano wiggled his cigarette at the Sewells.

"Sorry buddy, we don't smoke." Chris smiled dismissively.

"Well, not cigarettes anyways," Helen giggled, "we much prefer –"

Chris gave his wife's shoulder a sharp squeeze.

"Ouch!" she protested.

"It's okay." Gagliano smiled at them, his blue eyes crinkling at the corners. "I'm not a cop; in fact, I quite like the odd reefer myself." He lifted up his cigarette. "I think the off-duties here would frown on me somewhat if I lit up a few grams of Morocco's finest though." He laughed a low, grumbling laugh that seemed to begin somewhere below his slightly rounded belly.

"Can't help you, sorry," Chris said. "But there's a guy over by the kiddie rides selling *Bic* lighters four for a buck-fifty."

"Perfect," Gagliano said. "Thank you, both." He turned away and walked briskly in the opposite direction of where Chris had just pointed.

"What is it with the Y-Chromosome and no sense of direction?" Helen asked her husband, her eyes dancing in the bright sunlight; she'd perched her Ray-Bans on the top of her head to better see inside the gloom of Cano's art car and forgotten about them.

"Beats the fuck out of me," Chris growled. "Now let's go see the puppies."

The puppies were, as anticipated, painfully cute. Helen *ooh-ed* and *ahh-ed* over the tiny, squirming bundles. She held each one tightly and squealed with delight as they playfully nipped at her fingers and licked her face with their tiny pink tongues.

"I *love* this little guy," she cooed.

"I think he's quite fond of you too," Chris was forced to agree as he watched the spindly-legged, brindle pup nuzzling at his wife's face.

"His name's Tyson," the rather stern-faced woman in charge of the puppy stall said. "He's a Boxer."

"Ya don't say?" Chris laughed.

The woman just stared blankly at him.

"He is *so* adorable!" Helen said. She had that all-too familiar look on her face; the one Chris found impossible to say no to. "He reminds me of Buster."

Buster was the dog they'd gotten on doctor's orders almost five years ago.

"I suggest you look into adoption, and in the meantime, perhaps you might want to consider getting yourselves a dog." The sour-looking Doctor Evan P. Leger had told the Sewells.

Just what kind of insensitive thing is that to say to a young couple that you've just informed somewhat coldly would be most unlikely to conceive their own children? Sometimes the medical profession forgets that they are dealing with actual people.

Chris and Helen had been trying for a baby for over three years by that point in time.

"Trying for a baby?" Chris would say. "What a quaint euphemism for fucking by the biological clock." It was a fair assessment of what the Baby Obsession had done to their sex life by then.

And so, after a battery of tests so personal and invasive that they'd be frowned upon in Guantanamo, Dr. Evan P. Leger had sat there before them in his expensive office with his bad tie and Rudolf Hess face and suggested they get a dog.

"You mustn't blame yourselves," he'd said. "It's not really anyone's fault."

"So who's fault is it, exactly?" Chris had asked, but the good Doctor had just droned on, churning out his rote platitudes as if he'd been reading them from cue-cards.

Chris, apparently suffered from what they called in the trade 'immotile sperm'; which in layman's terms meant that he was firing blanks. Helen, as cruel happenstance would have it, had contracted a monster dose of Chlamydia in her late teens that had all-but destroyed her inner workings.

And that was pretty much that.

So, it was difficult, and somewhat superfluous to try to apportion blame for the Sewells' lack of reproductive success.

Despite the fact that the doctor's poorly placed advice had wounded them both deeply, Helen and Chris had gone ahead and adopted an appropriate child substitute from the local animal shelter. They'd decided to forego adopting an actual child as they had both come to the damning and inescapable conclusion that they were just too selfish to nurture someone else's chromosomes.

At first, Helen had taken to the dog, but then had quickly grown bored with him. After all, Buster was not the child that her hormones demanded – no matter how sweet and cuddly he was. She'd even gone so far as to admit to Chris one night after a bottle and a half of Chablis, that she was kind of switched off by the thought of ending her days driving a utilitarian SUV with a '*my children have four paws*' sticker on the rear bumper.

And then poor Buster had gotten sick, his neck lumpy with lymphoma, and he'd died.
And they'd both felt nothing.

Helen plopped the squirming Boxer pup back into the crate with its litter-mates and looked down at the puppies as they scampered around and yipping and yelping in the grubby cage. It was at times like these that it felt to her as if the Universe was mocking her; throwing up constant reminders that Helen Sewell would never have children – that she was *barren*, to give her condition its more blunt epithet.

Helen had read a short story that Chris had written long before they'd met and when he'd actually shown some promise as an author. The basic premise of the tale was that the human race had one day simply stopped reproducing. No reason, no great catastrophe; the species in its entirety had just quit making babies. The story had gone on to describe the inevitable decline of *Homo sapiens*, the desperate attempts to cultivate new people in laboratories, the infighting and the wars that ensued simply because there seemed to be little point in doing anything other than accelerating the inevitable end of the human race. Helen had once confessed to Sue Felchak that she wished the events of Chris's story were being played out in real life. That way, she wouldn't feel so totally alone in a world filled with babies. It was totally selfish thinking, of course, fuelled by being forced to watch her friends and colleagues push out one baby after another; each new arrival like a stab to her heart.

"I'd like to go now." Helen grasped Chris' arm to pull him close. "May we swing by the Crystal Lady's stall? I'd like to buy some rose quartz."

"Sure thing, baby," Chris answered with cheer, and it was clear that he was more than happy to get away from the puppies. He'd found that dogs always elicited one of two reactions from Helen; she'd either beg him to buy one, or she would get that melancholic look in her eyes and dip into depression. Thankfully, she'd been able to tear herself away before either had really taken hold, although Chris had seen just the faintest hint of sadness in his wife's eyes.

Chris allowed himself to be lead away. He bade a farewell nod to the puppy stall owner who looked decidedly pissed at what she clearly had figured as a sure-fire sale walking away.

"I think the Crystal Lady was over by the hot-dog stand," Helen said, her demeanor brightening with each step farther away from the puppies. "You don't mind, do you?"

"Not in the least, we have all the time in the world." Chris kissed the top of Helen's head and twitched his nose as her spiky hair tickled it.

"Yes, yes we do," Helen sounded happy. "And we're gonna enjoy every goddamned minute of it!"

"Here, here!" Chris laughed and put on his very best, clipped Disney English accent. "I do so love our adventures, Mrs. Sewell!"

"Pardon me?" a woman's voice from behind. Chris turned his head.

Walking several paces behind them was a couple. The lady of the pair – the owner of the voice – smiled at Chris.

"Can I help you?" Chris asked warily, and stopped in his tracks to eye the couple with suspicion. Helen turned and followed her husband's gaze

"We are *so* sorry to disturb you guys, but we just had to tell you just how cute you both are!" the woman gushed. "Ain't that so, Vernon?"

The guy – Vernon presumably – looked slightly embarrassed. "If ya say so, darlin'," he answered with an obedient tone in his voice that resonated with many years of agreeing with his woman in order to maintain a peaceful life.

"Err, thank you." Chris was nonplussed; it was quite possible that this was some kind of Northern Texas shake-down.

"Well, would ya look at me not mindin' ma manners!" The woman beamed and her gaudy scarlet lipstick parted to flash brilliant, white – most likely capped – teeth. "I'm Dixie-Lee Theuber, an' this here's ma other half, Vernon." She stepped forward and offered her hand for the shaking.

Politely, Chris shook hands with the lady, and then with her reluctant husband. Helen followed suit.

The woman – Dixie-Lee – was what Chris's Mom would have called *handsome*. She had long, bleached-blonde hair that she'd tied up into a loose bun (in a hurry by the looks of the escaping straggles that dangled either side of her tanned, lined face), bright blue eyes that sparkled from the midst of her generously-applied, blue eye shadow and the glossy lipstick that made the most of plumping out her thin lips. She was dressed in what appeared to be the local uniform of white tank top that strained over oversized, impossibly firm breasts, tight jeans and flip-flops.

"That's really nice of you to say so." Helen smiled at the woman. "Thank you." She puffed out her chest a little at the compliment.

"I'm sorry to disturb you nice folks," Vernon apologized, "Dixie-Lee's a little on the impetuous side. She's always stopping strangers for one reason or another." He gave Chris an apologetic glance on his wife's behalf; it was a look that husbands the world over would have recognized: *she's my wife. I love her more than life itself, but I* honestly *have no control.*

Chris smiled to reassure the man that all was okay, he understood. Theuber looked like he had ten years on Chris, but wore it well; he stood a little over six feet and was fit and tanned. He had mousey-brown hair, twinkling hazel eyes and wore the male counterpart of the local uniform; beige polo shirt, khaki shorts and sandals along with accompanying brown socks.

"It's not often we see such good-looking folk in Flanagan," the woman gushed. "Ain't that right Vernon?"

"Not often, nope. You're right there, hun."

"Would you two mind awfully if I took your picture?" Dixie-Lee asked with over-familiar bluntness.

This took Chris aback. His eyes met Theuber's and the man stared back at him as if this level of awkwardness were commonplace in his life, as if he'd been through this a thousand times before.

"I guess so," Helen said. Although she was enjoying the flattery, she'd picked up on Chris's obvious hesitance.

"Don't worry yerself," the woman laughed, "it's nothing creepy! I'm thinkin' of wearing ma hair short this summer and I'd like it to be like yours." She fished out her camera from her well-loved, brown ostrich skin purse. The camera was one of those quaint, old-fashioned cameras of yesteryear that took actual rolls of film that needed to be developed. Chris honestly didn't realize that people still had those.

"Then I guess it's okay," Helen laughed. "You want us both in your picture?"

"Of course!" Dixie-Lee's eyes sparkled playfully. "I want to show ma friends the gorgeous folk we met at the Flea Market; and they just won't believe me without real and proper proof."

Helen squashed herself up close to Chris. He put his arm around her and set his best false grin for the camera.

A click.

"That's just perfect, folks," Dixie-Lee said, "thank y'all so much."

"Don't mention it." It looked like Helen was actually warming to the woman. "It was our pleasure, wasn't it, babe?"

"Yeah. Our pleasure," Chris sounded wary, although this was, oddly enough not the first time Chris and Helen had been approached by complete strangers for a photograph. Sometimes it was because they had been mistaken for some famous couple or other, on other occasions it was simply for looking so damned cute together.

Chris figured that there still remained the chance of this being a hustle; perhaps Dixie-Lee and her painfully awkward husband would outright ask for money? Or were they going to try sell them something? Or maybe they were building up the patter to invite the Sewells to a private sex party with the swingin' folk of Flanagan?

The latter idea had crossed Chris's mind and in other circumstances, the Theubers were the pretty much the kind of couple that Chris and Helen may well have hooked up with in the right environment.

"Well, thank y'all again," Dixie-Lee effervesced as she shook Chris and Helen's hands in turn once again and with enthusiasm.

If there was some game behind this, now was the time the Theubers would show their hand.

"I hope your new hair style works out," Helen said.

"Thank ya', Ma'am. If'n I can look half as cute as you with it, then it'll be one heck of a happy day!" The woman grinned.

"For the both of us," Vernon added with a wry smile.

"And just what, precisely, do ya mean by that, Vernon Theuber?" Dixie-Lee laughed at her husband.

"You folks have a great day now," Dixie-Lee ordered. She slipped the camera back into her purse. "Come now, Vernon; we've taken up enough of these nice folk's time already," she said as if the whole thing had been *his* idea and not hers.

Theuber raised his eyebrows at Chris, a half-smile playing on his lips. Then Dixie-Lee tugged at his hand, and with a broad, face-splitting smile she ushered him away.

And there it was – perhaps the strangest thing of all about the odd encounter in Chris's mind was that there had been no hustle. No dragging Chris and Helen to some distant relative's stall to sell them a wildly expensive steak-rub or questionable second-hand electrical goods.

It was almost disappointing,

Secretly, Chris had always loved a hustle, and he admired the hustlers with their perfected trade. In truth, he was a bit of a soft-touch that even rookie grifters could spot coming a mile away; the perfect hustle-ee.

"I'd like to buy some steak rub before we go," Chris told Helen as they walked on. "Do you really think that your newest BFF really wanted to plagiarize your hair style?"

"Of course, why else would she want my picture?"

Chris gave his wife a sly grin; she really could be too naive for her own good sometimes.

Helen play-thumped his arm. "You really are too cynical sometimes, Christopher Sewell."

"It's just one on the long list of things that makes you love me," Chris replied, "I do hope that our picture doesn't end up on some seedy jerk-off website." He grinned.

"What? *Sweaty City Folk Fetish dot com*?" Helen laughed at him. "And what if it did?" She put on her faux-serious face, "It wouldn't be our first time on the world-wide-web now, would it?"

Chris looked sheepish. "Oh no, I guess it wouldn't," he said, "I'd forgotten all about that."

They laughed together and it felt good to share a private joke in their own private world; it was at times such as this that for the Sewells the rest of the universe simply melted away.

SEVEN

At the Gas Station

The sun-baked Texas wind slapped mischievously against their faces as Chris and Helen left the market and drove on into town. The Camaro's stereo blasted out the soaring orchestral might of *Roll Over Beethoven* at an incredible volume. This track was, in Helen's opinion at least, the crowning glory of the *Electric Light Orchestra's* entire back catalog and was best listened to at maximum decibels.

Helen rested her hand on Chris' leg as he drove away from the market. She gave him a smile and glanced down at the large tub of *Lunatic Dave's BBQ Beef Rub* that nestled in the center console cup holder; it would go nicely with the dozen or so others he had accumulated from flea markets over the years and would no doubt fit in nicely within Chris's Great Unused BBQ Rub Cupboard back home.

She lifted up the chunk of rose crystal she'd bought from the peculiar, Asian-looking woman with the harelip and held it up to the sunlight. Helen was more than delighted with the excellent price – thirty bucks – she'd haggled the stallholder down to for the baby-pink rock that glinted exquisitely as it refracted the harsh sunlight. She knew precisely what Chris thought of her crystal-healing kick – he'd certainly made no bones about letting her in on his derision. He always maintained that the whole thing was medieval quackery that should have died out along with anti-plague nosegays, pill bugs and leeches.

But Helen had always believed in the healing power of crystals, ever since reading about it in her Mom's new age magazines as she'd struggled through her own teenaged witch phase. The articles had explained in ethereal, earthy terms how a crystal's natural resonance could influence a living body by finding *harmony* at a cellular level. Sure, it sounded like hippy-dippy bullshit but even Chris's cynicism had taken a knock when Helen had used a tiny chuck of rose quartz to miraculously cure a headache he'd had that was so bad that he'd begged her to shoot him.

"I think I'll fill up with gas before we get to the motel," Chris shouted above the music and wind noise and pointed to what at first sight appeared to be an abandoned gas station up ahead. Were it not for the flickering neon **Open** sign, they would have just driven on by. "It'll save us some time tomorrow," he explained.Helen nodded her agreement, although it wasn't terribly clear to her as to why he would need to save time tomorrow; they had all the time in the world for their adventure, remember? Nonetheless, Helen winked at her husband and returned her attention to the pretty refracted light that danced from the crystal.

Chris turned off the pothole strewn main road and onto the forecourt of Flanagan's one and only gas station.

"Are you sure it's open?" Helen asked him, as she turned down the music.

"I'm guessing so," Chris sounded unsure, "there's a sign on the door." He looked around, peering for signs of life.

The sign above the main part of the gas station read:

Bakker's Gas Station & Convenience Store

And below that, hand painted in fading blue:

And Taco's

The gas station was a squat, wooden building, much like the majority of the dwellings they'd seen thus far in the town. And, like those buildings, it too was badly in need of a lick of paint and a little routine maintenance. The actual gas station part of the place appeared to be *really* ancient – easily nineteen twenties. And it looked as if it had last been painted bright white back in the day, when gas was but a few cents a gallon – if the sparse flakes of paint clinging stubbornly to the sun-bleached wood were any indication.

The convenience store section to the building, by contrast looked to be relatively modern – nineteen seventies perhaps – and seemed to have been added on with little thought as to aesthetics and painted in whatever color the construction company happened to have had going spare; some of it was a blood/rust red, some dark blue, some a sickly bile yellow. Standing in the dirt adjacent to the building was a grubby white minivan that had been amateurishly converted for the cooking and sale of the aforementioned tacos.

Chris pulled the Camaro gently up to the solitary gas pump that stood proud from the baked dirt floor. He got out of the car and studied the gas pump.

"I don't think you're supposed to help yourself," Helen informed her husband. She pointed to the small sign tied with frayed string to the post that supported the threadbare canopy that failed miserably in its mission to keep the sun from their heads.

The sign was curt, yet informative:

We Serve You

It was a quaint throwback, practically unique to backwater places such as Flanagan, which also served a convenient purpose as there was nowhere on the ancient pump to actually insert a credit card.

However, Chris thought to himself, the personalized service probably worked better when there was staff around who actually paid attention.

Chris leaned into his car and tapped the logo at centre of the steering wheel. The blast from the Camaro's horn broke the stifling, eerie silence with an abruptness that sounded stark and aggressive and made Helen visibly jump.

Nothing.

Chris hit the horn again.

"Alright, alright!" a gruff voice barked from somewhere beyond the gloom of the gas station. "I heard ya the first freakin' time!"

Startled, Chris turned around to face the gas station employee who walked towards him from the direction of the faded beige port-a-potty that lurked beneath an ancient oak across the road. He had on heavy boots, black baseball cap and denim overalls which sported an oblong button that declared his name to be Newman F Bakker.

"I'm sorry, I thought –"

"You city folks are all the same," Bakker said, his face serious. "Always in a goddamned hurry."

"I'm sorry –" Chris stammered, clearly embarrassed. The guy's face creased into a broad smile. "Only yankin' your chain, Sir. Trust ma' only custom of the day to turn up while I'm indisposed!" He laughed a hearty, carefree laugh that boomed through the hot, still air like a thunderclap.

Chris laughed along to mask his embarrassment.

"Now, what can I do for y'all?" Newman F Bakker asked. He removed his greasy baseball cap as he talked and wiped the sweat from his smooth, shaved head with it. He nodded in greeting to Helen who sat primly in the car, her knees pressed together.

"Fill her up, please."

"I assume you're referring to the *vee-hikal?*" Bakker winked at Helen as he drawled the last word.

Chris' mouth dropped wide open as Helen sputtered into a giggle at the expression on her husband's face. "Excuse me?" he said.

"I'm sorry, Sir. Just a little small-town banter is all, no offence meant." Bakker didn't really appear all that sorry.

Helen got out of the car.

"You'll have to forgive my husband." She smiled at the man. "He doesn't get out of the city that often."

"Houston?" Bakker undid the gas cap, pulled the nozzle from the pump and thrust it into the Camaro like he was making a point.

"Are we that obvious?"

"Yep." Bakker grinned. "That and the dealer name on your licence plate." He pointed towards the plate with a dusty boot. "I've known those snakes-in-the-goddamn-grass since they hawked beaters out of their front yard in Galveston." Bakker grinned as he pulled the trigger and began pumping gas.

Helen laughed. She was more at ease with Bakker than Chris, most likely because she didn't have the whole *protect my woman's honor* macho bullshit going on. This she did find somewhat amusing bearing in mind the fact that she had dressed according to her husband's tastes rather than her own. Helen stretched her legs and ran her fingers through her gritty hair. "I'm going to go grab a soda from the store," she informed Chris, "you want anything?"

Chris squinted at her. "Yeah, get me a Dr. Pepper," he said.

Although he was usually delighted to have his wife on display, Chris found himself feeling a little uncomfortable with Newman F. Bakker's close scrutiny and over-familiarity with Helen. Encouraging his wife's exhibitionist tendencies was all well and good but it always had to be on Chris's terms; whilst he loved to show the world just how hot his wife was – and she was more than pleased to accommodate her husband's vicarphilia fetish – to work for him it had to be in a controlled environment and populated by likeminded individuals; a swinger's club, fetish parties, private orgies and the like. For Chris, it was all about the anonymity of the crowd, which he found far less intimidating than situations such as this – one on one with the impossibly macho Newman F. Bakker really wasn't high on Chris Sewells' list of turn-ons. And for the first time in a long time, Chris wished his wife was dressed in something a little less skimpy.

"You got it, lover!" Helen leaned in and grabbed her purse from the car, seemingly oblivious to the fact that her breasts were threatening to spill out from her top.

"You just go on in, Missy," Newman smirked at Helen as his eyes roamed blatantly along the dark crack of her cleavage, "Ruthie-Peg will take real good care of you."

Helen thanked Bakker and made her way towards the store. She walked with the confident swagger of a woman watched, as if she sensed that the man's eyes were on her tight shorts every step of the way.

"Ruthie-Peg's ma kid sister," Newman seemed keen to keep up the chit-chat with Chris. "We've been takin' care of the place for our Daddy." Chris nodded politely; he didn't really want to engage the man in idle conversation any more than he had to. "There's a complimentary tire check and windshield wash," Bakker continued. "While ya' wait."

"Yeah, sure. Why not?" Chris replied with a fake smile and leaned against the car. At least that would give Bakker something other to do than make idle chit-chat.

Helen entered the cool interior of the convenience store, and a small bell hanging from the ceiling jangled merrily as the door hit it; a jolly, tinkling sound that resounded starkly in the still air. It felt unnaturally cold inside and the minute, downy hairs on Helen's arms stood to attention as gooseflesh crept along her exposed skin; the place was air-conditioned to somewhere around Arctic levels.

The store was deceptively bigger inside than it appeared from the outside; its farthermost wall appeared to be a thousand miles away, as if it were part of an elaborate optical illusion. The age-worn, metal shelves that filled the store were crammed with tinned foods of all descriptions, jars of innumerable colors and contents, dry goods, an array of fresh baked bagels and a wilting, limp selection of supposedly fresh produce that included passion fruit, pineapples, and ugli fruit; not exactly the kind of exotic fare Helen would have expected to see in a place like Bakker's.

"Hello?" Helen's voice was quickly absorbed by the dusty interior.

No reply.

At the left-hand side of the store there was a counter from which hunting rifles, shotguns and ammunition could be purchased, and beyond that a closed post office counter with adjoining UPS collection desk – also closed. Over to the right was a small collection of children's clothing displayed on three racks, beyond which Helen espied a curtained-off section that displayed the notice:

Gag Gifts and Novelties: Over 21's Only

Helen smirked at this; only in prudish, Bible-bashing Texas would they ever describe sex toys as *gag gifts* and *novelties*. It had something to do with an arcane law that prevented any intimation of sexual use, even when the items in question were shaped like monster dicks and vibrated.

The idea intrigued Helen no end, it was certainly mind-boggling to try imagining what kind of erotic playthings they could possibly be selling in a God-fearing, cattle-herding, spit-and-sawdust backwater town such as Flanagan. This was most certainly something she had to see for herself.

Glancing around for any sign of life and seeing none, Helen made her way towards the lure of Gag Gift Corner like a naughty schoolgirl perusing her first liquor store. She squeezed between the rack of kid's clothes and the empty magazine stand, her eyes set firmly on the grimy curtain. Perhaps there would be something fun behind said curtain? It would be nice to surprise Chris for their vacation.

"Feel free to go in and take a look-see if ya like," a disembodied voice startled her. Helen peered around the store and caught a movement behind the counter that boasted a cash register that looked even older than the gas station. It was one of those manual registers that had the big, clunky brass keys, pop-up numbers in the top window and a drawer that rings and then rattles the loose coins around when it opens.

"I take it you are over 21?" the voice sounded almost accusing.

"Y-yes, of course," Helen replied. It was always flattering for a lady to be asked that question, no matter how rudely.

The shape moved again and began to make its way from behind the register. "Sorry if I startled you, Ma'am," the girl behind the counter apologized, "I didn't see ya come in."

"That's okay, I didn't see you either," Helen said as the girl – what was her name again? *Peggy Sue?* – came into view.

How in the Good Lord's name hadn't Helen seen her?

Ruthie-Peg was vast; a huge mountain of a woman.

She was – at the very least – four hundred pounds, most likely four-fifty. She wore humongous, gray sweatpants and an amorphous, dark blue sweat top that accentuated her spreading pit stains to perfection. Ruthie-Peg's shoulder-length mouse-brown hair hung lank and lifeless around a face that looked like it had been inflated; her dark brown eyes squinting out from between puffy eyelids like gemstones set in dough.

Mother Nature had been a complete and utter bitch to poor Ruthie-Peg – there were some obese girls who were fine looking in their own right, and those one could easily imagine as beauties if only they would lose the excess weight.

Sadly, Ruthie-Peg Bakker fell into neither of these categories.

She smiled sweetly across at Helen and looked her up and down. Helen smiled back and tried her level-best not to stare at the enormous girl's chubby hamster cheeks, protruding front teeth and dark, fine-haired moustache.

"Why don't ya go along in and see if there's anything in there that tickles ya fancy?" Ruthie-Peg encouraged her. The big girl's words came out of her throat breathy, squeaky and labored from the exertion of having moved the entire three feet behind the counter. "While that good-looking husband of yours is out shootin' the breeze with ma' brother out there," Ruthie-Peg wheezed as she finally waddled out from behind her refuge. To do so, she had to force the rolls of shuddering fat that encircled her belly through the impractically narrow gap between the counter and the wall, which was no mean feat.

"Thank you, I will." Helen forced a smile. The air-conditioning puffed in her face as she neared a vent and she caught a sour whiff of the girl's body odor from way across the store. Helen ducked behind the curtain and into a small ante-room that was lit by a flickering striplight and adorned by shelves that carried a startling array of sex toys.

The imaginative display of adult playthings for sale was quite shocking for a small-town gas station store. There were the ubiquitous, generic-brand *Rabbit* style toys (*batteries* NOT *included!*), cheap nylon *Naughty*

Nurse outfits (One Size Fits *ALL* – although thinking about the delightfully aromatic Ruthie-Peg, Helen doubted that particular claim would stretch quite that far), a large selection of fake vaginas, blister-packed latex bras and panty sets, riding crops, whips and a shelf-full of solid latex anal-play toys that made the eyes water to just look at them. So, this is what God's Good Folk got up to when the kids were in Sunday school?!

Grinning to herself, Helen made her selection from the astonishing array of playthings; she picked out one for her and Chris and one that she simply *had* to get for Sue and Roger. It would be worth the sixty bucks just to see the look on their faces when they unwrapped their particularly inappropriate souvenir.

Sidestepping the dusty curtain, Helen exited the tiny room clutching the toys. She heard the store's bell tinkle and saw Chris walk in. Helen held her selection of toys aloft; a black leather riding crop and the life-sized, black latex fist with which she planned to embarrass her friends. "Hey, look what I've got!" she shouted across the store to her husband, totally oblivious to Ruthie-Peg's sensibilities and not noticing that Newman F. Bakker had entered the store not two steps behind Chris.

Chris looked suitably mortified and Newman grinned inanely, lifting a hand to his mouth to stifle the obvious snicker.

"Oh crap," Helen muttered as her face turned a quaint shade of puce. She dropped her hands to her sides and tried her best to pretend that she hadn't just waved the world's biggest sex toy over her head. "I am so sorry," she mumbled. She knew that Chris would find the whole scenario amusing – if not arousing to boot – and they'd no doubt laugh about it later; but right then Helen really wanted the earth to crack wide open and swallow her up.

"Ya can pay for those along with your gas," Bakker told her with a smirk. "Bring 'em over to the register an' Ruthie-Peg'll ring 'em up for ya." He nodded to his gargantuan sister who began the arduous three-foot trek to back behind the register. It was entirely possible that the fat woman had a judgmental smirk on her face, but it was difficult to tell for sure beneath the rolls of her chubby cheeks.

"Oh yeah, and Missy," Bakker called over to Helen. "If ya'll still wantin' that Dr. Pepper, the coke machine's over yonder." He pointed to the corner over by the USPS counter. "Only it's Pepsi." He smiled and winked and that made Helen's face flush all over again.

Helen took her walk of shame from Gag Gift Corner across to the checkout. Was she supposed to attempt to explain that the man-sized black fist was meant as a joke gift for friends, even if only to alleviate her own discomfort? Likewise, the riding crop? Under the circumstances, she figured that it really didn't matter. Apart from appeasing the little-girl part of Helen that still cared what strangers may think of her, an explanation was entirely unnecessary.

They'd probably heard it all before and anyway, after today, she'd never see these people again.

Helen got to the checkout under the scrutinizing gaze of Ruthie-Peg, her over-familiar brother and Chris, whose mortification on his wife's behalf had turned quickly to mirth. She wrinkled her nose at the acrid smell of stale sweat and body odor that wafted over the counter from the big girl and found it hard not to wonder just how much more unbearable Ruthie-Peg's stink would be without the cranked-up AC to cover for her. Helen placed the crop and the fist on the counter.

Ruthie-Peg glanced directly into Helen's eyes for the briefest of moments and she saw the big girl eyeing her up and down – was that the look of envy in the Ruthie-Peg's eyes?

"There's an adult theater over in Fort Stockton," Bakker offered, sounding like he was just trying to be helpful. "A couple o' our friends own it and it's always full of playful folks such as yourselves." He winked at Helen, further fuelling her discomfort. "Ya' should look it up – it's called Aphrodite's, an' it's couple's night on Mondays."

Helen said nothing, but wrinkled her nose to let Bakker know that degrading porn, leering old men and sticky carpets was most certainly not her idea of a good time.

"Thank you, but no," Chris said firmly. "We're just passing through; we're actually on our way to San Manuel."

"The nudist colony for swingin' folk?" Bakker grinned, "I thought so."

"Actually, it's clothing optional," Helen defended.

"Yep, that's what they all say."

"They?"

"We get a lot of folk passin' through here on the way there," Bakker explained. "An' they all say precisely the same thing – it ain't nudist, it's *clothing optional*." He laughed an affable laugh. "A couple of good looking folk like yourselves would get along real well there, what ya' reckon, Ruthie-Peg?"

Bakker's sister scrunched up her flabby face into something that kind of resembled a smile, but then again it *was* difficult to be sure. "You're not wrong there, Newman," she squeaked. "I heard they're crying out for some good- looking guys." She stared at Chris, blatantly checking him out head to toe. "They'd just love you, Mister." She flushed a little as her pudgy fingers busied themselves wrapping the giant latex fist in stiff brown paper.

"Hey, it looks like ma kid sister's taken quite a shine to ya, son," Bakker chortled. He gave Chris a hearty slap on the back. "What ya' say, Ruthie-Peg?"

Ruthie-Peg looked just like Helen had a few moments ago; as if she, too were praying that the ground would open up and swallow her.

It would need to be a very big hole.

Helen smiled sweetly at the fat girl's awkwardness in an attempt to show her a little solidarity; *mortally embarrassed women of the world unite!* But unfortunately, it came across on Helen's face as something more akin to pity.

Ruthie-Peg said nothing. She shot her teasing sibling a withering glance and rang up the gas and sex toys in silence. As she reached over the counter to hand Helen her purchases, Ruthie-Peg let out a strained fart that sounded like the mournful song of a marooned whale.

****

"I can't believe she just did that!" Helen finally cracked, as Chris drove off the gas station forecourt.

"I can't believe you held it together in there," Chris said admiringly. "You usually crack straight away at a fart."

Helen creased up laughing, her sides physically hurting. Chris was right, farts had always hit Helen's funny bone, and probably always would – it was a weakness that was all too often exploited by her more ruthless students. For Helen, it was the most hilarious thing about the entire episode – *including* the sex toy announcement – how the poor fat girl had kept her face painfully straight in the event of her own fart, nary a glimmer of embarrassment, a hint of a smile, or even an acknowledgement that she'd just passed gas like a dying cetacean. That was some rare talent right there.

"I don't know what was funnier," Chris continued, "that poor girl's unfortunate gas problem or her facial hair and Billy-Bob teeth!" He laughed. "At first, I thought she was wearing a disguise!"

They giggled together at this revelation and drowned out their hilarity with thunderous music from their favorite band.

The Camaro pulled away from the forecourt and onto the road and Chris headed towards where he figured the motel would be situated in a small hick town such as Flanagan. As they left the gas station behind, Chris gave the place one last glance in the rear-view.

Newman F. Bakker stood in the dirt next to the gas pump waving them off and speaking into the cell phone he had pressed to his ear. And behind the man, Chris saw a white *Mountaineer* pull up to the gas pump.

EIGHT

Flanagan's Last Barrel

"Welcome to the Flanagan's Last Barrel Motel," the sleazy-looking guy sitting behind the laminate reception desk greeted the Sewells with an odd-looking smile. "This your first time in our little town?" He pushed his wire-framed, tinted spectacles back up the bridge of his greasy nose and squinted through them at Helen's chest.

"Yeah, we're just passing through," Chris told him.

"That's what everyone says." The motel manager laughed. "There's folks that have lived here for three generations and more that still say they're just passin' through!" He laughed again, loudly.

"We have a room booked under Sewell." Helen interrupted the man's mirth. "We pre-booked last week, Mr. –?" Helen made a vain attempt to divert the man's attention from her breasts. Not that she minded too much that the manager was unashamedly staring at the delicious valley and supple flesh on display, she just wanted to get this over with and get to the room.

"I'm sorry, where *are* my manners?" The motel manager grinned. "Rizzo, Robbie Rizzo." Still seated, he extended a hand for Helen to shake and gave her what was most likely his very best professional face. "I'm the manager here – well, part-owner, kinda – it's complicated."

Helen shook Rizzo's hand, grimacing as his clammy palm pressed into hers.

"Pleased to make your acquaintance, Mrs. Sewell," Rizzo leered. "I do hope you enjoy your stay in our humble community." He finally, reluctantly let go of Helen's hand, and if he noticed the relief on her face, he didn't show it. "I'm afraid that for city folk such as your good selves, Flanagan's pretty much a one-horse town." He smiled at his guests. "Without the horse."

Chris and Helen laughed along with Rizzo on that one; the years of practice of forced hilarity at Roger Felchak's lame jokes had finally come in useful.

"Here we go." Rizzo said finally as he wiped a tear from his pock-marked cheek. "I've got your booking form." He lifted up a yellowed sheet of paper that had been unevenly torn from a legal pad. "We don't often get people making bookings; more often they just show up on their way to someplace else."

Chris was more than used to guys making an effort to shake hands with Helen and leaving him out, so much so that he wasn't in the least bit put out by Rizzo's apparent rudeness; he put it down to the fact that most men will go to any lengths for a touch of female skin and that Helen's breasts had a tendency to jiggle in a most alluring manner whenever she shook hands. Chris did, however find it difficult to take his eyes off of Rizzo's heavily acne-scarred face; he thought it resembled some ancient and remote moon from an asteroid-plagued corner of the Milky Way (an analogy that wasn't helped any by Rizzo's circular face that was topped by a buzz-cut so severe that it would be impossible to tell what color the man's hair was supposed to be were it not for the smattering of gray stubble on either side above his ears). By the look of him, poor old Robbie Rizzo had been plagued by bad skin since the day he'd discovered his first dick hair and even now, with teenagedom a long way behind him, the craters on Rizzo's forehead and chin were punctuated with angry-looking zits and yellowheads.

"You do know it's cash only?" Rizzo addressed Chris for the first time since the Sewells had walked into his cramped office; it stood to reason that the misogynistic bastard didn't believe in women carrying money.

"You did say. On the 'phone." Helen smiled her best smile at him. "Forty dollars for one night?" She pulled out the cash from her purse and Rizzo gave her the impression that a woman actually paying for something genuinely disarmed him. Was Flanagan just your typical, small Northern Texas town or a jolly jaunt back to the nineteen-fifties, she wondered?

"That's just fine, Ma'am." Rizzo forced a convivial smile and shot a glance at Chris, to let him know that he was an emasculated soft-dick who gave his woman far too much rein.

Chris said nothing and just smiled back at the guy.

Rizzo took the cash and stood up. "Okay, now that's all sorted, I'll show you to your room."

Helen's eyes widened.

Rizzo was perhaps the tallest human being she'd clapped eyes upon. Standing at least six-seven/six-eight, Rizzo was so tall in fact, that Helen had not even registered that he'd been *sitting down* this whole time; she had assumed that the man had been standing behind his crappy little counter. As Rizzo rose to his feet to tower above her and Chris, it was Helen's turn to stare at *his* chest. It was broad, muscular and clad in a tight-fitting, black thrash metal T-shirt that was emblazoned with an image of a pneumatically-breasted young woman clad in strategically placed, shredded clothes. The words *Anal Thrush* were printed over her head and *Thrash Metal* at her exquisitely bare feet; both phrases in an apocalyptic font that was somewhat difficult to read.

"It's my son's band, he's sixteen," Rizzo explained as he caught Helen's stare.

"You must be very proud," Helen said.

"Yeah, as a matter of fact I am," Rizzo said without a hint of irony in his voice. He made his way around to the Sewells' side of the counter, pulling up his ill- fitting jeans that sagged around his butt as he walked.

"It really is okay, I'm sure we can find it," Chris said. It shouldn't be too difficult a task since the motel had only about fifteen rooms, twenty at best.

Rizzo towered over his guests. "You guys have any luggage?" He blatantly ignored Chris, looking straight through him to ogle Helen's legs.

"In the car. We can get our bags once we get to the room," Chris deflected. "If you could just point us in the general direction – there really is no need to go to any trouble."

"No trouble at all, Sir," Rizzo was firm but polite. "It's all part of the service here at Flanagan's Last Barrel"

"You shouldn't leave your office on our account," Helen added. Although she was quite comfortable with the motel manager mentally undressing her, she'd picked up on her husband's reticence at being in the presence of Rizzo for any longer than was absolutely necessary – what attentive wife wouldn't? "What if someone calls to book a room?"

Rizzo laughed again, this time with a patronizing tone. "Like I said before, Ma'am, all of our business here is walk-ins. There's only been one phone booking in the two years I've worked here. And that was you," and so saying, Robbie Rizzo ushered the Sewells out of the cool sanctuary of the motel office and out into the sticky heat of the early evening.

Helen and Chris followed Rizzo out, passed an old, gray Camry that had seen far better days – the only other vehicle in the lot other than Chris's Camaro and therefore presumably Rizzo's – along the walkway towards the twin row of utilitarian rooms that comprised Flanagan's Last Barrel. Chris was forced to take long, quick steps in order to keep up with Rizzo's lanky gait – keen as he was to avoid the humiliation of being left behind by the taller man.

The motel's rooms were set out on either side of the dusty courtyard, a perfect mirror image of each other. Along the center of the courtyard was a crumbling, concrete walkway which had been cracked by uncounted years of ruthless Texan heat into unintentional crazy-paving. There were weeds in the cracks between the broken concrete, frazzled and brown where they'd been sprayed with *Roundup* and left to rot.

Nervous, tiny green lizards spooked by the unexpected presence of humans scampered up and along the walls. Occasionally, they would pause here and there to snap at the myriad mosquitoes that rested on the white stucco between blood dinners. The buzzing insects that were not resting continued to hum and whine hungrily around the heads of the three people dumb enough to be outside at that time of the day.

"I've put you in room eighteen," Rizzo informed the Sewells. He waved a lengthy arm in the direction of the farthest rooms along the row. "It's nearest the ice machine." He paused for breath as if the stifling heat had stolen it from him. "Ice machine's broken though, but at least you know where it's at." He smiled once more at Helen.

Helen reciprocated and shielded her eyes against the sun to look up into Rizzo's almost perfectly rounded face, and then around at the motel. The place boasted the style of accommodation that she'd been seen in an endless procession of movies featuring hick towns for almost as long as movies have been around. It was entirely generic, devoid of character and, one might even say soulless; even the Bates Motel had a certain charm by comparison.

It was easy to see that the place had been poorly maintained over the years. It sported sun-faded wood that had last been painted white a long, long time ago and many of its grimy window panes were cracked in the corners. As if to complete the cliché, every room at Flanagan's Last Barrel had an ancient, window-hanging air conditioning unit sticking out from a window – all of which were silent.

"Here you go," Rizzo announced as proudly as one would delivering guests to a suite at the Ritz and not room eighteen of the Flanagan's Last Barrel Motel in ass-end, Texas. "Now, are you sure you don't want help with your bags?"

Chris shook his head and stuck to his guns. "Thank you, no. I'll get them later." He said.

The room key Rizzo pulled from his pocket was attached to a six-inch piece of wood upon which was etched the motel's name and address. "You'd be surprised just how many folk walk off with our keys,"

Rizzo told them, wryly observing his guest's surprise at the size of the fob; folks like the Sewells were much more used to those electronic key cards that they used in the fancy la-di-da city hotels.

"Do they post them back to you?" Helen asked.

"Not one so far," Rizzo replied sternly, "but a man can hope."

Rizzo swung open the door to room eighteen and Rizzo stepped in. Chris and Helen followed close behind. "The dial for the AC is next to the bathroom door." Rizzo said and pointed to the yellowed door across the room. "There's a mini refrigerator under the credenza and the TV's all free."

Helen's eyes adjusted to the gloom that bore stark contrast to the glare outside. She surveyed the room and was pleased to note that the place really wasn't as bad as she'd been expecting. It was sparsely furnished – minimalist even – containing a king-sized bed adorned with a garish, floral top sheet, a burgundy faux-leather armchair that seemed like it had been stuck in the room as an afterthought, and the aforementioned laminate credenza upon which sat an old style cathode-ray TV. Casting a glance beneath the bed, Helen espied the bunch of sticky roach traps that were dotted with what looked like several months' worth of insect victims, some of whom were still alive.

As she stepped further into the room, Helen felt her K-Swiss sticking to the shabby old rug beneath her feet; the rug covering up a large patch of the cracked, peeling linoleum that spanned between the bottom of the bed and the credenza.

"Is this the biggest room you have?" Chris asked.

"No, Sir," Rizzo replied, with an offended frown.

"Would it be possible to upgrade to a bigger one?" Rizzo snorted at Chris and pushed his glasses back up his nose.

"Upgrade?" he spoke slowly. "I'm sorry, son, I think you misunderstood me." Rizzo shot a sly grin at Helen that spoke volumes.

"This is not the biggest room we have, but then again it's not the smallest neither." Rizzo absently picked at a ripe zit on his chin as he spoke. He popped it between his thumb and finger nails and wiped the resultant yellow fluid onto his shirt. He then made an exaggerated point of pulling back the dirty net curtain and peering outside. "You see, here at Flanagan's Last Barrel, the rooms are all the same size." He laughed at Chris's expense.

"Gotcha," Chris said with a nod. If Rizzo was trying to embarrass him, he certainly wasn't about to take the bait and lose face in front of Helen.

"But I tell you what I can do for you nice folks." Rizzo became animated. "I can upgrade you to a suite," he practically spat out *upgrade*.

"But I thought you said –" Helen began.

Rizzo held up a hand to silence Helen and stepped over to the door that faced the bathroom. He unlocked it, pushed it open.

"Ta-da!" Rizzo exclaimed, his face beaming with pride as if he'd unlocked the darkest secrets of the Higgs Boson and not just the door to room twenty.

"A *suite*?" Chris smiled at Rizzo. Now it was his turn to play the superiority card.

"Yes Sir," Rizzo replied, sounding like a snooty *Monty Python* character. He then gazed down through his smudged glasses at Chris, as if daring him to say something more.

"It's just perfect!" Helen exclaimed in anticipation of her husband's sardonic onslaught; experience had taught her that once cornered, Chris was not one to let such challenges slip by him without unleashing the full might of his sarcastic wit and vocabulary. "Thank you so much, Mr. Rizzo!" She fished out a twenty-dollar bill and pressed it into the tall man's hand, her fingers lingering on his moist palm; there's nothing quite like a woman's touch to diffuse masculine aggression.

"Thank *you*, Ma'am." Rizzo appeared to be genuinely pleased with the gratuity.

"Yes, thank you," Chris added.

"Like I said, all part of the service." Rizzo pocketed the cash.

Chris mumbled quietly to himself. He'd been looking forward to taking Rizzo guy down a peg or two after the snideness over his upgrade request, and now Helen had gone and spoiled his fun. It was clear that the oversized yokel considered Chris to be a spoiled city boy who never stayed anyplace in his coddled life where they didn't put a mint on your pillow and fold the first sheet of your three-ply lavatory paper into a triangle.

Chris *had* been going to ask about room service but already it was obvious that it would be moot point at Flanagan's Last Barrel, so he simply kept schtum to avoid more derision from Rizzo. Instead, he asked "Can you recommend a good place to get food around here?"

"Yeah," Rizzo answered without hesitation, "there's the taco wagon next to Bakker's gas station. Best tacos in town."

"We saw that earlier," Helen told the tall man. "It's the only tacos in town, isn't it?" She smiled again at Rizzo; he was enjoying having his fun with them both – that much was obvious.

"You got it Ma'am." Rizzo giggled with an almost child-like sound that sounded alien coming from such a huge frame. "In fact, it's pretty much the *only* food you can get around these parts that you don't have to cook yourself. They tend to open up around sundown."

"Tacos sound awesome," Chris said. "I didn't realize just how hungry I was until you said tacos." He smiled. "Do they deliver?"

Rizzo looked over his glasses at Helen and gave her an *'is this guy for real?'* look. Chris really was making this far too easy. "No Sir, they do not," Rizzo said. His words came out slow and deliberate, as if he were really putting a great deal of effort into controlling his mouth. "But then again, they are only a mile and a quarter along the road; shouldn't be too much trouble in that fancy car of yours."

Helen chuckled to herself. For as much as she loved her husband; he really could be a naive prick sometimes. Perhaps it would be good for them to venture out of the cities and away from four star hotels a little more often?

"That's no problem at all, Mr. Rizzo," Helen closed the conversation down before Chris's sometimes fragile ego could take another kicking. "I'll send my husband out later."

"Sounds like a plan, Ma'am," Rizzo agreed. "Now don't y'all forget that use of our pool is included in your price. You'll find it at the other side of the office," he told them. "We had the pool guy in to give it the once-over this afternoon so it's crystal clear and good to go." He eyed Helen down, up, then down again. "It's the perfect opportunity to strip down to your bikini and cool off after a hot day like today," he said with a wink. "After five PM, the water's so warm it's like taking a bath." And again, with the lascivious grin.

"We'll be sure to bear that in mind, thank you," Chris said, the firmness returning to his voice. "Now if you'll please excuse us –"

Taking the not so subtle hint for once, Rizzo backed out of the room. He placed the key and its monster fob on top of the TV. "If you need anything, just give me a holler, I'm here all night," he said, "anything at all." He winked at Helen one last time and finally made his exit.

"Well, this is not so bad." Helen sat herself down on the bed and bounced up and down to test its firmness, her breasts all but tumbling from her halter.

"I guess," Chris was forced to agree. "I've been dreading this part of the trip – you know crappy how these places can be," he said.

Past experience – before they were able to afford much, much better – had submitted the Sewells to bed bugs, filthy bed sheets, faulty plumbing, clogged toilets, cold hot water, no AC – they'd even had one motel room broken into while they were still asleep in it.

Chris left Helen to bounce on the bed and peered into the adjoining room of their 'suite'. Not surprisingly, it was absolutely identical to the one in which he was standing, right down to the crooked, framed marketing pamphlet on the wall next to the en-suite door and the mummified cockroaches under the bed. "It was nice of Lurch Addams to give us the executive upgrade," Chris said in a grand voice and began to giggle.

Helen smirked and burst out laughing. As used as she was to Chris's pampered exterior, there were times such as this that he never failed to amuse. She climbed from the bed, threw her arms around her husband and kissed him full on the mouth.

"I do love you, Mr. Sewell," she told him as she licked the salty taste of his sweat from her lips.

"Likewise, Mrs. Sewell."

Chris wrapped his arms around his wife and pulled her close; with Helen as his room mate, even the crappiest of motels could be bearable.

****

The bathroom was small and cramped, but clean. It boasted a cast iron, claw-foot bath into which the fat-headed shower cascaded. The shower curtain was three inches or so shorter than it needed to be and consequently much of Helen's shower spray had ended up on the concave bathroom floor where it gurgled away along the tiles into a small, stainless steel grate.

Helen stepped out from the foggy steam of the hot shower and wrapped a thick, white towel tightly around her chest, her damp body snuggling against the thick pile that cocooned her. Helen had been pleasantly surprised at the towels; they were of a far superior quality than she would have suspected for a place like the Last Barrel. Ever the cynic, she had actually caught herself examining each one to see if someone had picked off an embroidered *Best Western* or *Hilton* logo and replaced it with the Last Barrel's. There was no such chicanery and Helen chastised herself for being so damned snobbish. The Flanagan's Last Barrel logo sat discretely in the corner of each towel – a tiny embroidered brown barrel with *FLB* over it. What was more unusual to Helen was that the logo was nowhere else to be seen around the motel.

Tucking the end of the towel in on itself under one arm to keep it up in that way only women seem to know how, Helen shivered and stepped from the bathroom to check on the thermostat. It was cold and her skin crawled with gooseflesh, her nipples delightfully stiff.

Upon inspection of the antiquated, manual thermostat, Helen discovered that Chris had set the dial to sixty-seven degrees, as was his habit – there was no wonder that she was freezing! Helen flicked the dial around to a more bearable seventy-five and the air conditioner juddered to a reluctant stop, rattling the window through which it protruded in protest. This was typical Chris, setting the temperature to what would feel like absolute zero knowing full well that his poor wife – who felt the cold more than he did – was heading for the shower. Although, the cool air did feel kind of soothing on Helen's bare, sun-reddened shoulders and she was kind of grateful for the relief that it provided her in that respect.

Was it possible that Chris had actually thought of that and had set the AC accordingly? No – she knew her husband well enough to know that he'd not have given it a minute's thought and he'd just randomly cranked down the AC before heading out to play hunter-gatherer at Flanagan's one and only fast food outlet. Hiding his embarrassment at having asked Rizzo if the taco truck did deliveries, Chris had joked that the truck's marketing slogan should be; *You want tacos, you come and damn well get 'em!*

"Welcome to Hicksville, USA, baby". Chris had laughed, barely concealing his indignation at having to actually go fetch his own food.

But, dutiful husband that he was, Chris had gone anyways – had even managed to do so without grumping too much. It may only be a mile and a skip away, but the gesture had made Helen smile and she had *(almost)* forgiven him for attempting to freeze her to death.

Helen flicked quickly through all of the available – *free* – channels on the prehistoric TV. All freakin' six of them – Mr. Rizzo certainly hadn't done them too many favors there. Two of the channels showed season one *Family Guy* re-runs and the other four were in Spanish and featured silicone-breasted Latino girls in bikinis presiding over incomprehensible game shows. The – exclusively male, it transpired – contestants didn't really seem to care all that much whether they won or lost, they simply grinned inanely when they got the customary hug from the busty host girls at the end of the show.

Leaving the TV on just for the noise, Helen padded across the room to examine the framed promotional pamphlet that hung on the wall. Although, hung was not quite the operative word; it was in actually bolted on to the wall with four hefty screws, as if anyone would truly want to try stealing the thing.

WELCOME TO FLANAGAN'S LAST BARREL MOTEL!

The title exclaimed in dark blue, bold typeface. Beneath it was some faux-educational bullshit of dubious historical accuracy and photographs of happy, smiling families in expansive, spotless rooms that were devoid of cockroaches, sticky floors and inch-thick dust. Either these pictures had been taken a geological age ago, or in a different motel entirely.

The pamphlet itself was presented neatly in the dark wood frame and surrounded by a cream colored matte. It was dotted by hundreds of tiny, black bugs that had crawled under the glass to commit what appeared to have been a mass suicide, giving away the fact that it had been quite some time since the motel had last produced its marketing literature.

Helen's eye moved to a couple of paragraphs that were printed in black italics which made them stand out amidst the bland marketing-speak:

'How the Last Barrel Got Our Name'.

Helen cringed, this was just the sort of poor grammar that grated on her and she had to strongly resist the urge to mark it with a red cross and put *' SEE ME AFTER CLASS'* in the margin.

Once a teacher, always a teacher.

Helen read on.

'On January 16 1919, ratification of 18th amendment to the Constitution instituted Prohibition. On October 28 1919, Congress passed the Volstead Act to enforce the law. On October 29 1919, Francis Flanagan opened for business.

Of Irish descent, Flanagan was a colorful – if somewhat volatile – character; rumor had it that he was wanted in at least six states for crimes as diverse as bank robbing, fraud and manslaughter.'

Here was a grainy, sepia photograph of a diminutive, pointy-faced Francis Flanagan with a broad grin across his face, looking decidedly odd in a ridiculously wide Stetson. In each hand, he held aloft a ceramic jar.

'His popularity in the area grew steadily as he supplied illegal moonshine whiskey throughout Texas and up into most of Arizona, using his profits to build the town that was to bear his name.

The motel was one of the first buildings that Flanagan had built, both as a resting place for his customers who came from across two states to collect their moonshine, and as an illegal drinkery.'

Drinkery? Was that even a real word? Helen would have to ask Chris upon his return.

'During the years of the Great Depression, Flanagan continued to grow his town and take good care of its citizens, ensuring work where he could, and food on their tables where he couldn't offer paid employment. To the townsfolk, he became a hero.

When Prohibition was finally repealed with the passage of the 21st amendment to the constitution Dec 5 1933, Francis Flanagan set aside the final barrel of moonshine in a secret room beneath the Motel. It was subsequently built into the walls of the new Motel after it was rebuilt following the fire in 1964 that burned the entire building to the ground.

Flanagan's nemesis – a police officer by the name of Garrison Pemberton – hounded Flanagan throughout the prohibition years, until he mysteriously disappeared in June 1932, just six months before the end of Prohibition. Just before he was to mount a final assault on Flanagan's still.

Legend has it that Garrison Pemberton's body is in that last barrel that Flanagan made from the still and that the myth was put about by Flanagan himself to prevent anyone from opening it.

Francis Flanagan's personal superstition had it that as long as that last barrel remained in his town, Prohibition would never happen again – a belief that has held true for nearly eighty years.

With the end of Prohibition, and therefore his lucrative business, Francis Flanagan went on to

(continued over)'

There was just something to Helen's nature that made her desperate to know what Francis Flanagan had gone on to be after Prohibition. A respectable businessman? A lawyer? A murderer? She found instances such as this to be quite infuriating, inflaming as they did the natural curiosity that had driven her to become an educator in the first place; she was never content knowing just half the story. If only she could instil even a fraction of that love of learning into just a handful of her students!

It had been her own tenth grade biology teacher who always encouraged his students to research the subject in books, often by giving them a nebulous brief on a subject. His philosophy – one that Helen tried to adhere to herself – was that whilst a student was looking up one subject, they would accidentally hit upon others that caught their interest. This would, in turn, lead to another and another – and so on. *Learning by Osmosis*, he'd called it, and was totally proud of his play on words.

Sadly, in today's real world of teaching for test-passing and the instant-access information of the World Wide Web, her old teacher's philosophy was a dying, if not already deceased, one. As inspiring a teacher that Helen thought herself to be, she usually struggled to infuse even a passing interest of learning in her students, let alone a modicum of joy.

She rooted through Chris's travel bag and retrieved the folding hunting knife that he insisted on bringing along on every trip for what he called *just-in-cases*. She snapped the thing open and used the fine tip to unscrew the fastenings that held the pamphlet's frame to the wall. One of the screws – the second to be freed from its sheetrock prison – slipped from Helen's hand and bounced merrily across the floor and rolled behind the credenza.

"Shit," she grumbled beneath her breath and suddenly thought that vandalizing the motel room was not such a great idea after all. She dropped to her hands and knees and scrabbled a wary hand around behind the cheap unit, cringing at the thought of what unpleasant creepy-crawlies may be lurking there to greet her. Remarkably, and luckily for Helen, there were none. Instead she retrieved a corpulent dust bunny the size of a large hamster, a black match book with *Aphrodite's* emblazoned across its front in garish, neon pink, the errant screw she was looking for and a driver's license . She gave the license a cursory glance, wiping away the thick layer of dust from its front to peer at a smiling face with bright, white teeth and big, brown doe-eyes. And Helen couldn't help but wonder just how pissed Patricia Carey had been when she'd discovered that her driver's license was missing.

Helen placed the license on top of the TV – she'd hand it in to the motel manager in the morning – and went back to work on the picture frame.

Once all four screws were unfastened from the wall, Helen carefully lifted the frame down and placed it face down on the bed. She then saw that the rear of the frame itself was held in place with brass, flat-head screws; clearly the purloining of old promotional pamphlets was a serious problem for Flanagan's Last Barrel.

With a resigned sigh – she was beginning to wish she'd never started with this task – Helen dug the knife into the first of the screw heads and slowly turned it.

A sharp knock on the door startled her. She jumped and turned towards the door with guilt written all over her face. It was a rare occasion indeed that Helen did anything anywhere near as renegade as removing picture frames from motel walls, and her heart thumped like a kid caught stealing from the pantry between meals.

"I thought I told you to take the key," she admonished her husband as she walked to the door, the skin on her bare feet crawling at the touch of an unidentifiable sticky patch she stepped in on the floor next to the bed. "Those tacos better be good, Mister." She opened the door.

"Sorry to disturb you, Ma'am." It was Robbie Rizzo and not Chris who leered down at her from the doorway and framed by the dark, star-spotted Texas sky.

"Is there a problem, Mr. Rizzo?" Helen asked him. She pushed the door to minimise the gap, not wanting the motel manager to see that she was wantonly vandalizing his property.

"Er, no problem, no, nothing wrong at all, Ma'am. And call me Robbie." Rizzo smiled at Helen and the harsh light from the room accentuated the miniature peaks and craters of his acne-pitted face. "Is *Mr*. Sewell there?"

"He's out buying tacos from the gas station." Immediately Helen regretted telling the man that. Now Rizzo knew for certain that she was alone, although it wouldn't have taken a triple-digit IQ to notice that the Camaro was gone from the parking lot. There was just something about the way that Rizzo stared wide-eyed and blatant at her naked feet that was simply unnerving.

This was exactly the kind of situation that served well to make Helen feel both vulnerable and foolish at the same time; vulnerable because she had just confirmed to a complete stranger that she was alone and standing at the open door clad in only a towel, and foolish because she was a grown woman who could take care of herself. Plus, there was the fact that the towel itself was providing the most coverage her body had enjoyed all day.

"Just making sure you're happy with the *suite*, Ma'am," Rizzo said with a smile and as he spoke his jaw mashed a white blob of gum around in his broad mouth.

The word took Helen aback a little. She had forgotten that the nice Mr. Rizzo *(call me Robbie)* had rolled out the red carpet for her and Chris and had unlocked the door to the adjoining room.

"Everything's fine – just fine," she told Rizzo. "Thank you." She gave the man her sweetest smile and pushed at the door to close it.

"It's a quiet night." Rizzo clearly hadn't finished with his visit quite yet. Helen quit pushing at the door and smiled as politely as she could. "You're the only guests we got in tonight, so's you can feel free to make as much noise as ya like." Rizzo gave her the lascivious leer that he'd perfected. "Ain't nobody gonna complain."

Helen shuddered, *now* all too aware that she was utterly alone.

"Say, you folks ought to go visit the Bluebonnet fields tomorrow." Rizzo sounded chirpy. "They're a couple of miles due west of here, well worth the drive." Rizzo was obviously determined to keep the unwelcome conversation going, no matter how awkward his guest was feeling. He stared down at Helen and studied her pink-painted toe nails. "It's real romantic out there, a whole sea of blue as far as ya care to look."

"I don't think we'll have the time, we're not staying in town that long," Helen said. Of course, Rizzo knew that already because they were staying in his motel and had booked for just the one night.

"Ya can't pick 'em because they're the state flower an' that's illegal," Rizzo insisted. "But they're sure as hell perdy to look at."

"Thank you for the recommendation, Mr. Rizzo – *Robbie* – I'll make sure we make the time to drop by and take a look." She pushed on the door again.

Rizzo stepped forward and stuck his giant, soft-soled shoe in the door jamb. "While I'm here, I may as well check on your air conditioning, make sure it's working good and proper." He gave a cursory nod at the silent AC unit. "It don't seem to be on right now," he drawled.

Helen did her best to hide her panic and wished to fuck that she'd been wearing more than a towel when she'd opened the door. "That won't be necessary," she said with a firmness that surprised even herself. She, too glanced at the rickety unit that clung to the window like some giant, mechanical leach where earlier it had been rattling and humming like a 1980's boom-box. "Trust me, it's working just fine."

"That's as may be, Ma'am, but I still need to check it out." Rizzo leaned a little of his weight against the door, as if he were testing Helen's on the other side. "It's not been used for quite a while; you're the first folks in this room for a month or two."

"I can get my *husband* to take a look at it and give you a call if there's anything wrong," Helen emphasized and peered up at Rizzo.

The man was now dominating the doorway and Helen could smell the stale gum on his breath and the musky undertones of his sweat. "He'll be back any minute," she told him.

"Look, Ma'am," Rizzo's tone somehow managed to be both polite *and* menacing at the same time. "I'm just tryin' to do ma job here. If anything went wrong with that unit while you folks were in your bed, you'd soon be complainin' at me." He squinted down at Helen's cleavage that peeped so provocatively over her towel.

Rizzo pushed heavily on the door and it gave a little. Helen leaned her weight against her side, a worried expression across her face.

"Tacos!" Chris's voice piped up from the darkness behind the hotel manager. "Hey there, Mr. Rizzo, is everything okay here?"

Helen's relief was tangible as she felt Rizzo's weight shift away from the door as he stepped back from the doorway.

"Yes, Sir," Rizzo was pleasantness personified. "I was just checking that everything was to your good lady's satisfaction." He gave one final glare at Helen, as if he were committing to memory her every bump, curve and inch of skin that was visible around the towel. And then his eyes cast downwards to her feet again.

"Mr. Rizzo was just asking if he could check the air conditioning," Helen explained, knowing that the slight strain in her voice would portray to her husband just how uncomfortable this gum-chewing pizza-face was making her. "I told him it was all okay."

"Then I guess it's okay, Mr. Rizzo – sorry, *Robbie*." Chris smiled his broadest smile at the man. "Perhaps you would like to check it out in the morning, when we've gone." Of course, he'd picked up on his wife's discomfort; even Chris knew when the games should stop.

Rizzo backed off, in fact he *backed-the-fuck-off*, as Chris would have worded it. He flashed his wide, shit-eating grin at Chris and treated himself to one final letch at Helen's toes. "That's no problem at all, Mr. Sewell, happy to oblige," Rizzo's voice remained affable, as if he were the self-conscious one here. "You folks have a good night now, and remember what I said about the noise."

With that, he was gone, swallowed up by the darkness that lurked between the porch lights.

Chris walked into the room and with him came the heady scent of hot tacos that had Helen salivating on the spot. She slammed the door closed behind her husband and flicked down the latch on the lock. She also engaged the small, brass security chain in its tarnished cradle.

"What was that about the noise?" Chris wanted to know as he cast a quizzical glance at the displaced picture frame that lay prone upon the bed. "And what have we been up to, Mrs. Sewell?"

"Oh, that?" Helen looked sheepishly at her husband. "I got bored. And as far as the noise goes, the nice Mr. Rizzo informed me that since there's no other guests staying at the motel tonight; we can kick up as much ruckus as we want." She grinned her dirtiest grin at Chris, her eyes suddenly filled with wanton promise.

Chris pulled Helen to him and folded his long arms around her bare shoulders. "Then it would be rude not to take full advantage of said situation, my darling," Chris said before kissing his wife deeply, his tongue seeking out hers and with one hand buried in her damp hair.

NINE

Motel Sex

The tacos lasted all of fifteen minutes. They were greasy and literally dripping with fat but nonetheless they were outrageously delicious.

The fresh meat was so decadently moist that it simply dissolved on the tongue and was complimented by the spices that made it delightfully hot but so very much *more-ish*.

Helen and Chris had decided on eschewing seduction in favor of the food – partly because they were both ravenous and the tacos smelled so damned good and partly to prolong the anticipation of the physical delights to come – there was no reason to hurry since after all, they did have all night.

Gorged to satisfaction, Helen and Chris sat crossed-legged on the motel bed, their bellies full, appetites sated. Together, they watched a *CSI* rerun on the old TV set.

The picture frame was back in its rightful position on the wall; the inescapable lure of the tacos had beaten hands-down Helen's curiosity about the wonderful little town of Flanagan and all thoughts of its founder and his escapades had quickly evaporated.

"Well, this is predictable," Chris said without breaking his view of the TV show. "You can tell from the off who the killer is."

"Is it because they announced Robert Guillame as the guest star on the opening credits, and the killer is always the guest star?" Helen chuckled. This was a favorite beef of Chris's, so much so that it was a wonder as to why he ever bothered watching *CSI* in the first place.

"Nah, it's because the killer's pretty much always the black guy," Chris laughed.

"Or it could be that we've seen this episode a thousand times before." Helen laughed at her husband's well-worn repartee. "This one must be at least three seasons old, probably four."

Helen was watching the re-run with only a modicum of interest; she could mostly take TV or leave it and much preferred a good book. Chris was the big television viewer in their relationship. He'd always maintained that the hours he spent in front of the TV – *magic lantern* as his Grandmother used to call it – was research for some writing project or other that never actually seemed to materialize.

"Oh yeah," Chris said with an impish grin. "That would do it. So why *are* we watching this again?"

"Because it's the only thing I could find that's not in Spanish or doesn't have humongous breasts thrusting out of the screen." Helen pulled her very best disgusted face. "Or both."

"I quite like the thrusting breasts," Chris said, playfully tugging on Helen's towel to unveil hers. "But why would I want to watch them on TV when I have these magnificent specimens to play with?" He stroked the side of Helen's breast and watched as the tiny bumps of gooseflesh magically appeared at his touch.

"My thoughts exactly," Helen purred and lay herself down on the bed. She made a big deal of stretching, her arms above her head, her lithe legs taut and the action allowing the towel to fall completely away. She then pushed the taco wrappings off of the bottom of the bed with her feet and they plopped onto the floor where they would serve as torment for the surviving cockroaches that were stuck on the under-bed traps.

Chris scooted up to his wife and gazed down along her naked body. He found her to be so exquisitely beautiful that even after all of their years together he had never grown tired of looking at her. Helen quite simply took his breath away.

She smiled up at him, basking in the lustful look she had so easily created.

"Hey, Mr," her voice was breathy, her arousal more than transparent.

"Hey, Mrs." Chris twiddled one of his wife's nipples to stiffness.

"I was remembering London."

"Oh yeah?" Chris was an absolute sucker for their reminiscences of erotic adventures past. He always maintained that it was double the pleasure to have the brain aroused as well as the dick.

"Do you remember that dress we bought for me to wear at the fetish ball?"

Helen knew her husband all too well, knew precisely which buttons to press.

"How could I ever forget?" Chris's pulse quickened and his pants begin to feel constricting and uncomfortable. "That was the first time you ever wore latex." He cupped Helen's breast and massaged it gently.

"Hmmm, it felt so sexy against my skin." Helen writhed at his touch. "*Fucking* sexy," she corrected herself. "Cool and skin tight, and nothing left to the imagination."

For Helen, it had indeed been a night to remember. She had worn a red latex mini dress that covered from her neck to the top of her thighs – only just a fraction above the sensual curve of her buttocks – and was polished to such a high shine that Chris had been able to see the reflection of his face on her butt. The material itself had stretched and clung to Helen's curves and had enhanced her curvaceous figure to distraction.

Chris shifted his hand's attention to Helen's other breast, it was after all only good manners to make sure that it got the same treatment as its partner, plus this one had the added attraction of a nipple ring. This time, though his kneading at the pliant flesh was ever so slightly more urgent. Chris glanced down at the denuded mound between Helen's thighs and fought the primal urge to mount his wife then and there.

"It was so *fucking* hot the way everyone at the ball stared at me," Helen continued to press her husband's mental buttons.

"Me too." Chris forced himself away from Helen's breasts to undress. "What amazed me was that it was a fetish ball and practically everyone was wearing rubber - *and* there were people fucking all over the place, but all eyes were on my hot slut wife."

"There must have been more attractive women there than me." Helen was not above false modesty, nor fishing for compliments.

"No, there weren't," Chris gave the required answer. "Not even close." He leaned over and pressed his mouth to Helen's pierced breast. He sucked its taut tip into his mouth and danced his tongue around the cool metal ring that skewered through her nipple.

"I danced for you," Helen struggled to talk through the breath that caught in her throat. She let out a slight moan and squirmed on the bed. "On the dance floor in front of all of those people who just stared at me; wanting to fuck me," she whispered as she dug her hands into Chris's hair to pull him harder onto her tit. "They could all see that I was only wearing the latex dress and fuck-me stilettos. No underwear. Did you love the way my nipples poked out against the rubber and how the dress rode up to show off my ass?"

Chris moaned his reply, his mouth too full of Helen's flesh to make any sort of coherent sound. He drew her nipple deeper into his mouth and down towards his throat as if he was a suckling infant. Helen wriggled at his touch and squirmed her thighs together, craving pleasure from the pressure that her movements created on her pussy.

"And then," she murmured into Chris's ear, her voice throaty and lascivious, "I had to go to the bathroom."

Chris pulled his mouth away from Helen, releasing her soft, fleshy mound with a reluctant sucking sound. "Yes you did, you naughty slut." He stroked the soft skin on Helen's flat belly in ever increasing circles that ventured downward.

"And when I came back –" Helen gave him her dirtiest laugh. "– I was wearing only my shoes."

"Oh my God yes," Chris groaned at the memory – one of his absolute favorites of Helen. "You walked across that club like you owned the place and everyone in it." He slipped his hand between his wife's legs and found to his delight – and *relief* – that she was slick.

"I sat opposite you. That old leather chair was hellish cold on my naked skin." Helen breathed heavily as her husband's fingers toyed with an expert's touch at her clitoris. "I spread my legs for you –"

"– and everyone else," Chris reminded; as if Helen, would ever need reminding of that particular detail.

"For every *fucker* else." She licked his shoulder to enjoy the salty taste of her husband's sweat. "I wanted them *all* to watch me masturbate for you."

Helen squirmed at Chris's touch. She moved her thighs yet farther apart as if unable to get enough of the probing fingers that were slowly but surely driving her wild.

"They couldn't take their eyes off of you," Chris kept the game going, "the guys, the girls – all of them."

"And you *loved* me being an exhibitionist slut for you," Helen struggled to speak as a rising orgasm vied for her breath.

"I couldn't believe it when those four guys came over," Chris prompted as he slipped two fingers into Helen's vagina and rubbed at the rippled flesh inside.

"But you *wanted* them to," Helen gasped. "I could see it in your eyes. You wanted me to entertain them." Her eyes rolled back and closed. "Oh."

And with that simple sound, Helen came. Her body shuddered and she grabbed tightly at Chris's arm to press his hand down hard on her sex. Her hips thrust involuntarily against him as her breath *whooshed* out from her chest.

Taking his cue, Chris manoeuvered himself on top of Helen and in one smooth movement he slid his dick up to its hilt inside her. Helen climaxed again and her internal muscles squeezed him like they were trying to pull his cock away from his body. As she groaned,

Helen raked her fingernails down Chris's spine, breaking the skin in places.

"One cock in each hand, one in my mouth, and that black guy's mouth on my clit," she gasped as she stared with fierce intent into her husband's eyes. She could sense that he was close to his own release and as Chris's thrusting gained momentum, his face contorted and flushed a deep, dark pink. "And didn't you love it, you dirty bastard?" She licked his lower lip, sucked it into her mouth and bit down hard. "They came all over your cheap slut face," Chris growled against the sharp pain in his lip. "In your hair, on your tits." He worked his hips hard against Helen's, relishing the skin on skin of their epilated genitals and the way her vagina gripped him so incredibly tight.

"And then you came on that guy's face, so fucking hard that you damn near broke his nose," Chris grunted as he strained to hold off the orgasm that had become unavoidable.

"Oh yeah, that dirty fucker licked my pussy good and hard," Helen said. "I came like a bitch when his friends squirted their jizz all over me," Helen pressed her mouth close to Chris's ear, her breath warm and moist, "especially when they wiped their come-covered dicks on my filthy whore tits."

At this trigger, Chris could hold back no longer. With a loud, primal grunt he emptied himself deep into Helen, grimacing as he ejaculated, as if each spasm was agony.

Sated, they froze; their sweat-slicked bodies joined together and glistening wetly like some erotic ice carving. Chris supported his weight on his arms and gazed down at the sheen of sweat covering his wife's magnificent body whilst she in turn stared up at him and directly into his eyes.

It had been kind of fuck that once upon a time they would have hoped had resulted in a much-desired impregnation. That thought passed easily between them, no words necessary; not after so long of hoping. But no, that was not to be. All they had as the orgasm afterglow receded like a tsunami's floodwater was the post coital crash of the reality that they'd just participated in another mind-blowing but ultimately unproductive fuck.

And then, as with all such Sewell trysts, the moment passed.

Helen smiled up at her husband. "I have to pee," she announced and pushed him away and out of her body.

TEN

Helen at the Pool

It was only eight AM and already the unrelenting Texas sun was burning its way through the thin floral curtains of the motel suite. Helen stood alone in a narrow shaft of sunlight that snuck through the gap between the curtains; a concentrated beam of pure light that warmed the bare skin of her back and made her tingle all over.

She pulled her halter-top bikini over her head and wriggled it down onto her ample breasts, fighting to contain the bountiful mounds of flesh within the scant, twin triangles of black material. With proficient fingers, she tied the thin string of the garment behind her back, the flimsy bow she'd fashioned straining at the formidable task expected of it. She then rummaged through her overnight bag, searching for the equally inadequate bikini briefs that accompanied the top. The warm sun on her bare butt felt most enjoyable as she bent over to sort through her hastily- packed clothing.

"Aha!" she exclaimed triumphantly to herself as she pulled the tiny black briefs out from the deepest recess of her bag. "Gotcha!" She slipped the briefs on one leg at a time and thanked the Good Lord that she'd had a thorough Brazilian wax ahead of the trip. This particular bikini – one of hers and Chris's favorites – left absolutely no margin for error as regards to errant body hair. The bikini briefs themselves comprised little more than a minuscule pair of black fabric triangles joined at the sides by flimsy strings that were designed to ride high on the hip. The rear of the briefs left much of Helen's ass cheeks exposed and the front fit snug around her pussy to accentuate the cleft between her lips – and Helen knew from experience that just one false move and her labia could easily be making an appearance.

If Helen were to be completely honest with herself, her choice of swimwear was actually the least of her motivations for being completely smooth down below. The couples' retreat they were on their way to actively discouraged swimwear of any nature as a matter of policy, although they had stressed when she'd booked that they were *clothing optional* rather than an out and out nudist colony. If she were going to run the gauntlet of being naked around strangers, she wouldn't want to be the only one there with pubes. Nonetheless, she'd packed a couple of bikinis because there were occasions upon which it was nice to be able to wear something for the express intention of taking it off – one only had to look at the multi-billion-dollar lingerie industry for proof of that.

Helen grinned to herself as she padded around the room in her bikini, her naked feet catching on that sticky something on the floor and each time they did, she'd pull a disgusted face. Helen was confident that she looked as good as she felt, especially with a good ninety-five percent of her skin uncovered. Unlike most women of her age, Helen actually loved her own body. She was proud of her flawless skin – never had a pimple in her life - her firm flesh and perfectly proportioned curves. She certainly had been one of the lucky ones as far as Mother Nature's bounty had been concerned.

Earlier that morning, she'd despatched Chris to Bakker's gas station to buy bagels for breakfast. He'd protested of course, giving her his petulant lip and lame argument of *'why couldn't you have said something when we were there yesterday? We could have bought them then'*.

She'd placated him with a wet tongue kiss and a playful tweak of his dick and explained that she hadn't wanted bagels yesterday. Nor had she had any way of knowing that the desire would hit her today. What was she, a psychic? And then she'd smiled her most seductive smile at her husband to further diffuse his irritation.

"Besides which, they'll be fresh this morning," she'd assured him, "and you wouldn't want me to have stale bagels now, would you?" And then she had gone on to ask Chris if he could pick up a pot of cream cheese and some smoked salmon while he was at it. That, of course, had elicited the funny look down his nose that never failed to amuse her, along with a snort of derision and a wry laugh.

"Remember where we are, Babe. I'm more likely to pick up peanut butter chunky and flatmeat than cream cheese and smoked fucking salmon," he'd told her and that gorgeous, tell-tale curling of his mouth corners had let Helen know that it was his turn to laugh at *her* coddled naiveté.

She'd kissed her sweet, infinitely patient husband goodbye and sent him on his way with her taste lingering on his lips.

They'd both decided to hang on at the motel for the morning before heading out on the second and final leg of their journey. To be more precise, *Helen* had decided and Chris had gone along with her idea under cursory protest. They were in no big hurry to hit the road and had no time scale to adhere to, she'd explained, so why not enjoy a leisurely breakfast of cream cheese and salmon-less bagels? They were also free to enjoy the limited facilities that Flanagan's Last Barrel Motel had to offer and relax a little before disembarking.

Helen admired her body once more in the bathroom mirror and adjusted her top for the thousandth time. Sideways on, her breasts bulged out on either side of the inadequate material but Helen really didn't care; side-boob was very much *de rigueur* amongst the fashionistas these days.

She had had made the decision to catch some sun and if the fancy took her, maybe even take a dip in the motel pool that the creepy manager had told her was at the very least bleached clean. After their top-down trip yesterday, Helen's body was an odd patchwork of sun-tinged pink and glaring white and she figured that an hour or two of morning sun whilst wearing very little may help fill in the gaps a little.

She grabbed her cell phone from the bed and composed a quick text to Chris – *'Goin 2 pool, c u there'* – and hit the send button. She dropped her phone next to the lime scale encrusted washbasin and covered it with a hand towel. She then grabbed the one remaining, unused fluffy towel, her bottle of SF25 and headed outside.

Helen decided against the diaphanous pool dress that she'd picked out of her chaotic luggage to wear for her walk to the pool. After all, there would be no one around this early on a Sunday morning, especially so with her and Chris being the only guests; so, she concluded that that the black bikini's scant coverage would do.

Chris would no doubt have approved.

Clutching her towel and sun cream, Helen stepped out into the glare of the sunshine that lit up the walkway. After a night in the faintly musty, dimly lit room eighteen, it was wonderful to feel the warmth of the sun on her exposed skin and the deliciously contrasting cool morning breeze that caressed her body as she made her way down towards the pool. On her way by, Helen peered in to the motel's grubby site office as if she half-expected to see Creepy Rizzo (sorry, *Robbie*!) sitting at his desk and leering out at her with that stupid look on his big, round face. But the office was locked up and all appeared dark and deserted beyond the grimy window. There was a handwritten *CLOSED!* notice stuck to the window with cracked, graying blu-tack.

It can be difficult sometimes to picture certain people outside of their vocational environment, to imagine them having a life other than in the context to which one is exposed, such as teachers, for example. This was very much the case with the repugnant Robbie Rizzo as far as Helen was concerned, it was hard for her to imagine that he actually did exist beyond his little office and scarcely-patronised motel. It was entirely possible that there was a *Mrs.* Rizzo, a handful of kids, maybe even a mistress or two. He'd have a past, hopes and dreams, fears and sexual predilections just the same as everyone else. It was this latter thought that elicited a shiver from Helen as she walked by the man's crappy little office and followed the cracked pathway to the area behind the building.

Already Helen's skin was beginning to prickle in the sun's sharp light and she regretted her decision to put off the application of sun screen until she was poolside, at this rate her white bits were apt to turn pink and her pink bits likely to become even pinker.

The pool itself actually looked nice. In spite of Rizzo's assurances, the previous evening, Helen had been expecting to find a stagnant body of greenish water adorned with rotting leaves – floating and sunken – and perhaps even a dead squirrel or two. But no, the water was a crystal clear, inviting blue that twinkled like myriad diamonds in the sunlight. In compliment to the pool, the pale gray paving slabs around it had been scrubbed clean and denuded of weeds, the white plastic recliners were absolutely spotless and the potted sago palms were immaculately tended, freshly watered and positively verdant.

Helen did have the tendency to be an awful snob at times, as illustrated perfectly by her pleasant – if unexpected – revelation about the motel's towels. Hence it was no great surprise that she had been expecting to find some filthy piss hole of a pool in a place such as Flanagan's Last Barrel Motel. However, as opposed to the potential expenses involved in fixing the actual structure and décor of the motel, it probably had cost the owners almost next to nothing to scrub the flags, bleach the recliners and pay someone to throw chlorine in the water every couple of days or so.

See, still the inherent snob.

Helen picked out a recliner close to the pool and threw her towel down on it. She stood at the side of the pool and contemplated the brilliantly shimmering water that looked incredibly welcoming. Then again, so did the gleaming recliner and the warm sun that glinted from its stark, white plastic.

Common sense would dictate that Helen should really slap on the sun screen before she got burned, and *before* she hit the pool – instead, she gave a cursory glance at the orange SF25 bottle which had emblazoned upon it: *apply to wet skin.*

And that made up Helen's mind.

She gulped in a deep breath and held it, closed her eyes and braced herself against the anticipated sting of the cool water.

Then she jumped.

As the water closed in around Helen it shut off the outside world as it filled her ears and pressed lightly against her eyelids. She heard her heart thumping out its muffled beats in the darkness, felt the chilling embrace of the water on her skin and her nipples stiffen beneath the scant material that contained them.

Helen kicked upwards and thrust her head up and out of the water. As she surfaced, Helen wiped her face with one hand so that she could open her eyes without getting too much chlorine in them. She then squeezed the excess water from her hair and shook her head to empty out the water from her ears in order to restore her muted hearing.

"Good mornin', Ma'am," Rizzo's voice boomed behind her.

Startled, Helen turned around in the water. She squinted her eyes against the harsh light that shone by either side of Robbie Rizzo's head. "Good morning, Mr. Rizzo," Helen said in as pleasant a tone as she could muster. "I didn't think you'd be around this early in on a Sunday morning" She wiped more of the water from her eyes and looked up at the motel manager, noting with some amusement that his appearance had changed very little from when he'd booked her and Chris in the day before; his face still resembled an overcooked pizza and he wore the same ill-fitting jeans that threatened to slip down his hips. He also sported what appeared to be the same *Anal Thrush* T-shirt, although it did look to be clean and had neat crease lines as if it had come straight out of a packet; was it conceivable that the man had a garage full of his son's band's merchandise and this was a fresh one?

"I'm always around." Rizzo laughed. "In fact, I barely leave the freakin' place." He chewed on his wad of stale gum as he smiled down at Helen. "Hope you're enjoyin' the water, cleaned her out only yesterday."

"Yeah, it feels good."

"If I weren't so goddamned busy." Rizzo grinned at Helen. "I'd have half a mind to join ya."

It was a comment to chill the blood of even the hardest of people, let alone one that was just plain wrong on so many levels; the very thought of a motel's manager climbing in the pool with the customers?!

"Maybe some other time?" Helen said to Rizzo, more so because it seemed the polite thing to say than something she actually hoped would happen. She kicked off against the smooth pool bottom and began to swim.

"Yeah, maybe," Rizzo mumbled as he watched Helen swim away. He screwed up his eyes against the sun to better study her shapely, black-clad butt as it rose to the water's rippling surface. Then Helen's pale soles kicked against the water and she vanished beneath it.

Helen swam back and forth awhile. She'd always been a keen swimmer, enjoying the refreshing caress of cool water and the sense of freedom of isolation that the activity always afforded her. It also had the miraculous effect of clearing her head completely – as if by some magical trickery – of all thoughts of students and biology classes, of boring friends and life's repetitive, dull routines.

Of children and childlessness.

She looked up as she swam and noticed that Rizzo was still skulking around the pool, circling like a hungry vulture over roadkill, and doing his best to pretend not to be watching her swim. She'd seen his like before when she'd helped out at the school's dance recitals; the creepy Dads who would sit in the front row and pay just a little too much attention the tenth-grade dance troupe.

Helen smiled as she caught Rizzo looking and watched as he made himself busy sweeping away imaginary dirt from the paving stones with his mint condition, nylon broom. He then checked the already-watered palms and studied the pristine pool for God only knew what, all the while keeping one beady eye on her body. Undeterred, Helen continued her swim, determined not to be bothered by the tall man's scrutiny – besides, Helen Sewell was used to being looked at.

After a while, Helen looked up from the water and saw that Rizzo was no longer lurking and therefore it seemed an opportune moment for her to get out of the pool. Chris would be back any minute with breakfast and she wanted to catch some sun before they hit the road – also her finger ends were wrinkled like little pink raisins and Rizzo's chlorine overkill was beginning to make her eyes sting.

Helen climbed out of the pool and the warm air immediately began thawing out her chilled body. She padded over to the recliner she'd selected, leaving a wet trail of perfectly formed footprints on the spotless slabs. A cursory dab with the luxury towel and Helen was good to go.

She lay out the towel and began to fiddle with the tilt mechanism on the recliner, determined to get it to that perfect – yet seemingly unachievable – angle that was comfortable for the neck yet didn't mean burning out her retinas by pointing her face directly at the sun.

Bending over the recliner with her curvaceous rump raised skyward, Helen became aware that her audience of one had returned. She peeked over her shoulder and espied Rizzo hovering close to the corner of his office where the cracked concrete walkway met the fancy pool surround. Helen chose to ignore him.
She was happy enough to let him look.

Helen clicked the tilting end of the recliner into the slot that gave her as close to the best angle she was likely to get. She then laid herself out on the hard recliner, pleased that she'd grabbed the fluffy towel as a shield against the harsh plastic. Snatching the sun cream bottle from between her feet, Helen snapped open the lid and squirted a white blob of the stuff into her hand. She couldn't help but crack a girlish smile as the bottle made a wet farting sound as the thick cream sputtered out.

Rizzo studied Helen with hungry eyes as she applied the slick cream to her lithe body. Like a peeping teenager stealing a furtive glimpse of a neighbor's daughter, he was absolutely mesmerized by the way she smoothed the cream along the full length of her legs and how she lingered at her bulging calf muscles to take the time to massage in the slick lotion. And then he watched in awe as Helen moved on to her delectable feet and took great care to oil each and every toe individually until they all glistened wetly in the morning light.

Helen cast a glance over to her watcher and Rizzo's vacant stare told her in no uncertain terms that he'd died and gone to fantasy heaven.

Playing to her audience, Helen squeezed another blob of cream into her palm and rubbed it into her belly, working ever so slowly up towards her ample breasts and onto the exposed part of her décolletage. There she lingered, smoothing the cream with circular motions, and gradually working her hand to either breast where she slipped a finger beneath the edge of her bikini top to ensure maximum protection should it slip down a little.

She finished with her stomach, breasts and neck and daubed a little around her face and then she was all done – Chris could oil her back later. Helen laid back, closed her eyes and relaxed.

There's nothing to equal the delicious feel of fresh, morning sun on one's face. There is that way in which it makes the eyelids tingle and the delicate skin on the cheeks and forehead tighten with a most pleasant, prickling sensation that makes pent-up tensions in a body simply melt away in its warmth. And there is such a thrilling- delight at exposing parts of the body that have not seen real sunlight in far too many months.

It was at times such as these that Helen truly felt that life was good; if only every day could be like this.

Helen knew – and mostly appreciated – that she enjoyed an unprecedented freedom, the freedom to enjoy the adventures that life had on offer when you knew where to look, of having money in the bank, time away from the stresses of work, and of having no one to tie you down or hold you back.

Was she thinking about children again?

"You enjoyin' the sun there, Mrs. Sewell?" Rizzo's shadow fell across Helen's face, blocking out the heat of the sun. "Take care ya don't burn now."

Helen forced her eyes open to squint up at him, shielding them with an arm across her forehead. The man was standing as close as he possibly could to the recliner, his shins almost touching it, and of course he was staring down at her. "Yes I am, Mr. Rizzo. Thank you very much," Helen said politely. "And yes, I'm being careful not to burn."

There was a pause as Rizzo give the impression that he was struggling for something else to say, as if his power of speech had been dampened by his proximity to an attractive, near-naked woman. Helen was happy to allow the awkward pause to hang between them like a bad smell.

Rizzo cogitated and finally blurted out, "it'd be a shame to spoil that pretty skin of yours."

"Excuse me?" Helen was taken aback; she'd thought the motel manager a little too forward at her door the previous evening, but this was a whole new level.

"I said it'd be a shame if you sunburnt. You got nice skin." Rizzo smiled down at Helen and his eyes skittered the length and breath of her exposed body.

Helen fidgeted beneath Rizzo's scrutiny and was all of a sudden painfully conscious that her nipple ring was clearly visible through the bikini's thin material; it made her look like one side of her body was aroused and she remembered just how mortified her Mother had been upon discovering the piercing – even though Helen had turned thirty when she'd had it done. Nice girls didn't have holes punched in their private bits, apparently; it gave men the wrong impression and anyhoo, what *would* she do about breastfeeding?

"I'll be okay, Mr. Rizzo," Helen assured, deliberately keeping the discourse short and non-committal as Rizzo's eyes continued their crawl across Helen's skin. "Is there something you need?" she asked. "We'll be out of the room by eleven, if you were wondering."

Rizzo shook his head. "Nah, that's not a problem at all, Mrs. Sewell," he told her. "It's just that I was just tryin' to think back as to the last time I saw my good lady wife dressed like this." Something passed across his lips that may have been a smile and Helen thought it made him look a little wistful.

"Oh," Helen replied to the revelation, not at all sure how she should respond to such over-familiarity, having never been exposed to it in the safe anonymity of the city. Could it be that folk out here in the sticks were simply much less observant of personal boundaries and etiquette than they were back in Houston?

"She keeps herself pretty much covered up these days," Rizzo continued on. If the man was picking up on Helen's unease, he certainly wasn't showing it – or caring much. "Three kids and gravity ain't been so kind to her figure and such." Rizzo's jaw kind of rotated as he chewed and spoke at the same time which had the unfortunate effect of making his words sound even more hick as they came out.

"I'm sorry to hear that," Helen was genuine this time. She had vowed a long time ago to always make the effort to fight off the ravages of time and remain as attractive for her husband (and herself, of course) as she possibly could. She would most likely go under the knife if - and when - the time came, so it did tend to goad her that there were a lot of women who simply refused to make the effort.

"It don't matter none, Ma'am." Rizzo chewed as he spoke. "I ain't wanted to be with her since our littlest popped out. An' that was eleven years ago."

Again, with the over familiarity; what was it with this guy?

"They had to snip her open to get the little fucker out." Rizzo made an exaggerated scissor motion with his fingers. "Down there, if ya catch ma meaning?"

"Ouch." Helen winced at the very thought. If there was one benefit of being childless, it was that she had been spared the cruel touch of the cold steel of surgical scissors on her perineum, that sickening *snip* sound and a hot gush of blood between the legs. "That's awful," she said.

"Yep." Rizzo nodded his agreement. "Messed her up really bad down in her nether regions; made her labias and such all out of proportion. Looks like the last sandwich in Arby's now." His face showed no sign of humor at this. "So's they're not as conducive to the *maritals* as they once were, as ya can imagine," Rizzo sounded not quite as upset as Helen would have imagined one whose sex life was to all intents and purposes over to be. Perhaps his wife was an ugly old heifer and he was secretly pleased that he had an excuse not to fuck her anymore?

For someone like Helen – brought up in the more-polite echelons of society – it was difficult for her to guess at what the etiquette should be in circumstances such as this. Therefore, Helen had really found herself lost for words; here was a guy that she barely knew – the motel manager for Christ's sakes – regaling her with how crappy his marriage was and how he'd not poked his wife in over a decade on account of her episiotomy. In the modern lingo of her students, this entire exchange was most certainly *TMI*, quite possibly even a strong candidate for a definite *WTF*.

As Helen struggled for something less condescending to say than '*I'm so sorry to hear that*' to the guy who was dripping warm droplets of sweat onto her naked belly, Rizzo's attention was distracted.

Rizzo lifted his gaze from Helen's flesh. "Yo! Over here!" he shouted and raised an arm in greeting.

Helen followed his gaze and fully expected to see her husband bearing bagels.

Instead, she saw, at the other side of the pool a dishevelled figure appear, which she immediately recognised as the guy who'd pumped gas for them the day before at the gas station; the creepy, overly-macho mechanic guy who had the fat sister.

"Hey, Newman! Over here!" Rizzo shouted over Helen's body. "Jesus H, that man's deafer n' a fucking post some days," he grumbled to both himself and Helen. "Nuttier than squirrel shit, too." He grinned.

Helen looked on with mounting dread as the inimitable Newman F. Bakker made his way over towards her and Rizzo. He wore his work overalls, his greasy hat hiding his sweaty, bald pate and he had a fatuous grin across his face. He swung a half dozen tins of *Bud Lite* by their perf-pack; which by the way Bakker shuffled his feet as he walked would appear to be by no means his first beers of the day.

Whilst Rizzo's attention had been a source of flattering amusement – even though she'd not expected the motel manager to have been around quite this early – Bakker's arrival was a turn of events Helen hadn't foreseen. If she had, she would have at the very least dressed a little more appropriately for an impromptu poolside six-pack party.

Helen was comfortable with her state of undress in the presence of Rizzo – and now Bakker – but her nervousness was for what Chris would make of her redneck audience should he return and catch the soiree (and where the hell was he, by the way? Just how long *does* it take to buy bagels?). Whilst Helen knew that Chris revelled in her ability to turn every head in a room, he was only happy when he could call the shots and bring an end to the games when he needed to. But this – total strangers out of Chris's preferred context and with zero means of him manipulating the situation – Helen knew all too well that this was way out of her husband's comfort zone and she was already beginning to regret a few of the decisions she'd made.

"Hey, Robbie." Bakker stopped at the opposite side of Helen's recliner to the motel manager. He reached over and slapped Rizzo's shoulder as hard as he could, the sound like a distant thunder clap. "How's it hanging, man?" He grinned as he peered down at Helen over his mirrored sunglasses. "Howdy, Ma'am. Good to see ya'll again."

"Hi," Helen replied as friendly as she could manage. She sat up and drew her knees up to her chin to hide her chest. She saw her bikini-clad body reflected in Bakker's shades and decided that although she looked vulnerable, she was still most decidedly hot.

"I was just tellin' Mrs. Sewell here that she ought not to burn that pretty skin of hers," Rizzo talked over Helen's body as one would a pool table in a dive bar.

"It's all too easily done, Ma'am." Bakker took over the conversation and Rizzo visibly shrank back from the man, very much as a dog will do in the presence of the pack's alpha male.

Bakker grinned and tore another can free from the six-pack. He popped the tab and a fine spray of chilled beer sprayed over Helen's torso. Bakker thrust the opened can into Rizzo's outstretched hand and droplets of chilly condensation and Rizzo's arm sweat dripped down onto Helen's thigh. "The sun here is fiercer than it is in the city, ya know," Bakker's voice took on the distinctive, authoritative tone of the bar room know-it-all. "On account of we don't have that thick layer of petrochemical smog protectin' us out here in the boonies." He chuckled as his eyes roamed wild and free over Helen's body. "I thought you guys were headin' up North?"

It was a welcome change of subject for a Helen, who was torn between staying put and weathering out the unwanted attention or making her excuses and leaving –

knowing that Chris would be along any minute; as much as she was enjoying the attention on her husband's behalf, she remained unsure as to what his reaction might be. "We'll be setting off as soon as Chris – my husband – gets here," she told Bakker and Rizzo, her voice firm as she made the clumsy effort to reference the fact that her man would be appearing shortly, even if he were already somewhat overdue.

"Well, that's real nice, Mrs. Sewell. It's a good idea to get some miles behind you before the desert heat really kicks in," Rizzo said quietly and blinked down at Helen's toes.

What was it about this guy and her feet?

Sure, Helen's long toes looked extra cute with the fresh, French manicure she'd had done especially for the trip, and the smooth skin of her bare feet shimmered with the sun oil that gave them that alluring, sensual look, but Helen had never really cared much for her own feet - they were quite possibly the least favorite part of her body. She'd never understood the attraction that feet held for some men – to her they were one of the more practical accessories to the human body – although on more than one occasion in their marriage she had masturbated Chris between their soft soles, even though she hated the slippery feel of his come squidging between her toes; so much so that she would dash to the bathroom immediately after to rinse it off, with Chris laughing at that comical walk she did on the sides of her feet to keep her messy toes off of the floor.

Seemingly oblivious to Helen's unease, or the impending arrival of her husband, Bakker and Rizzo chugged steadily at their beers. They downed them in one and crumpled up the cans with sweating, meaty hands. Rizzo tossed his can at an empty trash can behind them. It hit the side and rattled noisily to the ground.

"Goddammit!" he cussed.

"Never were much of a shot, were ya, Robbie?" Bakker threw his own can and made the perfect shot. "P'raps if ya' put hair 'round the trash can, you'd have got it in first time!" Bakker roared at his own joke and had his back slapped by the grinning Rizzo. Helen joined in, although her laugh was more nervous than mirthful.

"Say, lady," Bakker said as he struggled to get his laughter under control. "How come you're botherin' to cover up?" He leaned over and tugged at Helen's thin bikini strap with his grubby fingers. "There's more folk than us two gonna see everythin' you've got where you're going; and you're gonna git yourself those embarrassing white bits and such."

"Really!?" Helen slapped his hand away. She hugged her knees a little tighter to her chest.

"I must to apologize for my friend." Rizzo looked a tad embarrassed and shot Bakker a stern look – Bakker grimaced back at him like he really couldn't give much of a shit what the motel manager thought. "He's never really been one for talking right to the ladies," Bakker growled at Rizzo and thumped his friend's arm. Rizzo recoiled and rubbed at the spot as if it had really hurt.

"Hey!" a chirpy voice danced across the pool, and Helen couldn't have been any more delighted to hear her husband's dulcet tones.

"Over here!" Helen waved Chris over and with her arms no longer around her knees, she gave Bakker and Rizzo a more than generous eyeful of her jiggling breasts.

Chris jogged over clutching the bulging brown bag of bagels like his life depended on them. "Hi, Babe," he said and bent over to kiss Helen full on the lips. "Sorry it took me so long, service was a bit slow."

"That's okay, sweetie, Mr. Rizzo and his friend have been keeping me company." A relived smile played across her lips.

"Good to see ya again, Son." Bakker stretched out a hand for the shaking. "Sorry if Ruthie-Peg kept ya waiting for your breakfast."

Chris shook Bakker's hand and told him that it really was nothing to worry about.

"Ya want a beer, son?" Bakker asked.

"I'm good, thank you," Chris replied. "It's a little too early for me."

"Please yourself, cunt," Bakker grumbled. He thrust another beer at Rizzo who pulled eagerly at the tab with a bitten fingernail, raised the can in a silent toast and chugged at the cold liquid with his Adam's apple bobbing up and down like a fishing float.

"Pardon me?" Chris said, not really believing what he *thought* he'd just heard.

"Swim?" Helen interjected, her eyes darting between the two rednecks and her husband whose hackles were predictably well and truly on the rise.

"Sure," Chris said, quizzically, although he already doubted what he'd thought Bakker had called him. He dropped the bag of bagels at the bottom end of Helen's recliner and stripped off his shirt. He offered a helping hand to Helen who took it and let him haul her upright. Once free of the recliner, she wrapped her arms around his neck and stretched out her legs with a sigh.

"If you two gentlemen would excuse us." Chris smiled at Rizzo and Bakker. "My wife and I are going to take a swim before *our* breakfast." He gave a sardonic grin and nodded at the beers that both men clutched and couldn't fail but to notice that the two men were too distracted staring at Helen's – well, *everything*.

"It's your prerogative, Son," Rizzo mumbled. "Pool's all part of the price." He half-heartedly raised his can at the couple and had the action mirrored by his drinking buddy.

Helen squealed as Chris carried her over to the edge of the pool and with little ceremony threw her in. As Helen flew through the air, she flailed in a most unladylike way, her arms and legs waving wildly about as she hit the water with a huge and undignified splash.

Chris plunged in after her and covered half the width of the pool underwater. He surfaced and swam with long, lazy strokes over to Helen. He lifted her out of the water and then took her in his arms, both of them giggling like love-struck school kids.

Bakker and Rizzo, beverages firmly in hand sat themselves down across from Helen's empty recliner from where they still had an uninterrupted voyeur's view of the couple frolicking in the pool.

"I'm sure the hotel manager guy has a thing for me," Helen sniggered as she wrapped her long, trim legs tight around her husband's waist. "If you hadn't come along when you did, I may have just run away with him."

The laughed together and glanced across at the sweating hillbillies who raised their beer cans in acknowledgement of the joke they had to have figured was on them.

"I wouldn't blame you at all, my love." Chris added. "He does seem quite the catch."

Helen unwound her legs from Chris and let them float up to break the surface of the crystal blue water. She poked her toes out of the water and pointed them skyward, spreading and stretching them and sneaking a sideways glance at Rizzo whose eyes were practically on stalks at her blatant display; much more and the poor man would be in danger of a heart attack. Helen then lay back in Chris's strong, protective arms and her breasts bobbed around weightlessly in the water in front of his face and she saw in her husband's eyes his aroused state.

"Don't know why you're holding on to her so tight, Son!" Bakker called out, his voice slurred. "It's not like she's gonna sink is she?" He laughed out loud, a deep, raucous guffaw that boomed across the pool. "

"Least not with those floatation deee-vices!" He slurred the last word and the somewhat superfluous footnote seemed to rile Chris.

"Is that redneck serious?" Chris growled.

"Aw, leave him be," Helen soothed. "It's just the beer talking." She nuzzled Chris's neck, nibbling on the soft skin.

"Yeah!" Rizzo joined in, the alcohol raising both his voice and his bravado, "he means your titties, lady!"

The two rednecks laughed together. They slapped their thighs and held their bellies like this was the funniest thing that had ever been said in the whole history of forever.

Helen grinned at Chris. "You can't really blame them, Hun," she purred. "I'll bet it's been a long time since either of them saw a body like this that wasn't on a computer screen." She wiggled in his arms and her breasts broke the surface once more, swaying in the water with a hypnotically liquid motion. "And besides which, you know that a gal like me loves a little attention from time to time."

"Even if it is from the Drunk Brothers?" Chris smiled.

"Gotta get it where you can at my age, lover." Helen pushed away from her husband and swam slowly just out of his reach. She winked at Chris and dived under the water, her shapely backside breaching the water like some graceful aquatic mammal. Chris glanced over at the two men, amused by and proud of the mesmerized looks on their faces. He swam after his wife.

Helen and Chris bobbed back up together and in unison wiped the over-chlorinated water from their smarting eyes. Helen leaned in and kissed Chris with a full on-the-mouth, lingering tongue kiss that served well to stir his loins in the cool water.

"Was that for my benefit?" Chris asked once the kiss was broken. "Or theirs?" He nodded across the pool.

Bakker and Rizzo were gone.

"Too bad if it was for them, they missed it." Helen had a tinge of disappointment in her voice. "I'll bet they've either gone to jerk off or get more beers."

"Or both," Chris offered, "there's nothing quite like a little multitasking."

Helen snorted in amusement and looked directly into her husband's eyes. "I love you, Chris," she said.

"And I love you too, Helen."

"I love this version of us, we really are fun."

"Me too, baby, we should do more of this."
Helen pressed herself tight against her husband's body, moulding into him with an eagerness like she was attempting to make one person out of two. She kissed him again, her tongue probing for his, the warmth between her legs grinding against his thigh.

Gently, Chris pushed her away.

"Don't tell me you're getting shy on me, Mr. Sewell?" Helen teased. "Scared of getting caught fucking by the nasty, rough men?"

Chris laughed. "Oh yeah, like those two watching us getting it on would be a turn-off." He flashed a wicked grin at his wife. "We've performed for worse."

Helen smiled and nodded, reached for him again.

"Sorry to spoil the moment baby, but I really *do* need to go to the restroom." Chris looked a tad sheepish.

Helen wriggled her leg between his, her thigh squeezing his cock and balls, feeling the stiffness that sprouted there. "Why don't you just go here?" she whispered in her most sultry tone. "Think of it as foreplay."

Chris smiled at his wife, his eyes twinkled. "I don't want to get too graphic, my love, but I really don't think that Norman-fucking-Bates would take too kindly to me downloading last night's tacos into his freshly-cleaned pool."

"Eww, that's gross!" Helen grimaced and play-slapped her husband's bare chest, the sexy moment dissipating like an ice cube on a hotplate – albeit temporarily. "You really can be quite disgusting, Chris."

"And don't you just love it?" Chris kissed his wife's cute button nose and swam to the edge of the pool.

He climbed out.

With an admiring glance back and a self congratulatory smile at Helen who floated effortlessly on her back – boobs-skyward – in the pool, Chris made his way over to the bathrooms, his wet feet squishing on the sun-warmed slabs.

Helen watched him go, ogling his broad, tanned back and the way his muscular ass moved beneath the clinging, wet swim shorts. It was at moments such as these that all Helen wanted, more than anything in the world, was her husband's skin on hers and his dick buried deep inside her.

****

Chris finished up and flushed the toilet, then idly watched as it filled up again with dark blue, scummy water. He let himself out of the stall and washed his hands in the tepid water that sputtered out from lone working faucet. He tried – but soon gave up – drying his hands beneath the hand-dryer; the breeze it generated was comparable both in sound and strength to an asthmatic wasp.

He exited the restroom and stepped back into the sunlight that hurt his eyes after the cool gloom.

Chris heard voices and his heart sank a little. Rizzo and his grubby mechanic friend were back and by the sounds of their raucous laughter, drunker than ever. He quickened his step and headed back to the pool where Rizzo and Bakker had reclaimed their spectator positions by Helen's recliner, no doubt attracted like bees around honey the second his wife had exited the pool.

"Hey there, Son," Rizzo greeted Chris with a fat, drunken grin.

"Oh, hi again," Chris said. He glanced down at Helen who met his eyes with what he thought was meant to be a reassuring look.

"I do hope you and your good lady wife are enjoying our hospitality." Rizzo lifted his beer can to his lips and took a noisy slurp from it.

"We are, Mr. Rizzo, thank you." Chris joined the two men by his wife's feet. "Call me *Robbie*, ever'one else does." The redneck belched beneath his breath and blasted Chris in the face with the rancid stench of beer and low quality weed.

"You got it, Robbie."

"And I do hope that my friend's ribald nature didn't offend your Missus any," Rizzo said and took a sideways step as if to block Chris's view of Helen. "Only, he doesn't get the company of good lookin' folks that much, so he doesn't know how to behave exactly." Rizzo grinned. "He spends so much time with that fat elephant of a sister of his that he prob'ly forgets what a real woman's supposed to look like." Rizzo's speech slurred again; elephant sounding something akin to *elerr-phunt.*

"And she does look like she's *all* real to me," Bakker sniggered aggressively as he leaned over Helen. "Them's some fine titties ya got there, Ma'am." He tugged at Helen's top, breathing his foul liquor fumes into her face and revealing the rose pink of the very edge of Helen's areola before she knocked his hand away.

"No!" she barked.

Bakker ignored her and ran a dirty fingernail along the side of Helen's breast and down along her rib cage. Helen slapped the hand away again and made as if to get up off of the recliner.

"Hey!" Chris snapped.

Rizzo turned to face Chris who stood just short of eyelevel with his chest. "Calm yourself down, son," he growled, "it's jus' the beers talkin, is all." He placed a broad hand on Chris's chest and gave him a firm but gentle push to indicate that he really ought to sit down.

As Helen clambered from the recliner, Bakker grabbed at her bikini briefs to yank her back down. The thin material pulled away in his hand to reveal what little of her ass it had covered and the front dug hard into her pussy. Helen yelped and plopped back onto her recliner.

"That's enough!" Chris growled, and attempted to sidestep Rizzo.

"I said, sit the fuck *down.*" Rizzo kneed Chris hard in the balls and he crumpled down hard on the recliner by Helen's feet. Something snapped on the seat's frame which gave out a loud cracking noise.

Helen struggled against Bakker who had now her pinned to the recliner with one knee on her solar plexus. She lashed out a flailing hand at Bakker's face, but he bobbed his head to one side and Helen's fist hit nothing but thin air.

"Like to play rough, do we?" Bakker grinned. He slapped the side of Helen's breasts full force with a flat hand and she squealed. Then he slapped her again, as if her crying out had actually been encouragement.

"What the fuck?!" Chris scrabbled to his feet, and pushed at Rizzo's seemingly immovable frame.

"I did ask you to sit down," Rizzo said, almost apologetically and shoved Chris in the chest. Chris staggered backwards and flew head over ass over the recliner, his arms windmilling as he tried in vain to maintain balance. He landed hard on the stone slabs next to the recliner, his legs entangling with the thing as he struggled to extricate himself from the hard plastic.

In a couple of strides, Rizzo was upon him.

Bakker climbed on top of Helen and the recliner creaked under their combined weight. He positioned himself with his crotch on her belly and her hands pinned beneath his knees. From the bulge in his scruffy jeans that dug into the smooth flesh of her stomach, his arousal at Helen's all but naked, oiled body was all too apparent.

Chris freed himself from the recliner and scrambled to his feet. "Leave my wife alone!" he shouted with all the bravado he could muster, although his voice betrayed him as fear added a distinct quiver. Then Rizzo punched Chris in the side of the head and white sparks shot across his vision as he went down once more, his bare skin slapping on the hot flags. He scrambled to get back up but Rizzo lashed out with a foot that caught Chris on the back of the head and this time he went down and lay perfectly still.

Pinned beneath Bakker's weight, Helen watched helplessly as Chris was knocked out cold by the motel manager. She wriggled the best she could, but was no match for Bakker's sheer weight and brawn. Bakker ground his groin against the smooth dip of Helen's belly, he was hard and she could see his dick straining against his jeans to be free. "Is this what you want, you prick-teasing bitch?" Bakker snarled. "You want me to fuck you?" He then pulled out a scruffy rag from the back pocket of his oily jeans.

It was just the everyday dirty shred of cloth Helen would have expected any self-respecting gas station attendant to carry; tattered, oil-stained and well-used – only this one was in a sealed baggie.

Bakker extricated the rag from the baggie. "Say, lady," he said with a sinister grin, pressing the pungent material firm against Helen's nose, "does this smell like chloroform to you?"

ELEVEN

At the Hands of the Assailants

Chris jolted awake with a nauseating abruptness and a head that throbbed like a bastard in the spot where Rizzo had thumped him. His eyes snapped open and he took in the view of the all too familiar drabness of room eighteen of Flanagan's Last Barrel Motel; the severe sunlight that filtered through the shabby curtains, the outdated, fading décor and the deceased and dying cockroaches beneath the bed.

He was still wearing his swim shorts which were all but dry, belying the fact that he'd been unconscious for quite some time. He was sitting on the sticky, faded carpet propped up – back to back – against Helen. There was the unmistakeable, faint but acrid whiff of chloroform drifting over from her that stung his eyes. He could feel his wife's cool, damp skin against his, the thin spaghetti strap of her bikini top, her hair tickling his shoulders. Chris was also alarmed to discover that his hands were tied behind his back. "You okay, Hun?" he croaked, his mouth dry. It hurt to talk and the side of his face where he'd been punched felt tight and bruised.

"Yeah, you?" Helen replied with a tremble in her voice.

"What the fuck's going on, Helen?"

"What the fuck does it look like, Mister?" Rizzo's voice emulated Chris's. Accurately, as it happened.

Chris spun his head around to face the door. There, he saw Rizzo standing with his arms folded and that smug, shit-eating grin on his gum-chewing face. The man in the *Anal Thrush* T' nodded a polite hello to his captives.

Chris wriggled his hands. A little of the feeling was returning to them and the painful prickle of pins and needles heralded the recommencement of blood supply. He discovered that whatever was binding his hands together had been applied quite loosely; as if Rizzo hadn't had the wherewithal or the common sense to tie his captive's hands together properly.

"I don't know what you think you are doing here, Mr. Rizzo," Chris's voice struggled to remain calm. "But you won't get away with it."

"Nothing to get away with, Son. Not yet, anyhow." Rizzo grinned. "And I distinctly remember asking ya'll to call me *Robbie*."

"Mr. – Robbie," Chris continued "If you let us go –"

"– if this is the part where ya tell me if I let ya go now, you'll not tell on us, y'all can save your bullshit." Rizzo snorted and his smile slipped as his face adopted an unpleasant snarl. "I seen enough TV to know that if I let you go now, you'd run to the first po-leece that ya could find and sing like a couple o' canary birds." He leaned his tall frame against the door's. "Whatever ya do from here on in, don't take me for stupid, Son."

Chris wriggled his hands free of their binding and by leaning his weight against Helen's back, he levered himself up to his feet. He ran at Rizzo and before the man had time to react, Chris was upon him. Chris pushed Rizzo away from the door frame, and crashed him hard against the credenza.

"Chris!" Helen cried out.

Rizzo attempted to push Chris off of him, but Chris had a hold of his T-shirt with one hand which distorted the *Anal Thrush* girl's lissom legs into looking like something like Dali would paint. With his free hand, Chris punched wildly at Rizzo's face.

Struggling to defend himself against Chris's onslaught, Rizzo had a comically startled look on his face, as if he were none too sure as to how this could possibly be happening. Chris had him pinned down with the TV sticking in his back and the door had been left unguarded and he kept casting anxious glances towards the open doorway. Still, Rizzo managed to block all but Chris's odd lucky punch with his forearms, and even those that got through lacked power and fighting experience.

"Chris!" Helen again, panic in her tone.

"I got this!" Chris panted through his exertion. He didn't dare take his eyes off of his quarry, Rizzo had half-heartedly begun to fight back and their scrap was turning into more of a lame schoolyard scuffle than anything else.

"CHRIS!"

"Better mind your wife, Son," Rizzo sputtered between blocking Chris's punches.

Chris twisted his head around towards Helen.

"I said I got –"

What Chris saw next knocked the fight right out of him as sure as if Rizzo had landed him a punch in the balls. Chris dropped his fists and stepped back from the motel manager, the color visibly drained from his face and he looked as if he wanted nothing more than to throw up.

"Well howdy there, Mr. Sewell," Newman Bakker greeted Chris as pleasantly as you like. He smiled as he pressed the Glock muzzle so hard into Helen's temple that it left a neat, red indent. "Why don't you come sit back down like a good boy?"

Like a beaten dog, Chris slunk back to his place on the carpet. He offered Helen an apologetic smile and whilst her eyes told him that it was okay that he'd at least tried; Chris was sure he could detect just a hint of disappointment there.

Rizzo followed Chris across the room as he sat back down with his bare back pressed once more against Helen's. Rizzo joined his shaven-headed gas station buddy in standing over their captives and whilst much of their attention was understandably drawn to Helen's state of undress, they both eyed Chris as one would a recently landed fish.

"Nice of y'all to join Newman and me," Rizzo said. He smirked at Chris as if somehow he *knew* damned well he'd made a grammatical mistake and that it had been a deliberate one just to irritate the English teacher.

"Sure is," Bakker sounded absurdly like an archetypal, local news co-anchor. "We've been lookin' forward to getting to know y'all better." He crouched down low next to Helen, his face in hers. "'Specially you, darlin'."

"You dare touch her, and I'll –" Chris growled.

"– you'll do what, exactly?" Bakker poked the gun in Helen's throat and slowly traced the cool metal down her damp cleavage.

Helen shivered against Chris's back, her entire body rough with raised gooseflesh.

"Seems to me like you're in no position to be making threats, Son." Rizzo chewed on his gum loudly for emphasis. "So I'd recommend ya keep your fuckin' mouth shut." He delivered a sharp, swift kick to Chris's thigh which made the quad muscle go numb. Chris ground his teeth together and refused to give Rizzo the satisfaction of showing his pain.

"I think we should all just relax and get to know one another." Bakker stood back up and towered over Chris and Helen. "And I think we should begin by getting you out of those wet clothes." He smirked down at Helen. "Which in your case, really shouldn't take too long."

Rizzo cracked a laugh so hard that he almost choked back his gum. Looking down, he caught the look on Chris's face that told him in no uncertain terms that given the chance he'd rip out Rizzo's heart and feed it to him.

Bakker wiggled the gun at Helen's upturned face. Of the two captors, he seemed to be most enjoying the empowerment the weapon offered, absolutely relishing the fear on the woman's face. "Come along now, on your feet," he barked. "We'd hate for you to catch your death," he virtually purred the final word, as if savoring it.

Helen struggled to her feet and stood before the two men with a defiant look in her eyes. Her left arm, she wrapped across her chest, her right went down to cover between her legs; despite the bravado, Helen Sewell had never felt more vulnerable in her entire life.

This moment was inevitable, Helen had figured that it would be coming along sooner or later. Of course Rizzo and Bakker would want to see her undressed, it was beginning to feel like they were being held hostage in a cliché.

"Now, why are you doing that Ma'am?" Rizzo tugged at Helen's arms. "Ya should be proud of what ya got going on there, not hide it all away."

"Yeah," Bakker joined in. "And Newman and me have seen pretty much all of it anyways, barring the fine details." He laughed again, spraying the top of Chris's head with spittle. He then waggled the gun towards Chris, and Helen flinched.

"As I was sayin' –" Bakker left the sentence hanging and conveyed the remainder of the message with his eyes. He scanned Helen's body top to toe, lingering on the terrified look in her eyes.

Helen sighed.

She'd seen enough home invasion movies – they were a particular favorite of Chris's – wherein this particular scenario would invariably lead to sexual motives. So, Bakker's request really hadn't come as a big surprise. So, with a little embarrassed hesitation, Helen moved her arms away from her body and spread them out to her sides. She gave a weak smile at the reaction she'd elicited on Bakker's and Rizzo's faces as they feasted their greedy eyes upon her body; they looked to her like a couple of teens who'd snuck in the back door of their first titty bar. As if encouraged by the power her physique was exhibiting over the two men, Helen sucked in her belly a little and pushed out her chest to impress them even more.

"Now, ain't that better?" Rizzo said as his eyes crawled across Helen's ample bosom. They then cast downwards once again to study her feet so intently that it looked like he was counting her toes.

"Yep, sure is," Bakker agreed. "What say you, Son?" He leered at Chris over the gun barrel.

"Yeah," Chris said, his voice little more than a whisper.

"You could show a little more enthusiasm!" Bakker spat. He poked the gun hard into Chris's forehead. Chris's head jerked back and already an angry red circle was forming between his eyes.

"Yes, it's better!" Chris yelped. "Are you fucking happy now?!"

"Yes, Sir," Bakker smiled, "yes I am." He nodded at Helen. "And I'll be even happier when your good lady steps out of her wet clothing."

Helen fixed her eyes on Bakker's and ignored Rizzo completely. From experience with meathead guys such as these two – all testosterone and puffed up posturing – Helen knew that to disregard one in favor of his cohort would serve well to create some tension between the two. Maybe then the balance of power would tilt more in her and Chris's favor. Helen reached both hands behind her back to tug at the thin bow that held her bikini top in place.

"No, no, no!" Rizzo's sharp intonation made Helen freeze. "Not like this!" He manoeuvered himself to Helen's left side and leaned his pock-marked face close into hers. "Where's your sense of occasion, Ma'am?"

Bakker nodded in silent agreement. He reached a hand under Chris's armpit and pulled him to his feet. "Robbie's right, ya know," he said. "We should have ourselves a little shindig, seeing as though it's just us four friends an' all."

"Why are you doing this to us?" Chris struggled to appear strong, but his voice betrayed him with its slight tremor.

"Well…" Rizzo pondered for a second or two and leaned in so close to Helen that his nose pressed into her cheek. "It's most likely because we can."

"And after your wifey was so kind as to parade her goodies out by the pool for our delectation an' all –" Bakker offered by means of a justification.

"– and givin' us both the glad-eye, too," Rizzo chimed in.

"And *that* – thank you, Robbie." Bakker appeared to be getting more irritated by the second by his friend. "I figured Robbie and me are entitled. We just want a little fun, is all." He cast a smile at Helen that would have been convivial under (much) different circumstances. "What say you make a start, Ma'am?"

Helen really had little choice but to capitulate.

Bakker began to slow-clap and Rizzo followed suit, joining in with a uniquely out of tune *da-de-da* version of *The Stripper*. "Come on Son! Don't be shy!" Bakker encouraged Chris's participation with a prod of the Glock to the ribs. Chris clapped along a little out of time and added his voice to theirs as Helen began to dance.

Helen had frequented enough strip joints in her time to know all the moves; she and Chris had been through a phase of patronising Chris's favorite gentleman's club at least one night a week. It had been entirely Chris's doing, of course – his idea of a romantic night out and a means by which to cater to Helen's sapphic fantasies. Although, she had told him at the time that her fantasies – sapphic or otherwise – didn't quite extend to past-their-sell-by drug addicts waving their saggy, tired old tits and c-section scars in her face.

This had meant that they frequented one of the more upscale establishments on the outskirts of town. Helen had enjoyed their excursions and actually made friends with some of the girls who worked there. Sometimes she and Chris would invite them home for fun and games and on occasion, the strippers would invite Helen up on stage to strut her stuff and give Chris one hell of a show.

Therefore, her impromptu performance for Rizzo and Bakker was not even the first time Helen had stripped for an audience.

Ignoring the guy's tuneless beat in favor of her own internal rhythm, Helen swayed her hips side to side and began to gyrate her pelvis and bend her knees ever so slightly. She ran her fingers suggestively through her hair, down along her neck, and on to the sides of her breasts, which she pushed tightly together to create a deeper, exaggerated crevasse between them. Then she snaked her hands ran down along the smooth skin of her flanks and belly, stopping teasingly short of the tiny black triangle of material that covered her pussy.

"Oh yeah baby!" Rizzo shouted his encouragement like some self-conscious, redneck version of Austin Powers, the gray wad of gum visible on his tongue as he chomped on it.

Helen undid the bikini's tie, grabbing quickly at the front of the top to keep it covering her breasts as she danced. Then with an expert flick of the wrist, the bikini top flew off and into Rizzo's face to leave her tits startlingly bare, much to the sheer delight of two-thirds of her audience. That said, she noted that Chris was no longer looking overly uncomfortable, if anything he was clapping along with some enthusiasm; Helen knew that it was entirely possible that her show was actually beginning to excite him, despite the bizarre circumstances.

Staying with her own beat the best she could, Helen thrust her crotch in Bakker's direction. Making eye contact with the man, she stroked her breasts and tweaked her nipples into hard arousal. She then smiled at Bakker and he grinned back at her like an asylum inmate.

With a long, deep breath for courage, Helen hooked a thumb either side of her black briefs and turned her back to the men. She heard Rizzo let out a groaning sigh as she slid the scant material over her buttocks and down to her ankles. She gave a cheeky wiggle of her ass as she stepped out of the briefs and then trailed them back up along the inside of her leg from ankle to thigh and rubbed the black cloth along her crotch. Helen took one more deep breath and turned around to face her audience.

The clapping and singing silenced.

Helen Sewell stood there stark naked, damp bikini briefs in one hand, in front of her husband and two complete strangers.

Whilst this wasn't by any means Helen's first time being naked in company, and it was to be hoped that it wouldn't be her last, this instance was perhaps the most surreal. Possibly because this was Helen's first time – for *anything* – at gun point.

"Jeeeeees-us!" Bakker exhaled, taking in every inch of Helen's denuded body as he did so. "An' you're as smooth as a baby's *bee-haand* too." Bakker actually licked his lips at the sight of Helen's bare slit and the delicious folds of labia that pouted out at him like the delicate petals of an exotic desert flower.

Not finished yet, Helen turned to Rizzo and deliberately brushed her bare breasts against his arm. She then draped her bikini bottoms over his nose and wrinkled hers with distaste as he inhaled deeply to take in her intimate scent.

Bakker applauded, whistled and stomped his feet. "That was one heck of a show, lady!" He nudged Chris with his elbow. "You're one lucky sonofabitch, catching yourself a hot piece o' prize ass like that!"

"I'm sayin'," Rizzo agreed. He plucked Helen's briefs from his face and tucked them down the front of his jeans where they further exaggerated the bulge that had already formed there. "Ya'd almost believe the slut's done this before!" He laughed and stepped back to take in Helen as naked as the day she was born; everything on show and looking for all the world like she scarcely felt self conscious at all.

Helen had always thought that there was something quite unique about the effect that naked female flesh has on a man; she could sense the almost tangible spell her nudity had cast over her captors, and felt a warm, blossoming sensation of *control*.

"Now you," Bakker said as he stared directly into Chris's eyes and swung the gun towards Helen's chest. He began again with the tuneless tune and once more Rizzo added his own *da-de-das*.

Chris blanched, reluctant to comply, as if he was essentially terrified of appearing foolish. He then cast a nervous glance at the gun that pointed between his wife's breasts and began to dance. Unlike Helen's, Chris's was an awkward dance, his body all out of rhythm.

Bakker cackled. "Nah, just messing with ya!"

Rizzo gave out a hearty, head-back roar of a laugh and grabbed at his own dick as if to prevent himself peeing in his pants.

Bakker lowered the gun with a wink at Helen. He elbowed Chris in the ribs in a jovial gesture. Chris laughed along with them; it was a strained, almost forced laugh.

"Seriously though." Bakker's laughing ceased with startling abruptness and he stared dead straight into Chris's face. The gun was once more pointed at Helen's pierced nipple. "Lose the fucking shorts, Mr. Sewell."

****

"The problem we have now," Newman F. Bakker explained with a smirk, "is that Robbie and me have both got a hard-on like fourteen-year-old boys who found their Daddy's Viagra stash."

Rizzo nodded his own agreement and grabbed at his crotch for emphasis, just in case anyone else in the room may have missed the point.

Bakker looked over at Chris, who they'd made sit in the shabby armchair. He had his legs crossed to hide his genitals.

"Question is, what are we going to do about it?" Bakker's question was, of course a predictable one; this was clearly all part of the game.

Helen rolled her eyes at this; the two were getting to be so clichéd that it was almost comical.

She sat primly in the center of the bed with knees pulled up to her chin to hide as much of her nakedness as was possible. She faced Bakker and Rizzo who were perched on the end of the bed and the way she had her legs arranged, she was denying them even the view of her bare ass. The two men looked positively adolescent sitting there, simply oozing anticipation and each with one leg on the floor like this was some nineteen-fifties film set.

"You ever saw your lady fucking another man?" Bakker's aimed his blunt question at Chris.

Chris nodded.

"Can't hear ya, Mr. Sewell!"

"Yes. I said *yes*."

"Yes, what?"

"I've seen Helen with another man." Chris told Helen *sorry* with his eyes.

"How 'bout *two*?" Rizzo chipped in with a hopeful tone and a lascivious look crept across his face.

"No," Chris admitted, "I've always been the second guy." He offered up a shy smile. "It's kind of our thing."

"Well, I'm focussed on *my* thing right now." Rizzo grabbed his crotch once again; it appeared to be becoming a bit of a habit with the man.

"I bet you just love it when she performs with other men for you?" Bakker seemed to be getting into his stride now, revelling in Chris's obvious discomfort. "Well?"

Chris shook his head, knowing full well where this was all heading.

"My friend asked you a question, son!" Rizzo snarled, getting into a stride of his own.

Bakker pointed the gun at Helen. "You gonna answer me?" he growled at Chris. "Or am I gonna have to start shooting people?"

"Alright! Yes! I like it when she performs for me," Chris spat back, "are you fucking happy now?"

Bakker loosened his belt, and then unbuttoned his jeans. "No, Sir – but I soon will be." He smirked. And so saying, Bakker slid his belt, jeans and underpants down over his hips in one smooth movement, one-handed and with some expertise. His penis was quite the impressive sight as it bounced up erect and to full attention from its sparse clump of dark, wiry pubic hair that had been flattened against Bakker's sweaty crotch by his tight underwear. "Now, why don't you tell your wife what you'd like to watch her doing?" Bakker said. "How you'd like for her to pleasure us two gentlemen for your entertainment?"

Chris stared at the three of them on the bed. Helen – his beautiful wife – and the two Hicksvillians; one with the unleashed his dick he clearly intended to use, the other obviously straining at the leash to follow suit.

Helen fidgeted slightly on the bed, shivering as if a chill breeze was caressing her bare skin despite the thick, humid heat that smothered the motel room. Of all the exploratory sex she had experienced with Chris, Helen had never done this before; not with two strange men. Her pleasure – and reassurance – in three-ways had always been that Chris was right there with her.

This was to be an altogether different experience for her, way out of her own comfort zone, let alone Chris's.

Rizzo struggled out of his jeans. He pulled down his pristine, white Y-fronts to release their contents and his thin, uncircumcised penis flopped out, along with Helen's screwed up, damp bikini briefs.

Bakker leaned across the bed and poked Helen in the breast with a rough nudge of the gun. She squealed and shuffled backwards and this appeared to please Bakker no end. He poised once more with the gun's muzzle over Helen's tit, his dick twitching with the anticipation.

"Okay, okay!" Chris cried out. "Helen, I'd like for you to pleasure Mr. Bakker and Mr. Rizzo for my entertainment."

"Manners?" Rizzo giggled.

"Please." Chris bowed his head to hide the blush of humiliation that pinked his cheeks.

"Now, that's better," Bakker added as he crawled across the bed towards Helen. "My Mom always said to mind your P's and Q's." He manhandled Helen onto all fours on the bed and positioned himself to her rear. He paused to feast his eyes on the roundness of her rump, the pink rawness of her sex.

"If you'd care to take that end, good buddy." Bakker smiled at Rizzo. "I'm sure Mrs. Sewell would be only too willing to oblige."

"Don't mind if I do, Newman, old friend." Rizzo adopted a high-class Southern accent that sounded not unlike something one would hear in a Tennessee Williams play. He ground his teeth hard against the gum in his mouth, as if determined to extract every last molecule of flavor from it. He manoeuvered himself to stand at the side of the bed with his pasty white – almost translucent – dick six inches or so from Helen's face. "If that's okay with Mr. Sewell, that is."

The rhetorical question really required no reply but Chris was evidently obliged. "Yeah, go right ahead," he said quietly.

Rizzo wiggled his hips to flap his hardening dick in front of Helen's eyes like it was a toy for a puppy to chase. "You heard your husband, lady. Go right ahead."

Helen screwed up her eyes and took Rizzo's dick into her mouth.

"And don't you go thinking about chomping down on my friend's dick neither," Bakker instructed. "I'd hate for anything untoward to happen to that nice husband of yours." He swung the gun around and aimed it squarely at Chris's head.

Helen, of course couldn't see the gun, but she knew exactly what Bakker had meant by his threat.

Bakker slid his free hand over Helen's rump to stroke and knead at the firm flesh there, as if he were assessing a prize heifer for market. His rough hands circled around her buttocks, easing them ever so gently apart as he massaged, exposing her puckered hole. Bakker slid his fingers down between Helen's cheeks to sneak them down towards her vagina and once there, his probing fingers poked and explored Helen's most intimate flesh.

"Heck, she's wetter'n Bin Laden's coffin!" Bakker exclaimed as his fingers sank knuckle-deep into the slippery warmth between Helen's legs. He grunted out loud and pushed two fingers inside her and smiled as

Helen squirmed at his invasion and let out an involuntary whimper.

"She feelin' good at that end, Newman?" Rizzo's breath was quickening as Helen worked on him.

"What kind of dumb-ass question is that supposed to be?" Bakker laughed. "It's goddamned pussy, of course it feels fuckin' good!" He finger-fucked Helen as he spoke, his dick slapping against her ass.

"You got yourself a real tight pussy going on here, Mrs. Sewell," Bakker said to Helen in a most casual manner, as if he were complimenting her on a new hair-do. "Especially considering your age and all." He wriggled his fingers deep inside her and Helen pushed back to meet them, driving them still deeper. "How many kids have y'all had? One, two, three?" He paused, pensive. "Now, I ain't no gynecologist, but this sure don't feel like a three-kid vagina to me. Hell, after two, going up my wife's pussy is like sliding a cocktail wiener along Broadway."

Rizzo giggled at this but was cut short by a gasp as Helen poked her inquisitive tongue into the hole at the tip of his penis.

"And you ain't got a C-scar, so it's my guess that y'all don't have any kids at all." He felt Helen tense up inside, her vagina gripping his fingers as if she were trying to wrench them from his hand.

Helen forced open her eyes to look beyond Rizzo's sweat-sheened belly with its coarse black hair, and over at Chris who sat naked and motionless in the armchair, watching her – watching Rizzo and Bakker as they used her body to take their pleasure. She could see that his erection was stirring between his own legs as his body betrayed its arousal at the scene that unfolded before him.

"So, how come y'all don't have any kids yet, son?" Bakker directed his attention at Chris as he almost absently finger-fucked Helen. "You really didn't ought to wait much longer; your good lady here is a fine specimen and all, but she's no spring chicken." He wriggled a third finger inside Helen, gently screwing her with his hand and grinding his erection on her smooth thigh.

"We – er, we can't have children," Chris said, his voice trembling.

"Why in God's name not?" Rizzo seemed genuinely astounded at this revelation. "You firing blanks, son?"

Chris shrugged and looked blankly at the guy with his dick in Helen's mouth.

"Robbie asked you a fuckin' question." Bakker nudged at Helen's anus with the gun and she whimpered. "May I suggest you show some good manners and reply?" He applied a little pressure and the cold steel tip of the gun entered Helen.

"Okay!" Chris cried out. "Helen had a *Chlamydia* infection when she was younger," he told the stranger the one thing he'd never even confided to his closest friend, "and it messed up her insides."

Bakker appeared pleased with the response and withdrew the Glock from Helen's ass. He lifted the gun to his nose and sniffed at it.

Helen pulled Rizzo's cock from her mouth and it slopped out with a loud slurping sound. "Don't forget to tell them about your immotile sperm, Chris," she sounded indignant which came across as ever so slightly droll, given her current circumstance.

"You got poor swimmers, son?" Rizzo sounded almost sympathetic. "That's nothing to be ashamed of."

"It is if you want kids," Helen spat. She grabbed Rizzo's dick in her hand and jerked on it in front of her face. "His sperm's so fucked up it's not even any good for *in vitro* procedures."

Bakker laid the gun on the bed and gave Helen's ass a hearty slap that left a large, red imprint of his hand on her white skin. "Well said, Mrs. Sewell!" he said.

Helen grunted and bore down even harder on Bakker's wriggling fingers that had inadvertently found her G-spot.

"Well, at least *my* problem is congenital and not something I caught screwing around like some cheap whore in my freshman year of collage," Chris sounded petulant now. "*That* was entirely your fault."

"Really?" Helen raised her voice, her breath quickening as Bakker's thumb located her clitoris. "It's not fair to hold me accountable for things I did before I even met you! It's not my fucking *fault*, Chris!" She maintained her hand's rhythm on Rizzo's skinny penis that was now twitching against her fingers.

"Then who's fault is it, Helen?" Chris sat forward in his chair with his hands on his lap – as if he were trying to conceal his own arousal. "You screwed around like sex was going out of style and now we'll never have kids. I'd say that was pretty, damned conclusive as to whose fucking fault it is, wouldn't you?" Chris's eyes brimmed with tears and he turned his head away.

"I think your husband may have a good point there, Ma'am," Bakker said. He increased the pressure on Helen's clit whilst at the same time driving his chunky, busy fingers deep inside her. "Perhaps if you hadn't been such a filthy teenage whore back in the day, you'd have had a houseful of young 'uns by now." He gazed down at Helen's butt with an appreciative smile. "Mind, it would have been a goddamned *tragedy* to have spoiled this exquisite pussy of yours, Mrs. Sewell."

"Fuck you, Chris!" Helen spat, close to tears herself by now. This was a peculiar sensation indeed – to be on the verge of orgasm yet angry and lachrymose all at the same time. "If your sperm did more than just *crawl* out of your fucking ball sack, we might have had a chance," she snarled.

"That's bullshit, and you know it!" Chris retaliated, his masculine pride on the line. "Even if I had the most vigorous sperm on the planet, your rotten insides couldn't carry a baby. Or weren't you listening to every doctor we've spoken to, *ever?*"

Bakker smirked across at Rizzo. He increased the intensity of his fingers in Helen's vagina and dug his prick so hard into her thigh that she yelped, as his own climax approached. For Bakker, listening to the Sewells fight appeared to be more erotic than even the filthiest of dirty sex talk.

"Vigorous sperm?" Helen scoffed. "That's not even funny!" she panted as her climax raced towards her.

"You have no idea how emasculating all those motherfucking fertility tests were for me, Helen," Chris whined, his voice clogged with emotion. "It was all so – fucking *intrusive.*"

"Intrusive!" Helen laughed at him. "They stuck a catheter up my cunt and ripped out bits of my fucking uterus, Chris!" she screamed. "How fucking *intrusive* do you think that felt, you cocksucker!?" Helen's breath caught in her throat as the inevitable orgasm built inside her and she gripped Rizzo's dick so hard that he gasped. "You've always blamed me for this, and it's not fucking fair. You know damn well that even if f I had the most fecund womb on the fucking planet, your useless sperm couldn't have made it up there even if they'd caught a fucking cab!"

Rizzo grunted out a laugh at this and then, "Sorry." His face flushed as he neared release.

"Bitch," Chris snapped.

"Limpdick." Tears welled from Helen's eyes and dripped down onto Rizzo's dick, moistening its rumpled skin.

At this, Rizzo grunted like some feral, primitive animal and ejaculated hard into Helen's face, which served to trigger Helen's own orgasm. She squealed and humped Bakker's hand as she worked industriously on her own pleasure. In turn, Bakker shot his load on to her thigh, his semen hot and slimy against her skin.

Riding high from the waves of pleasure that continued to roar through her body, her face sticky with fat globs of ejaculate, Helen wriggled free of Bakker's fingers which slipped out of her to leave her vagina gaping, sodden and deliciously throbbing. She then released Rizzo from her grip and scrambled from the bed.

Through her tears Helen could see that Chris was crying too but she had only one thing on her mind at that moment. With a glance at her husband's heartbreaking face, and a look that spoke a thousand volumes, Helen dashed into the bathroom and slammed the door shut behind her.

TWELVE

New Friends and Old

"There's no need to be embarrassed about what y'all said there." Bakker called after Helen. "These things are better out than in, is what I always say."

Helen grabbed at the toilet roll. She missed her first attempt; her tear-filled eyes had blurred her vision and somewhat skewed her depth perception. On her second shot, Helen unrolled a fistful of the harsh paper and wiped roughly at the streaks of Rizzo's semen that mixed with her tears and ran in slow motion down her face.

As much as Helen was the adventurous type when it came to all things sexual, she had never really enjoyed the feel of come on her skin, especially so on her face. Although she'd grown accustomed to her husband's emissions, the way the stuff clung like slime from some disgusting mollusc, and its cloying, salty smell – the whole thing just made her skin crawl and she couldn't wait to be rid of it.

Much more than the violated feeling Rizzo and Bakker's semen had left Helen with was the abject *hurt* she had felt at Chris's ugly words. In their eleven years of marriage, Helen had never known her husband to be so venomous on the subject of children, or lack thereof. Naturally she blamed herself for their predicament; she'd been young and dumb and stupid in her college years, and there wasn't a day went by without self-reproach. But to hear it voiced so blunt and hateful like that from Chris – despite their extraordinary circumstances – was like a punch in the guts. Still, as Rizzo had so eloquently put it, better out than in; for as brutal as her exchange had been with Chris back there, Helen found that she did actually feel a little better for having got it off of her chest.

Sniffling up the last of her tears, Helen scraped the last of Bakker's come from her thigh and turned on the washbasin faucet. She would have done anything right then for a long, hot shower, but she didn't dare risk incurring the wrath of her captors by spending too long in the bathroom – she had an inkling that they had more plans.Helen splashed her face with the cold water that coughed out from the faucet in fits and starts, rinsing away the cloying stink from her face. Done, she reached for the towel and knocked her cell phone to the floor where it skittered under the bath tub. Helen plonked herself down on the lavatory with her face buried in the towel. There she took a little time to compose herself.

She heard a knock on the door from the other room. At first she thought it was Bakker or Rizzo checking up on her, but then realized the knock was on the door to the outside; it was a faint yet more *solid* rap as if on thick wood. Then she heard the *new* voices – other than those of the men who had just had their fun with her – enter the room beyond her little sanctuary.

Helen cocked her head dog-like – and listened. She thought that the arriving voices *did* sound awfully familiar.

****

Chris watched from the armchair as Robbie Rizzo pulled on his pants to go answer the door. Rizzo struggled to contain his dick in the faded denim as it was still mostly hard. He wore a look of deep concentration on his face as he slowly did up the zipper, obviously wary of trapping his dick in the metal teeth. Behind him, Bakker had climbed from the rumpled bed and pulled his shorts on over his own wilting cock.

Helen was still in the restroom – probably would be for sometime – Chris figured that she was likely washing both Rizzo's and Bakker's stink from her skin; he knew only too well just how much she detested semen on her body, most especially on her face.

Rizzo held open the door, which let in the outside heat and a handful of fat, striped mosquitoes. "Don't y'all stand on ceremony, come on in," he said, relishing playing the role of *mine host*. He peered out through the doorway with an impatient expression on his sweaty face and absently swatted at a mosquito that settled on his arm. The insect's bulbous, humbug body popped under Rizzo's palm and matted blood in his arm hairs. Rizzo grimaced and rubbed it in.

Ruthie-Peg Bakker waddled past Rizzo and into the motel room, carrying a large pile of pizza boxes in her plump, wobbling arms. As she walked by Chris, her vast bulk cast a heavy shadow over his naked body. She smiled down at him. "We brought pizza!" she squeaked.

"Of course ya' did," Rizzo teased. "Now we can *really* get this freakin' party started!" He let out a hearty guffaw that made Chris jump.

"You remember my lovely sister, of course," Bakker addressed Chris, the cheer back in his voice. He'd dressed and now stalked across the room to greet the new arrivals.

Chris gazed up at Ruthie-Peg with a look on his face gave away just how self-conscious he was of his own state of undress. "Hi," was all he could muster.

If it was at all possible, Ruthie-Peg – the girl-mountain – appeared to Chris to be bigger than she had been at the gas station. Most likely because she was away from the relatively flattering low light of the convenience store and its concealing counter. But, either way you looked at it, Ruthie-Peg was on the morbid obesity scale somewhere around *'Welcome to the Circus'*.

"Vernon, my good buddy," Rizzo effervesced as Vernon Theuber stepped over the threshold, his eyes instinctively hunting around for a cold beer.

"And if it isn't the delectable Dixie-Lee." Bakker grinned as Rizzo ushered Theuber's wife into the room. Bakker stepped up and planted a decisive kiss on the woman's lips whilst giving her butt a playful pat, resting his palm against the curve of her buttock.

Dixie-Lee Theuber looked pretty much the same as she had when Chris and Helen had seen her and Vernon at the flea market. She had on a fresh, white tank top and had exchanged her jeans for jeans shorts that were cut so high that the pockets hung down below the denim. A large, silver safety pin held the shorts together at the front in the absence of a button, and as far as Chris could make out, the gal was going commando.

"Why Newman Bakker, that's awful forward of ya - in front of my husband and all," Dixie-Lee gushed as she lackadaisically swiped Bakker's hand away from her ass. "And in front of your guest, too." She kicked off her flip-flops and dropped her ostrich skin bag on to the floor where it landed with a dull thud. She addressed Chris, "Why, I do believe we've already had the pleasure." She extended a hand. "Only y'all had on more clothes at the flea market!" Dixie-Lee laughed a hoarse, phlegmy, smoker's laugh.

Chris shook her hand. There was really little else he could have done.

"Hope ya'll don't mind, but we kinda started without you," Rizzo announced as he stood holding the door ajar, as if he were expecting more people to arrive.

"Yeah, we had us a little fun while we were waiting on y'all," Bakker added. "Robbie and me got ourselves better familiarized with Mr. Sewells' better half." He raised his hand to Dixie-Lee's lips and pushed a couple of fingers into her mouth.

Dixie-Lee sucked on them like they were Popsicles.

"Now ain't that just the sweetest thing you ever tasted in your life?" Bakker smirked at the woman. "Better even than you, Dixie-Lee." He chortled at the woman's disdain and quickly withdrew his fingers as if suddenly afraid she would bite him for his insolence.

"Well, I'll be sure to remember that the next time you want some Dixie-lovin' for free at our theater, Newman F. Bakker – you dirty old bastard." Her words were harsh but Dixie-Lee couldn't help but crack a reluctant smile and lick her lips to relish the musty taste of another woman on her tongue.

The bathroom door flew open.

Helen, with her modesty wrapped the best she could manage in a fluffy white bath towel, ran out with an ear-piercing scream. She aimed herself squarely towards Dixie-Lee, who was the only thing that stood between her and the freedom of the open door.

Vernon Theuber stepped towards Helen in an attempt to hinder her progress but she shoved him away with such force that his scrawny frame was sent sprawling over the bed and he crumpled onto the floor on the opposite side with a winded *oomph!*

Singularly focussed on the startled Dixie-Lee, Helen lowered her head and charged like she was prepared to go *through* the trashy bitch if necessary.

Timing it just right, Dixie-Lee shot out her leg in a well aimed kick at her would be attacker's cunt, and Helen went down like a head-shot deer.

Chris reacted in an instant and jumped from his chair, only to be pushed back down by Ruthie-Peg's humongous, flabby hand, her sausage fingers digging into his bare chest.

Dixie-Lee pounced. She perched on Helen's chest just below her breasts and pinned her arms to the floor with toned, muscular thighs that rendered Helen immobile. Rummaging through her ostrich skin bag, Dixie-Lee pulled out a collar and chain leash, a pair of red latex pants, something evil-looking constructed of leather straps and buckles, a folded switchblade and an alarm clock.

"Ain't it always the way that it's the last thing ya' get is the thing ya need?" She declared with a wicked grin as she pulled out from the depths of her bag a rusted-up pair of pliers. Holding Helen's head still by a fistful of hair, Dixie-Lee forced the pliers into Helen's mouth and clamped them down tight on the top, left incisor.

Still in considerable pain from the kick, Helen tried her damndest to struggle against Dixie-Lee's assault, but the woman's weight and sheer strength had her less than helpless.

Dixie-Lee gave a skilful twist of her wrist and there came a sharp *crack* as Helen's tooth leapt from her mouth amidst a fine spray of bright blood and saliva. It skittered across the floor and came to rest at Rizzo's feet. He stared down at it with a look on his face like he might just be about to throw up.

Helen screamed out in pain. She thrashed her legs and bucked her body like a tormented bronco attempting to dislodge its rider.

Dixie-Lee grabbed a bigger fistful of Helen's short hair and used it to thump the woman's head down hard on the floor. She then leaned forward until her face was but an inch from Helen's dazed eyes.

"Now, you can keep on tryin' to get away, Missy," Dixie-Lee snarled. "You've got another thirty-one teeth in that pretty little head of yours; but I'm not sure how much more punishment your pussy's gonna take."

Helen spat blood into Dixie-Lee's face.

"Now, that's no way to treat my good lady wife," Vernon Theuber castigated. "Ain't that right, Newman?"

"Damn right," Bakker agreed. "But ya gotta admit, Vernon – there's something freakin' hot about the feisty ones." Bakker's laugh was a menacing, deep rumble.

Helen saw that Bakker's gun was once again pointing at Chris's face and she quit struggling, despite the agonising pain that shot through her face and all the way to the back of her skull. "You *bitch*!" she snarled at Dixie-Lee and blood tainted saliva bubbles frothed from her mouth like she was some rabid wild animal.

The redneck woman just laughed in her face. "I've been called worse, Ma'am, and by tougher than you." Dixie-Lee grinned and reaffirmed her grip on Helen's arms with her bare thighs. "Much, much fuckin' worse".

She twisted her head to address her husband, "Ain't that right, Vernon?"

No reply from Vernon, he was too busy staring slack-jawed at Helen's exposed breasts.

The motel towel (resplendent with its tiny embroidered barrel) had fallen away from Helen's body during her rather one-sided fight with Dixie-Lee. It lay open beneath her, dotted with speckles of blood, and once again Helen Sewell was stark naked and exposing her body to the world.

"Ya like what ya see, do ya?" Dixie-lee chastised her husband who stood over Helen with his mouth agape and an all too obvious bulge in the front of his pants.

Vernon nodded and grinned inanely and Rizzo slapped his back and split one of his grins.

"Are those *really* real?" Dixie-Lee asked, and gave a nod towards Helen's chest.

"Fuck you," Helen replied. The pain in her mouth had abated a little, although the slimy trickle of congealing blood down the back of her throat made her feel nauseous.

"Well, I'll be," Dixie-Lee marvelled as she gawped down at Helen's bare breasts. "They're nearly as good as mine." To further make her point, she pulled her tank top up over her head to set her own breasts free.

Dixie-Lee's breasts were indeed quite formidable, if somewhat motionless. They perched on her chest less than a foot away from Helen's face, their skin taut and cherry-red nipples standing proud – and it looked just like someone had glued two flesh-colored pudding basins to the woman's rib cage.

"These babies are all mine, too!" Dixie-Lee announced as she juggled her tits, much to the mirth of her husband and his friends. "I got the receipt in ma purse to prove it!" They all laughed, Dixie-Lee the hardest, and still those improbable breasts barely moved. "I had 'em done," she confessed to Helen as if this were some great and secret revelation between old friends. "Had to. It's fair criminal what a pair 'a kids and thirty-odd years'll do to a woman's *tiddies*." She smiled. "Ain't that right, boys?"

The three men nodded their agreement but didn't take their eyes away from Helen.

Dixie-Lee extended a finger and prodded at Helen's breasts. She examined the soft, liquid flesh with childlike curiosity.

"Hope ya don't mind," she said.

Helen had little else to do but shake her head. "Be my fucking guest, bitch," she growled, much to Dixie-Lee's amusement.

Dixie-Lee spread her fingers over Helen's breasts as if to grasp as much of them as was possible. She squished and kneaded them with firm, circular motions and took the time to pinch and tweak at the stiffening nipples that pouted up at her. All the while she glanced over her shoulder at her silent, enraptured audience.

"Now, what do you want to go spoiling these beauties with that for?" Dixie-Lee's voice was schoolmarm stern. She tugged gently at Helen's nipple ring, extending the nipple until Helen grunted and strained beneath her weight.

"Ya like a little pain, eh?" Dixie-Lee smirked. "Is that why ya had it done? Or was it to please that sexy man o'yours?" She nodded towards Chris who was helpless to do anything other than glower at her from behind Ruthie-Peg's bulk.

Helen said nothing and stared defiantly up at the woman.

Dixie-Lee leaned forward again to thrust her face into Helen's; her solid breasts crushing into Helen's. "I asked you a question, Bitch," she growled. "You'd be best off replyin'." She plucked the switchblade from where it lay on the floor next to her bag and flicked it open with a resounding *snap*.

"Both," Helen's voice quivered as the knife came into view. "Chris thinks it's sexy. And I enjoyed getting it done." The truth being that Helen had gone through with the piercing on Chris's insistence and whilst he'd relished watching her have it done, she'd actually cried a little when the needle stabbed through her nipple; the pain had been almost more than she could stand, but at the same time she'd found herself more than a tad wet afterwards.

As if delighted with her answer, Dixie-Lee sat back up to rest her full weight on Helen's flat stomach.

"Thought so," she said.

Dixie-Lee traced the tip of the knife across the top of Helen's right breast, the blade creating a thin, red trail on the flawless white skin. She then followed the rounded contour down into Helen's cleavage and up over the left breast.

"If ya like pain so much, ya should have done what I had done, Missy," Dixie-Lee said. "They cut me here to put ma' tiddies in," she explained as she ran the knife along the underside of each Helen's breasts, "and here." The knife pressed a little harder and left behind it an angrier red line where Helen's breasts met her underarm.

Of course, Dixie-Lee's demonstration was rather superfluous – Helen could plainly see the vivid pink scarring where Dixie-Lee's tits had been sliced open under the name of vanity. Sadly, rather than enhancing Dixie-Lee's sexuality, it looked more like someone had taken a chainsaw to the poor woman.

"Please, n-no," Helen stammered. She wriggled her arms, but found them to be perfectly trapped beneath the firm, sweaty flesh of her tormentor; the feel of the chilled metal on her skin made Helen feel increasingly uncomfortable.

"And –" Dixie-Lee continued, wetting her lips with a moist tongue. " – here." She circled the tip of the blade around Helen's pierced nipple. "See, they had to relocate ma' nipples because once they put the silicone bags in, the darned things were practically under ma' freakin' chin." She toyed with Helen's nipple ring, slipped the tip of the knife through its hoop. "And I think that must have been the most painful part of the whole *pro-ceeedure* right there."

Dixie-Lee yanked the switchblade up and back and ripped out Helen's nipple ring.

Helen screamed out in agony as her delicate flesh tore and she rolled her head side to side as waves of white-hot pain shot through her body.

Even Vernon, Bakker and Rizzo winced.

"Stop it!" Chris shouted, the anger in his voice anger raising it an octave or two. He scrambled to his feet only to be pushed down once more by the formidable weight of Ruthie-Peg Bakker. And this time the fat woman sat down on his lap to render him as immobile and helpless as his wife. "Please!" Chris implored, unable to bear seeing Helen's pain.

Dixie-Lee stared down at Helen with a satisfied smile on her lips; plainly revelling in the woman's hurt. She studied with sadistic delight the welling pool of thick blood that flowed from the tip of Helen's breast and trickled down along its sides; it looked very much like one of those kid's science fair volcanoes they made with *papier-mâché,* baking soda and vinegar.

"You bitch!" Helen finally found her voice and screeched at Dixie-Lee. "You *fucking* bitch!"

"Steady on there, tiger," Dixie-Lee scolded, "y'all just admitted that ya like a little pain." She stood up, taking care to keep Helen's wriggling body between her feet. "I'm just playin' is all."

Helen grasped at her throbbing breast with her newly liberated hands in an attempt to sooth the pain from her torn nipple and stem the blood flow that quickly turned her fingers all red and sticky.

Dixie-Lee looked down at Helen and took in the entirety of her vulnerable, naked body with a lascivious expression on her handsome face.

"Leave my wife alone, you sick whore!" Chris's command from beneath Ruthie-Peg's blubber garnered the amused derision of his captors. The obese woman shifted her weight a little and one of her stomach's fat rolls compressed Chris's diaphragm and rendered him silent.

"You're a fine one to be name-calling, Mister," Dixie-Lee chastised, "seeing as though ya make your wife shave off her George Dubya." She pointed with distaste at Helen's hairless pudendum. "*I* think it makes her look like a ten-year old. Ya like little girls, do ya', Mr. Sewell?"

Chris shook his head and tried to speak but his words were suffocated by the volume of flab that pressed hard into his chest.

"Well, I wouldn't let ya within a mile of ma' daughters!" Dixie-Lee winked at Chris. She unhooked the safety pin that held her shorts together and wriggled them down over her hips; and as Chris had earlier suspected, it was thus confirmed that she was not wearing underpants.

"*This* is what a woman's supposed to look like," Dixie-Lee announced with pride as she stood naked over Helen.

"Amen!" Rizzo joined in, somewhat enthusiastically.

"Ain't that the truth?" Bakker smiled and his eyes feasted on the thick, black clod of pubic hair that sprouted out between Dixie-Lee's legs.

"I'll bet y'all would like to see Mrs. Sewell here with a real woman, wouldn't ya?" Dixie-Lee played to her audience, feeding from the nods and libidinous expressions. Even Ruthie-Peg was starting to look horny, her attention momentarily distracted from the pizzas.

Dixie-Lee bent over and parted Helen's legs.

Helen struggled against Dixie-Lee's efforts and clamped her thighs firmly together.

"I wouldn't do that, if I were you, Missy," Dixie-Lee's tone was quite matter of fact, as if she were merely passing the time of day with Helen and not threatening her. She inclined her head towards Bakker.

Bakker made a big show of flicking the Glock's safety to *off* and took a step or two closer to Chris.

Helen had no other choice than to relax. "Redneck skank," she cursed Dixie-Lee beneath her breath as the woman prised her legs wide apart.

Ignoring the insult, Dixie-Lee lifted Helen's right leg up into the air and held it tight against her own belly. She thought that Helen's foot looked cold, her toes a little white as if their circulation had been cut off, but she really wasn't all that focussed on the woman's feet. Slowly, Dixie-Lee lowered herself down and positioned herself between Helen's legs, lowering her hirsute vulva onto the warm, smooth skin of Helen's.

Helen shuddered at Dixie-Lee's touch. Although she had been with women before – the sapphic aspects of her and Chris's sexual exploration had always rated amongst her favorites – and she did enjoy the feel of female skin against her own, she was as discerning about her female lovers as she was about her men; if not more so. Dixie-Lee was most definitely not Helen's type at all; the woman's coarse, trailer-park hands, comically fake tits, and out of control pubic hair that resembled neglected topiary had the redneck firmly placed on Helen's '*NO*' list. Even so, there was just something about being pushed out of one's comfort zone every once in a while.

"Let's do this!" Dixie-Lee groaned and began to scissor her pussy against Helen's.

Theuber, Rizzo and Bakker stepped closer to secure themselves a better view of the impromptu floor show. Ruthie-Peg leaned her bulk towards Dixie-Lee and Helen so that she too could watch whilst at the same time ensuring that Chris remained pinned down and helpless. Even Chris found himself unable to avert his eyes, Helen indulging her bisexual tendencies had always delighted him, however bizarre the circumstances – he simply couldn't help himself.

Helen grimaced at the sensation of Dixie-Lee's thick bush as the woman ground it on her soft skin; it had the feel of someone scraping away at her sensitive lips with a pan scrubber, although there was something oddly pleasurable about the contrast of the wiry hair and the warm, wet flesh that poked through it.

Rizzo was – quite literally – drooling. He'd quit working at his gum mid-chew and stood there with his mouth agape with a long drip of saliva stringing down onto the semi-naked woman on his T-shirt. Rizzo's eyes bulged along with his jeans, his arousal at Dixie-Lee's antics unashamedly obvious to everyone else in the room.

"You likin' this?" Ruthie-Peg asked Chris in that inimitable squeaky voice that made her sound like a cartoon character. "Seein' your wife tribbin' another lady?" She wheezed out something that could have been a laugh. Or gas. "That's performing *tribidage*, scissoring if ya' will." She giggled. "See, I'm not as stupid as y'all think I am." She turned her face towards Chris and blasted her hot, foul breath in his face.

Chris shook his head. He was still struggling to breathe, let alone talk.

"Don't you go givin' me all that coy bullshit, Mister," the fat girl chided. "There's not a man alive who doesn't like all o'those lesbian goings-on, and I just know you'll be no different. Why, I can feel your dick poking in my thigh right now," she sounded like a coy, southern belle and Chris couldn't discern whether she was putting it on or not. Ruthie-Peg fidgeted her considerable weight a little to one side. She fished in her sweats pocket and pulled out a crumpled cigarette pack and cheap Zippo lighter.

The fat woman was right; Chris *was* becoming aroused watching his wife grinding vaginas with the dreadful redneck woman. And as much as he hated himself for doing so, he kept on telling himself that his erection was nothing more than an involuntary biological response to the visual stimuli – Helen would have been proud at his pragmatism. It also looked to Chris as though Helen was actually starting actual enjoy her ordeal; her face had flushed pink and she had half-closed her eyes as she often did in the initial throes of ecstasy.

Ruthie-Peg fired up the lighter and lit her cigarette. She took a deep, long draw from it – held it in her lungs awhile – and exhaled the lot in to Chris's face.

Chris wrinkled his nose and shot the flesh mountain a malevolent look.

Take it outside, Buddy?

All things given, it was an absurd reaction to have amidst the escalating, over-dramatic moaning from

Dixie-Lee, the lecherous attention directed at Helen by the rednecks, the gun aimed at Chris's face, along with the obese woman slowly crushing the life out of Chris's legs - But Chris just couldn't help himself, he simply didn't like cigarette smoke – it was why they'd booked a *non-smoking* room at the Last Barrel Motel in the first place.

"Well, *pardon me*," Ruthie-Peg snarled at Chris in that ludicrous squeak of hers, the offending cigarette dangling from the corner of her cavernous mouth. "I happen to need to smoke – medically speaking – to help keep my weight down," she said with no hint of irony whatsoever. "So I'm sorry to have slighted your sensibilities." She pulled the cancer stick from her mouth and stubbed it out on Chris's bare nipple.

"You fat cow!" Chris yelped and struggled beneath Ruthie-Peg like a kicked dog.

"What the–?" Dixie-Lee exclaimed, perturbed at the distraction from her rubbing at Helen's pussy. Angrily, she looked over at Chris and Ruthie-Peg.

Rizzo and the others also turned their attention to Chris, their eyes burning into him like he was *that guy* who answered his cell in the movie theater.

"She fucking burned me!" Chris whined as he clutched at his sore, blackened nipple.

Even Helen cast him a dirty look.

"Well, you've gone and interrupted the ladies now," Bakker sounded especially irritated. "And that's just plain fuckin' rude." He took a step closer to Chris with the gun, his trigger finger twitching.

"It's okay, no harm done," Theuber mediated. "You carry on, my love," he coaxed Dixie-Lee.

"There's no need, Vernon," Dixie-Lee was petulant. "The mood's gone." She let go of Helen's leg, climbed off and faced Chris. "We were just getting to our orgasms there as well, Mr. Sewell – and you went and spoiled the moment."

"Perhaps he's jealous that you're giving his missus all the attention an' neglectin' him?" Bakker ventured.

"Perhaps so," Dixie-lee grumbled, "all I know is that his – *impolite* – interruption has left me all pissed off and with an itch in my groin." Her voice took on an angry tone as her eyes flashed displeasure at Chris. "But if Mr. Sewell here is feeling left out because we're having some fun with his wife and not him, then I guess we really ought to include him a little."

Taking their cue, Rizzo and Theuber moved on Chris. Ruthie-Peg struggled to shift her immense body off of him, leaving him once more naked and vulnerable. Chris attempted to back away by pressing himself into the back of the armchair. But, of course, there was nowhere to go.

The two men grabbed Chris, one arm each, and lifted him bodily out of the chair. They escorted *(dragged)* him over to the bed and made him stand next to it like a soldier at inspection. Terrified, Chris stole a glance over at his wife, perhaps he was in need of some of her resolve?

Helen had sat herself upright on the floor with her knees drawn protectively up to her chin. Her chest and all down along her flanks were streaked with drying blood and there was a dribble of pinky-red snaking its way down from the corner of her mouth.

Their eyes met briefly.

"Well, would ya just looky here!" Theuber exclaimed with great amusement. "Come take a look-see at this, Dixie-Lee!" He pointed a trembling finger at Chris's smooth, freshly-shaved genitals. "What is it with you city folk and body hair? Ya look like a little boy."

"There's no wonder pubic lice are a dying species," Bakker added sagely, "it's because of folk like you killing off all of their habitats." He smirked at Chris and nodded towards Helen. "It's a small wonder that Greenpeace don't stage a protest of some sort."

"Yeah, like a *'Save the Crabs'* campaign," Rizzo threw in his two cents' worth. "They could form human chains around the waxing salons. Ya know, to raise awareness and such."

Given their deadpan delivery, it was difficult for Chris to ascertain if the men were actually serious or not.

"Ya know what gets my goat?" Bakker persisted, "is that those saving the earth, tree-hugging types get all up in arms when the rain forests get pulled down and it kills off some dumb motherfucking' frog." He adopted a serious tone, "Their argument is that said frog might just hold the secret to curing cancer or Alzheimer's or some such and when it's gone, that cure dies with it."

"Ya got a valid point, there, Newman," Rizzo sounded rather like a man trying too hard to appear clever in front of his superiors.

"So, what if the humble pubic hair louse just so happened to hold a secret cure for something big?" Bakker mused. "And I'm sure nobody even bothered to check – but what if it did, and you folk with your Brazilians and *Nair* and laser hair removal have killed 'em all off?"

Chris stared into Bakker's eyes with fear in his own; it was not out of the question that the man was a total lunatic.

"Never mind that," Dixie-Lee cut in. "I do declare that Mr. Sewell here ain't circumcised!"

"Well, I'll be!" Rizzo exclaimed. "You some kind of *English*, Son?"

Chris shook his head.

"My Dixie-Lee fucked an English fella a couple of years back," Theuber chipped in. "Ain't that right, my lover?"

Dixie-Lee poked at Chris's flaccid penis with a bony finger. "Yeah, I did," She answered. "Freakiest thing I ever had in my mouth, I can tell ya'! It was like unravelling one of those magician's 'kerchiefs, only in pink and veiny." She laughed a filthy laugh that seemed to delight her friends.

Bakker nodded to Rizzo who stepped over to Helen and helped her to her feet. He guided her over to the bed, stood her to face her husband.

The mechanic retrieved Chris's hunting knife from the travel bag and handed it to Rizzo, handle first.

Chris watched with mounting terror as the knife changed hands. "Whatever it is you're planning, please don't," his voice sounded small. He cupped his shrinking penis with shaking hands; felt his balls cowering so close to his body it was like they were trying to get back in.

Rizzo took Ruthie-Peg's lighter from her pudgy hand, flicked it to life.

"You really are a whiny little prick, ain't ya?" Bakker taunted Chris. "Look at what your wife's been through, and she's not snivelling one bit." He cupped Helen's chin and lifted her face up. She forced a weak smile which showed off the fresh, bloodied gap between her perfect teeth. "And all we're going to do is what's done to millions of little *babies* every day." He grinned at Chris.

"Oh sweet Jesus, no," Chris gasped.

Rizzo wafted the lighter flame along the length of the hunting knife to heat up the blade.

"It's gonna take a while to sterilize your knife, son, so I think we should find something to do to take your mind of what's coming your way," Bakker managed something in his voice that resembled concern. He pulled the riding crop from Helen's bag and swished it in the air close to Chris's ear.

Chris winced at the cruel noise the crop made and looked at Helen for some form of reassurance.

Dixie-Lee grabbed Helen and bent her over the edge of the bed with her face buried in the sheets and rump in the air. Helen struggled against the woman, but quickly gave up as she was overpowered.

Bakker handed the crop to Chris, forcing it into the hand that wasn't gripping his dick and balls. "Have at it, son," he said with a wicked grin.

Chris glanced down at Helen's flawless behind that was thrust so indelicately skyward, couldn't help but admire its exquisite curvature and soft, downy skin. "No," He said, dropping the riding crop on the floor. "I won't do this."

"You mean to tell me that you've never played school teachers, Son? You've never taken a whip to your wife's behind in the bedroom?"

"No," Chris lied.

"Then, that's a cryin' shame." Bakker stared Chris down as he toyed absently with the gun. "We were looking forward to seeing some stripes on your wife's perfect behind."

Dixie-Lee pulled Helen from the bed. Helen pulled herself from the woman's grip and stood to face her. She thrust out her formidable chest, despite the dull, throbbing ache in her torn, bleeding nipple – as if to deliberately irk the redneck woman with her perfect, full and one hundred percent natural breasts.

"Looks like you're good to go." Bakker motioned for Helen to pick up the riding crop. As she did so, Bakker punched Chris hard in the solar plexus, doubling him over with an accompanying *whoosh* of breath forced from his lungs. Dixie-Lee guided Chris's fall onto the bed, folding his arms beneath him as he went down so that they were pinned by his own weight. Then she pressed hard on the back of Chris's head, forcing his face into the hard mattress to keep him still and stifle his protests.

"I have never hit my husband, and I'm not going to start now," Helen told Bakker.

"Then I'll shoot him in the fuckin' head," Bakker replied as calm as you like and emphasised his point by pointing the gun at Chris. "It's your choice, lady."

Theuber picked up Dixie-Lee's alarm clock from the sticky bloodstain Helen's tooth extraction had made on the floor. He set it. "I say we give it five minutes, what ya think, Newman?"

Bakker nodded.

Tears forced themselves into Helen's eyes as she gripped the crop tight, raised it high above her head and swished it down on Chris's bare buttocks where it made a loud, resounding *thwack!*

Chris let out a muffled yelp against the bed and wriggled his butt as if trying to move it out of the way.

Helen looked down at the red stripe she'd made across her husband's buttocks. It was an angry contrast that looked sore against the white skin. So, this was what it felt like?

"Keep going," Bakker instructed.

She brought the down crop again, harder this time and Chris cried out in pain.

"That's a good girl," Bakker encouraged as Theuber and Ruthie-Peg shuffled closer to view the spectacle. "Do it again and don't stop 'till the alarm goes off."

Helen swiped the crop at Chris's backside again and again, grunting with the exertion. With each stroke,

Chris ground his pelvis into the edge of the bed to escape the torment which gave the unfortunate appearance that he was fucking the mattress. And it wasn't long before the whip marks on Chris's butt cheeks had crisscrossed and were running into each other like an aerial photograph of mystical lay-lines. Some of the welts were already bruising up a plum-purple color and others oozed crimson blood where Helen had inadvertently hit the same place more than once and split her husband's skin.

"Well then," Vernon Theuber reflected as he looked on and took a slurp on his beer. "Don't this just make Fifty Shades of Grey look like Harry fuckin' Potter?" He laughed at his own joke and looked around for approval, although sadly no one laughed with him.

"Don't stop now," Bakker commanded. "Your husband's enjoying himself."

Helen studied Chris's limp form; his bloodied ass, the muffled whimpers, the gun aimed at his head, and to her it actually looked otherwise. She lifted the riding crop high above her head. Held it there.

"Why are you hesitating?" Bakker asked, smoothing a hand over his hairless pate. "He did nothing to help you when Dixie-Lee tore up your titty and rubbed your pussy raw with that thatch of hers," he goaded and glanced down at the chafing between Helen's legs. "He let *you* get hurt, Helen."

Helen brought the crop down hard on Chris.

Again, and again.

"He's happy to see *you* in pain, but can't take it himself. What kind of fucking man is that?" Bakker's voice boomed as Helen thrashed at Chris's behind with a blood lust she would never have thought herself capable of. "Do it for all the perverse things he's made you do just so he can get hard -"

Trrrrrrrr.

The shrill voice of the alarm clock filled the room.

Bakker seized Helen's arm halfway through a down stroke, gripping her wrist so tight as to cut off the blood to her fingers, he plucked the riding crop from her hand.

Dixie-Lee turned Chris's limp body over on the bed, his legs still draped over the side. She looked surprised to see that Chris was fully erect, his dick standing rigid and proud. She grabbed a hold of it and pulled the foreskin up over its bulbous head as far as it would stretch. She held out her other hand and Rizzo handed over the heated hunting knife. Dixie-Lee placed the knife into Helen's hand.

"Oh, no," Helen whimpered, a flash of regret skittering across her face.

Ruthie-Peg waddled over and placed her hands on Chris's chest to press him down on the mattress. Bakker slipped his gun between Helen's legs and ran its cold barrel the length of her slit. "Do it," he growled and pressed the muzzle hard against Helen's clitoris.

With a sharp intake of breath, Helen drew the razor-sharp blade across the taut hood of her husband's penis. The hot steel sliced though the tender foreskin like a knife through butter with a hot, wet *tsssssssss*. Delicate wisps of pinkish-black smoke wafted up from the cauterized skin and in the blink of an eye Dixie-Lee pulled it free of Chris's dick.

Chris squealed and bucked against the pain but couldn't break away from Ruthie-Peg's strength. Instead, he flailed his arms, lifted up and slammed his head against the bed. "You fucking bitch!" he cried out. "You cut my fucking dick off!"

Dixie-Lee held the smoking, wrinkled foreskin up in front of his face and wiggled it a little. "No we didn't, ya' big freakin' baby; we just took off the bit God stuck on as one of his little jokes!"

Helen was a surprised to see that there was so little blood; Dixie-Lee's removal of her nipple ring had caused far more than this. But, nonetheless it did look incredibly painful. Plus, Chris's prick looked weird without its protective hood – all naked, angry and exposed.

Helen screamed.

She dropped the knife – almost stabbing into her own bare foot – and climbed onto the bed with Chris. She took him into her arms and held him tight and they both sobbed.

Rough, calloused hands pried Helen and Chris apart. At first they resisted the separation from the sanctuary of each other's arms, but in the end, they had no choice but to succumb to the strength of the others, even without Ruthie-Peg who had wandered off in the direction of the pizza boxes.

Rizzo and Bakker manhandled Chris and Helen over onto their backs on the bed.

"We got one more surprise for y'all," Bakker announced.

"Only, it ain't much of a surprise," Ruthie-Peg added from the armchair as she stuffed rolled-up pizza into her mouth, "seein' as though you bought the thing in ma' shop an' all."

Bakker lifted up the brown paper-wrapped rubber fist and unwrapped it with all the zeal of a small child on Christmas morning.

"Oh, sweet mother of God, no," Chris groaned. "You can't be fucking serious."

"Deadly," Bakker said. He bent over to rummage through Helen's valise. As he did so, he made a big deal out of casting aside the skimpy underwear and bikinis that were packed therein.

"Nothin' to be afraid of," Theuber said. "*You* bought it, after all."

"I bought it for a friend," Helen explained, her throat clogged with thick mucus and tears. "As a joke."

"Strange sense of humor, if y'ask me," Dixie-Lee cackled as she delved into her bag. She yanked out a set of leather BDSM underwear which was resplendent with thick straps, silver buckles and studs. She threw it on the bed next to Helen. "Put these on, you're gonna have to look the part."

"You didn't buy any lubrication to go with this?" Bakker said with disappointment in his voice. He waved the black latex fist in Helen's direction and its clumped fingers pointed at Helen in an accusatory manner. "Just what kind of fucking friends are you?"

"I told you, I bought it as a –"

"Joke -– I know," Bakker stared at Helen. "Which means that you, Sir," he addressed Chris with a broad grin as he plucked a family-sized bottle of shampoo from Helen's travel bag, "will be farting bubbles for a day or two."

****

Helen had always felt self-conscious – silly even – wearing bondage gear, although she was the first to admit that she actually looked quite stunning in it; there was just something about her trim, curvaceous frame that complimented black leather, straps and silver buckles.

The outfit – if it could be called that – given to her by Dixie-Lee fit Helen well enough. It provided a covering of rough leather over her crotch and breasts –

the latter of which rubbed without mercy on her lacerated nipple and made every movement a painful one – and was just enough to add a soupcon of eroticism. There were wide straps that traversed Helen's body to give her a fierce, bondage-bitch appearance, along with fat buckles that dug into the soft flesh of her belly. The one glaring omission from the ensemble were shoes; in anyone's book, it was the six-inch, spiked heel, strappy stilettos that made a dominatrix look complete.

"I don't think I can do this," Helen said quietly.

Bakker sighed and pointed the gun towards Chris with a nonchalant flick of the wrist. His expression was one of bored resignation, as if he had already grown tired of coaxing Helen with threats to her husband.

Theuber and Rizzo manoeuvered Chris back into the face down position with his legs draped over the side of the bed and his bloodied butt poking into the air. Dixie-Lee lay across him to hold onto his head and her silicone chest dug hard into his back.

"You really are going to have to stop fucking whining when we ask you to do something," Rizzo menaced Helen. "We want to have fun, not listen to you moan."

"Unless it's the *good* kind of moaning." Ruthie-Peg squeaked and followed on with an emulation of an orgasm that sounded like Meg Ryan on helium.

"I just can't –" Helen protested and dropped the latex fist onto the bed.

"Oh, for fuck's sake!" Bakker exclaimed. He grabbed the thing from the bed and shoved it back into Helen's hand.

"No!" Helen tried to back away, once more dropping the fist onto the bed.

Theuber stepped in and grabbed Helen's wrist so hard that everyone heard the bones crack. He slapped the sex toy into her hand. "You don't get to say *no*, lady," he snarled. He then twisted Helen's arm up and around to maneuver the fist towards her husband's exposed backside and pressed the end of it against the delicate, puckered flesh of Chris's anus.

Chris gave out a muffled cry and struggled under the weight of Dixie-Lee and Rizzo's strong arms that were holding him down. Ruthie-Peg had torn herself away from the food to lend her considerable weight to Chris's legs and Bakker added his free hand to Chris's thigh to further contain the struggle.

Helen positioned the fake fist against Chris's anus and flinched along with him as it made contact. All Helen could do at this point was to hope that Chris could relax his body enough to go through with this.

"Best get started, lady," Rizzo whispered in Helen's ear. "I think Newman's starting to get antsy with that gun of his."

Chris twisted his head to one side the best he could, straining for a gulp of air that didn't stink of Dixie-Lee Theuber's beer breath, and watched as Helen poured a liberal amount of shampoo – *and conditioner (two in one) for distressed hair* – over the latex fist and down the crack between his butt cheeks. The touch of cool liquid made him shiver involuntarily.

"I am so sorry about this, babe," Helen said as she pressed the stiff latex fingers gently against his puckered hole.

Chris bore down as the tapered fingers slipped inside him, their journey eased by the slickness of the shampoo. He knew that it was essential that he fight the natural urge to tense up, to do that would deliver insurmountable pain. So, Chris forced himself to relax as he felt the discomfort of the toy (*gag gift* – this was Texas, after all!) sliding into his ass with more ease than one would think possible. Shifting his rump's position ever so slightly, Chris let his body guide the invading latex as he worked with his wife to complete their warped challenge.

The wider knuckles of the fist strained Chris's sphincter muscle to its limit and it stopped there. Helen pushed a little and Chris let out a loud moan. He buried his face in the bed and his fists balled against the pressure.

"What ya waitin' for, Mrs. Sewell?" Chris heard a voice say. It may have been Rizzo but to him the hillbillies were all starting to sound very much the same.

"I can't –" Helen spluttered, "it's too big." There was anger and frustration in her voice that made her sound shaky and almost on the verge of tears.

Bakker pressed the muzzle of the gun into the back of Chris's head. "Well, I *really* don't think you're trying hard enough," he growled.

"I'm hurting him!"

"That, Mrs. Sewell is the fucking point," Theuber snarled.

Chris heard a swish and the all-too familiar *thwack* of harsh leather on bare skin. He heard Helen yelp as the riding crop stung her ass and he felt her body jump. And then there came the stretching, tearing, searing torment that flooded his lower body as his sphincter split beneath the assault of the giant fist, allowing the toy to invade his body and fill up into his rectum with cold, unforgiving rubber.

Chris screamed.

Helen screamed along with her husband as blood gurgled out from Chris's split flesh and out onto her hands. She'd actually *heard* the moment Chris's body had torn; a sickening, renting noise that she would never be able to forget. She stepped away from the terrible damage she had orchestrated with a nauseated look in her eyes as like some grotesque birthing, the fist slopped out of Chris and on to the floor as his body expelled it. Helen watched him with tears dribbling down her cheeks as he slumped down on the bed and she could see that his eyes were rolling towards the back of his head.

"I'm sorry, I am *so* sorry," Helen's voice returned to her as Chris passed out and went limp in the sticky fluids that welled out of his body and soaked through the bed sheets.

****

"Come on now, let the dog see the rabbit," the still naked Dixie-Lee's voice was the first one that Chris heard upon awakening. She planted her calloused hands on his sore buttocks and spread him apart to see the damage done by the latex fist. Chris flinched as a sharp spark of pain flashed through him.

"Ya really need to learn to relax, Hun," Dixie-Lee admonished. "If ya'd relaxed like you were asked before, this wouldn't be necessary now." Carefully she examined the split in Chris's ass; it had all but stopped bleeding but was incredibly angry and sore. "Pass me the bottle, will ya?" she asked Rizzo.

Rizzo obliged and handed Dixie-Lee a liter bottle of vodka. Dixie-Lee unscrewed the cap and poured a liberal amount of the pungent liquid onto a wad of cotton balls she'd liberated from Helen's makeup bag. Then, she began to wipe away the congealing blood from Chris's butt.

Chris cried out with the harsh sting of the cheap liquor and squirmed against Dixie-Lee's ministration.

"Don't ya worry, son, I used to be a nurse," she comforted.

"Yeah, a *vit-nery nurse,*" Rizzo derided.

"Don't matter a damn, Robbie Rizzo, stitches is stitches," Dixie-Lee defended, "no matter what animal you're puttin' 'em in."

At the word *stitches* Chris groaned and tried to crawl away across the bed.

"Hold him down and keep 'em spread," Dixie-Lee ordered Rizzo and Theuber.

They did as instructed without complaint and pinned Chris to the bed with his legs splayed in a most ungainly fashion. He tried to protest but his face was buried into the mattress that was sour with the stink of his own sweat.

Dixie-Lee produced a curved needle and surgical thread as if from thin air. She busied herself threading the needle, holding its eye close to the bridge of her nose as if she really ought to have been wearing spectacles. "You, git your ass over here," she barked and looked over her needle at Helen who sat next to Ruthie-Peg's armchair, knees hugged tight to her chest. "Come hold your man's hand," Dixie-Lee's tone made it quite clear that the request was not optional. "It's the least ya can do, considerin' this was all your doin'."

Helen stood up and made her way across the room. She sat on the edge of the bed and took hold of Chris's hand and he gave her a tentative smile.

"Gonna have ya' as good as new in no time at all," Dixie-Lee purred as she stabbed the needle's keen point into Chris's ass.

Each sharp prick of the needle through the torn, rubbery muscle elicited a guttural groan from Chris as it delivered its exquisite sparks of pain. Again, and again the sharp steel punctured his delicate flesh as Dixie-Lee stitched him back together. Chris gripped his wife's hand tightly; almost crushing her fingers with each stab of the needle as he moaned quietly into the mattress.

And when she'd finished the intricate trio of stitches and tied off the black thread in a neat, miniature butterfly, Dixie-Lee admired her handiwork with a satisfied smile on her scarlet lips. "Perfect," she congratulated herself. "Ya' can roll him over now," she instructed Theuber.

Rizzo joined in to help flip Chris on to his back.

"Take this," Dixie-Lee pressed a small, nondescript pill against Chris's lips. "It'll help with the pain."

Chris looked at the woman with a grateful expression and swallowed the pill dry. Almost immediately it began to take effect and his eyes began to close.

"Well, would ya look at that?" Dixie-Lee smiled, pointing to the huge, bloodied erection that Chris was sporting.

****

Chris regained consciousness with a strange, fuzzy feeling in his head. The drug that Dixie-Lee had given him had proved to be effective in numbing the pain in both his ass and his dick; the only thing Chris could feel in his damaged nether regions was the urgent need to visit the restroom.

As the darkness receded, Chris saw that Helen was back in her spot by the armchair. She was still wearing the miniscule leather outfit and she wore it well; in some odd, sadistic way her tear-streaked face and the blood smears on her breasts seemed somehow to enhance it. Rizzo, Bakker and Theuber were standing around to ogle Helen's exposed body whilst they chugged on cold beers, whilst Ruthie-Peg and a now dressed Dixie-Lee were sitting on the floor by the armchair and munching on pizza.

"I need the bathroom," Chris announced as he struggled from the bed, the drug-dulled twinge in his ass only just bordering upon bearable.

"Best go with him," Rizzo instructed Helen.

"No, it's okay, I'll manage," Chris said.

"You'd be best advised to do as Robbie says," Bakker told Helen with a tone to his voice that did not invite argument.

"I can't – we don't."

"You've *never* seen each other in the bathroom before?" Theuber sounded intrigued. "Now, ain't that romantic."

"That, right?" Bakker asked Helen

Helen nodded.

"Well, if this ain't just a weekend for firsts?" Bakker laughed out loud and his friends joined in. Then to Helen, "you'd better hurry, before your man craps himself on the bed." He prodded her bare thigh with the toe of his boot.

Helen arose slowly from beside the chair, now painfully self conscious of the tiny leather costume that clung precariously to her body; she actually felt more exposed wearing the bondage outfit than she had done being stark naked in front of Bakker and his motley gang.

She helped Chris from the bed and escorted him to the bathroom. There, she sat him down on the lavatory and turned to leave.

"No, ya don't." Dixie-Lee had followed closely behind and pushed Helen back into the cramped bathroom. She smiled her sweetest smile, unmistakably enjoying her captive's discomfort.

"I told you, we don't do that," Helen protested.

"And we're telling you that you do now." The smile slipped and menace glowered through. "My Mom always used to say that a man and wife ain't properly married 'till they've stunk each other's shit. Ain't that right, Vernon?"

"Right as ya can be, my lover," Theuber agreed.

"Take my Vernon there." Dixie-Lee flicked her eyes over to her husband like he was some odd side show curiosity. "I don't know how he does it, but he always manages to need to drop a goddamn deuce when I'm in the motherfuckin' bath!"

Theuber grinned gingerly and Rizzo, Bakker and Ruthie-Peg giggled at him.

Dixie-Lee followed Helen back into the bathroom and closed the door.

"Well, fancy that," Rizzo broke the silence, "married how many years and never shared the bathroom."

"They probably got one of those fancy big houses with two restrooms," Theuber speculated.

"Or maybe more," Rizzo added. "I heard that some of them big houses have more lavatorials than there are people."

"Why?" Theuber sounded genuinely puzzled; as if the moneyed folk's conundrum was far too much for his country bumpkin brain to fathom.

As Dixie-Lee closed the bathroom door, she shut out her friends' banal banter. "It's for the best," she told Helen, "considerin' his injuries an' all." She gave Helen an expression that could easily have passed for a compassionate smile.

"It's okay, baby," Chris did his best to reassure his wife. "Like they said, it's a weekend for firsts."

Helen was uncomfortable – more so than Chris – being in the restroom with him sitting on the lavatory. She had never shared what her mother referred to as *bathroom moments* with any of her partners; having been brought up to think it not conducive to maintaining the romantic mystique within a relationship. "I guess I have no choice, do I?" She glanced from Chris to Dixie-Lee who shook her head *no*.

"A little support here," Chris groaned as his bowels began to move. "Please, baby."

With great reluctance and a look of sheer disgust on her face, Helen crouched down beside her husband and held his hand.

Back in the motel room, Bakker and his cohorts heard Chris's agonized scream from the bathroom; a sound so shrill that it was nigh-on impossible to believe its originator to be male. Everyone in the room turned their attention towards the bathroom door.

"Oh my God!" cried Helen's distinctive voice and that was quickly followed by Dixie-Lee's maniacal cackle.

"Well, now ya seen him do that, ya can get over it," they heard Dixie-Lee saying. "Now, help your husband get cleaned up and don't forget to flush that fuckin' thing away."

"That's one hell of a woman ya got there, Vernon," Bakker said to his friend and cracked a wry smile.

THIRTEEN

A Brief Respite

They'd locked Helen and Chris in the adjoining room, the one Rizzo had so proudly declared had transformed the room they'd booked into a *suite*. Bakker and the two other guys had frogmarched them in to the room once they'd finished up with Chris's ablutions in the bathroom and had thrown a barely adequate first aid kit in after them.

The minute the connecting door was closed behind them, Chris had tried the door to the outside – of course it was locked. Then he'd tried to open the solitary window only to discover that it had been nailed shut and glazed with toughened safety glass. He'd actually been about to hit it with the old, bulky TV set when Helen had stopped him.

"They'll come running the first sound they hear," she'd told him. "And just how far do you think we'd get *if* you managed to smash the window?" And then she'd killed off any argument Chris may have countered with, "they have a gun, remember?"

So instead, they'd showered together and cleaned themselves up and for the first time since their vacation had begun to go astray by the motel pool, they'd had some time alone.

Helen had taken the time to smear Chris's striped butt with the cool, soothing hydrocortisone cream she'd dug out of the first aid kit that Bakker had so thoughtfully donated; she'd tested it first on her own ass-stripe and it seemed to be working just fine on Chris. Before attending to her husband's thrashed rump, Helen had bandaged up his freshly circumcised penis after applying a generous dollop of the antiseptic salve that was also to be found in the kit. For herself, Helen had popped a bunch of ibuprofen caplets to dull the ache in her mouth and the twinges from her torn nipple.

Upon Helen's close inspection, the stitches Dixie-Lee had sewn into Chris's backside appeared to have been expertly executed and had held fast through Chris's bathroom moment. Added to that the potent painkiller Dixie-Lee had given him, the wound there didn't appear to be giving him too much pain.

Bakker had informed the Sewells upon their incarceration that '*Funtime*' (his word, not theirs) would recommence upon the sound of the alarm clock Dixie-Lee had brought along in that seemingly bottomless bag of hers. He'd made a big deal out of setting the alarm time on the clock for the following morning and derived great pleasure from informing his captives that when the alarm sounded, their brief respite would be over. He'd placed the clock close to the door on his side and Helen and Chris had been able to hear its ominous and imposing *tick-tick-tick*; Bakker had made sure that there would be no escape from the clock's tinny ring when the time came.

At first, Helen and Chris had been able to hear the clock ticking through the door, but as Bakker's gang's antics had escalated, all they had been able to hear were raucous voices.

And by the sound of things, Bakker and his cohorts were in the process of getting royally drunk, high and horny as hell. Bottles clinked, voices were raised and quickly turned from high-spirited to belligerent; at one point Helen and Chris had listened with suppressed mirth as they heard Vernon Theuber begging his wife for a blow-job. Ruthie-Peg had then volunteered her services when Dixie-Lee had told her husband in no uncertain terms to fuck off and go blow the disgusting little thing himself.

"It would take one hell of a brave – or incredibly foolish – man to put anything in that glutton's mouth." Chris had said and he and Helen had shared a giggle.

They lay in the bed in each other's arms, naked and engulfed in the cool sheets. As they watched, the night beyond their grubby window turned a pitch, brooding black, punctuated by countless twinkling stars.

"I'm sorry for what I said," Chris broke the silence between them. "Before, I mean – about us not being able to conceive."

"Me too, baby," Helen murmured, her head snuggled against his chest. "I know that it's not your fault, I was just angry."

"I'm not entirely blameless," Chris sighed. "Which is why I lashed out at you back there. Sometimes I just feel so damned useless."

"You shouldn't." Helen lifted her head to look into her husband's face. "If there's anyone to blame, it has to be me. I'm the one with the ruined insides, remember?"

"You need to quit punishing yourself, babe." Chris stroked his wife's hair. "I'm glad that I know how you *truly* feel now."

The exchange Helen and Chris had been forced into at the hands of Bakker and Rizzo had been their first real, unreserved talk since discovering their inability to have children. And, although one would have thought the circumstances had been less than ideally conducive to such a conversation, it had at least been an honest one – brutally so.

"Yeah, likewise." Helen smiled. "It felt good to get it all out, it was cathartic."

Chris craned his neck downwards and they shared a tender kiss.

"You do realize that they are unlikely to let us go, don't you?" Chris broke the kiss.

"It had crossed my mind," Helen replied, "I'm trying not to think about that."

"I think that they're planning to kill us once they've had their fun."

"You're probably right, babe. But what can we do?"

"Nothing much we can do right now," Chris replied with a tremble in his voice. "I guess we just go along with their games and hope that they get careless before they get bored. If they do, we may have a chance," Chris said, his voice lowered.

A coarse, strident laugh – Dixie-Lee's – burst through from the adjoining room and made the Sewells jump.

"Quit your hoggin' the pipe, Robbie and pass me another one of those motherfucking rocks!" She cackled. Ribald laughter from Rizzo and the others ensued. Moments later, the unmistakable stench of crystal meth' crept beneath the connecting door like a malignant fart.

"If there's any way we can get a hold of that gun, or even my hunting knife, we may have more of chance," Chris whispered.

"There are two of us and five of them, Chris. And you're pretty messed up," Helen kept her voice low.

"I'm fine," Chris reassured, "all thanks to you and Nurse Dixie-fucking-Lee."

They shared a laugh and whilst it was brave, it sounded hollow and somehow inappropriate within the confines of their dusty little room.

"I can't see either of us getting the gun off of Bakker though, he holds onto it like it's glued to his hand," Helen said.

"True, but he's a guy. And you do have your own weapons of mass distraction, baby." Chris gave Helen a half-hearted smile and pointed at Helen's breasts that were pressed tight against his chest. "You play up to him and his defenses are bound to drop sooner or later. And then, pow!"

"*Pow*? What do you think this is? Batman?" Helen smirked. "And how do we know what they have planned for us? We may not get the chance."

"They're guys, and we guys think with our dicks." Chris smiled. "You should have that figured out by now, my love." He gave his wife a fond smile. "So whatever it is that they have in store for us, there's bound to be an opportunity to get a hold of that gun. Then let's see how quickly the balance of power shifts."

Helen murmured something against Chris's chest that he *felt* rather than heard and he realized that his wife was drifting off to sleep. Soon, he followed her and his own sleep was deep and fitful.

****

Chris awoke with a start, Helen roused next to him; they'd not strayed from each others' arms all night. The day's fresh light flooded in through the grimy window and filled their room with warmth.

It was beautiful.

Yet all the Sewells could focus on was the relentless ringing of the wretched alarm clock on the other side of the connecting door. They looked at each other with anxious faces.

Chris extricated himself from his wife's arms and struggled from the bed, wincing with each movement as his body complained. He padded over to the closet and saw that there was a note pinned to the door that had most definitely not been there the night before.

"It's from the rednecks." Chris ripped the note from the door. "They say we're to wear what they've left for us in here." He glanced at the closet with wary eyes.

"And they spelled *wear* incorrectly." Chris screwed up the note and tossed it across the room. "I'm sure those bastards are trying to wind me up." He gave Helen a brave smile although his nervous, trembling hands betrayed his true feelings.

Chris pulled open the closet doors.

There were two outfits hanging inside. For Helen, a black, shimmering, backless mini dress that looked incredibly expensive, French and at least two sizes too small. On the other hanger, there hung a pair of red latex underpants along with a collar and leash, presumably for Chris's adornment. Below the hanging items stood a pair of black patent shoes with vertiginous metal heels and the thinnest of shiny leather straps; they looked like bondage for feet, no doubt Robbie Rizzo's contribution to the proceedings.

Raucous laughter from next door arose above the tinny clanging of the alarm clock. It was a scary, illicit substance-fuelled hilarity – most likely at something incredibly inane.

"Well, I guess this makes things painfully clear." Helen forced a smile as she picked the dress from the closet.

"I'm scared, babe." Chris wrapped his arms around Helen's waist and held her tight, his voice small and weak.

"I know, baby," Helen said with a thin smile. "But at least we're in this together."

The look of terror in Chris's eyes told her that this was cold comfort.

It didn't take either of them long to dress, the alarm had barely had time to run down before they were finished. Once suitably attired, Helen took her husband's hand and squeezed it tight.

"It's show time," she said.

FOURTEEN

Showtime Indeed

Bakker, Theuber and Rizzo let loose a string of wolf-whistles and cat-calls as Helen strutted in from the adjoining room pulling Chris along behind her on the leash. She looked lusciously breathtaking as the tight dress accentuated each and every one of her curves, her endless legs, the silky-smooth skin of her back, and the subtle sway of her unfettered breasts.

At the sight of Chris in his state of undress, Ruthie-Peg and Dixie-Lee joined in with their own cacophonous shrieks of approval. Chris looked suitably subservient in the tight latex pants that clung like a second skin to his sore backside and his exposed, muscular body was tense as he strained against the leash that bit harshly into his neck.

Chris stubbed his toe on the alarm clock which had fallen over when Helen had opened the adjoining door –

they'd actually had the damned thing leaning up against the door – he cursed it beneath his breath and when he looked down he was surprised to see that it was almost four in the afternoon.

The mood amongst the Sewells' captors had certainly changed whilst they had been locked away; their sadistic playfulness replaced by something so sexually charged and intense that it was practically palpable. It was the combination of the discarded drug paraphernalia and beer bottles, along with the blatant, animalistic look in each of their eyes that was the chief cause for concern; it exuded an uneasy feeling of *no control.*

"Well, don't you two look as *perdy* as a picture?" Dixie-Lee enthused. She approached Helen. "This dress makes ya' tiddies look almost as good as mine." She slapped Helen's breasts with the flat of her hand.

Helen batted the woman's hand away, an action that appeared half-hearted at best.

Dixie-Lee took exception to this and pulled out her blade, snapping it open. "Don't you dare raise your hand to me, bitch," she snarled and jabbed the blade at Helen's arm, drawing blood. Another slash and the front of Helen's dress opened up, along with a thin, red stripe that ran the length of Helen's left breast. Helen yelped and jumped backwards.

Rizzo moved up behind Helen, slipped his arm around her neck. He snaked a sweaty hand down into the slash in the fabric to grasp at her breasts. "Y'all got to play nice now," he whispered in Helen's ear, his breath hot and reeking of alcohol and meth'.

Helen struggled against the man's grip but his fingers found her wounded nipple and latched onto it. She ground her teeth against the pain and wriggled to shrug him off. Then, she felt the hunting knife against her throat and quit her struggling.

"That is really no way to treat your host," Bakker chastened Helen. He grinned, his face glistening with a slick sheen of sweat. "If I were you, I'd pay heed to Robbie and play real nice."

Helen glowered at Bakker, who was fiddling with the buttons at the back of the alarm clock. He checked its face and plopped the thing down on the bed.

Dixie-Lee snatched the leash from Helen's hand and led Chris over to the armchair that Ruthie-Peg had filled with her corpulent bulk. The fat girl was – somewhat predictably – eating cold, leftover pizza.

As he neared the armchair, Chris saw that Ruthie-Peg was as naked as the day God made her. Without the voluminous clothing to conceal her gargantuan body, her obese frame showed off the rolls of fat that layered over other rolls of fat and the places around her stomach and flanks where her flab was calloused over and resembled thick, reptilian scales. Ruthie-Peg's huge breasts hung downwards, thick, elongated and pendulous. They flopped like long-dead sea creatures either side of her immense belly and were adorned with huge, irregular shaped nipples that looked like dark pink Rorschach tests. Sitting there with her pale, podgy body, wide face and squinting eyes, Chris thought that poor old Ruthie-Peg looked very much like *Jabba the Hutt's* fat sister.

As enormous and unsightly as the corpulent woman was, the smell that emanated from Ruthie-Peg actually surpassed her grotesque appearance. She gave off the unmistakable stink of stale sweat mixed in with the acrid tang of body odor of long-unwashed skin. It was a stench tinged with none so subtle hints of food grease, bodily waste and some long-defunct perfume.

As Dixie-Lee led Chris closer to Ruthie-Peg he pulled a disgusted face as his stomach turned somersaults.

Meanwhile, Vernon Theuber was running an exploratory hand up along Helen's thigh. He squealed with delight upon discovering the absence of panties and Helen slapped that hand away too.

Bakker pushed his face into Helen's. She met his eyes with hers, defiantly refusing to break the contact. He, too was rank with sour sweat, his hot breath snorting in and out of his flared nostrils as he seethed, "I said. Play nice." Bakker pressed his lips on to Helen's and forced his tongue into her mouth.

It took much of Helen's resolve not to bite down on the invading appendage; it was hard, bullying and had a disgusting chemical taste to it. Still, the ever-present gun that Bakker clutched in his greasy hand to jab into her guts guaranteed her compliance. So, Helen responded to the unwelcome kiss, moving her lips around his and stroking his rough, urgent tongue with hers as if he were a lover. As they kissed, Bakker's hand crept up Helen's body and enclosed her breast – mercifully the unviolated one – digging his fingers into the supple flesh to knead it as a master baker manipulates his dough. Theuber's hand returned to Helen's exposed thigh and Rizzo stepped in to lick the salty sweat from her bare back and smiled with great delight at the shudder that wracked her body.

"Say there, lover boy," Dixie-Lee sidled up to Chris and stroked his tender, throbbing penis through the cool, taut latex. She sighed as she heard him groan in pain. They were standing next to Ruthie-Peg, and she looked up at Chris with an expectant look in her squinting little eyes. "Ya like what ya see?" Dixie-Lee rubbed her hard tits against his arm and squeezed her thigh against his.

Chris had little option but to nod. Although he far from liked the sight – and smell – of what he was being presented with, he knew that it would have been foolish to antagonize either woman at that juncture.

Dixie-Lee perched herself upon Ruthie-Peg's thigh – plenty of room there. One hand clutching Chris's leash, with her other she grabbed a handful of the obese woman's breast and her fingers disappeared into its abundant, wobbling flesh.

"What say Ruthie-Peg 'n me give y'all a *lesbitanian* show, Mr. Sewell?" Dixie-Lee purred. "Would ya like that?"

Chris stared at the woman, horrified.

"If I could have everyone's attention!" Bakker's baritone voice bounced around the room and made everyone start. He stepped away from Helen and his hand lingered on her breast, reluctant to leave the supple flesh. "Before we all get carried away here, I have a little announcement to make." He waved the gun around over his head to emphasise his authority.

He picked the alarm clock off of the bed and lifted it up high. He addressed Helen directly, "I know we've been having ourselves a whole lot of fun an' all." He grinned. "But when this here alarm clock goes off in precisely one hour, I am real sorry, but it'll be time for me to kill the two of you," he said and with it he managed to sound almost friendly.

Helen glanced over at Chris and saw terror lurking in his eyes.

Bakker's declaration came as little surprise to Chris - there had always been that certain inevitability about this entire scenario from the moment Bakker and Rizzo had overpowered them at the pool; and he knew that these things rarely ended with a pleasant smile and a handshake. But there was still something about hearing it put quite as bluntly as that which had come as a shock.

Chris stole a glance at Bakker's gun.

"I do hope I've not spoiled the moment too much." Bakker looked as if he were really enjoying himself now. "I suggest that y'all enjoy yourselves as much as ya can, while ya can." He placed the clock gently on the bedside table, as if it were the most delicate timepiece in the world.

Rizzo sidled up to Helen's side. "Like the man said, let's have us some fun," he leered, his lips slippery and moist on Helen's ear. "I think you'll be amazed at just how pliable folk can be when death comes a'callin'." He pulled Helen backwards by her neck and guided her towards the armchair, Ruthie-Peg, Dixie-Lee and Chris.

Chris visibly shuddered with repulsion as Dixie-Lee continued to paw at the rippling mound of quivering flesh that was Ruthie-Peg. The big girl moaned and writhed and her flab shifted and wobbled as if it had a life all of its own. Dixie-Lee pulled on Chris's leash to invite him to join her. Of course, Chris had little alternative but to allow himself to be drawn slowly towards Ruthie-Peg's disgusting body as the collar bit into his throat. As he got closer to the fat woman, one of her saucer-sized rose-pink nipples entirely filled his view.

Bakker grabbed Helen's hair and forced her to her knees. Rizzo and Theuber pulled out their dicks and presented them, semi-erect to Helen's face.

"Please, no," Helen groaned, but her protest was quickly muffled by the two men pushing their dicks into her mouth.

Bakker reached down and pulled Helen's dress apart to fully expose her breasts. He ripped away the band aid that covered the ripped flesh of her nipple and the torn flesh oozed crimson blood once more.

Helen spat out the uninvited dicks.

Bakker slapped her face.

Hard.

"Ow-w!" Helen cried out, the shock of the assault made her see bright stars that danced across her vision.

"You need to do as you're told, bitch," Bakker snarled. He slapped her again and the reverberating sound of flesh hitting flesh filled the room. Bakker's erection twitched and bounced – aroused still further by the violence.

Chris pulled away from his own torment at the monstrous breast of Ruthie-Peg. "Hey!" he growled at Bakker. "Quit that!"

"What? This?" Bakker smirked at Chris and hit Helen's cheek again. This time she lost her balance and fell to the floor. Her breasts spilled out of the rip in her inadequate dress and the hemline rode up to expose her bare pussy and pouting labia.

Dixie-Lee gave Chris's leash a hard yank to pull him back and in to line and back onto the fat woman's tit.

Then Rizzo and Theuber fell upon Helen like a starving pack of wild animals; all mouths and hands and dicks. She struggled against their onslaught; lashing out, kicking, bucking her body as she tried her damndest to prevent them from pinning her arms and legs.

Roughly and without apology, Bakker pushed his two friends aside. He dragged Helen by her arms over to the armchair and towards her husband. Helen yelped as she banged against a leg of the bed and the rough floor chafed her bare behind.

"You wanna play the hero?" Bakker yelled in Chris's face. "Then let's play fucking heroes!"

Dixie-Lee pushed Chris down onto the floor next to his wife.

Bakker snapped his fingers and Dixie-Lee pulled out a pair of secateurs from her seemingly bottomless ostrich bag. She handed them to the Bakker with a conspiratorial smile.

"No!" Helen screamed, her eyes fixed on the vicious looking implement; was that dried blood staining its jaws? "I'll do whatever you want!"

"Well, that goes without saying," Bakker said to Helen with a sharp, coughing laugh as Rizzo and Theuber held her down.

Chris attempted to struggle away but was held immobile by a combination of Dixie-Lee kneeling on his chest and Ruthie-Peg's gargantuan foot resting on his rubber-clad crotch.

"We're gonna play us a little game." Bakker crouched down beside Chris. "I call it *fingers or toes* – it's how we find out who our foot fetish folks are." He flashed a cheesy game show host smile. "Now, *you* get to choose." He snip-snipped the secateurs in front of Chris's face. "Which of your wife's digits do ya prefer?"

"You sick fuck!" Chris spat. "I won't play your fucking game!"

Bakker tut-tutted. "Now, that *is* a shame. I was kinda hoping you'd enter into the spirit of the occasion." That smile again, it dripped malevolence. "Because, if ya don't, we'll all choose one each." Pause for effect. "An' there's five of us."

"What's it to be, City Boy?" Rizzo asked and his mouth sounded dry with anticipation but still he smacked around the stale glob of discolored gum.

"I won't –"

Bakker smacked Helen's face again. It was more than an open-handed slap this time – he used the back of his hand and his knuckles left an angry red mark on the soft skin of her cheek.

"Bastard!" she barked.

In response to her protest, Theuber grabbed Helen's wounded nipple and gave it a sharp twist.

Helen howled.

Another twist, harder this time and blood squirted out between Theuber's finger and thumb.

Helen screamed out again and pushed against the men who held her down. *"Cunts!"* she screeched as blood ran down her breast and soaked into what remained of the dress, making it glisten wetly.

"One simple decision and your wife's pain stops," Bakker reiterated, "now which is it to be? *Fingers or toes?"*

Chris fought back tears and tried to move. He was expertly pinned, his view of Helen's face all but obscured by Dixie-Lee's implausibly solid boobs. Dixie-Lee crawled off of Chris, leaving Ruthie-Peg to provide all of the weight necessary to prevent him from moving. She knelt down between Helen's legs. "Hold her steady, boys," she instructed, tugging at the safety pin that held her tiny denim shorts together. It took a little pulling but finally she pulled the thing free of the stiff material. "I'm gonna help focus these good folks' minds some."

As much as Helen wriggled and squealed, Theuber and Rizzo held her tight as Dixie-Lee's fingers worked between her legs, pushing her thighs further apart to spread her wide open.

"Quit fussin', and think of this as compensation for us losing your nipple ring." Dixie-Lee bent down close to Helen's vagina with the safety pin opened and poised.

"Go on, bitch, do it!" Helen screamed her defiance.

The sharp stab of the pin as it pierced through her clitoris was perhaps the most intensely agonizing thing Helen had ever experienced in her life. It drove shards of searing white pain deep into her body and threatened to detach her from consciousness itself. Helen screamed long and loud.

"Stop it! Please!" Chris cried out, distressed to see his wife in so much pain. *"Please!"*

"Only *you* can make it stop. You know the rules," Bakker said in an eerily pleasant tone.

Chris shook his head. "I can't, I won't –"

"For Christ's sakes, Chris!" Helen screamed at her husband as Dixie-Lee positioned herself once more over her pussy with the safety pin.

"I'm so sorry babe –"

"I don't need *sorry*, Chris!" Helen sobbed. "I need you to just make a fucking decision." She screamed again as Dixie-Lee jabbed the pin a second time and a spray of blood arced up over her body.

"Fingers!" Chris screamed, his throat thick with tears and snot. "I choose her fingers!"

Dixie-Lee sat up and examined the bloodied mess between Helen's legs, and was clearly proud of her handiwork. The safety pin remained skewered through Helen's clitoris hood and Dixie-Lee's bloodied fingers dripped a thin rivulet of scarlet onto her own thigh.

"Now, that was an easy decision, wasn't it?" Bakker praised. "Perhaps if you'd made it a little sooner, your poor lady wife wouldn't have had to have gone through all of that, would she now?" He stroked Helen's toes that were exposed at the ends of the shoes they'd made her wear. "Between you and me, I had you figured as a foot man all along."

Dixie-Lee shifted herself back to Chris to regain her spot perched upon his bare chest. This gave Chris a clear view of his wife and he saw that onne side of her face was red and swollen with the imprint of Bakker's rough hand and her breasts and between her thighs were snaked with blood.

"And now for round two; your starter for ten points." Bakker was in his element now. He pressed the secateurs into Chris's hand. "Who do you think your wife would rather have do this?" he asked. "Us or you?"

"Jesus Christ," Chris grunted.

"Our Lord and Savior is not an option, I'm afraid." Bakker smirked at his own lame joke and the others giggled along. "Some folk prefer that we do it – abdication of responsibility an' all that," he said. "Others want to be the one to do it, so no one else is giving pain to their loved one." He stroked Helen's hair, a tender gesture, and looked somewhat amused as she flinched at his touch. "What say you, Mrs. Sewell?"

Helen remained silent, but something in her eyes told him that she so very badly wanted this to be Chris.

Desperate, Chris lashed out at Bakker with the secateurs, aiming for the man's eyes, fully intent on blinding him.

Bakker reacted in an instant. He grabbed Chris's wrist so tight that the bones and tendons ground together and made him yelp. Bakker grappled with Chris with the sharp implement dangerously close to his face and he barely managed to avoid the curved blades plunging into his eye.

Overpowering Chris with relative ease, Bakker pinned Chris's arm to the floor. He kept a firm grip on the wrist as Chris writhed with the pain that was causing him – the best he could do with Ruthie-Peg's obese foot pressing down on his balls. "Ya really don't want to be doing that," Bakker growled and for the first time he appeared to be genuinely riled. Then with a vicious sneer that curled the corner of his lip, Bakker cast a glance at Rizzo. "Let's do this."

Rizzo lifted up Helen's arm.

Instinctively Helen struggled against him and attempted to pull her limb back towards the relative sanctuary of her body, but she was no match for Rizzo's wiry brawn. Rizzo manoeuvered her hand to where Bakker held Chris's hard against the linoleum, bending open her pinkie finger to place into the secateurs' tarnished jaws.

"No," Chris said.

"Look," Bakker's temper bubbled to the surface, "do you really want to spend what's left of your last hour on God's green earth procrastinating?!" He waved the Glock at Helen's head to further emphasize his point.

Helen glanced over at the alarm clock. She rolled her head to meet her husband's eyes. "Just do it, Chris," she said, quietly.

Chris scrunched his eyes tight shut and squeezed down on the rubber coated handle and felt the blades slice through the skin at the base of Helen's finger. Chris sobbed as Helen let out a low, throaty groan and bright crimson blood flooded from the wound he'd inflicted.

"I can't fucking do this!" Chris shouted at Bakker, feeling resistance as the metal jaws bit down to the bone in his wife's finger. He eased off the pressure, his hands shaking.

"Bastard!" Helen snarled. "Quit being a fucking pussy and just do it!" she sounded angry now, her voice laced with venom. And she stared at Chris like she'd kill him there and then if she got the chance.

Chris bore down on the secateurs with all the strength in his hand, then added his other hand and squeezed with all of his might.

Helen screamed and cussed, her body bucking so wildly that she almost broke free of the strong hands that held her down.

"There ya go!" Bakker shouted his encouragement. "Nearly there!"

Chris pumped at the secateurs again and then once more as the blades literally chewed their way through his wife's finger. There was one final, sickening *crack* as the secateurs clamped shut and Helen's severed finger tumbled onto Chris's bare leg. He looked down at the thing like it was burning a hole in his flesh and Helen screamed and yelled at him that he was a *motherfucker*.

Chris began to sob.

Bakker dealt Chris a hearty slap on the shoulder. "Well done – I honestly didn't think ya'd have the balls go through with it!"

Helen slumped back against the armchair and Ruthie-Peg's fat-rolled ankles. She watched, stunned and in shock as Dixie-Lee wrapped a rubber band around the finger stump to stem the blood. Even without the band, the fresh wound wasn't bleeding anywhere near as much as Helen had expected; there was just a thick dribble of blood seeping out around the white nub of splintered bone that nestled in the center of the wound. She guessed that the secateurs had clamped the blood vessels shut as they'd munched through her pinkie.

"You *fuckers*!" Chris exploded, fighting hard against Dixie-Lee's weight on his rib cage and managed to catch her by surprise. She toppled off of him and fell down hard, the wind knocked from her lungs with a wheezing grunt. Chris tried his best to scrabble to his feet but Ruthie-Peg's humongous foot pressed down hard on his balls and stopped him dead in his tracks.

Dixie-Lee picked herself up, she'd landed hard and unladylike on her ass and she seemed to take umbrage at the way the others were smirking at her. She pulled back her arm, made a fist and thumped Chris square on his nose. Chris's head fell backwards and knocked with a wet *crunch* against the hard floor. He gazed up at Dixie-Lee with a dazed look in his eyes and blood leaking from both nostrils.

Then Dixie-Lee pulled her switchblade. She pushed Ruthie-Peg's foot up onto Chris's belly and out of her way so she could slash at his rubber pants. The knife sliced effortlessly through the tight latex, parting it like taut skin to leave a bloodied cut over the curve of Chris's hip bone.

Dixie-Lee ripped the pants away. Grinning like a maniac she grabbed hold of Chris's penis and squeezed it extra hard, delighting in the anguished howl this drew from her victim and surprised that she actually felt the thing stiffen in her hand. She pulled off her halter-top and then wriggled out of her own shorts with expert ease and straddled Chris's thighs; there really was to be no doubt as to what was coming next.

Encouraged by his wife's burst of action, Theuber pulled at the jagged slash in Helen's dress and ripped the front of the flimsy garment wide open. Helen slapped at his hands and clawed at his face until Rizzo seized her injured hand and gave the stump a cruel *scrunch* between his powerful fingers. Helen cried out with the pain and the three men descended upon her.

Rizzo clamped his mouth around Helen's nipple – mercifully her right one – and sucked it deep into his mouth. Rizzo tore away the remaining fabric that shielded part of Helen's crotch and pawed at her vagina like a jock on prom night. He smiled a sadistic smile as Helen squirmed and arched her pelvis at his touch, not giving much of a damn that her fresh piercing was adding to the torment he was dishing out.Bakker pushed his lips onto Helen's and his tongue penetrated her mouth. It tasted foul and was insistent, probing and demanded reciprocation. He tapped the chill metal of the gun to Helen's temple to ensure the latter.

Dixie-Lee pulled the bandage away from Chris's freshly circumcised dick and delighted in the yelp that her action solicited. She stroked his twitching prick with one hand and reached out to Ruthie-Peg with her other to beckon her friend to come join in.

Keen to be not excluded from the fun, Ruthie-Peg puffed and panted and squeaked out a thin, reedy fart as she shifted her bulk to the edge of the chair. Utilizing Dixie-Lee's hand as leverage, she positioned her formidable undercarriage over Chris's head with the broad expanse of her back to her friend.

Revolted by the sight but too afraid to look away, Chris stared up at the thick rolls of fat and sparse tufts of wiry pubic hair that bore down on him like some ghastly, monstrous and incredibly ravenous animal.

Chris could smell her. Over-ripe and under washed, Ruthie-Peg had that cloying, gamey smell of deer meat left on the hook for way too long. In day's long past, Chris had often mused as to just how people as obese as Ruthie-Peg managed to wipe their own asses. And as Ruthie-Peg lowered herself onto his face, Chris saw for himself that it appeared that they didn't all that much.

"Make sure ya lick me good and strong, Mr. Sewell," Ruthie-Peg instructed, her would-be seductress tone somewhat marred by her queer, high-pitched voice. "Mamma needs to come."

The gargantuan thighs that enveloped his head quickly muffled Chris's hearing, but he heard Ruthie-Peg's demands well enough, along with the animalistic grunts of the three men working their pleasures on Helen. Fighting against the nausea that swam alongside the pain

Dixie-Lee was creating in his dick, Chris ventured his tongue towards where he guessed the fat woman's pussy might be. In response, the corpulent Ruthie-Peg ground herself into Chris's face and let out a gassy fart that made him gag.

Dixie-Lee positioned her vagina directly over Chris's penis. He was still not fully tumescent but she was impatient to have him inside her so she guided him in to her slick hole with her hand that was sticky with Chris's fresh blood.

Chris screamed as he felt himself slip inside Dixie-Lee. And muffled as his scream was through the many folds and flaps of Ruthie-Peg, it was still loud. The sharp agony of Dixie-Lee's vagina as it gripped along the raw edge of his dick was like raging sheets of flame shooting through his groin. Chris thrashed and wriggled and each movement served only to enhance the agony and in his throes, Chris flung out his arm and found Helen's hand.

He held it.

Bakker's thick, brutish tongue felt alien and rough and didn't belong in Helen's mouth; he was clamped down tight on her lips and his nose crushed hers and was making it increasingly difficult for her to breathe. He had a hand buried in the short hair at the back of her head, and was pulling so hard on it that Helen could barely move.

Rizzo renewed his efforts on Helen's vagina, amusing himself by sliding his fingers in and out, pausing only to increase their number one at a time. He was already up to four and Helen's sex was beginning to stretch and look sore.

Theuber broke away from his suckling to slap at Helen's breasts with the palm of his clammy hands, beaming away to himself like a kid with a new play center. He slapped her left boob several times as hard as he could and grunted with the exertion, pleased when he heard her moan inside Bakker's mouth.

One slap too many and Helen snarled at the pain and hit out at Theuber with her injured hand, her other not leaving Chris's. She connected hard with Theuber's bicep and shrieked at the fresh pain that it generated in the raw stump of her finger.

"Ouch!" Theuber yelped and rubbed at his arm. In retaliation he hit Helen in the gut with a clenched fist and knocked the wind out of her – but still she lashed out at him.

Bakker unzipped his pants and wriggled them down to his knees. All the while he kept his mouth pressed tight against Helen's, probing the soft inside with his tormenting, sour-tasting tongue. Finally, Bakker broke the kiss and with no more than a grunt, he pushed Theuber off of Helen and swatted Rizzo's hand out of her vagina. He shuffled around and positioned himself between Helen's legs, studying her raw, exposed sex with wicked intent as he did so.

Instinctively, Helen closed her legs.

Bakker slapped Helen's face, his open hand stinging her skin and sending twinkling lights darting to and fro behind her eyes. Then, as if working to a choreographed routine, Rizzo and Theuber took hold of a leg each and spread Helen apart once more, countering her attempts to fight them off with their sheer brute force.

Helen clamored and cried out, still hanging on to her husband's hand. She struggled against the three men as best she could but knew that she would be unable to avoid the inevitable.

Bakker rammed his gun hard into Helen's navel. This caused her to gasp and stunned, she quit struggling. In that instant Bakker had plunged his penis inside her, rough and deep. Helen forced out a cry that came from somewhere between pain and pleasure.

As Helen endured her torment, Dixie-Lee rode Chris's dick like a rodeo champion. As she fucked him, her hands pushed down heavy on Chris's chest and blood from his wounded dick seeped out of her cunt to mat in her thicket of pubic hair. In tune with her friend's sexual rhythm, Ruthie-Peg's voluminous flesh enveloped Chris's head and much of his upper body as she writhed against his face. Her body quivered and shook as her moans of ecstasy reached an ever-increasing pitch; any higher and only dogs and bats would be able to hear her.

Helen squeezed her husband's hand as Bakker thrust in and out of her body.

There was no response.

Chris's hand rested limp and lifeless in hers.

As Bakker plunged hard and fast into Helen, his pubic bone scraping against the safety pin in her clitoris, Helen found the pain that emanated from her new piercing to be not entirely unpleasant and much to her chagrin, she could feel her own orgasm building. She bucked against Bakker's single-minded assault, her free hand slapping at his face – which served only to increase his fervour – and kicked to pull her legs free of the hands that gripped her ankles.

Helen gave Chris's hand another squeeze and there was still no response. He wasn't moving at all. "Stop! No!" Helen cried out and twisted her hips in an attempt to dislodge Bakker's invasion.

Bakker grinned, interpreting Helen's resistance as encouragement and upped his pace, driving harder and deeper into her. As he fucked, Bakker's face blushed vivid red and dripped fat beads of sweat onto Helen's breasts as he careened towards release.

"They're killing him!" Helen yelled as she tugged on Chris's lifeless hand.

"Shut it, Bitch!" Theuber said and reached over to deliver another stinging slap to her breasts.

Helen's body tensed at the sudden shock of the slap and the tight squeeze of her internal muscles tipped Bakker over his precipice. A deep, rumbling groan forced itself from his mouth and the tendons and veins stood proud in his neck as he came. A fresh sheen of exertion sweat popped out on Bakker's flushed chest and he closed his eyes, engrossed in the moment.

Helen let go of Chris's hand. She snatched the gun from Bakker's limp fingers and thrust her hips upwards, hard and high. This had the effect of throwing Bakker off of her, his penis slipping out with a gush of slippery fluids as he fell away. Startled, Rizzo and Theuber loosened their grip on Helen's legs and her flailing foot connected with Rizzo's face to send him reeling backwards. Shocked by this turn of events, Theuber let go of Helen's leg and shuffled backwards with a look of abject fear on his face.

As Bakker toppled sideways there was a bewildered look in his eyes; a fusion of post-orgasm and *what-the-fuck*. His dick pulsed with its own rhythm as he fell and sprayed thick strings of ejaculate across the filthy floor.

Helen scrabbled to her feet. Her legs were still a little wobbly and thin trickles of blood and come ran down them and stained her feet. She stood over Ruthie-Peg and Dixie-Lee who were oblivious of what was going on, so lost were they in their own pleasures.

"Get off my husband!" Helen yelled and pointed the Glock down at the two women.

Bakker picked himself up from the floor and made a move towards Helen, his eyes blazing with humiliation. Helen waved the gun at the man, and then at the other two men to ensure their full cooperation. Bakker raised his hands and returned to the floor.

"Get. Off. My. Husband," Helen snarled at the fat woman and poked at her giant, flabby tit with the gun. Finally, Ruthie-Peg opened her eyes. She squinted up at Helen, not breaking off undulating her grotesque undercarriage on Chris's face; it was as if she really couldn't help herself.

Dixie-Lee had quit screwing Chris and was staring wide-eyed up at Helen with Chris's dick still inside her.

"Are you people really that stupid?" Helen rolled her eyes.

Dixie-Lee lunged for the gun, grabbing Helen's hand with both of hers.

And that was when the gun went off.

It bucked in Helen's hand like a thing possessed and almost jumped out of her – and Dixie-Lee's – hand. Dixie-Lee let go and sat back down on Chris's cock.

The room fell silent.

Bakker, Theuber, Rizzo and Dixie-Lee joined Helen in gawping at Ruthie-Peg each one of them open-mouthed in disbelief.

Ruthie-Peg lowered her head and studied the small hole that had appeared between the third fat roll of her considerable breast. A trickle of blood and greasy, yellow adipose tissue dribbled out from the hole and formed a gruesome rivulet that snaked towards the huge cleft in her belly where her navel lay buried.

"Oh my," she said.

That was it – a simple *oh my*.

The alarm clock went off, splitting the silence with its disrespectful urgency. No one in the room seemed to notice the harsh sound, as all attention was transfixed on the gruesome scene.

The bullet had made its way downwards through Ruthie-Peg's heart and out through the small of her back. There, it had punched a fist-sized hole through the folds of her fat. There the skin, stretched drum-taut, had split wide open in a thick spider web of ripped skin that looked like a cracked window. The force of the shot had pushed out a loop of Ruthie-Peg's small intestine which glistened pink and wet as it draped out of her like a sodden crepe bunting, over Chris's stomach and onto the floor. Amidst the viscous, yellow fat that oozed out of the exit wound there also protruded a ragged chunk of colon, its contents thick, brown and oozing down over her colossal ass. It filled the entire room with the unmistakable stink of ruined innards.

As the alarm clock ran down its urgency and timbre declined in a wholly inappropriate Last Post for Ruthie-Peg.

Death is never instant, as it takes the brain roughly three minutes to die. The organ shuts down one section at a time, much in the same way in which they switch off a stadium's lights once everyone has gone home; and even when a body loses outward consciousness, that doesn't mean that you are not thinking about stuff. It was impossible for Helen with her biologist's curiosity not to wonder what was going through Ruthie-Peg's mind as her body closed down.

The big woman's eyes stilled and her jaw flopped open. Gracelessly she slumped to one side and her immense body slid off Chris in one monstrous, fluid movement. And with little by the way of dignity, Ruthie-Peg Bakker hit the floor face-down with a resounding, wet *smack*.

FIFTEEN

What to Do With Ruthie-Peg

The clock finally lost all of its momentum. Its trill noise became a dull, slow motion clanging until finally, it came to a halting, grating stop.

In a final show of humiliation, Ruthie-Peg passed out a sizeable volume of gas from her ruined guts as her body settled. Everyone stared quiet and dumbfounded at her colossal corpse.

Dixie-Lee began to scream, loud and shrill. From her position as she'd fucked Chris, she'd caught the majority of the blood and gloop that had exited Ruthie-Peg and she was spattered belly to scalp with her friend's fluids. She wailed her hysteria and disgust as slivers of Ruthie-Peg's guts and congealing gobbets of fat dripped from her naked body in slippery wet clumps. They plopped onto her bare thighs like fat, repulsive slugs and slid their way slowly down to the floor. And between her thighs, Chris came 'round, gasping desperately for a lungful of air. He looked up at Dixie-Lee with a puzzled expression on his grotesquely-stained face, not at all sure as to what had just transpired; all he knew was that the repulsive, smothering weight of flesh was no longer pressing the life out of him.

"You fucking killed her!" Dixie-Lee screeched at Helen. "You *shot* Ruthie-Peg!"

"If you hadn't grabbed the gun–" Helen looked down at the thing in her hand as if seeing it for the first time; there was still a thin wisp of smoke wafting from the cold eye of its muzzle and its cordite stink filled her nostrils.

"Calm the fuck down!" Theuber grabbed Dixie-Lee by the shoulders. He shook her hard with little regard for the fact that Chris's violated dick was still inside her.

"She's fucking dead! *What the fuck!*" Still Dixie-Lee refused to be placated.

It would appear that a firm slap to the face was the way things most were dealt with out here in the sticks, and Theuber was more than happy to oblige. He administered a hard swipe across his wife's cheek and she slid off Chris in stunned silence whilst Chris let out a loud gasp at the renewed pain in his dick. Dixie-Lee remained quiet and slumped against the armchair and stared wildly at the oozing, bleeding corpse by her feet.

Chris struggled upright, gasping for breath and wiping the filthy taste from his mouth. There was a throbbing, burning pain that enveloped his entire lower body but he was determined not to show any sign of weakness in front of Bakker and the others, especially since the tables appeared to have turned.

"The gun was loaded?" Vernon Theuber aimed the rhetorical question at Bakker.

"Of course it was fucking loaded!" Bakker defended. "What did you expect?"

"You fucking prick," Theuber spat, as if the epithet were entirely necessary. "You *absolute*, fucking prick!"

"Oh my God," Helen mumbled. "It was an accident. You all saw what happened." She placed the gun ever so carefully on the bed, handling it gingerly - as if it were a venomous, living thing making ready to bite.

"Accident or not, you shot Ruthie-Peg," Rizzo's voice had calmed somewhat, his tone one of controlled panic.

"How was I supposed to know the gun was fucking loaded?" Helen growled at him.

"It's a gun, Mrs. Sewell," Theuber snarled as he helped a distressed, gore-soaked Dixie-Lee to her feet. The woman had begun trembling uncontrollably as shock began to settle in. "You should always assume that a gun is loaded, and handle it accordingly," he condescended.

"So, what the fuck do we do now?" Helen asked. She put a steadying arm around Chris, who was still unsteady on his feet.

"We?" Bakker stared intensely at Helen, and then glanced down at the obese corpse on the floor. "There's no *we*, Mrs. Sewell." He guided Dixie-Lee towards the door, her husband and Rizzo followed on. "We're just the hired help. *We* are all done here."

"You can't just leave us with – this!" Helen kicked out a bare foot at Ruthie-Peg, slapping the acres of pink jello-flesh into ripples of motion.

Chris looked on, nonplussed at the exchange. "What the hell is going on Helen?" he croaked. "What does he mean by *hired help*?"

"I *mean* that this was all one big game, Mr. Sewell," Bakker told him with firmness in his voice. "A game that's just gone too far. And now it's over."

Chris stared at his wife, eyes wide as if questioning what he was *sure* he was hearing. "You arranged all this?" his voice was barely audible.

"Surprise!" Helen replied with a weak smile and a tiny trickle of blood ran from the corner of her mouth.

Chris looked over at Bakker and the others who hovered by the door anxious to leave, at the immensity of Ruthie-Peg's corpse, and he shook his head. He looked in to Helen's worried face with tears welling in his eyes.

"You've got to be fucking kidding me?"

"Nope." Helen shook her head slowly; she looked worried.

"You put me – *us* – through all that for me, just for kicks?" Chris dragged a hand through his hair, disbelief etched on his face. "Even the finger?" He pointed at the raw stump on Helen's hand.

"Even the finger," she said.

"I don't fucking believe it."

"I'm sorry baby, I thought –"

"You are awesome," Chris said, his voice choked with emotion. "You really are the very best of everything, Mrs. Sewell, thank you so much." He hugged his wife close and kissed her delicious lips and tasted the tears and the faint smear of blood that had streaked there.

"Happy Anniversary, darling." Helen whispered in his ear.

****

"I paid your people for the entire weekend," Helen's hackles rose as she addressed Bakker. Her tender moment with Chris had been rapidly superseded by the painfully obvious matter of the business that needed taking care of.

Bakker was the appointed leader of the group for the fantasy experience she'd booked and he was on his way out of the door, along with the remaining three. This pissed Helen off no end, the contract she'd signed with the Agency had distinctly stated that in the event of anything going astray with their experience, the Agency's representatives were contracted to sort things out; she'd paid out enough cash to be able to expect that any and all eventualities would be catered for.

"We weren't paid for getting killed," Bakker replied. "The Agency is responsible for *this*." Helen nodded down once again at the unfortunate Ruthie-Peg's lifeless body. "*You* have to help us deal with it."

"*We* didn't sign up for this, Mrs. Sewell," Bakker told her. "You're on your own. We're not paid enough to deal with this crap; I suggest you take it up with the Agency."

The statement was bullshit of course, Helen could see that the man was panicking because things had gone awry and he just wanted to be as far away from Helen, Chris and Flanagan as he could get. She knew that these people were paid handsomely for enacting fantasy role-play scenarios for the Agency's exclusive clientele, and were expected to deal with *all* eventualities.

This particular eventuality though, appeared to be way above their collective pay grades.

Theuber unlocked the door and escorted Dixie-Lee into the warmth that waited for them beyond room eighteen. Rizzo and Bakker followed him out in silence, with not even a glance back at the Sewells. The door slammed shut behind them and Helen and Chris were left alone with the corpulent and decidedly dead Ruthie-Peg.

A brief moment of peace passed between the two.

"I think I shall write a stiff letter of complaint to the Agency about those people," Helen said.

"I think you should," Chris agreed and they laughed

together – long and hard.

****

"So, how was it for you, my love?" Helen asked her husband as she finished up re-bandaging his penis. She had him sitting on the edge of the bed whilst she knelt on the floor between his legs to administer first aid to his poor, wounded dick. She hadn't changed out of the dress and its torn, blood soaked fabric clung wetly to her body and yet she still managed to look incredibly hot – even with the stump of her pinkie finger she'd had to bandage up herself that now looked like a small, bloodstained mushroom.

"I had fun, babe, thank you," Chris leaned over to kiss his wife's hair. "But then, you knew that I would."

"I had an inkling." Helen smiled up at Chris. "And I had to surpass last year's surprise."

"Well, you certainly achieved that, my love. I hope you enjoyed yourself too," a loaded question. Chris knew that this adventure had been *way* beyond Helen's comfort zone and whilst it was astounding the trouble she had gone to in order to spoil him and embrace his predilections, Chris was concerned that she may have gone a little too far out of character this time.

"It was our best yet," Helen assured her husband, "although I think I'll be replacing my new clit piercing with something gold to match the tooth I have my eye on; quite possibly something with a diamond or two in it." She lifted the hem of her tattered dress and twiddled the safety pin in her clit, which made her gasp a little. She smiled up at her husband and lust smouldered in her eyes.

Chris dug his hands in Helen's hair and lifted her face up to meet his. He leaned down to kiss his wife's full lips and his painful arousal made itself apparent in her hand.

Helen let go of Chris's penis and grasped his hands, pulling them gently from her head. "You're not thinking that *this* is part of the adventure?" She nodded toward the dead woman, shaking her head. "Playtime is over, Chris," she let him down as gently as she could. "We have things that we need to deal with."

"Okay, so what are we supposed to do?" Chris asked. Whilst Helen's anniversary surprise had been a most enjoyable journey for him on many levels, the unplanned and unfortunate demise of the fat woman had kind of dampened the proceedings a little for him. He looked over at Ruthie-Peg's body, which lay oozing its gross, unpleasant fluids across the motel room floor and was already beginning to stink the room out.

"We can't just leave her here, not in a motel room booked in our name. I doubt the Agency will be too pleased with us for actually killing one of their employees and even Hicksville cops wouldn't take too long to follow a clue that fucking obvious," Chris said. "I guess we have no choice but to dispose of the body, but God only knows how were going to do that."

"You're right," Helen agreed. "But right now, I'm more concerned about Bakker and the others."

"Really? Ouch!" Chris yelped a protest as Helen tied off the bandage around his dick.

"They're witnesses, Chris," Helen's voice had that serious tone that always seemed to raise the hairs on the back of Chris's neck – this time being no exception. "They saw me shoot Ruthie-Peg, accident or not. What if they went to the police?"

"And say what?" Chris suppressed a wry laugh. "That they were paid to kidnap and assault us in some crappy motel room?"

Helen took his hands; her wonderfully naive husband.

"People talk, Chris." She looked deep into his eyes. "No matter how well paid they may be for their silence, they always do. One word of this gets out – *any of it* – and we're finished." Helen gave Chris her most stern face.

"What are you saying, Helen?"

"What I'm saying is that we have to protect ourselves, our future." Helen reached for the gun that lay next to Chris on the bed. "We're going to have to finish this."

Chris was horrified by what he was hearing. Was Helen *actually* proposing what he thought she was proposing? Role playing and sexual adventures were one thing, but hunting down four people to dispose of them in cold blood was another matter entirely.

"Chris," Helen squeezed his hands tight; she could sense his reticence, the fear that seeped from his pores – she always could. "You're going to have to trust me on this one."

And Chris knew at that point that he really had no choice in the matter. "Okay, babe," his voice was quiet, shaky. "Meantime, we really can't ignore the elephant in the room for too much longer."

Helen grinned and stood up in front of her husband. "Christopher Sewell, that is incredibly bad taste!" she said as she play-slapped his arm and laughed, at the same time wrinkling her nose; Ruthie-Peg's body smelled bad, way beyond the capabilities of the room's ancient air conditioner. "We're going to have to bury her out in the desert," Helen said.

"An admirable plan, my love." Chris frowned. "But how the hell do you propose we get all of *that* into the car?" He nodded towards the gigantic corpse. He'd made a good, valid and practical point of course. Ruthie-Peg weighed in at around four hundred pounds, quite possibly much more. So, assuming of course, they could manage to manoeuver her, how in God's name do you fit said four-hundred-pound *(plus!)* woman into the trunk of a Camaro soft top?

"That's the easy part," Helen said and gave Chris that disarming smile of hers. "We dismember the body."

"Are you serious?" Chris – who up until an hour ago had thought he knew his wife incredibly well – was, to put it mildly, incredulous.

"Deadly." Helen winked at him. "If we remove her limbs it will make her easier to carry," she explained as matter of fact as if she were outlining dinner plans. "And we'll be able to fit her in the trunk – it'll be a little like playing body *Tetris* but I'm confident she'll fit."

Chris shook his head. "You make it sound so easy, babe," he said. "And I'm sure it might be if we had the proper tools. We don't even have a saw."

"Don't need one," Helen sounded almost cheerful, or perhaps she was just better at hiding her panic than her husband? "If we slice through the limbs at the joints, there'll be no bones to have to cut through, only tendons." Ever the biologist, Helen was unfazed by her ghoulish proposal. "And for that, we have these." She kicked at the secateurs that Chris had used not so long ago to remove her pinkie finger.

"Sounds like you have it all figured out." Chris was still somewhat subdued, things were moving much too quickly for him and although he was slipping into self-preservation mode, his wife was well ahead of him in that respect.

"One of us has to," Helen said with just the slightest hint of derision in her voice. "Now, I'm guessing that the hardest part is going to be digging through all of that blubber." She glanced down at Ruthie-Peg's corpse. "So I suggest we make a start," so saying, Helen picked the hunting knife up from the floor – the knife that Chris always brought along on their trips for *just-in-cases;* if ever there was ever a classic *just-in-case*, this was surely it.

Helen kicked off her heels and padded barefoot and with purpose and determination over to Ruthie-Peg.

****

Ruthie-Peg's nude body proved to be far harder to handle than either Chris or Helen had initially thought; her thick rolls of fat were difficult to grip and she was slick with sweat and blood and Christ only knew what. Added to that, of course, was the fact that the woman was the weight of at least three people.

Even allowing for the fact that she was dead, Ruthie-Peg looked terrible. Blood had pooled along her front under the pull of gravity to give the flesh there a mottled, bruised appearance and the exit wound from the flab on her back looked like a raw, gaping and toothless mouth. Ruthie-Peg's glassy eyes had frozen half-open and her face wore a kind of surprised countenance – as if she were actually shocked to find herself deceased.

Chris and Helen decided to strip naked to go about their business of disposing of the fat woman. The outfits that Bakker *et al* had forced them to wear were all but trashed anyway and there seemed to be little point in messing up fresh clothes that they would then have to destroy later.

Working together as a gruesomely efficient team, and sweating profusely with exertion, they managed to roll Ruthie-Peg into the bathroom and manoeuver her close to its concave center. As they heaved and shoved and tugged her corpulent body it flopped lifelessly onto the stained tiles and more of her bowel slopped out of the gaping hole in her back. Much to the Sewells' disgust, it perforated and squirted a foul, stinking liquid out across the floor.

"We'd best start with the legs," Helen said to Chris and he thought that she sounded matter of fact – disturbingly so – almost to the point of clinical; as if simply refusing to allow herself the luxury of panic. "That way we get the hard work out of the way first," she grunted as she knelt down next to Ruthie-Peg and hacked at the wobbling roll of fat that encircled the woman's hip with Chris's hunting knife. To Practical Helen, the fat woman was nothing more to her now than an oversized laboratory frog, all pinned out and awaiting dissection.

Chris grabbed a hold of Ruthie-Peg's foot and pulled the leg out at a forty-five degree angle to allow Helen access to the hip joint. Ruthie-Peg's thigh spread out on the cool floor like she was some beached sea creature and her sparsely-haired pussy pouted and oozed. The sight and stink of the corpulent cadaver brought Chris perilously close to throwing up. He twisted his head to one side and gulped down long, deep breaths of relatively fresh air in his attempt to bring his churning stomach into check and the nausea subsided some.

It took Helen less than twenty minutes to separate Ruthie-Peg's legs from her body. She sliced Chris's keen blade through the thick rolls of fatty tissue at the top of the thighs like a hot knife through butter, the bulging layers of slippery yellow tissue sliding apart as if they were nothing. She made an incision that encircled the top of Ruthie-Peg's thigh, keeping track with her free hand – the fat was thick and slippery and had the tendency to fill in each cut and would otherwise have made it difficult for her to see where she had made the incisions. Once she'd made it down to the muscle layer, Helen traced the tapered end of the quad muscle up to the hip joint and sliced away the tissues there to expose the ligaments that held the joint together; cutting up Ruthie-Peg in much the same way as she had uncountable lab rats.

"Hold this," she instructed Chris, and had him hold open the deep wound with the knife. She then went to work on the taut, pinky-white ligaments with the secateurs and their honed jaws snipped through the triumvirate of wiry ligaments far easier than they had done through Helen's finger. Once that was done, Helen had Chris help her pop the ball of Ruthie-Peg's femur out from its corresponding pelvic socket and all at once the woman's right leg lay on the bathroom floor – completely separate from her body.

Chris cut a strip from the plastic shower curtain and wrapped Ruthie-Peg's leg up in it. He then placed the limb carefully to one side whilst Helen got to work on the big woman's remaining leg. All the while, he kept his silence, his mind away with his own thoughts and still fighting to convince himself that any of this was a good idea. It all had that fuzzy *unreal* feeling, as if he were experiencing a bad and particularly vivid dream, as if he would soon awaken in the bed he and Helen shared in their familiar, cosy home and be all excited about their pending road trip to Flanagan.

Thanks to the Sewells' foresight to go about their gruesome business in the motel room's bathroom, Ruthie-Peg's blood and various other spilled fluids drained away nicely down the grate in the center of the room. Occasionally though, Chris had had to poke accumulating jellied clumps of clotting blood and globs of bile-colored fat down through the grating.

Before too long, both of Ruthie-Peg's legs lay together, each wrapped in their clear, makeshift shrouds on the bathroom floor. And once Helen had detached the obese woman's gargantuan arms both she and Chris sat back to study their handiwork.

Now all of Ruthie-Peg's limbs lay in a neat pile next to the grating – each one wrapped in a slice of the shower curtain that Chris had sacrificed to the cause – and together they looked like a particularly macabre pile of party gifts. Ruthie-Peg's dismembered corpse continued to ooze clotting blood and yellow gunk from the gaping wounds where her arms and legs had once been, as well as the foul-smelling gloop from the gaping hole in her back. Luckily for the Sewells, all of that trickled slowly down the grating with a phlegmy, gurgling noise.

Helen glanced over at Chris's bloodied, sweating body with something akin to fiery lust in her eyes – it was a look that he really couldn't remember seeing before, although it was hard to tell with her face smeared as it was with blood and gore. Helen leaned in and gave him a lingering, wanton kiss. As she did so, her knee slid in a puddle of blood and she lost her balance. Helen slipped along the tiled floor and onto Ruthie-Peg's mutilated torso, her lips far from her husband's.

And as Helen knocked into her, Ruthie-Peg's huge head lolled to its side and stared at her with cold, dead eyes that looked angry and accusing.

Using Ruthie-Peg's mountainous body to gain leverage, Helen struggled to her feet. "Would you mind dealing with the head, darling?" Helen asked as her amorous mood evaporated. "I really could do with some fresh air."

"Me?" Chris actually sounded put out – and somewhat appalled – by his wife's suggestion.

"You'll be just fine," Helen placated but there was impatience in her tone. "If you cut *between* the vertebrae in the neck, it'll be easy," she instructed. "You probably won't even need the secateurs."

Chris pulled that face again. He was an English teacher for heaven's sake and unlike his wife, Chris was not accustomed to the blood-and-guts horror that was inherent in her chosen subject.

"You can do it, sweetheart," Helen cajoled as her bare feet struggled to find their grip on the blood-slicked floor. "I'll look for a shovel while I'm out. I'd guess there has to be a maintenance room somewhere around this god-awful place." She stepped over to the tub. "But I do think I need to clean up a little first, though."

Chris nodded his reluctant agreement and broke off from his grim contemplation of Ruthie-Peg's fat neck to look over at his wife. Helen was smeared from head to toe with blood, gore and sweat like the nefarious antagonist of some cheap schlock-horror film; she was of course right and was unquestionably in need of a rinse before venturing outside.

Helen stepped into the tub and twisted the shower lever upwards to *hot*. The initial blast of cold water made her gasp but it soon turned warm and she rubbed hard at the bloody stains on her body.

Ignoring the thin sprays of water that strayed across from the now curtainless shower, Chris set about removing Ruthie-Peg's head. Firstly, he twisted it to one side so that her eyes weren't looking up at him as he contemplated where best to make the initial cut. As he did so, Ruthie-Peg's tongue lolled out from between her thin lips and a whisper of fetid breath puffed out of her mouth.

As with the dead woman's legs, the main problem was finding a suitable place amongst the blubber; all of

Ruthie-Peg's many chins were all kind of blended into one solid roll that joined her real chin to her chest like a bloated goitre. Finally, Chris decided upon a deep incision across the throat and dug the knife down into the soft meat of Ruthie-Peg's neck with a sawing motion. Congealing blood that had been trapped in her jugular veins bubbled out with the stale breath from her throat and coated Chris's hands with a slick, stinking mess.

Helen stepped from the shower, her body shining wet and clean. She skirted around Chris, Ruthie-Peg and the blood pool. "Remember to cut *between* the vertebrae," she reminded.

"I know, I know," Chris replied without being distracted from his work. There was the faintest hint of a smile on his lips, and there was something quite unmistakable in the way in which he glanced up at Helen from Ruthie-Peg's dismembered body that made Helen think that he was enjoying himself.

Helen left her husband to it and padded over to the bedroom. She tried to slip on her K-Swiss, wiggling her bare feet to force the things on but quickly gave up; wet feet into tennis shoes were always going to be a tricky equation. She pulled on her shorts and one of Chris's black T-shirts - which she tied in a tight knot at the back to make it fit tight over her slender stomach and bra-less chest and still the thing covered her like a small dress.

"I shouldn't be too long," she called over to Chris. She bent down to pluck Dixie-Lee's switchblade from the floor, pressed the sliver button on its cool flank and snapped the blade back into the mother-of-pearl handle.

Once outside room eighteen, Helen was surprised to see that the day's light was all but gone; neither she nor Chris had realized that it had gotten so late. The sky was clear and cloudless, dotted with the first of the early stars and a thin crescent moon. The worst of the suppressive heat had dissipated from the air to leave it stale and damp; nonetheless, it was a most welcome change from the cloying stench of blood and death she'd left behind her. Helen padded along the walkway, the cracked pavers warm and comfortable beneath her bare feet.

She made her way towards the reception office; if there was a caretaker's store anywhere to be found at Flanagan's Last Barrel Motel, she figured that it would be near there. She hoped that there'd be a shovel secreted within – better still, two – burying Ruthie-Peg's body was going to take a hell of a lot of digging.

As Helen rounded the corner with the black, shimmering water of the motel pool at her back, she saw the familiar, beat-up Camry parked up outside the office. The car's door was open and its engine rattled along with a juddering, hesitant thrumming sound, as if it were misfiring or was about to run out of gas.

There was movement in the office, the intermittent shock of a flashlight's beam coupled with the sounds of someone searching for something.

Rizzo had come back to the motel.

As Helen watched from her hiding place in the shadows, Rizzo's tall shape stepped from the tiny office with his arms filled with beige files. Rizzo gave a nervous, furtive look around the car park and down along the empty road before scurrying to his car like a skittish wild animal. He plopped his butt into the driver's seat, keeping one leg on the blacktop as if ready for a return journey to the office. He twisted around to add the files to the pile of paperwork that cascaded from the shotgun seat into the foot well.

Helen kicked the car door as hard as she could manage with the ball of her bare foot; three years' worth of Taebo putting extraordinary power into the motion.

The door slammed into Rizzo's leg and splintered his shin so thoroughly that shards of bone stuck out through both his skin and his pants leg. Rizzo howled in both pain and surprise and Helen wrenched open the car door to face the man.

Moaning in agony and no longer capable of playing the tough guy, Rizzo snivelled like a scared kid and scrabbled over to the passenger seat to get away from the crazy lady bearing down on him. As he did so, his smashed leg scraped limply against the door jamb and made him cry. "Oh, sweet Jesus, no," Rizzo sobbed through the tears and snot that bubbled from his nose.

"Please no –"

Helen climbed into the car after Rizzo and punched him square in the face, splitting his nose and knocking him all but senseless. Rizzo held up his hands in a protective gesture but Helen just knocked them aside. She punched him again and again, her attack brutal and frenzied until she felt the bones of Rizzo's face shifting beneath her fist and his teeth snapped loose and Helen felt a twinge of exhilaration that made her clit tingle and she wondered if this is how Chris had felt that night in Vegas.

Finally, Rizzo's protests grew weak and he became still. Pausing to catch her breath, Helen contemplated the man, watching with growing annoyance as his chest rose and fell in an irregular rhythm. She could hear the air rattling through his smashed nose as he exhaled and the bubbling of thick fluids deep down in his throat; she hadn't realized just how difficult it was to kill a human being – they were certainly far more resilient than was portrayed in the movies.

Swallowing a deep gulp of the tepid air that reeked of Rizzo's sour sweat and spilled urine, Helen thumped her fist repeatedly into the man's ugly mug, maintaining a steady rhythm which she hoped would beat the life out of him. Rizzo's body writhed and squirmed beneath Helen, his weakening body struggling against her weight to be free from the relentless assault on his collapsing face.

And still Rizzo insisted upon being a stubborn sonofabitch, so much so that Helen's impatience finally got the better of her. She pulled Dixie-Lee's switchblade out of her ass pocket, clicked it open and plunged the blade hilt-deep into the side of Rizzo's neck, slicing it forward. Rizzo's gasping, gurgling throat opened up like a second mouth and sprayed Helen and the car's interior with bright, arterial blood. Helen stabbed him in the chest – twice, three times just to make sure and at the fourth thrust of the knife Rizzo's body fell still and the blood quit spurting.

Helen scrambled away from Rizzo and out of the bloodstained vehicle. She kicked Rizzo's crushed leg into the car and slammed the door closed behind it. She then leaned her hands against the car's roof, doubled over and threw up nothing but a stream of acrid, stinging bile and cloggy mucus as she'd not eaten a scrap since the tacos two nights ago.

Dazzling white headlight beams illuminated Helen and cast her shadow, long and spindly against Rizzo's car. Startled, heart thumping, Helen whipped her head around and saw an SUV making its way across the motel lot. "Shit," Helen whispered to herself and she ducked down to hide behind Rizzo's car.

The SUV – a *Mountaineer* that appeared to be a flat, dirty cream color given an orange tinge in the dim overhead lights – drove nonchalantly by the car that contained the recently deceased Robbie Rizzo and parked up at the far end of the lot; its brake lights painted Helen a glowing red as she broke cover and ran back to Chris.

****

"We have to go!" Helen burst back into room eighteen, startling Chris. "Someone's here!"

Chris stopped dead in his tracks and stood there, bloodied and naked adjacent to the neat pile of legs and arms in the middle of the bathroom. He'd removed Ruthie-Peg's oversized head as Helen had instructed and had it wrapped in the square of clear plastic and balanced neatly on top of the limbs. "What the hell happened to you?" Chris asked as he stared at Helen's shirt which was soaked through and glimmering with fresh blood.

"That's not important right now; didn't you hear what I just said?" Helen barked as she pulled the bloodied shirt off over her head, dropping it to the bathroom floor with a wet *splat*.

"Yeah. Who's here?"

"How the hell should I know who it is, Chris?" Helen raised her voice and panic laced her breathlessness. "A car just pulled into the parking lot and we're here with this mess. We have to get the fuck out of here – now."

"But what about *this mess*?" Chris looked scared, his face growing paler by the second. "If we can't get her out, we should burn the place."

"There's no time, Chris." Helen fought to retain her composure. "And what if the fire department put out the fire before it destroyed all of this?" She pointed at the dismembered corpse by her husband's feet. "All that would do is draw attention to what we did here."

Chris looked down and contemplated his hands, which were red and matted with tiny shreds of flesh.

"Then we have to get Ruthie-Peg to the car," he said quietly.

"No, babe, we have to go *now*," she said firmly. "We tie up the loose ends and come back and finish the job later, maybe we can speak to the Agency." There was hope in her voice. "They'll be pissed about Ruthie-Peg for sure but they have to be obliged to help us out."

Chris's mouth flapped open as if he had something important to add, but no sound came out. With a little effort, he spoke quietly, "but –"

"Are you not listening to me?" What little there remained of Helen's patience was dwindling fast. "Someone is coming. There's no time for worrying about the fat woman, there's no time for *anything*." She perched her hands on her hips in a final and dominant gesture, her bare, blood smeared breasts thrust towards her husband. "So get dressed, Chris," she ordered.

Obediently, Chris rinsed his hands off in the sink and wiped away the worse of Ruthie-Peg's blood from his body with a fluffy towel. He made his way over to the bed and dug through his travel bag for fresh jeans and a shirt.

Helen pulled another T-shirt from Chris's bag – had he *only* packed black ones? – and tugged it down over her breasts. Quickly she checked her shorts, they'd been mostly covered by the other shirt when she'd despatched Rizzo and so had but a few blood smears, so Helen decided against using up precious time changing them. She peeped through the curtains and although she saw nothing, there was that gut-certainty that whoever it was in the SUV, they were coming ready or not.Quickly, Helen slipped on her K-Swiss and she and Chris crammed everything that didn't belong to the motel into their travel bags, checking and double-checking to make sure that nothing was being left behind. They picked up the alarm clock, the gun and Dixie-Lee's ostrich skin bag and Helen retrieved her cell phone from beneath the tub – absolutely nothing was left to chance.

"This is why we have to finish this," it was Helen who broke the silence between them.

"Eh?" Chris grunted. He was rummaging under the bed to retrieve a stray sock whilst trying desperately to avoid touching the sticky cockroach traps and their macabre contents.

"Because if we don't, this is how we get to spend the rest of our lives; scared to death of a knock on the door and forever looking over our shoulders." Helen said. "And that's not to mention – no more adventures like this, ever."

Chris looked at his wife and saw the little-girl-lost look in her eyes. Despite all the big talk and bravado, to him Helen looked truly scared. He stood up and embraced her, pulling her body close to his.

"You're right, my love," Chris whispered, his lips touching the warmth of her ear. "We have to find the others, but how the hell do we find out where they are?"

"It's Monday night, isn't it?" Helen replied and gave Chris a knowing smile and broke the embrace. "And Monday night is couple's night."

Helen and Chris gathered their bags and headed for the door. Chris did an abrupt half-turn and dashed into the bathroom, only to emerge carrying one of Ruthie-Peg Bakker's severed arms. "I thought maybe if we left less –" he offered.

"Really, Chris?" Helen snorted.

Chris shrugged, gave her a sheepish grin and dropped Ruthie-Peg's arm onto the floor. He followed his wife from the room and they both raced towards the Camaro.

Behind them and partially hidden by the motel's

eerie shadows walked a dark figure; Helen's bogeyman was on his way.

Chris and Helen climbed into their car without so much as a backwards glance. Chris gunned the engine and drove away from the Flanagan's Last Barrel Motel parking lot with the lights off. He didn't dare flick them on until they were some way along the highway.

****

Ronnie Gagliano made his way slowly along the motel walkway, heading directly towards room eighteen. He'd heard the Sewells' car driving away, but had seen no other signs of life since his arrival. He drew hard on his cigarette and the orange glow shone bright and lit up his weary face in the darkness that pooled between the overhead lights.

He pushed open the door to room eighteen with his foot. Although his nose had forewarned him of what he was to find in there, Gagliano grimaced and his stomach churned at the sight that greeted him. As he surveyed the carnage, he actually found it difficult to equate the butchery with the nice couple he'd briefly acquainted himself with at the flea market; there really was no accounting for some tastes.

"Goddammit," Gagliano growled as he eyed the blood- soaked floor, the severed arm on the rug and the makeshift abattoir that the bathroom had become. "This wasn't supposed to happen." He pulled his smart phone from an inside pocket and brought it to life with a thumbprint.

Gagliano punched a couple of virtual buttons on the touch screen and held the phone to his ear. As he did so, he walked into the bathroom, taking great care to step around the congealing puddles of blood and smears of crud on the tiled floor. He studied Ruthie-Peg's mutilated body that lay before him in a flaccid, gargantuan heap in the center of the room, at her fluids that drained as if in slow motion into the tarnished grate in the middle of the concave floor.

"It's me," Gagliano grumbled into the phone, "we gotta clean up. Something went wrong here." He then hung up the phone and headed out of the room and back into the stale air of the dark Texas night.

SIXTEEN

Aphrodite's Adult Theater

It took twenty minutes for Chris to drive them the eight miles from Flanagan to Stockton. The poorly-maintained roads were littered with potholes that had made for a particularly uncomfortable ride for Chris's wounded backside. Added to that, he'd insisted on sticking to the speed limit even though the highway had been practically empty; it would have been foolish to court the attention of the law enforcement community by breaking the speed limit smeared with the dried blood of a woman his wife had recently killed and with Helen looking like she'd taken a bath in the stuff.

Once they'd reached Stockton, a town of greater magnitude and civilization than Flanagan, Chris had allowed himself to relax a little. There had been no wailing of sirens, no blue flashing lights to feed his paranoia, just the sparse smattering of regular evening traffic into which they blended as well as was possible in a bright yellow Camaro that was moving at precisely the legal speed limit.

They had found what they were looking for by the side of the main road, sandwiched between an *Arby's* and a *Micro Center*. It was an unassuming, gray prefabricated cube of a building with a neon purple stripe that ran all the way around the top edge. There was a small, red neon sign that read –

APHRODITE'S ADULT THEATER

– which let the Sewells know that they were in the right place.

Chris pulled up in the parking lot at the farthest end away from the two other vehicles that were parked there. One was a hybrid of some description – it was hard to tell in the fading light, since to Chris all Japanese eco-cars looked pretty much the same – and the other was the ridiculously decorated hearse they'd seen at the flea market art car show; in the garish red light of the theater's sign he could make out the lumpy knobbles of the jumbled bric-a-brac that adorned the vehicle's bodywork.

"I should have figured," Chris said with a groan.

"I guess this is it," Helen said.

"Yeah, I guess it is," Chris replied with a weighty sigh. "Are you *sure* you want to do this, babe?"

"I don't *want* to, Chris," Helen said with a frown. She pulled on the leather gloves she kept in the glove compartment and retrieved the Glock from the bag down by her feet. She checked the gun's clip – it was full, notably minus one round of course – then handed Chris the hunting knife. It still had dried gobbets of Ruthie-Peg's blood clinging to it and stank to high heaven of raw flesh and shit.

Helen pocketed the switchblade and declared them both ready. "But we both agreed that we really have no choice," Helen's voice was quiet, controlled – calm even. "We can't rely on the Agency to make this all go away and we just can't risk any of this getting out." She squeezed her husband's knee and said, "besides which, this is my mess and I've never been one not to tidy up after myself."

Chris nodded and smiled at his beautiful wife; after so many years married, he knew best when not to argue with her.

****

"He should be here by now," Dixie-Lee Theuber said as she glanced up at the clock on the back wall of the empty theater. It had been an age since Rizzo had driven back to the motel to pick up his stuff and there was no reply from his cell.

Dixie-Lee sat back in the cheap velour theater chair and watched with scant interest the porn movie that played out on the screen. There was a skinny white girl with horrendously fake boobs that were somehow managing to sag being gang banged by three hung black guys – one of whom seemed to be having trouble maintaining his erection – whilst trying to pretend like she was enjoying herself; and of course, White Chick was fooling no one. This was your typical low-cost, nasty porn fare and Dixie-Lee couldn't help but scoff when they zoomed in for the close up shot of the girl's well-used vagina; would it have killed them to have added a squirt of lubricant under the pretext of realism?

"Perhaps he went on home," Bakker suggested.

"Rizzo knows damn well that we were all told to stay here," Vernon Theuber spat, "*and* what would happen if he went against instructions." He cast a cursory glance at the clock, saw that it was a quarter till nine and sighed. "We can only assume that something has happened to him – *now* what the hell are we supposed to do?"

"We calm the fuck down, is what we do," Donny Cano spoke up, his impatience shining through loud and clear; the Theubers had done nothing but complain since the minute they'd set foot in the theater and it was really getting on his nerves now. It was as well that he'd remained here in the background for this one, Collins to their Aldrin and Armstrong, his job to liaise between Bakker's team and the Agency facilitator – Christ himself only knew what state these three would have gotten themselves into had he not been; although in Cano's book the circumstances surrounding the Sewells' adventure going so tragically awry did seem to warrant a certain amount of panic. It was Cano's job to maintain calm the best he could and avoid any further mishaps; the Agency would be in touch with their instructions all in good time.

Dixie-Lee continued her protest, "But, what if –"

"What if nothing, Mrs. Theuber," Cano cut her dead. "You know full well that the Agency's directives are perfectly clear insomuch what we are to do in the eventuality of things not going entirely to plan."

"So, you expect us to just sit tight and wait for Rizzo to show up?" Theuber chipped in, his mouth curled into a most unpleasant half-snarl.

"That is exactly what I expect you to do," Cano told him, his voice firm and almost preternaturally calm.

"This just ain't right. We should go," Dixie-Lee added.

"Look, Cano," Theuber spat, "we have a *situation* going on here, unless you've not listened to anything we've told you." He squared up to Cano, not giving a damn as to who was supposed to be leading whom right now. "And I know that we have our directions and God help us if we don't stick to them – but for Christ's sakes, somebody just got killed!"

Dixie-Lee's lower lip quivered. "And that stupid woman damn near killed me too!" she threw in her two-cent's worth.

"It was a fucking *accident*," Theuber said, "we all saw that." He shot a glance at Dixie-Lee who shrivelled under his gaze. "So quit your belly-aching."

"This is the last time; I swear it's the last," Dixie-Lee grumbled. "I can still feel her blood and shit on my face." Upon arrival, Dixie-Lee had scrubbed herself down in the theater's bathroom to be rid of the fat woman's gore – had done so until her skin was raw and glowing pink. "This is what happens when you go cheap, Garry!" She snapped at her husband who stood with his mouth agape and with a look of total shock on his face.

"You–you're not supposed to –" he stammered.

"Seriously?" Dixie-Lee stared at her husband as if he'd just wandered in from the funny farm. "You don't think that we've gone a little beyond worrying about using our real names, *Garry*?" She took great delight in watching her husband flinch at her blatant use of his name. "Somebody actually *died* – unless you missed that part of the proceedings back there – and we don't know what the fuck's coming next!"

"You didn't seem to mind people getting killed too much last year, *darling*," Theuber refused to follow suit and use Dixie-Lee's given name. "As I recall, you couldn't wait to cut that guy's throat in the bluebonnet fields when your dumb little alarm clock went off."

"That was *different*," Dixie-Lee retorted with anger and frustration in her voice. "That was *our* adventure, and that couple were just random people we met at the lifestyle club."

"And who told you that?" Bakker joined in the marital melee, seemingly for the sport of it.

"The Agency," Dixie-Lee told him.

"Oh fuck…" Theuber – *Garry* – said quietly as the harsh realization of Bakker's intimation sucker-punched him. "But if they were previous clients, how come they said nothing when we – when we did what we did to them?"

"Who knows what people are capable of once the Agency gets their hooks into them?" Cano said, his tone low and menacing. "Perhaps their own adventure was worthy of blackmail in the extreme, or maybe their families were under the direst of threats?" He gave the Theubers what could easily have been misconstrued as a smile. "Or maybe they *were* nothing more than a random couple of people in the right place at the wrong time?"

"And maybe we wouldn't be part of this clusterfuck if you'd bought us the Platinum Package, Garry – then we wouldn't have been obliged to muck in with the fucking *staff* to pay it off!" Dixie-Lee cast a glance at Bakker. "No offence."

"None taken," Bakker said quietly and shrugged.

Cano listened to the Theuber's raised voices with a gnawing irritation. This was precisely what he'd said would happen when the Agency began to use past clients to staff their adventures; the slightest hint of things going off track and these people wig out. It had been a relatively recent move by the Agency's higher echelons in an attempt to broaden the client base; one that Cano had considered a tad tacky as in his mind it had brought the Agency's unique offering down to the levels of a Disney cruise. It was not that the *Standard* package was inexpensive by any stretch of the imagination, and its introduction had had the effect of attracting fresh blood for the creation of the Agency's adventures; but Cano really wished they'd just leave the whole thing to professionals such as himself, Bakker and Rizzo.

And speaking of which – Cano punched up Rizzo's number on speed dial and held his phone to his ear, the dial tone a welcome respite from Dixie-Lee's bitching at her husband.

"There's no reply," Cano informed the others, cutting Dixie-Lee dead in her whining tracks once more. "I'll head over to the Motel and see if he's still there." He made his way back towards the theater door, the contrasting skin tones of the porn actors projected on his face. "Make sure none of you leave," he aimed his parting shot at Bakker, his tone quite unmistakable.

"You got it, boss," Bakker said as the door swung shut and Cano vanished in to the night.

Bakker was beginning to have his own doubts. He'd worked for the Agency for the best part of six years, and had never once seen things go so terribly wrong – accident or no. Sure, sometimes the hired help got hurt – when you played rough that was an occupational hazard – but what had happened to Ruthie-Peg had been a wake-up call; any one of them could have taken that damned bullet.

Maybe it was time to quit while he was ahead? He'd been growing weary of the sick fucks that he was forced to deal with, and whilst the money was good, it was no longer sufficient compensation for the things he'd had to bear witness to. As adventurous as he considered himself, Bakker had experienced repulsive and perverse things that he quite simply didn't understand at all.

"I don't know why I let ya' talk me into doing this anyways, pandering to sick bastards like those two," Dixie-Lee continued to berate her husband.

"Nobody *forced* you into this, Dixie-Lee," Theuber raised his voice to her and for a split second he seemed tempted to raise a hand too. "You knew the terms when we signed up."

"Yeah, well maybe I didn't know what kinda' people I'd have to deal with," his wife complained.

"And what kind of people would that be then?" Helen Sewells' voice made all three of the people in the dingy theater jump. Dixie-lee, Theuber and Bakker looked around in disbelief as Helen made her way from the door at the rear of the theater with the gun aimed at Dixie-Lee's head. Her other hand, she held behind her back as if concealing a jolly surprise.

Chris saw all too clearly the panic that crawled across the three faces at the front of the theater and framed against the backdrop of the porn film, he thought they cut rather absurd figures.

"Oh shit," Bakker muttered.

Aphrodite's was, as far as adult theaters go, much less seedy than Helen would have expected; the carpets were certainly less sticky for one thing. The unmanned entrance was a disappointing excuse for an adult store and actually had a far less adventurous selection of sex toys – *gag-gifts* – than the gas station in Flanagan. As Helen made her way down the aisle, the grainy skin-flick played on and she saw that all three of the black men were attempting to get their dicks into the actress's vagina at the same time; it really was looking quite uncomfortable for the poor girl.

"*Shit* just about sums this whole situation up," Helen said, looking at Bakker with the gun trained on Dixie-Lee. "We're really sorry about this, folks, but we can't just leave this unfortunate – *incident* – unfinished." She strode with confidence towards Bakker, Theuber and Dixie-Lee, enjoying the newfound power that the firearm afforded.

"You can't be serious?" Bakker said, with a nervous tremble in his voice.

"You fucking *raped* me!" Helen screamed at him, her voice loud and startling in the enclosed space.

"But it's what you –" Theuber began to say but his voice petered out as Helen's attention returned to Dixie-Lee.

Chris followed along behind Helen, an unmistakable limp in his step as his wounded ass served well to remind him of what these people had been paid to do to him.

Helen pulled out the alarm clock from behind her back and watched with interest as a look of abject terror crept across Dixie-Lee's face. Balancing the clock with great care on the back of a chair, Helen moved towards the redneck woman with the gun held steady at eye-height.

"You assholes ran off like scared kids and left us to clean up the mess," Helen growled.

"It wasn't our mess to clean up," Bakker told her, his voice a low growl. "And maybe we shouldn't have run out on ya'll like that," he reasoned, "but that ain't no reason to come in here waving a gun around." Bakker kept his unwavering eye on the gun that pointed at Dixie-Lee's face; he looked scared.

"I hear you, Mr. Bakker, and believe me we have considered all of our options. Isn't that right, babe?" Helen addressed her husband.

"Yeah. Sorry guys," Chris sounded genuinely apologetic, and he kept his eyes lowered ever so slightly.

"I'm afraid that we just can't live the rest of our lives waiting for the day that all of this pops up to bite us on the ass," Helen lapsed into teacher-voice; she was actually making her explanation sound reasonable.

"We're teachers, and you know just how far up their own asses School Boards can be; last semester a Home Ec. teacher was fired in our district because she accidentally posted a topless vacation picture on Instagram." Helen shook her head.

"And if I became a famous author, I'd imagine the temptation for blackmail would be pretty strong for you guys," Chris added. It was an unlikely scenario, given his inability to knuckle down and actually finish anything, but he thought it to be worthy of mention.

Helen snorted at Chris and shot him a look as if in the middle of everything they were dealing with, he'd finally stepped off of the crazy train.

"And just who the fuck do you think we are going to tell?" Theuber asked her and there was fear in his words. "And if we *did* talk, who in God's name would believe any of this?"

"I'm sorry, but we're just not going to take the risk," Helen replied, "so in the spirit of our adventure, I set the alarm for nine-thirty; it should give you all time to say your good-byes."

"You can't do this." Bakker's eye was still on the gun.

"We *can*, but only because we have to, Mr. Bakker," Helen sounded strangely calm. "Believe me, we are truly sorry."

"Like fuck you are, you sick bitch," Dixie-Lee spat and her venom made Helen recoil, almost imperceptibly. Bakker took advantage of Helen's fleeting distraction and made his move. Closing the gap between them in an instant, he lunged with his arms outstretched and grabbed for the Glock.

But Helen was quicker to react than he'd anticipated. She spun around to face him and squeezed the trigger, the gun roared and bucked wildly.

Bakker screamed in pain as a bullet ripped through the fingers of his left hand and sent two of them spinning through the air in a delicate mist of blood. He fell to the floor sobbing and clutching at his ruined hand.

The sudden, sharp report startled everyone in the theater and Theuber, jolted into action by the burst of adrenaline provided by the gunshot seized his own moment. He made a dash for the rear of the theater, screaming like a banshee at the top of his voice, hoping someone outside would hear him. He raced full speed towards the door that swung tantalizingly half open.

Theuber made it almost as far as the door when it slammed shut in his face. "What the f–?" he gasped and turned around to see that Chris was behind him.

In one swift, smooth motion, Chris thrust the hunting knife up into Theuber's belly and sliced him from pubic bone to sternum. The knife's keen blade plunged deep, slashing through organs and severing Theuber's aorta which let loose with a gushing torrent of bright crimson blood. Theuber let out a low, guttural moan and grabbed at the gaping tear in his abdomen in a futile attempt to stem the flow of blood and escaping viscera.

"Fucker!" Theuber screamed in Chris's face as the life drained from him. He collapsed to his knees in the spreading pool of blood and innards and the sudden jerk as he hit the floor dislodged a looping string of small intestine that slopped to the ground with a watery slap.

"No!" Dixie-Lee hollered and made as if to run to Theuber but Helen pointed the gun at her face once more to suggest otherwise.

Chris wrinkled his nose up at the stench of Theuber's slit insides. It was a stink that he'd endured for as much as he'd cared to today and he wanted nothing more than to be away from it. Theuber stared up at Chris, eyes imploring as his hands grappled with the slippery pink coils that escaped amidst the wash of blood. In Theuber's eyes Chris could see the glimmer of the slightest hope that he could still somehow get through this.

"Please," he begged Chris. "help m–"

Chris slashed at Theuber's throat, his knife slicing through the dying man's final words. Blood cascaded from the slit in Theuber's neck in a thin, red curtain, bubbling like a mountain brook with the air that escaped from his windpipe. Chris bent over to wipe the blood from his knife on Theuber's shoulder and watched as the man slumped to the floor to die in front of him. A hint of a smile played across Chris's lips, as if Theuber's demise had sparked some fond memory or other.

"You crazy bastards!" Bakker roared. He lay on the floor at Helen's feet nursing his mangled hand close to his chest. Along with severing the two fingers, Helen's bullet had also shattered Bakker's thumb so that sharp slivers of bone stuck out at crazy angles from the skin, and his entire hand was bleeding profusely into his shirt, soaking it through. He was also blubbering like a kid that just scraped his knee falling off the monkey bars.

"Oh, for Christ's sakes," Helen rolled her eyes at Bakker; her patience for cry babies had always been thin. "Man up, Newman." She waved at Bakker with her own damaged hand; blood had soaked all the way through the fresh bandage she'd put on the pinkie stump – the wound aggravated by the Glock's recoil. "I didn't cry when you made my husband do this, and I'm *just a fucking girl*." She mocked Bakker with the faintest hint of a smile that danced upon her lips.

Dixie-Lee helped Bakker to his feet and held him upright. She offered him a snot-encrusted tissue with which to wrap the bleeding hand.

"This has gone too far, Mrs. Sewell," Dixie-Lee

addressed Helen, peering with defiance down the gun's barrel. "An accident is one thing, but – this." She pointed at her husband's blood soaked body and struggled to keep her composure. "None of us signed up to be murdered by you two sick fuckers," Dixie-Lee's voice was raised, anger and despair making her words tremble.

Dixie-Lee began to walk towards the theater door, taking Bakker along with her. She was forced to support most of Bakker's weight as his legs appeared to have forsaken him, and he leaned in to her body as if he were trying to push her over. Behind them, Helen waved the gun at Dixie-Lee's back, scowling as one would at a defiant child.

"We're leaving now," Dixie-Lee told her, her voice flat and emotionless. "It's a couple of minutes to nine-thirty now; there really is nothing more you can threaten us with." She continued on towards the door.

Without hesitation, Helen shot out Dixie-Lee's right knee and watched with morbid fascination as the woman went down hard, her head bouncing on the floor with a resonant *thunk!* Bakker fell down alongside her and the two fell into a tangled heap. Dixie-Lee screamed and clutched at her knee, her hands bloodied and covered in fragments of bone and flesh.

Bakker struggled to get himself upright and there was bloody murder in his eyes.

Helen put a slug in Bakker's right knee too.

"Fucking *cunt*!" Bakker ululated as he collapsed back on top of Dixie-Lee. "You fucking shot me!" he screamed, as if Helen's actions really required further narration.

Dixie-Lee attempted to crawl away, and despite the squirming weight of Bakker that pinned her down she was actually making good progress.

Helen stood over Bakker and Dixie-Lee with her gun poised. She studied them, curious about their pain and taking in the terror that wafted up in the stench of blood, adrenaline-sweat and piss. There was something rather profound behind her puzzled, child-like expression; Helen felt as if something deep inside her own psyche had in that moment quite fundamentally *changed*.

"That's some good shooting, babe," Chris praised as he slipped an arm around his wife's shoulders and looked down at the two who squirmed in pain at Helen's feet.

Helen looked up at her husband and smiled at him with her eyes, her face eager to please. "It's a shame about him." She nodded towards Theuber's body over by the theater door. "I would have liked to have had some fun with that one."

"I'm sorry," Chris apologized. "I got a little carried away."

"Nah, it's all good." Helen reached up and pulled Chris's face towards hers in a kiss. It was a deep, delicious kiss in which Helen devoured the taste and earthy scent of her husband and moulded her body into his with a primal urge.

The alarm clock rang out, its shrill voice echoing loudly within the confines of the theater and drowning out Bakker and Dixie-Lee's pained moaning, along with much of the fake moans that wafted over from the screen. Upon the ominous sound of the alarm, the rednecks resumed their agonized attempt to escape, scrabbling and wriggling across the floor the best their shattered limbs would allow.

It was with some reluctance that Helen broke the kiss. Clutching the Glock firmly, she braced herself over Dixie-Lee and Bakker. "I love you, Mr. Sewell," Helen purred.

"And I love you, Mrs. Sewell." Chris smiled at his wife, his eyes twinkling and his dick painfully erect within the confines of his pants.

Helen felt a warm, tingling sensation spread through her body, setting her nerve endings alight and prickling the back of her skull. She felt alive – stimulated as she had never experienced never before, and finally Helen Sewell knew just what her husband found so exhilarating about such sheer, unadulterated brutality.

And with any further ado, Helen shot the people she knew as Dixie-Lee Theuber and Newman F Bakker in the back of their respective heads.

Job done.

Helen dropped the Glock to the floor and turned to Chris. She kissed him, so forceful and urgent that her teeth clattered on his, her tongue wild and invasive in his mouth. Breaking the kiss with reluctance, she undressed Chris, pulled her shirt up over her head and stepped out of her shorts so they were both lusciously naked amongst the carnage.

The alarm clock's tinny chime wound slowly down as Chris gently coaxed Helen to the floor. There he kissed and caressed every inch of her naked body, savoring the coppery taste of the thin smears of blood that adorned her, the pungent saltiness of her delicate sheen of sweat and the exhilarating flavors of her sex. Lost in the moment, themselves and each other, Helen and Chris frolicked and rolled around on the theater floor like two teenagers frolicking in the surf on a balmy summer's day.

And then Helen unbandaged Chris's wounded dick and they fucked.

Chris and Helen slammed their bodies into each other, their wounds adding exquisite pain to their ecstasy. Chris climbed on top of her, pushing Bakker and Dixie-Lee's corpses out of the way with little reverence and entirely oblivious to the carpet that was soaked with their blood. Chris stabbed his penis at Helen's denuded cunt, entering her body with ease as her tight muscles sucked him in deep with a savage voracity.

Helen moaned and bucked her hips to meet his, cried out as the sharp stab of pain from her newly pierced clitoris added to her pleasure.

Chris pressed his mouth to Helen's tit. He sucked its taut, puckered tip into his mouth and danced his tongue around the jagged rip in the nipple.

"That hurts, you fucker," Helen whispered and she dug her hands into Chris's hair and pulled him down harder on her breast.

Chris moaned something by means of reply but his mouth was too full of Helen's delicious, bleeding flesh to make any sort of coherent sound. He drew her nipple deeper into his mouth and down towards his throat as if he was a suckling infant.

As their fucking grew in intensity, their bodies locked together in one sweat-soaked, grinding mass; Chris's aggressive thrusting met by Helen's equally fierce response, their primal grunts an audible illustration of their pleasures and pain.

Then, Helen's eyes closed and she cried out, *"oh!"* And with that one, simple sound, Helen came. Her body shuddered and she grabbed at Chris's striped ass and pressed him down hard on to her sex. Her hips thrust up to meet him and lifted his entire weight up from the floor as her labored breath rushed out from her chest.

Chris thrust hard into Helen's body once more. She climaxed a second time and her internal muscles squeezed him like they were trying to tear his cock away from his body. She raked her fingernails down along her husband's spine, their sharp points snagging on his skin and drawing tiny pinpricks of blood.

Helen stared with fierce intent into her husband's eyes, sensing that he was close to his own release – his hips gained momentum, his face contorted and he flushed a deep pink. Helen licked his lower lip, sucked it into her mouth and bit down hard.

Chris growled against the pain in his lip which tipped him over the edge and he grimaced as Helen squeezed his sore dick with her inner muscles as if to milk every last drop from of his body, wanting all of him inside of her.

Finally, sated, they both froze, their sweat-slicked, bloodied bodies joined together and glistening wet like some grotesque ice carving.

"What the fuck –?" a strange voice broke into their moment.

The cop walked through the theater door, stepped gingerly over Theuber's corpse and made his way slowly down the aisle, the dark blue of his uniform making him virtually invisible in the gloom. He fumbled with trembling hands to retrieve his gun from its holster as his eyes darted between the naked people who appeared to be actually *fucking* in front of the screen and the money shots that heralded the finale of the dire porn film that played above them.

"Don't. Fucking. Move," the cop instructed. He sounded to Helen and Chris like he was dangerously close to losing his lunch. "Just don't!"

"Shit!" Helen mouthed at Chris.

"What the fuck do we do?" Chris whispered as he looked around frantically for Bakker's gun. Panic drained the color from his face when he saw that the gun was well beyond his reach.

"This is not what it looks like, Officer," Helen

ventured.

"I don't even *know* what this looks like," the cop stammered as he visibly fought to keep the bile from flooding the back of his throat. "Just what the fuck is going on here?" He kept his gun steady and aimed at Chris. "Did you kill those people?"

"I can explain, Officer." Chris attempted to get up.

"I said, don't move!" the cop repeated himself – louder this time – and the queasiness in his voice was unmistakable. "I *will* fucking shoot you. Both of you." He paused a couple of yards away from the Sewells, his face crumpled in disgust. "You were actually fucking each other?" he said.

"You were watching us?" Helen smiled and puffed out her gleaming, bloodied chest. "Did you like what you saw, officer?"

"You killed these people." The cop aimed his gun at Helen's head. "I thought they were fake until –"

Helen shot a knowing wink at Chris. "You don't know just how close you are with that one, Officer." She twisted her torso a little more to face the cop, presenting him with her blood-stained breasts.

"You really are sick people." The cop actually – visibly – gagged. "I should shoot the pair of you now and save the state the cost of a fucking trial."

"You could." Helen pouted at the cop. "Or you could come join us?"

"Fucking perverts." The cop clearly didn't know what he was supposed to do next; there fell a blank expression across his paling features and there was a pronounced tremble to his hands. After what seemed to be a long, silent age, he fumbled for the radio that was pinned to his shoulder. Grabbing it, he pressed the button and it crackled to life. "Requesting backup –"

The shot that silenced the cop rang out from over by

the theater doorway. One side of his head exploded and sprayed blood, gray brain gloop and shards of skull across the theater. The cop's legs collapsed from beneath him and he crumpled loosely to the floor, his left eye lolling from its shattered socket and flapping against his cheek.

Helen gave out a huge sigh of relief and grasped her husband's hand. Chris took it and looked as if he was going to cry.

"Mr. and Mrs. Sewell," a polite voice greeted them. "How very nice to meet you again." A man of mature years with a shock of white hair and twinkling blue eyes stepped out from the shadows and made his way down the aisle towards Helen and Chris. Seemingly oblivious to – or unmoved by – the carnage and the bloodied, naked state Helen and Chris were in, he had a hand outstretched to shake. The other, he used to surreptitiously return his small revolver to his inside jacket pocket.

SEVENTEEN

Customer Satisfaction

Ronnie Gagliano – the guy Helen and Chris had *literally* bumped into at the flea market – introduced himself with a respectful smile. "I have been your personal facilitator for this particular adventure." He told them in a manner most professional. Both Chris and Helen declined his offer of a handshake.

"We're still a little messy," Helen apologized as she pulled on her shorts.

"I appreciate that, Ma'am." Gagliano gave her a warm smile and like a true gentleman he averted his eyes from her bare, blood-smeared breasts as she tugged the oversized T' over them. "Y'all had yourselves a good time?" It was, of course, a rhetorical question.

Chris studied Gagliano with a wary look. He glanced down at the bodies that lay by his feet. "I'm sorry about this mess," he said, "and at the motel – that was an accident, I swear." He offered an appeasing smile. "We thought we could clear things up ourselves but things kind of got a little out of hand."

"Don't mention it, Sir – it's all part of the service," Gagliano assured and a look passed between he and Helen.

"Thank you for taking such good care of us, Mr. Gagliano," Helen said with a smile that showed off her missing tooth. "It's been worth every dollar." She then smiled at Chris who stood silently beside her, naked and looking so painfully vulnerable. She took hold of her husband's hand and squeezed it. "Especially this," she said as she looked around, "I'm tempted to say that this was the best part of the whole experience."

"Helen?" Chris said.

"Surprise again, my darling." Helen smiled and planted a soft kiss on her husband's lips.

"They – *this* was all part of the –?" Chris stalled, as if he simply couldn't find the word.

Helen nodded. "Adventure?" She looked like the cat that got the canary.

"The fat woman?"

Helen nodded.

"But you said she wasn't."

"I lied." Helen smiled.

"The cop?"

"Even the cop," Helen reassured as her eyes searched for Chris's for the approval that she so desperately craved.

"No way," Now he just sounded like the kid who just received the best Christmas gift ever.

"Happy anniversary, baby," Helen whispered. "This was all for you."

"Wow," was all Chris could manage, "you *really are* the best of everything, sweetheart. I love you so much," and with that, Chris Sewell took his wife in his arms and held her tightly.

****

For Ronnie Gagliano, this was just another job well done. His sole purpose as facilitator was to ensure that the Agency's clientele received precisely everything they had so handsomely paid for, had a wonderful time living out their fantasy scenarios and didn't fall foul of any law enforcement. And of course, he'd ticked each and every box with his requisite professionalism.

All that remained now was to clean up after the Sewells.

The cop had been Gagliano's own flourish to the adventure. He'd served as both an added adrenaline kick and a natural stopping point to the proceedings. And whilst it went against Gagliano's grain to have had to kill a real cop, it had been nonetheless an inevitability. Besides, Helen Sewell had paid for five corpses, so what was one more? The Agency would consider it a bonus for their treasured clients.

But now, Gagliano wanted nothing more than to be away from the theater, to be smoking a soothing cigarette and out of the death-stink. Once he'd seen the Sewells on their way, he'd hand over to the clean-up crew to deal with the mess – they had already sanitized the motel in their own inimitable, proficient manner – and his job would be done.

Of the countless adventures Gagliano had overseen in his ten years with the Agency – the highly elusive and fiercely exclusive *Velvet Society* if one were to give them their proper and correct title – this would be the one that would sit most uncomfortably at the top of his *very worst* list; Mr. and Mrs. Sewell were some seriously fucked-up people. As world-weary and jaded as Gagliano had become over his years of witnessing the very worst of human behaviour he had rarely experienced anything quite as extreme as this – the Sewells had certainly scored a resounding ten out of ten on Gagliano's weirdshitometer.

Of course, he had no idea as to whether the Sewells had booked the Standard or the Platinum for their adventure – that was something that was kept strictly between the Agency and the clients during this part of the proceedings – nor if he'd see them again as clients or players. But Gagliano did hope that if they were ever to be a part of somebody else's adventure, knowing now what Helen and Chris Sewell were capable of – heaven help those people.

It galled Gagliano to lose good people like this, and he hated the lies that he had to spin to secure their involvement. Of course, they never knew *exactly* how things were going to end when their own demise came as part of someone's adventure package but thankfully there were not that many clients that had the Sewells' particular tastes. On the more practical level, it was never easy to replace good, reliable people for this kind of work – hence the Agency's policy to involve previous clients in return for a discounted adventure – although there seemed to be no shortage of wannabee actors and actresses, and clients for whom being the villains of the piece was *their* adventure; the challenge was always to find those who could be both discrete *and* comfortable with the freaky stuff. Those that Gagliano did recruit on behalf of the Agency tended to stick around for the exceptional pay, generous health plan, world travel and the wild, crazy experiences.

"You gave us quite a fright back at the motel," Helen broke into Gagliano's reverie. "I saw your car pull into the lot and I thought we were going to be caught red-handed with the fat woman."

"Entirely my fault for arriving too soon," Gagliano apologised sweetly, with a wry smile. "I got to the motel a little sooner than expected. Although I honestly thought that I'd given you both enough time to dispose of her."

"That was not as easy at you may think, she was *huge*," Chris said with a gentle laugh; he was dressed now and looked more at ease. "But what about the guy with the hearse, he left before we could –?" Chris sounded worried.

"Nothing for you to worry about on that score, Mr. Sewell," Gagliano reassured him. "All loose ends have been taken care of."

"And *thank you* for the cop at the end," Helen added. "He scared the crap out of me, but a nice touch."

Gagliano accepted the compliment with good grace and even forced the flicker of a smile. "If you would be so kind as to oblige, Ma'am," he said. "I'd be grateful if you and Mr. Sewell would fill out our customer satisfaction form after you get cleaned up. It should only take you about five minutes." He handed Helen two blank, white envelopes that contained the four-page form.

"Consider it done," Helen said as she stepped over Bakker's body to retrieve the envelopes. "You really did make this a memorable adventure."

"I'm very pleased to hear that, Mrs. Sewell," Gagliano replied. "But then again, you did give us wonderfully detailed notes to work from. The Agency always takes pleasure in a job well done – and satisfied clients, of course." Gagliano ventured a rare smile. "If you don't mind my asking – will we be arranging your next adventure?" he enquired.

"Yes, Sir," Helen Sewell beamed at the facilitator. "We've already booked."

EPILOGUE

One Year On

A polished, jet black Maserati GranTurismo pulled up at the gas station's one and only pump. The doors either side opened in unison and the handsome driver and his equally stunning passenger climbed out.

The driver was a tall guy, six two/six three and had a dark complexion that made him look like he was of Pakistani descent. He wore black Aviators, fashionably distressed jeans, Converse shoes and a short-sleeved, button-down designer shirt that simply screamed *expensive*. His wife, of equal stature in her towering heels, had chosen to defy the merciless Texas heat in shiny, footless leggings that made her endless legs shimmer like liquid black. In compliment, she had on a pale blue, cowl neck top that plunged way down beyond her pierced navel to display to perfection her braless cleavage and surgically enhanced breasts.

The guy peered at the notice pinned to the gas pump that declared that there was attendant service and then he looked around, nonplussed for the promised employee.

"Howdy, folks!" The attendant materialized from

somewhere behind the closed up taco truck. He tucked his stained shirt into his pants as he walked and ran a grubby hand through his unruly mop of pitch-black hair. "Sorry to keep y'all waiting," he said.

"That's okay," the tall man replied and peered over the top of his sunglasses. "If you wouldn't mind filling her up for me?"

The attendant nodded towards the leggy wife and gave the guy a sly wink. "I'm assuming by that ya' mean the car?" he chuckled.

"Of course the car." The guy missed the *double entendre* completely and looked offended. "And if you could point my wife in the direction of the rest room?"

"Well, just look at me forgettin' the manners ma' Mamma taught me!" The attendant beamed and stretched out an oil stained hand for the shaking. "I'm Newman F. Bakker," he lied, and pointed to his name button by means of confirmation. "Pleased to make your acquaintance, Sir," Chris Sewell said with his well-practised Redneck Texan drawl. "And if your good lady would care to call in at the store, ma sister'll be only too happy to furnish her with the restroom key. Her name's Ruthie-Peg, and she's always glad of a little female company."

He waved across at the attractive, short haired woman who sat behind the antiquated cash register and she peered back out at him through the filthy window.

Helen Sewell smiled the sweetest of smiles that showed off a glinting hint of gold as she waved back at her husband and their new visitors with a hand that was missing its pinkie.

"Oh yeah," Chris added with a wink and a broad grin, "and welcome to Flanagan."

END

A Note From The Author

I would like to say a massive thank you to you – yes, you, Dear Reader – for spending an hour or three in the company of the Sewells.

I hope that my novel has entertained you, turned your stomach a little in the way only good, disturbing horror can do, and made you reflect a little on the diverse nature of the human animal. Please do take a little of your precious time to write a review, and to tell your fellow horror-lovers about *Flanagan*.

As a horror writer, I have explored the worlds – and *nether*worlds – of ghosts, demons and devils, of people who possess hellish powers and those lethal members of the animal kingdom that make even my skin crawl. But, over and above all of these, shining bright, are people like Chris and Helen; individual examples of our species for whom the word humanity is a misnomer at best.

I once owned a company in the UK that specialised in fantasy fulfilment – nothing quite as extreme as what you have just experienced, but sometimes pretty damned close. We had clients of all persuasions and perversities who desired to push their own boundaries and experience the taboo; and just when we thought we had seen everything, someone would contact us with a request that that reminded us, in no uncertain terms, we most certainly had not.

Whilst we should most certainly maintain our healthy respect for the nightmare things that lurk beneath the bed and those slithering, creeping creatures that skulk in the darkest shadows of our imagination, it is important to always keep in mind that sometimes the worst monsters of all may well be living in that nice, neat house next door…

About Your Author

James hails originally from Yorkshire, England having relocated with his family to Houston, Texas in 2010. He has an honors degree in Zoology and a background in sales, marketing and business. Relatively new to the writing arena, his writing style and story telling have already been compared to James Herbert, Richard Laymon, Stephen King, Dan Brown and Robert Ludlum.

An Affiliate Member of the Horror Writer's Association, James has to date five novels published, in addition to three novellas and myriad short stories dotted about in myriad anthologies.

James also writes screenplays and currently has three under option (a spine-chilling horror, a Tarantino-esque crime caper and an animated family movie). In 2014 he was commissioned by Spectra Records to write a biopic feature on the early life of Bob Marley, and in 2015 was writer for hire on the Kenyan sitcom '*The Samaritans*'.

As if that weren't enough, James has written and directed a bunch of short movies, winning Best Director in the 2013 *Splatterfest* film competition and Remi awards at Houston's *Worldfest* Film Festival in 2012, 2014 and 2015.

James' writing style has been described as uncompromising, unique and entertaining; he combines highly original ideas with brilliant vocabulary and highly effective yarn spinning in which the story always comes first! Be warned, his work does have a tendency towards the dark side – usually with a rich vein of humor – and there is *always* that delicious twist at the end!

www.jameslongmore.com

Also by James H Longmore

Tenebrion

Amateur film makers inadvertently invoke a demon when they break into an abandoned elementary school to perform and film an authentic Black Mass for their entry into a short movie competition!

Dave Priestley reveals his plan to his the movie-making friends – to film an authentic Black Mass in Watsonville's abandoned elementary school – the site of a horrific tragedy nine years before.

Tenebrion – the demon of darkness – makes preparations of its own within the darkness of hell. It requires a specific set of circumstances and human victims to split open a fissure between the worlds and set free its brethren. Tenebrion has been manipulating humans for centuries in order to put things into place and the movie makers are the unfortunate, final pieces of its nefarious puzzle.

Priestley, ever the stickler for authenticity and detail, prepares the Mass and accidentally sets the denizen of Hell free. And whilst Priestley and his skeptical friends attempt to recapture Tenebrion and return it to the dark shadows of the netherworld, it hunts them all down – one by one – for inclusion in its hellish gateway.

<u>Pede</u>

A true homage to the Creature Feature genre!

Once luxurious, the Mountainview Spa Hotel in the heart of California's Coachella valley lies decaying, abandoned and heavily boarded up. Its secret; it is the site of a radioactive, 'dirty' bomb explosion five years' previous.

Zoology Professor Jane Lucas has a lifelong phobia of Scolopendra gigantea, the Giant Centipede, despite being the world's leading authority on it. Following the savage deaths of two young lovers who broke into the hotel for its natural underground spa, and the discovery of centipede remains almost three times its natural size, the professor teams up with four of her students to investigate. But their expedition becomes a fight for survival when they are trapped in the hotel with a gang of violent thugs – including the boyfriend of one of the female students with whom the professor has been having an illicit affair.

They soon discover a voracious swarm of the oversized centipedes that has spawned within the hotel, but are horrified to learn that another creature even more terrifying hunts in the Mountainview's deserted hallways - a centipede of seemingly impossibly monstrous proportions; and it is ravenous and desperate to feed.

<u>Blood and Kisses</u>

The definitive short story collection from James H Longmore - an eclectic mix of dark horror, bizarro and Twilight-Zone style tales of the downright disturbing.

Welcome to the long awaited collection from the writer of horror novels 'Pede and Tenebrion; a forword by Richard Chizmar (co-author of Gwendy's Button Box and author of A Long December), 18 short stories, 5 flash fiction and even a poem - all skin-crawling, soul-shredding tales of terror, of the darkest things that skulk amongst the night's inky shadows, and of the everyday gone horribly awry.

There is more, Dear Reader, much, much more; for within these pages we have devils, demons and ghosts, lycanthropes and demi-gods, all rubbing nefarious shoulders with vilest of Hell's offspring who have slithered from the netherworld to doff their caps and wish us all the sweetest of dreams…

Other Books From HellBound Books
www.hellboundbookspublishing.com

The Pleasure Hunt

After meeting the mysterious *Dark Dance* on the casual encounters website, The Pleasure Hunters Club, *Sexy Cupid* finds himself enchanted by a enigmatic seductress – *Dark Dance*.

After experiencing bizarre, nightmarish visions during their first physical liaison, *Cupid* awakes on a bench somewhere in Louisville, unable to get the mystifying creature off his mind. As he begins to search both online and through the seedy streets of the city for her, he uncovers harrowing truths about the object of his obsession, truths which fill him with both indomitable dread and inexplicable love for her.

By the time *Cupid* begins to understand the terror he faces, the shackles on his soul are already too tight as the ancient monster has her talons dug well into his flesh.

Every time he is swept away to her world of Theia - the Moon Realm - she extracts and devours yet another piece of his very essence, and despite the merciless torment of his encounters with his obsession - and the warnings of, a menacing stranger - he presses on to find her, dragging himself deeper into her darkened realm.

Cupid soon finds that he may have but one opportunity to escape the demonic *Dark Dance*, but the bewitchment she has cast upon his heart may deter him from making a stand; with his soul about to slip down the gullet of the beast, *Cupid* has to make a decision before he is forever wrapped in the wicked thaumaturge's wings of eternal damnation.

The Waning

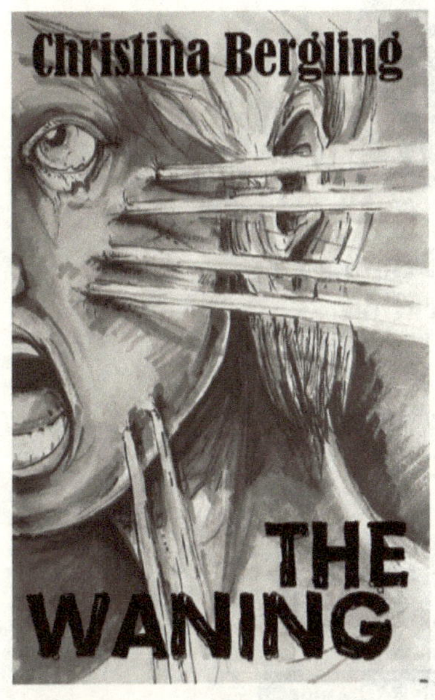

Beatrix woke up in a small metal cage, Lost in the darkness, a persistent dripping sound her only company.

She was celebrating a promotion that was the culmination of her entire ruthless, driven career; a promotion that would cement her status enough for her to take her relationship with her girlfriend out of the lesbian closet; Beatrix had finally made it.

And then she was here, disoriented and petrified in a blackness she could not define. Yet the reality of her Master may be even more terrifying than the crushing darkness and enveloping isolation. He appears as an ominous shadow in the doorway of her cell, never speaking. Instead, he teaches Beatrix the language of pain and torture, of submission and obedience, of domination and possession

With each passing day, the fight and hope in Beatrix begins to shrivel and wane. With each savage beating, her survivalist instincts rise up to overwhelm the person she was. With each dehumanizing condition, she begins to forget who she was and the life from which she was ripped. Can Beatrix ward off the psychological breakdown of her Master? Can she resist the temptation to survive and thrive through submission? Either Beatrix will succeed at surviving and escaping the torments of her Master or her Master will succeed at breaking her completely and reforming her into his design for a human possession…

**A HellBound Books LLC
Publication**

www.hellboundbookspublishing.com

Printed in the United States of America

www.ingramcontent.com/pod-product-compliance
Lightning Source LLC
Chambersburg PA
CBHW030603170726
48283CB00002B/453